A Heron Books Collection

CONTENTS.

CHAPTER LI.

CHAPTER LII.

CHAPTER LIII.

CHAPTER LIV.

CHAPTER LV.

CHAPTER LVI.

CHAPTER LVII.

CONTENTS.

CHAPTER XLIII.

CHAPTER XLIV.

CHAPTER XLV.

CHAPTER XLVI.

CHAPTER XLVII.

CHAPTER XLVIII.

CHAPTER XLIX.

CHAPTER L.

CONTENTS.

CONTENTS OF VOL. II.

PORTSMOUTH CITY COUNCIL
LIBRARY SERVICE

WITHDRAWN

C 00222 881

P100206662

Dickens Collection.
PORTSMOUTH LIBRARIES

Central Library
Tel. 819311

R 889558 5101

823 DIC

© 1967 Heron Books, London

CHARLES DICKENS

THE POSTHUMOUS PAPERS
OF
THE PICKWICK CLUB
II

Illustrations
by Seymour and Phiz

HERON BOOKS

Charles Dickens

CHARLES DICKENS

COMPLETE
WORKS

CENTENNIAL EDITION

LIST OF ILLUSTRATIONS

CHAPTER XXX.

HOW THE PICKWICKIANS MADE AND CULTIVATED THE ACQUAINT-
ANCE OF A COUPLE OF NICE YOUNG MEN BELONGING TO ONE
OF THE LIBERAL PROFESSIONS; HOW THEY DISPORTED THEM-
SELVES ON THE ICE; AND HOW THEIR FIRST VISIT CAME TO
A CONCLUSION.

"WELL, Sam," said Mr. Pickwick as that favoured servitor
entered his bed-chamber with his warm water, on the morning
of Christmas Day, "Still frosty?"

"Water in the wash-hand basin's a mask o' ice, sir," responded Sam.

"Severe weather, Sam," observed Mr. Pickwick.

"Fine time for them as is well wropped up, as the Polar
Bear said to himself, ven he was practising his skating," replied
Mr. Weller.

"I shall be down in a quarter of an hour, Sam," said Mr.
Pickwick, untying his nightcap.

"Wery good, sir," replied Sam. "There's a couple o'
Sawbones down stairs."

"A couple of what!" exclaimed Mr. Pickwick, sitting up
in bed.

"A couple o' Sawbones," said Sam.

"What's a Sawbones?" inquired Mr. Pickwick, not quite certain whether it was a live animal, or something to eat.

"What! Don't you know what a Sawbones is, sir?" inquired Mr. Weller. "I thought everybody know'd as a Sawbones was a Surgeon."

"Oh, a Surgeon, eh?" said Mr. Pickwick, with a smile.

"Just that, sir," replied Sam. "These here ones as is below, though, aint reg'lar thorough-bred Sawbones; they're only in trainin'."

"In other words they're Medical Students, I suppose?" said Mr. Pickwick.

Sam Weller nodded assent.

"I am glad of it," said Mr. Pickwick, casting his nightcap energetically on the counterpane, "They are fine fellows; very fine fellows; with judgments matured by observation and reflection; tastes refined by reading and study. I am very glad of it."

"They're a smokin' cigars by the kitchen fire," said Sam.

"Ah!" observed Mr. Pickwick, rubbing his hands, "overflowing with kindly feelings and animal spirits. Just what I like to see."

"And one on 'em," said Sam, not noticing his master's interruption, "one on 'em's got his legs on the table, and is a drinkin' brandy neat, vile the t'other one—him in the barnacles—has got a barrel o' oysters atween his knees, wich he's a openin' like steam, and as fast as he eats 'em, he takes a aim vith the shells at young dropsy, who's a sittin' down fast asleep, in the chimbley corner."

"Eccentricities of genius, Sam," said Mr. Pickwick. "You may retire."

Sam did retire accordingly; Mr. Pickwick, at the expiration of the quarter of an hour, went down to breakfast.

"Here he is at last!" said old Mr. Wardle. "Pickwick, this is Miss Allen's brother, Mr. Benjamin Allen. Ben we call him, and so may you if you like. This gentleman is his very particular friend, Mr. ——"

2

MR. BOB SAWYER.

"Mr. Bob Sawyer," interposed Mr. Benjamin Allen; whereupon Mr. Bob Sawyer and Mr. Benjamin Allen laughed in concert.

Mr. Pickwick bowed to Bob Sawyer, and Bob Sawyer bowed to Mr. Pickwick; Bob and his very particular friend then applied themselves most assiduously to the eatables before them; and Mr. Pickwick had an opportunity of glancing at them both.

Mr. Benjamin Allen was a coarse, stout, thick-set young man, with black hair cut rather short, and a white face cut rather long. He was embellished with spectacles, and wore a white neckerchief. Below his single-breasted black surtout, which was buttoned up to his chin, appeared the usual number of pepper-and-salt coloured legs, terminating in a pair of imperfectly polished boots. Although his coat was short in the sleeves, it disclosed no vestige of a linen wristband; and although there was quite enough of his face to admit of the encroachment of a shirt collar, it was not graced by the smallest approach to that appendage. He presented, altogether, rather a mildewy appearance, and emitted a fragrant odour of full-flavoured Cubas.

Mr. Bob Sawyer, who was habited in a coarse blue coat, which, without being either a great-coat or a surtout, partook of the nature and qualities of both, had about him that sort of slovenly smartness, and swaggering gait, which is peculiar to young gentlemen who smoke in the streets by day, shout and scream in the same by night, call waiters by their Christian names, and do various other acts and deeds of an equally facetious description. He wore a pair of plaid trousers, and a large rough double-breasted waistcoat; out of doors, he carried a thick stick with a big top. He eschewed gloves, and looked, upon the whole, something like a dissipated Robinson Crusoe.

Such were the two worthies to whom Mr. Pickwick was introduced, as he took his seat at the breakfast table on Christmas morning.

3

"Splendid morning, gentlemen," said Mr. Pickwick.

Mr. Bob Sawyer slightly nodded his assent to the proposition, and asked Mr. Benjamin Allen for the mustard.

"Have you come far this morning, gentlemen?" inquired Mr. Pickwick.

"Blue Lion at Muggleton," briefly responded Mr. Allen.

"You should have joined us last night," said Mr. Pickwick.

"So we should," replied Bob Sawyer, "but the brandy was too good to leave in a hurry: wasn't it, Ben?"

"Certainly," said Mr. Benjamin Allen; "and the cigars were not bad, or the pork chops either: were they, Bob?"

"Decidedly not," said Bob. The particular friends resumed their attack upon the breakfast, more freely than before, as if the recollection of last night's supper had imparted a new relish to the meal.

"Peg away, Bob," said Mr. Allen to his companion, encouragingly.

"So I do," replied Bob Sawyer. And so, to do him justice, he did.

"Nothing like dissecting, to give one an appetite," said Mr. Bob Sawyer, looking round the table.

Mr. Pickwick slightly shuddered.

"By the bye, Bob," said Mr. Allen, "have you finished that leg yet?"

"Nearly," replied Sawyer, helping himself to half a fowl as he spoke. "It's a very muscular one for a child's."

"Is it?" inquired Mr. Allen, carelessly.

"Very," said Bob Sawyer, with his mouth full.

"I've put my name down for an arm, at our place," said Mr. Allen. "We're clubbing for a subject, and the list is nearly full, only we can't get hold of any fellow that wants a head. I wish you'd take it."

"No," replied Bob Sawyer; "can't afford expensive luxuries."

"Nonsense!" said Allen.

"Can't indeed," rejoined Bob Sawyer. "I wouldn't mind a brain, but I couldn't stand a whole head."

4

ARABELLA AND HER BROTHER.

"Hush, hush, gentlemen, pray," said Mr. Pickwick, "I hear the ladies."

As Mr. Pickwick spoke, the ladies, gallantly escorted by Messrs. Snodgrass, Winkle, and Tupman, returned from an early walk.

"Why, Ben!" said Arabella, in a tone which expressed more surprise than pleasure at the sight of her brother.

"Come to take you home to-morrow," replied Benjamin.

Mr. Winkle turned pale.

"Don't you see Bob Sawyer, Arabella?" inquired Mr. Benjamin Allen, somewhat reproachfully. Arabella gracefully held out her hand, in acknowledgement of Bob Sawyer's presence. A thrill of hatred struck to Mr. Winkle's heart, as Bob Sawyer inflicted on the proffered hand a perceptible squeeze.

"Ben, dear!" said Arabella, blushing; "have—have—you been introduced to Mr. Winkle?"

"I have not been, but I shall be very happy to be, Arabella," replied her brother gravely. Here Mr. Allen bowed grimly to Mr. Winkle, while Mr. Winkle and Mr. Bob Sawyer glanced mutual distrust out of the corners of their eyes.

The arrival of the two new visitors, and the consequent check upon Mr. Winkle and the young lady with the fur round her boots, would in all probability have proved a very unpleasant interruption to the hilarity of the party, had not the cheerfulness of Mr. Pickwick, and the good humour of the host, been exerted to the very utmost for the common weal. Mr. Winkle gradually insinuated himself into the good graces of Mr. Benjamin Allen, and even joined in a friendly conversation with Mr. Bob Sawyer; who, enlivened with the brandy, and the breakfast, and the talking, gradually ripened into a state of extreme facetiousness, and related with much glee an agreeable anecdote, about the removal of a tumour on some gentleman's head: which he illustrated by means of an oyster-knife and a half-quartern loaf, to the great edification of the assembled company. Then, the whole train went to

5

church, where Mr. Benjamin Allen fell fast asleep: while Mr. Bob Sawyer abstracted his thoughts from worldly matters, by the ingenious process of carving his name on the seat of the pew, in corpulent letters of four inches long.

"Now," said Wardle, after a substantial lunch, with the agreeable items of strong-beer and cherry-brandy, had been done ample justice to; "what say you to an hour on the ice? We shall have plenty of time."

"Capital!" said Mr. Benjamin Allen.

"Prime!" ejaculated Mr. Bob Sawyer.

"You skate, of course, Winkle?" said Wardle.

"Ye-yes; oh, yes," replied Mr. Winkle. "I—I—am *rather* out of practice."

"Oh, *do* skate, Mr. Winkle," said Arabella. "I like to see it so much."

"Oh, it is *so* graceful," said another young lady.

A third young lady said it was elegant, and a fourth expressed her opinion that it was "swan-like."

"I should be very happy, I'm sure," said Mr. Winkle, reddening; "but I have no skates."

This objection was at once overruled. Trundle had a couple of pair, and the fat boy announced that there were half-a-dozen more down stairs: whereat Mr. Winkle expressed exquisite delight, and looked exquisitely uncomfortable.

Old Wardle led the way to a pretty large sheet of ice; and the fat boy and Mr. Weller, having shovelled and swept away the snow which had fallen on it during the night, Mr. Bob Sawyer adjusted his skates with a dexterity which to Mr. Winkle was perfectly marvellous, and described circles with his left leg, and cut figures of eight, and inscribed upon the ice, without once stopping for breath, a great many other pleasant and astonishing devices, to the excessive satisfaction of Mr. Pickwick, Mr. Tupman, and the ladies: which reached a pitch of positive enthusiasm, when old Wardle and Benjamin Allen, assisted by the aforesaid Bob Sawyer, performed some mystic evolutions, which they called a reel.

6

MR. WINKLE ON SKATES.

All this time, Mr. Winkle, with his face and hands blue with the cold, had been forcing a gimlet into the soles of his feet, and putting his skates on, with the points behind, and getting the straps into a very complicated and entangled state, with the assistance of Mr. Snodgrass, who knew rather less about skates than a Hindoo. At length, however, with the assistance of Mr. Weller, the unfortunate skates were firmly screwed and buckled on, and Mr. Winkle was raised to his feet.

"Now, then, sir," said Sam, in an encouraging tone; "off vith you, and show 'em how to do it."

"Stop, Sam, stop!" said Mr. Winkle, trembling violently, and clutching hold of Sam's arms with the grasp of a drowning man. "How slippery it is, Sam!"

"Not an uncommon thing upon ice, sir," replied Mr. Weller. "Hold up, sir!"

This last observation of Mr. Weller's bore reference to a demonstration Mr. Winkle made at the instant, of a frantic desire to throw his feet in the air, and dash the back of his head on the ice.

"These—these—are very awkward skates; ain't they, Sam?" inquired Mr. Winkle, staggering.

"I'm afeerd there's a orkard gen'l'm'n in 'em, sir," replied Sam.

"Now, Winkle," cried Mr. Pickwick, quite unconscious that there was anything the matter. "Come; the ladies are all anxiety."

"Yes, yes," replied Mr. Winkle, with a ghastly smile. "I'm coming."

"Just a goin' to begin," said Sam, endeavouring to disengage himself. "Now, sir, start off!"

"Stop an instant, Sam," gasped Mr. Winkle, clinging most affectionately to Mr. Weller. "I find I've got a couple of coats at home that I don't want, Sam. You may have them, Sam."

"Thank'ee, sir," replied Mr. Weller.

7

"Never mind touching your hat, Sam," said Mr. Winkle, hastily. "You needn't take your hand away to do that. I meant to have given you five shillings this morning for a Christmas-box, Sam. I'll give it you this afternoon, Sam."

"You're wery good, sir," replied Mr. Weller.

"Just hold me at first, Sam; will you?" said Mr. Winkle. "There—that's right. I shall soon get in the way of it, Sam. Not too fast, Sam; not too fast."

Mr. Winkle stooping forward, with his body half doubled up, was being assisted over the ice by Mr. Weller, in a very singular and un-swan-like manner, when Mr. Pickwick most innocently shouted from the opposite bank:

"Sam!"

"Sir?"

"Here. I want you."

"Let go, sir," said Sam. "Don't you hear the governor a callin'? Let go, sir."

With a violent effort, Mr. Weller disengaged himself from the grasp of the agonised Pickwickian, and, in so doing, administered a considerable impetus to the unhappy Mr. Winkle. With an accuracy which no degree of dexterity or practice could have insured, that unfortunate gentleman bore swiftly down into the centre of the reel, at the very moment when Mr. Bob Sawyer was performing a flourish of unparalleled beauty. Mr. Winkle struck wildly against him, and with a loud crash they both fell heavily down. Mr. Pickwick ran to the spot. Bob Sawyer had risen to his feet, but Mr. Winkle was far too wise to do anything of the kind, in skates. He was seated on the ice, making spasmodic efforts to smile; but anguish was depicted on every lineament of his countenance.

"Are you hurt?" inquired Mr. Benjamin Allen, with great anxiety.

"Not much," said Mr. Winkle, rubbing his back very hard.

"I wish you'd let me bleed you," said Mr. Benjamin, with great eagerness.

"No, thank you," replied Mr. Winkle hurriedly.

"I really think you had better," said Allen.

"Thank you," replied Mr. Winkle; "I'd rather not."

"What do *you* think, Mr. Pickwick?" inquired Bob Sawyer.

Mr. Pickwick was excited and indignant. He beckoned to Mr. Weller, and said in a stern voice, "Take his skates off."

"No; but really I had scarcely begun," remonstrated Mr. Winkle.

"Take his skates off," repeated Mr. Pickwick firmly.

The command was not to be resisted. Mr. Winkle allowed Sam to obey it in silence.

"Lift him up," said Mr. Pickwick. Sam assisted him to rise.

Mr. Pickwick retired a few paces apart from the by-standers; and, beckoning his friend to approach, fixed a searching look upon him, and uttered in a low, but distinct and emphatic tone, these remarkable words:

"You're a humbug, sir."

"A what?" said Mr. Winkle, starting.

"A humbug, sir. I will speak plainer, if you wish it. An impostor, sir."

With those words, Mr. Pickwick turned slowly on his heel, and rejoined his friends.

While Mr. Pickwick was delivering himself of the sentiment just recorded, Mr. Weller and the fat boy, having by their joint endeavours cut out a slide, were exercising themselves thereupon, in a very masterly and brilliant manner. Sam Weller, in particular, was displaying that beautiful feat of fancy-sliding which is currently denominated "knocking at the cobbler's door," and which is achieved by skimming over the ice on one foot, and occasionally giving a postman's knock upon it with the other. It was a good long slide, and there was something in the motion which Mr. Pickwick, who was very cold with standing still, could not help envying.

"It looks a nice warm exercise that, doesn't it?" he inquired of Wardle, when that gentleman was thoroughly out of breath, by reason of the indefatigable manner in which he had converted his legs into a pair of compasses, and drawn complicated problems on the ice.

"Ah, it does indeed," replied Wardle. "Do you slide?"

"I used to do so, on the gutters, when I was a boy," replied Mr. Pickwick.

"Try it now," said Wardle.

"Oh do please, Mr. Pickwick!" cried all the ladies.

"I should be very happy to afford you any amusement," replied Mr. Pickwick, "but I haven't done such a thing these thirty years."

"Pooh! pooh! Nonsense!" said Wardle, dragging off his skates with the impetuosity which characterised all his proceedings. "Here; I'll keep you company; come along!" And away went the good tempered old fellow down the slide, with a rapidity which came very close upon Mr. Weller, and beat the fat boy all to nothing.

Mr. Pickwick paused, considered, pulled off his gloves and put them in his hat: took two or three short runs, baulked himself as often, and at last took another run, and went slowly and gravely down the slide, with his feet about a yard and a quarter apart, amidst the gratified shouts of all the spectators.

"Keep the pot a bilin', sir!" said Sam; and down went Wardle again, and then Mr. Pickwick, and then Sam, and then Mr. Winkle, and then Mr. Bob Sawyer, and then the fat boy, and then Mr. Snodgrass, following closely upon each other's heels, and running after each other with as much eagerness as if all their future prospects in life depended on their expedition.

It was the most intensely interesting thing, to observe the manner in which Mr. Pickwick performed his share in the ceremony; to watch the torture of anxiety with which he viewed the person behind, gaining upon him at the imminent hazard of tripping him up; to see him gradually expend the painful force he had put on at first, and turn slowly round

10

on the slide, with his face towards the point from which he
had started; to contemplate the playful smile which mantled
on his face when he had accomplished the distance, and the
eagerness with which he turned round when he had done so,
and ran after his predecessor: his black gaiters tripping
pleasantly through the snow, and his eyes beaming cheerfulness
and gladness through his spectacles. And when he was
knocked down (which happened upon the average every third
round), it was the most invigorating sight that can possibly
be imagined, to behold him gather up his hat, gloves, and
handkerchief, with a glowing countenance, and resume his
station in the rank, with an ardour and enthusiasm that
nothing could abate.

The sport was at its height, the sliding was at the quickest,
the laughter was at the loudest, when a sharp smart crack
was heard. There was a quick rush towards the bank, a wild
scream from the ladies, and a shout from Mr. Tupman. A
large mass of ice disappeared; the water bubbled up over it;
Mr. Pickwick's hat, gloves, and handkerchief were floating
on the surface; and this was all of Mr. Pickwick that anybody could see.

Dismay and anguish were depicted on every countenance,
the males turned pale, and the females fainted, Mr. Snodgrass
and Mr. Winkle grasped each other by the hand, and gazed
at the spot where their leader had gone down, with frenzied
eagerness: while Mr. Tupman, by way of rendering the
promptest assistance, and at the same time conveying to any
persons who might be within hearing, the clearest possible
notion of the catastrophe, ran off across the country at his
utmost speed, screaming "Fire!" with all his might.

It was at this moment, when old Wardle and Sam Weller
were approaching the hole with cautious steps, and Mr.
Benjamin Allen was holding a hurried consultation with Mr.
Bob Sawyer, on the advisability of bleeding the company
generally, as an improving little bit of professional practice
—it was at this very moment, that a face, head, and shoulders,

emerged from beneath the water, and disclosed the features and spectacles of Mr. Pickwick.

"Keep yourself up for an instant—for only one instant!" bawled Mr. Snodgrass.

"Yes, do; let me implore you—for my sake!" roared Mr. Winkle, deeply affected. The adjuration was rather unnecessary; the probability being, that if Mr. Pickwick had declined to keep himself up for anybody else's sake, it would have occurred to him that he might as well do so, for his own.

"Do you feel the bottom there, old fellow?" said Wardle.

"Yes, certainly," replied Mr. Pickwick, wringing the water from his head and face, and gasping for breath. "I fell upon my back. I couldn't get on my feet at first."

The clay upon so much of Mr. Pickwick's coat as was yet visible, bore testimony to the accuracy of this statement; and as the fears of the spectators were still further relieved by the fat boy's suddenly recollecting that the water was nowhere more than five feet deep, prodigies of valour were performed to get him out. After a vast quantity of splashing, and cracking, and struggling, Mr. Pickwick was at length fairly extricated from his unpleasant position, and once more stood on dry land.

"Oh, he'll catch his death of cold," said Emily.

"Dear old thing!" said Arabella. "Let me wrap this shawl round you, Mr. Pickwick."

"Ah, that's the best thing you can do," said Wardle; "and when you've got it on, run home as fast as your legs can carry you, and jump into bed directly."

A dozen shawls were offered on the instant. Three or four of the thickest having been selected, Mr. Pickwick was wrapped up, and started off, under the guidance of Mr. Weller: presenting the singular phenomenon of an elderly gentleman, dripping wet, and without a hat, with his arms bound down to his sides, skimming over the ground, without any clearly defined purpose, at the rate of six good English miles an hour.

But Mr. Pickwick cared not for appearances in such an extreme case, and urged on by Sam Weller, he kept at the very top of his speed until he reached the door of Manor Farm, where Mr. Tupman had arrived some five minutes before, and had frightened the old lady into palpitations of the heart by impressing her with the unalterable conviction that the kitchen chimney was on fire—a calamity which always presented itself in glowing colours to the old lady's mind, when anybody about her evinced the smallest agitation.

Mr. Pickwick paused not an instant until he was snug in bed. Sam Weller lighted a blazing fire in the room, and took up his dinner; a bowl of punch was carried up afterwards, and a grand carouse held in honour of his safety. Old Wardle would not hear of his rising, so they made the bed the chair, and Mr. Pickwick presided. A second and a third bowl were ordered in; and when Mr. Pickwick awoke next morning, there was not a symptom of rheumatism about him: which proves, as Mr. Bob Sawyer very justly observed, that there is nothing like hot punch in such cases: and that if ever hot punch did fail to act as a preventive, it was merely because the patient fell into the vulgar error of not taking enough of it.

The jovial party broke up next morning. Breakings up are capital things in our school days, but in after life they are painful enough. Death, self-interest, and fortune's changes, are every day breaking up many a happy group, and scattering them far and wide; and the boys and girls never come back again. We do not mean to say that it was exactly the case in this particular instance; all we wish to inform the reader is, that the different members of the party dispersed to their several homes; that Mr. Pickwick and his friends once more took their seats on the top of the Muggleton coach; and that Arabella Allen repaired to her place of destination, wherever it might have been—we dare say Mr. Winkle knew, but we confess we don't—under the care and guardianship of her brother Benjamin, and his most intimate and particular friend, Mr. Bob Sawyer.

Before they separated, however, that gentleman and Mr.

13

THE PICKWICK CLUB.

Benjamin Allen drew Mr. Pickwick aside with an air of some mystery: and Mr. Bob Sawyer thrusting his forefinger between two of Mr. Pickwick's ribs, and thereby displaying his native drollery, and his knowledge of the anatomy of the human frame, at one and the same time, inquired:

"I say, old boy, where do you hang out?"

Mr. Pickwick replied that he was at present suspended at the George and Vulture.

"I wish you'd come and see me," said Bob Sawyer.

"Nothing would give me greater pleasure," replied Mr. Pickwick.

"There's my lodgings," said Mr. Bob Sawyer, producing a card. "Lant Street, Borough; it's near Guy's, and handy for me, you know. Little distance after you've passed Saint George's Church—turns out of the High Street on the right hand side the way."

"I shall find it," said Mr. Pickwick.

"Come on Thursday fortnight, and bring the other chaps with you," said Mr. Bob Sawyer, "I'm going to have a few medical fellows that night.

Mr. Pickwick expressed the pleasure it would afford him to meet the medical fellows; and after Mr. Bob Sawyer had informed him that he meant to be very cosey, and that his friend Ben was to be one of the party, they shook hands and separated.

We feel that in this place we lay ourself open to the inquiry whether Mr. Winkle was whispering, during this brief conversation, to Arabella Allen; and if so, what he said; and furthermore, whether Mr. Snodgrass was conversing apart with Emily Wardle; and if so, what *he* said. To this, we reply, that whatever they might have said to the ladies, they said nothing at all to Mr. Pickwick or Mr. Tupman for eight-and-twenty miles, and that they sighed very often, refused ale and brandy, and looked gloomy. If our observant lady readers can deduce any satisfactory inferences from these facts, we beg them by all means to do so.

14

CHAPTER XXXI.

THE PICKWICK CLUB.

WHICH IS ALL ABOUT THE LAW, AND SUNDRY GREAT AUTHORITIES
LEARNED THEREIN.

SCATTERED about, in various holes and corners of the
Temple, are certain dark and dirty chambers, in and out of
which, all the morning in Vacation, and half the evening too
in Term time, there may be seen constantly hurrying with
bundles of papers under their arms, and protruding from their
pockets, an almost uninterrupted succession of Lawyers' Clerks.
There are several grades of Lawyers' Clerks. There is the
Articled Clerk, who has paid a premium, and is an attorney
in perspective, who runs a tailor's bill, receives invitations
to parties, knows a family in Gower Street, and another in
Tavistock Square: who goes out of town every Long Vacation
to see his father, who keeps live horses innumerable; and who
is, in short, the very aristocrat of clerks. There is the salaried
clerk—out of door, or in door, as the case may be—who
devotes the major part of his thirty shillings a week to his
personal pleasure and adornment, repairs half-price to the
Adelphi Theatre at least three times a week, dissipates
majestically at the cider cellars afterwards, and is a dirty
caricature of the fashion which expired six months ago.
There is the middle-aged copying clerk, with a large family,
who is always shabby, and often drunk. And there are the
office lads in their first surtouts, who feel a befitting contempt
for boys at day-schools: club as they go home at night, for

15

saveloys and porter: and think there's nothing like "life."
There are varieties of the genus, too numerous to recapitulate,
but however numerous they may be, they are all to be seen,
at certain regulated business hours, hurrying to and from the
places we have just mentioned.

These sequestered nooks are the public offices of the legal
profession, where writs are issued, judgments signed, declarations
filed, and numerous other ingenious machines put in motion
for the torture and torment of His Majesty's liege subjects,
and the comfort and emolument of the practitioners of the
law. They are, for the most part, low-roofed, mouldy rooms,
where innumerable rolls of parchment, which have been
perspiring in secret for the last century, send forth an
agreeable odour, which is mingled by day with the scent of
the dry rot, and by night with the various exhalations which
arise from damp cloaks, festering umbrellas, and the coarsest
tallow candles.

About half-past seven o'clock in the evening, some ten days
or a fortnight after Mr. Pickwick and his friends returned to
London, there hurried into one of these offices, an individual
in a brown coat and brass buttons, whose long hair was
scrupulously twisted round the rim of his napless hat, and
whose soiled drab trousers were so tightly strapped over his
Blucher boots, that his knees threatened every moment to
start from their concealment. He produced from his coat
pockets a long and narrow strip of parchment, on which the
presiding functionary impressed an illegible black stamp. He
then drew forth four scraps of paper, of similar dimensions,
each containing a printed copy of the strip of parchment
with blanks for a name; and having filled up the blanks,
put all the five documents in his pocket, and hurried away.

The man in the brown coat, with the cabalistic documents
in his pocket, was no other than our old acquaintance Mr.
Jackson, of the house of Dodson and Fogg, Freeman's Court,
Cornhill. Instead of returning to the office from whence he
came, however, he bent his steps direct to Sun Court, and

walking straight into the George and Vulture, demanded to know whether one Mr. Pickwick was within.

"Call Mr. Pickwick's servant, Tom," said the barmaid of the George and Vulture.

"Don't trouble yourself," said Mr. Jackson, "I've come on business. If you'll show me Mr. Pickwick's room I'll step up myself."

"What name, sir?" said the waiter.

"Jackson," replied the clerk.

The waiter stepped up stairs to announce Mr. Jackson; but Mr. Jackson saved him the trouble by following close at his heels, and walking into the apartment before he could articulate a syllable.

Mr. Pickwick had, that day, invited his three friends to dinner; they were all seated round the fire, drinking their wine, when Mr. Jackson presented himself, as above described.

"How de do, sir?" said Mr. Jackson, nodding to Mr. Pickwick.

That gentleman bowed, and looked somewhat surprised, for the physiognomy of Mr. Jackson dwelt not in his recollection.

"I have called from Dodson and Fogg's," said Mr. Jackson, in an explanatory tone.

Mr. Pickwick roused at the name. "I refer you to my attorney, sir: Mr. Perker, of Gray's Inn," said he. "Waiter, show this gentleman out."

"Beg your pardon, Mr. Pickwick," said Jackson, deliberately depositing his hat on the floor, and drawing from his pocket the strip of parchment. "But personal service, by clerk or agent, in these cases, you know, Mr. Pickwick—nothing like caution, sir, in all legal forms?"

Here Mr. Jackson cast his eye on the parchment; and, resting his hands on the table, and looking round with a winning and persuasive smile, said: "Now, come; don't let's have no words about such a little matter as this. Which of you gentlemen's name's Snodgrass?"

At this inquiry Mr. Snodgrass gave such a very undisguised and palpable start, that no further reply was needed.

"Ah! I thought so," said Mr. Jackson, more affably than before. "I've got a little something to trouble you with, sir."

"Me! exclaimed Mr. Snodgrass.

"It's only a *subpœna* in Bardell and Pickwick on behalf of the plaintiff," replied Jackson, singling out one of the slips of paper, and producing a shilling from his waistcoat pocket. "It'll come on, in the settens after Term; fourteenth of Febooary, we expect; we've marked it a special jury cause, and it's only ten down the paper. That's yours, Mr. Snodgrass." As Jackson said this he presented the parchment before the eyes of Mr. Snodgrass, and slipped the paper and the shilling into his hand.

Mr. Tupman had witnessed this process in silent astonishment, when Jackson, turning sharply upon him, said:

"I think I ain't mistaken when I say your name's Tupman, am I?"

Mr. Tupman looked at Mr. Pickwick; but, perceiving no encouragement in that gentleman's widely-opened eyes to deny his name, said:

"Yes, my name *is* Tupman, sir."

"And that other gentleman's Mr. Winkle, I think?" said Jackson.

Mr. Winkle faltered out a reply in the affirmative; and both gentlemen were forthwith invested with a slip of paper, and a shilling each, by the dexterous Mr. Jackson.

"Now," said Jackson, "I'm afraid you'll think me rather troublesome, but I want somebody else, if it ain't inconvenient. I *have* Samuel Weller's name here, Mr. Pickwick."

"Send my servant here, waiter," said Mr. Pickwick. The waiter retired, considerably astonished, and Mr. Pickwick motioned Jackson to a seat.

There was a painful pause, which was at length broken by the innocent defendant.

18

" I suppose, sir,' said Mr. Pickwick, his indignation rising while he spoke; " I suppose, sir, that it is the intention of your employers to seek to criminate me upon the testimony of my own friends ? "

Mr. Jackson struck his forefinger several times against the left side of his nose, to intimate that he was not there to disclose the secrets of the prison-house, and playfully rejoined :

" Not knowin', can't say."

" For what other reason, sir," pursued Mr. Pickwick, " are these subpœnas served upon them, if not for this ? "

" Very good plant, Mr. Pickwick," replied Jackson, slowly shaking his head. " But it won't do. No harm in trying, but there's little to be got out of me."

Here Mr. Jackson smiled once more upon the company, and, applying his left thumb to the tip of his nose, worked a visionary coffee-mill with his right hand : thereby performing a very graceful piece of pantomime (then much in vogue, but now, unhappily, almost obsolete) which was familiarly denominated " taking a grinder.'

" No, no, Mr. Pickwick," said Jackson, in conclusion ; " Perker's people must guess what we've served these subpœnas for. If they can't, they must wait till the action comes on, and then they'll find out."

Mr. Pickwick bestowed a look of excessive disgust on his unwelcome visitor, and would probably have hurled some tremendous anathema at the heads of Messrs. Dodson and Fogg, had not Sam's entrance at the instant interrupted him.

" Samuel Weller ? " said Mr. Jackson, inquiringly.

" Vun o' the truest things as you've said for many a long year," replied Sam, in a most composed manner.

" Here's a subpœna for you, Mr. Weller," said Jackson.

" What's that in English ? " inquired Sam.

" Here's the original," said Jackson, declining the required explanation.

" Which ? " said Sam.

" This," replied Jackson, shaking the parchment.

"Oh, that's the 'rig'nal, is it?' said Sam. "Well, I'm wery glad I've seen the 'rig'nal, cos it's a gratifyin' sort o' thing, and eases vun's mind so much."

"And here's the shilling," said Jackson. "It's from Dodson and Fogg's.'

"And it's uncommon handsome o' Dodson and Fogg, as knows so little of me, to come down vith a present," said Sam. "I feel it as a wery high compliment, sir; it's a wery hon'rable thing to them, as they knows how to reward merit werever they meets it. Besides wich, it's affectin' to one's feelin's."

As Mr. Weller said this, he inflicted a little friction on his right eye-lid, with the sleeve of his coat, after the most approved manner of actors when they are in domestic pathetics.

Mr. Jackson seemed rather puzzled by Sam's proceedings; but, as he had served the subpœnas, and had nothing more to say, he made a feint of putting on the one glove which he usually carried in his hand, for the sake of appearances; and returned to the office to report progress.

Mr. Pickwick slept little that night; his memory had received a very disagreeable refresher on the subject of Mrs. Bardell's action. He breakfasted betimes next morning, and, desiring Sam to accompany him, set forth towards Gray's Inn Square.

"Sam!" said Mr. Pickwick, looking round, when they got to the end of Cheapside.

"Sir?' said Sam, stepping up to his master.

"Which way?"

"Up Newgate Street."

Mr. Pickwick did not turn round immediately, but looked vacantly in Sam's face for a few seconds, and heaved a deep sigh.

"What's the matter, sir?" inquired Sam.

"This action, Sam," said Mr. Pickwick, "is expected to come on, on the fourteenth of next month."

CELEBRATED SASSAGE FACTORY.

" Remarkable coin*ci*dence that 'ere, sir," replied Sam.

" Why remarkable, Sam ? " inquired Mr. Pickwick.

" Walentine's day, sir," responded Sam ; " reg'lar good day for a breach o' promise trial."

Mr. Weller's smile awakened no gleam of mirth in his master's countenance. Mr. Pickwick turned abruptly round, and led the way in silence.

They had walked some distance : Mr. Pickwick trotting on before, plunged in profound meditation, and Sam following behind, with a countenance expressive of the most enviable and easy defiance of everything and everybody : when the latter, who was always especially anxious to impart to his master any exclusive information he possessed, quickened his pace until he was close at Mr. Pickwick's heels ; and, pointing up at a house they were passing, said :

" Wery nice pork-shop that 'ere, sir."

" Yes, it seems so," said Mr. Pickwick.

" Celebrated Sassage factory," said Sam.

" Is it ? " said Mr. Pickwick.

" Is it ! " reiterated Sam, with some indignation ; " I should rayther think it was. Why, sir, bless your innocent eyebrows, that's where the mysterious disappearance of a 'spectable tradesman took place four year ago."

" You don't mean to say he was burked, Sam ? " said Mr. Pickwick, looking hastily round.

" No, I don't indeed, sir," replied Mr. Weller, " I wish I did ; far worse than that. He was the master o' that 'ere shop, sir, and the inwenter o' the patent-never-leavin'-off sassage steam ingine, as ud swaller up a pavin' stone if you put it too near, and grind it into sassages as easy as if it was a tender young babby. Wery proud o' that machine he was, as it was nat'ral he should be, and he'd stand down in the celler a lookin' at it wen it was in full play, till he got quite melancholy with joy. A wery happy man he'd ha' been, sir, in the procession o' that 'ere ingine and two more lovely hinfants besides, if it hadn't been for his wife, who was a most

ow-dacious wixin. She was always a follerin' him about, and
dinnin' in his ears, 'till at last he couldn't stand it no longer.
'I'll tell you what it is, my dear,' he says one day; 'if you
persewere in this here sort of amusement,' he says, 'I'm
blessed if I don't go away to 'Merriker; and that's all about
it.' 'You're a idle willin,' says she, 'and I wish the 'Merrikins
joy of their bargain.' Arter wich she keeps on abusin' of
him for half an hour, and then runs into the little parlour
behind the shop, sets to a screamin', says he'll be the death
on her, and falls in a fit, which lasts for three good hours—
one o' them fits wich is all screamin' and kickin'. Well, next
mornin', the husband was missin'. He hadn't taken nothin'
from the till,—hadn't even put on his great-coat—so it was
quite clear he warn't gone to 'Merriker. Didn't come back
next day; didn't come back next week; Missis had bills
printed, sayin' that, if he'd come back, he should be forgiven
everythin' (which was very liberal, seein' that he hadn't done
nothin' at all); the canals was dragged, and for two months
artervards, wenever a body turned up, it was carried, as a
reg'lar thing, straight off to the sassage shop. Hows'ever,
none on 'em answered; so they gave out that he'd run avay,
and she kep on the bis'ness. One Saturday night, a little
thin old gen l'm'n comes into the shop in a great passion and
says, 'Are you the missis o' this here shop?' 'Yes, I am,'
says she. 'Well, ma'am,' says he, 'then I've just looked in
to say that me and my family ain't a goin' to be choked for
nothin'; and more than that, ma'am,' he says, 'you'll allow
me to observe, that as you don't use the primest parts of
the meat in the manafacter o' sassages, I think you'd find
beef come nearly as cheap as buttons.' 'As buttons, sir!'
says she. 'Buttons, ma'am,' says the little old gentleman,
unfolding a bit of paper, and shewin' twenty or thirty halves
o' buttons. 'Nice seasonin' for sassages, is trousers' buttons,
ma'am.' 'They're my husband's buttons!' says the widder,
beginnin' to faint. 'What!' screams the little old gen'l'm'n,
turnin' wery pale. 'I see it all,' says the widder; 'in a fit

of temporary insanity he rashly converted his-self into sassages !' And so he had, sir," said Mr. Weller, looking steadily into Mr. Pickwick's horror-stricken countenance, "or else he'd been draw'd into the ingine; but however that might ha' been, the little old gen'l'm'n, who had been remarkably partial to sassages all his life, rushed out o' the shop in a wild state, and was never heerd on artervards !"

The relation of this affecting incident of private life brought master and man to Mr. Perker's chambers. Lowten, holding the door half open, was in conversation with a rustily-clad, miserable-looking man, in boots without toes and gloves without fingers. There were traces of privation and suffering —almost of despair—in his lank and care-worn countenance; he felt his poverty, for he shrunk to the dark side of the staircase as Mr. Pickwick approached.

"It's very unfortunate," said the stranger, with a sigh.

"Very," said Lowten, scribbling his name on the door-post with his pen, and rubbing it out again with the feather. "Will you leave a message for him?"

"When do you think he'll be back?" inquired the stranger.

"Quite uncertain," replied Lowten, winking at Mr. Pickwick, as the stranger cast his eyes towards the ground.

"You don't think it would be of any use my waiting for him?" said the stranger, looking wistfully into the office.

"Oh no, I'm sure it wouldn't," replied the clerk, moving a little more into the centre of the door-way. "He's certain not to be back this week, and it's a chance whether he will be next; for when Perker once gets out of town, he's never in a hurry to come back again."

"Out of town!" said Mr. Pickwick; "dear me, how unfortunate!"

"Don't go away, Mr. Pickwick," said Lowten, "I've got a letter for you." The stranger seeming to hesitate, once more looked towards the ground, and the clerk winked slyly at Mr. Pickwick, as if to intimate that some exquisite piece of humour was going forward, though what it was Mr. Pickwick could not for the life of him divine.

"Step in, Mr. Pickwick," said Lowten. "Well, will you leave a message, Mr. Watty, or will you call again?"

"Ask him to be so kind as to leave out word what has been done in my business,' said the man; "for God's sake don't neglect it, Mr. Lowten."

"No, no; I won't forget it," replied the clerk. "Walk in, Mr. Pickwick. Good morning, Mr. Watty; it's a fine day for walking, isn't it?" Seeing that the stranger still lingered, he beckoned Sam Weller to follow his master in, and shut the door in his face.

"There never was such a pestering bankrupt as that since the world began, I do believe!" said Lowten, throwing down his pen with the air of an injured man. "His affairs haven't been in Chancery quite four years yet, and I'm d—d if he don't come worrying here twice a week. Step this way, Mr. Pickwick. Perker *is* in, and he'll see you, I know. Devilish cold," he added, pettishly, "standing at that door, wasting one's time with such seedy vagabonds!" Having very vehemently stirred a particularly large fire with a particularly small poker, the clerk led the way to his principal's private room, and announced Mr. Pickwick.

"Ah, my dear sir," said little Mr. Perker, bustling up from his chair. "Well, my dear sir, and what's the news about your matter, eh? Anything more about our friends in Freeman's Court? They've not been sleeping, *I* know that. Ah, they're very smart fellows; very smart, indeed."

As the little man concluded, he took an emphatic pinch of snuff, as a tribute to the smartness of Messrs. Dodson and Fogg.

"They are great scoundrels," said Mr. Pickwick.

"Aye, aye," said the little man; "that's a matter of opinion, you know, and we won't dispute about terms; because of course you can't be expected to view these subjects with a professional eye. Well, we've done everything that's necessary. I have retained Serjeant Snubbin."

"Is he a good man?" inquired Mr. Pickwick.

"Good man!" replied Perker; "bless your heart and soul, my dear sir, Serjeant Snubbin is at the very top of his profession. Gets treble the business of any man in court— engaged in every case. You needn't mention it abroad; but we say—we of the profession—that Serjeant Snubbin leads the court by the nose."

The little man took another pinch of snuff as he made this communication, and nodded mysteriously to Mr. Pickwick.

"They have subpœna'd my three friends," said Mr. Pickwick.

"Ah! of course they would," replied Perker. "Important witnesses; saw you in a delicate situation."

"But she fainted of her own accord," said Mr. Pickwick. "She threw herself into my arms."

"Very likely, my dear sir," replied Perker; "very likely and very natural. Nothing more so, my dear sir, nothing. But who's to prove it?"

"They have subpœna'd my servant too," said Mr. Pickwick, quitting the other point; for there Mr. Perker's question had somewhat staggered him.

"Sam?' said Perker.

Mr. Pickwick replied in the affirmative.

" Of course, my dear sir; of course. I knew they would. I could have told *you* that, a month ago. You know, my dear sir, if you *will* take the management of your affairs into your own hands after intrusting them to your solicitor, you must also take the consequences." Here Mr. Perker drew himself up with conscious dignity, and brushed some stray grains of snuff from his shirt frill.

"And what do they want him to prove?" asked Mr. Pickwick, after two or three minutes' silence.

"That you sent him up to the plaintiff's to make some offer of a compromise, I suppose," replied Perker. "It don't matter much, though; I don't think many counsel could get a great deal out of *him*."

"I don't think they could," said Mr. Pickwick; smiling,

despite his vexation, at the idea of Sam's appearance as a witness. "What course do we pursue?"

"We have only one to adopt, my dear sir," replied Perker; "cross-examine the witnesses; trust to Snubbin's eloquence; throw dust in the eyes of the judge; throw ourselves on the jury."

"And suppose the verdict is against me?" said Mr. Pickwick.

Mr. Perker smiled, took a very long pinch of snuff, stirred the fire, shrugged his shoulders, and remained expressively silent.

"You mean that in that case I must pay the damages?" said Mr. Pickwick, who had watched this telegraphic answer with considerable sternness.

Perker gave the fire another very unnecessary poke, and said "I am afraid so.'

"Then I beg to announce to you, my unalterable determination to pay no damages whatever," said Mr. Pickwick, most emphatically. "None, Perker. Not a pound, not a penny, of my money, shall find its way into the pockets of Dodson and Fogg. That is my deliberate and irrevocable determination." Mr. Pickwick gave a heavy blow on the table before him, in confirmation of the irrevocability of his intention.

"Very well, my dear sir, very well," said Perker. "You know best, of course."

"Of course," replied Mr. Pickwick hastily. "Where does Serjeant Snubbin live?"

"In Lincoln's Inn Old Square," replied Perker.

"I should like to see him," said Mr. Pickwick.

"See Serjeant Snubbin, my dear sir!" rejoined Perker, in utter amazement. "Pooh, pooh, my dear sir, impossible. See Serjeant Snubbin! Bless you, my dear sir, such a thing was never heard of, without a consultation fee being previously paid, and a consultation fixed. It couldn't be done, my dear sir; it couldn't be done."

Mr. Pickwick, however, had made up his mind not only

that it could be done, but that it should be done; and the consequence was, that within ten minutes after he had received the assurance that the thing was impossible, he was conducted by his solicitor into the outer office of the great Serjeant Snubbin himself.

It was an uncarpeted room of tolerable dimensions, with a large writing-table drawn up near the fire: the baize top of which had long since lost all claim to its original hue of green, and had gradually grown grey with dust and age, except where all traces of its natural colour were obliterated by ink-stains. Upon the table were numerous little bundles of papers tied with red tape; and behind it, sat an elderly clerk, whose sleek appearance, and heavy gold watch-chain, presented imposing indications of the extensive and lucrative practice of Mr. Serjeant Snubbin.

"Is the Serjeant in his room, Mr. Mallard?" inquired Perker, offering his box with all imaginable courtesy.

"Yes, he is," was the reply, "but he's very busy. Look here; not an opinion given yet, on any one of these cases; and an expedition fee paid with all of 'em." The clerk smiled as he said this, and inhaled the pinch of snuff with a zest which seemed to be compounded of a fondness for snuff and a relish for fees.

"Something like practice that," said Perker.

"Yes," said the barrister's clerk, producing his own box, and offering it with the greatest cordiality; "and the best of it is, that as nobody alive except myself can read the Serjeant's writing, they are obliged to wait for the opinions, when he has given them, till I have copied 'em, ha—ha—ha!"

"Which makes good for we know who, besides the Serjeant, and draws a little more out of the clients, eh?" said Perker; "Ha, ha, ha!" At this the Serjeant's clerk laughed again; not a noisy boisterous laugh, but a silent, internal chuckle, which Mr. Pickwick disliked to hear. When a man bleeds inwardly, it is a dangerous thing for himself; but when he laughs inwardly, it bodes no good to other people.

" You haven't made me out that little list of the fees that I'm in your debt, have you?" said Perker.

"No, I have not," replied the clerk.

" I wish you would," said Perker. "Let me have them, and I'll send you a cheque. But I suppose you're too busy pocketing the ready money, to think of the debtors, eh? ha, ha, ha!" This sally seemed to tickle the clerk amazingly, and he once more enjoyed a little quiet laugh to himself.

" But, Mr. Mallard, my dear friend," said Perker, suddenly recovering his gravity, and drawing the great man's great man into a corner, by the lappel of his coat; "you must persuade the Serjeant to see me, and my client here."

" Come, come," said the clerk, "that's not bad either. See the Serjeant! come, that's too absurd." Notwithstanding the absurdity of the proposal, however, the clerk allowed himself to be gently drawn beyond the hearing of Mr. Pickwick; and after a short conversation conducted in whispers, walked softly down a little dark passage, and disappeared into the legal luminary's sanctum: whence he shortly returned on tiptoe, and informed Mr. Perker and Mr. Pickwick that the Serjeant had been prevailed upon, in violation of all established rules and customs, to admit them at once.

Mr. Serjeant Snubbin was a lantern-faced, sallow-complexioned man, of about five-and-forty, or—as the novels say —he might be fifty. He had that dull-looking boiled eye which is often to be seen in the heads of people who have applied themselves during many years to a weary and laborious course of study; and which would have been sufficient, without the additional eye-glass which dangled from a broad black riband round his neck, to warn a stranger that he was very near-sighted. His hair was thin and weak, which was partly attributable to his having never devoted much time to its arrangement, and partly to his having worn for five-and-twenty years the forensic wig which hung on a block beside him. The marks of hair-powder on his coat-collar, and the ill-washed and worse tied white handkerchief round his throat, showed that he had not found leisure since he left the court to make any alteration in his dress: while the slovenly style of the remainder of his costume warranted the inference that his personal appearance would not have been very much improved if he had. Books of practice, heaps of papers, and opened letters, were scattered over the table, without any attempt at order or arrangement; the furniture of the room was old and ricketty; the doors of the book-case were rotting on their hinges; the dust flew out from the carpet in little clouds at every step; the blinds were yellow with age and dirt; the state of everything in the room showed, with a clearness not to be mistaken, that Mr. Serjeant Snubbin was far too much occupied with his professional pursuits to take any great heed or regard of his personal comforts.

The Serjeant was writing when his clients entered; he bowed abstractedly when Mr. Pickwick was introduced by his solicitor; and then, motioning them to a seat, put his pen carefully in the inkstand, nursed his left leg, and waited to be spoken to.

"Mr. Pickwick is the defendant in Bardell and Pickwick, Serjeant Snubbin," said Perker.

"I am retained in that, am I?" said the Serjeant.

"You are, sir," replied Perker.

The Serjeant nodded his head, and waited for something else.

"Mr. Pickwick was anxious to call upon you, Serjeant Snubbin," said Perker, "to state to you, before you entered upon the case, that he denies there being any ground or pretence whatever for the action against him; and that unless he came into court with clean hands, and without the most conscientious conviction that he was right in resisting the plaintiff's demand, he would not be there at all. I believe I state your views correctly; do I not, my dear sir?" said the little man, turning to Mr. Pickwick.

"Quite so," replied that gentleman.

Mr. Serjeant Snubbin unfolded his glasses, raised them to

his eyes; and, after looking at Mr. Pickwick for a few seconds with great curiosity, turned to Mr. Perker, and said, smiling slightly as he spoke:

"Has Mr. Pickwick a strong case?"

The attorney shrugged his shoulders.

"Do you purpose calling witnesses?"

"No."

The smile on the Serjeant's countenance became more defined; he rocked his leg with increased violence; and, throwing himself back in his easy-chair, coughed dubiously.

These tokens of the Serjeant's presentiments on the subject, slight as they were, were not lost on Mr. Pickwick. He settled the spectacles, through which he had attentively regarded such demonstrations of the barrister's feelings as he had permitted himself to exhibit, more firmly on his nose; and said with great energy, and in utter disregard of all Mr. Perker's admonitory winkings and frownings:

"My wishing to wait upon you, for such a purpose as this, sir, appears, I have no doubt, to a gentleman who sees so much of these matters as you must necessarily do, a very extraordinary circumstance."

The Serjeant tried to look gravely at the fire, but the smile came back again.

"Gentlemen of your profession, sir," continued Mr. Pickwick, "see the worst side of human nature. All its disputes, all its ill-will and bad blood, rise up before you. You know from your experience of juries (I mean no disparagement to you, or them) how much depends upon *effect*: and you are apt to attribute to others, a desire to use, for purposes of deception and self-interest, the very instruments which you, in pure honesty and honour of purpose, and with a laudable desire to do your utmost for your client, know the temper and worth of so well, from constantly employing them yourselves. I really believe that to this circumstance may be attributed the vulgar but very general notion of your being, as a body, suspicious, distrustful, and over-cautious. Conscious as I am,

The First Interview with Mr. Serjeant Snubbin

sir, of the disadvantage of making such a declaration to you, under such circumstances, I have come here, because I wish you distinctly to understand, as my friend Mr. Perker has said, that I am innocent of the falsehood laid to my charge; and although I am very well aware of the inestimable value of your assistance, sir, I must beg to add, that unless you sincerely believe this, I would rather be deprived of the aid of your talents than have the advantage of them."

Long before the close of this address, which we are bound to say was of a very prosy character for Mr. Pickwick, the Serjeant had relapsed into a state of abstraction. After some minutes, however, during which he had reassumed his pen, he appeared to be again aware of the presence of his clients; raising his head from the paper, he said, rather snappishly,

" Who is with me in this case ? "

" Mr. Phunky, Serjeant Snubbin," replied the attorney.

" Phunky, Phunky," said the Serjeant, " I never heard the name before. He must be a very young man."

" Yes, he is a very young man," replied the attorney. " He was only called the other day. Let me see—he has not been at the Bar eight years yet."

" Ah, I thought not," said the Sergeant, in that sort of pitying tone in which ordinary folks would speak of a very helpless little child. " Mr. Mallard, send round to Mr. — Mr. —."

" Phunky's—Holborn Court, Gray's Inn," interposed Perker. (Holborn Court, by the bye, is South Square now). " Mr. Phunky, and say I should be glad if he'd step here, a moment."

Mr. Mallard departed to execute his commission; and Serjeant Snubbin relapsed into abstraction until Mr. Phunky himself was introduced.

Although an infant barrister, he was a full-grown man. He had a very nervous manner, and a painful hesitation in his speech; it did not appear to be a natural defect, but seemed rather the result of timidity, arising from the consciousness of being "kept down" by want of means, or interest, or connexion, or impudence, as the case might be. He was overawed by the Serjeant, and profoundly courteous to the attorney.

"I have not had the pleasure of seeing you before, Mr. Phunky," said Serjeant Snubbin, with haughty condescension.

Mr. Phunky bowed. He *had* had the pleasure of seeing the Serjeant, and of envying him too, with all a poor man's envy, for eight years and a quarter.

"You are with me in this case, I understand?" said the Serjeant.

If Mr. Phunky had been a rich man, he would have instantly sent for his clerk to remind him; if he had been a wise one, he would have applied his fore-finger to his forehead, and endeavoured to recollect, whether, in the multiplicity of his engagements he had undertaken this one, or not; but as he was neither rich nor wise (in this sense at all events) he turned red, and bowed.

"Have you read the papers, Mr. Phunky?" inquired the Serjeant.

Here again, Mr. Phunky should have professed to have forgotten all about the merits of the case; but as he had read such papers as had been laid before him in the course of the action, and had thought of nothing else, waking or sleeping, throughout the two months during which he had been retained as Mr. Serjeant Snubbin's junior, he turned a deeper red, and bowed again.

"This is Mr. Pickwick," said the Serjeant, waving his pen in the direction in which that gentleman was standing.

Mr. Phunky bowed to Mr. Pickwick with a reverence which a first client must ever awaken; and again inclined his head towards his leader.

"Perhaps you will take Mr. Pickwick away," said the Serjeant, "and—and—and—hear anything Mr. Pickwick may wish to communicate. We shall have a consultation, of course." With this hint that he had been interrupted quite long enough, Mr. Serjeant Snubbin, who had been gradually growing more and more abstracted, applied his glass to his eyes for an instant, bowed slightly round, and was once more deeply immersed in the case before him : which arose out of an interminable lawsuit, originating in the act of an individual, deceased a century or so ago, who had stopped up a pathway leading from some place which nobody ever came from, to some other place which nobody ever went to.

Mr. Phunky would not hear of passing through any door until Mr. Pickwick and his solicitor had passed through before him, so it was some time before they got into the Square ; and when they did reach it, they walked up and down, and held a long conference, the result of which was, that it was a very difficult matter to say how the verdict would go ; that nobody could presume to calculate on the issue of an action ; that it was very lucky they had prevented the other party from getting Serjeant Snubbin ; and other topics of doubt and consolation, common in such a position of affairs.

Mr. Weller was then roused by his master from a sweet sleep of an hour's duration ; and, bidding adieu to Lowten, they returned to the City.

CHAPTER XXXII.

THERE is a repose about Lant Street, in the Borough, which
sheds a gentle melancholy upon the soul. There are always
a good many houses to let in the street: it is a bye-street
too, and its dulness is soothing. A house in Lant Street
would not come within the denomination of a first-rate
residence, in the strict acceptation of the term; but it is a
most desirable spot nevertheless. If a man wished to abstract
himself from the world—to remove himself from within the
reach of temptation—to place himself beyond the possibility
of any inducement to look out of the window—he should by
all means go to Lant Street.

In this happy retreat are colonised a few clear-starchers, a
sprinkling of journeymen bookbinders, one or two prison
agents for the Insolvent Court, several small housekeepers
who are employed in the Docks, a handful of mantua-makers,
and a seasoning of jobbing tailors. The majority of the
inhabitants either direct their energies to the letting of
furnished apartments, or devote themselves to the healthful
and invigorating pursuit of mangling. The chief features in
the still life of the street are green shutters, lodging-bills,
brass door-plates, and bell-handles; the principal specimens of
animated nature, the pot-boy, the muffin youth, and the

34

baked-potato man. The population is migratory, usually disappearing on the verge of quarter-day, and generally by night. His Majesty's revenues are seldom collected in this happy valley; the rents are dubious; and the water communication is very frequently cut off.

Mr. Bob Sawyer embellished one side of the fire, in his first-floor front, early on the evening for which he had invited Mr. Pickwick; and Mr. Ben Allen the other. The preparations for the reception of visitors appeared to be completed. The umbrellas in the passage had been heaped into the little corner outside the back-parlour door; the bonnet and shawl of the landlady's servant had been removed from the bannisters; there were not more than two pairs of pattens on the street-door mat, and a kitchen candle, with a very long snuff, burnt cheerfully on the ledge of the staircase window. Mr. Bob Sawyer had himself purchased the spirits at a wine vaults in High Street, and had returned home preceding the bearer thereof, to preclude the possibility of their delivery at the wrong house. The punch was ready-made in a red pan in the bed-room; a little table, covered with a green baize cloth, had been borrowed from the parlour, to play at cards on; and the glasses of the establishment, together with those which had been borrowed for the occasion from the public-house, were all drawn up in a tray, which was deposited on the landing outside the door.

Notwithstanding the highly satisfactory nature of all these arrangements, there was a cloud on the countenance of Mr. Bob Sawyer, as he sat by the fireside. There was a sympathising expression, too, in the features of Mr. Ben Allen, as he gazed intently on the coals; and a tone of melancholy in his voice, as he said, after a long silence:

"Well, it *is* unlucky she should have taken it in her head to turn sour, just on this occasion. She might at least have waited till to-morrow."

"That's her malevolence, that's her malevolence," returned Mr. Bob Sawyer, vehemently. "She says that if I can afford to give a party I ought to be able to pay her confounded 'little bill.'"

"How long has it been running?" inquired Mr. Ben Allen. A bill, by the bye, is the most extraordinary locomotive engine that the genius of man ever produced. It would keep on running during the longest lifetime, without ever once stopping of its own accord.

"Only a quarter, and a month or so," replied Mr. Bob Sawyer.

Ben Allen coughed hopelessly, and directed a searching look between the two top bars of the stove.

"It'll be a deuced unpleasant thing if she takes it into her head to let out, when those fellows are here, won't it?" said Mr. Ben Allen at length.

"Horrible," replied Bob Sawyer, "horrible."

A low tap was heard at the room door. Mr. Bob Sawyer looked expressively at his friend, and bade the tapper come in; whereupon a dirty slipshod girl in black cotton stockings, who might have passed for the neglected daughter of a superannuated dustman in very reduced circumstances, thrust in her head, and said,

"Please, Mister Sawyer, Missis Raddle wants to speak to *you*."

Before Mr. Bob Sawyer could return any answer, the girl suddenly disappeared with a jerk, as if somebody had given her a violent pull behind; this mysterious exit was no sooner accomplished, than there was another tap at the door—a smart pointed tap, which seemed to say, "Here I am, and in I'm coming."

Mr. Bob Sawyer glanced at his friend with a look of abject apprehension, and once more cried "Come in."

The permission was not at all necessary, for, before Mr. Bob Sawyer had uttered the words, a little fierce woman bounced into the room, all in a tremble with passion, and pale with rage.

"Now, Mr. Sawyer," said the little fierce woman, trying to appear very calm, "if you'll have the kindness to settle

36

that little bill of mine I'll thank you, because I've got my rent to pay this afternoon, and my landlord's a waiting below now." Here the little woman rubbed her hands, and looked steadily over Mr. Bob Sawyer's head, at the wall behind him.

"I am very sorry to put you to any inconvenience, Mrs. Raddle," said Bob Sawyer, deferentially, "but——'

"Oh, it isn't any inconvenience," replied the little woman, with a shrill titter. "I didn't want it particular before to-day; leastways, as it has to go to my landlord directly, it was as well for you to keep it as me. You promised me this afternoon, Mr. Sawyer, and every gentleman as has ever lived here, has kept his word, sir, as of course anybody as calls himself a gentleman, does." Mrs. Raddle tossed her head, bit her lips, rubbed her hands harder, and looked at the wall more steadily than ever. It was plain to see, as Mr. Bob Sawyer remarked in a style of eastern allegory on a subsequent occasion, that she was "getting the steam up."

"I am very sorry, Mrs. Raddle," said Bob Sawyer with all imaginable humility, "but the fact is, that I have been disappointed in the City to-day."—Extraordinary place that City. An astonishing number of men always *are* getting disappointed there.

"Well, Mr. Sawyer," said Mrs. Raddle, planting herself firmly on a purple cauliflower in the Kidderminster carpet, "and what's that to me, sir?"

"I—I—have no doubt, Mrs. Raddle," said Bob Sawyer, blinking this last question, "that before the middle of next week we shall be able to set ourselves quite square, and go on, on a better system, afterwards."

This was all Mrs. Raddle wanted. She had bustled up to the apartment of the unlucky Bob Sawyer, so bent upon going into a passion, that, in all probability, payment would have rather disappointed her than otherwise. She was in excellent order for a little relaxation of the kind: having just exchanged a few introductory compliments with Mr. R. in the front kitchen.

"Do you suppose, Mr. Sawyer," said Mrs. Raddle, elevating her voice for the information of the neighbours, "do you suppose that I'm a-going day after day to let a fellar occupy my lodgings as never thinks of paying his rent, nor even the very money laid out for the fresh butter and lump sugar that's bought for his breakfast, and the very milk that's took in, at the street door? Do you suppose a hard-working and industrious woman as has lived in this street for twenty year (ten year over the way, and nine year and three quarter in this very house) has nothing else to do but to work herself to death after a parcel of lazy idle fellars, that are always smoking and drinking, and lounging, when they ought to be glad to turn their hands to anything that would help 'em to pay their bills? Do you——"

"My good soul," interposed Mr. Benjamin Allen, soothingly.

"Have the goodness to keep your observashuns to yourself, sir, I beg," said Mrs. Raddle, suddenly arresting the rapid torrent of her speech, and addressing the third party with impressive slowness and solemnity. "I am not aweer, sir, that you have any right to address your conversation to me. I don't think I let these apartments to you, sir."

"No, you certainly did not," said Mr. Benjamin Allen.

"Very good, sir," responded Mrs. Raddle, with lofty politeness. "Then p'raps, sir, you'll confine yourself to breaking the arms and legs of the poor people in the hospitals, and keep yourself *to* yourself, sir, or there may be some persons here as will make you, sir."

"But you are such an unreasonable woman," remonstrated Mr. Benjamin Allen.

"I beg your parding, young man," said Mrs. Raddle, in a cold perspiration of anger. "But will you have the goodness just to call me that again, sir?"

"I didn't make use of the word in any invidious sense, ma'am," replied Mr. Benjamin Allen, growing somewhat uneasy on his own account.

"I beg your parding, young man," demanded Mrs. Raddle in a louder and more imperative tone. "But who do you call a woman? Did you make that remark to me, sir?"

"Why, bless my heart!" said Mr. Benjamin Allen.

"Did you apply that name to me, I ask of you, sir?" interrupted Mrs. Raddle, with intense fierceness, throwing the door wide open.

"Why, of course I did," replied Mr. Benjamin Allen.

"Yes, of course you did," said Mrs. Raddle, backing gradually to the door, and raising her voice to its loudest pitch, for the special behoof of Mr. Raddle in the kitchen. "Yes, of course you did! And everybody knows that they may safely insult me in my own 'ouse while my husband sits sleeping down stairs, and taking no more notice than if I was a dog in the streets. He ought to be ashamed of himself (here Mrs. Raddle sobbed) to allow his wife to be treated in this way by a parcel of young cutters and carvers of live people's bodies, that disgraces the lodgings (another sob), and leaving her exposed to all manner of abuse; a base, faint-hearted, timorous wretch, that's afraid to come up stairs, and face the ruffinly creatures—that's afraid—that's afraid to come!" Mrs. Raddle paused to listen whether the repetition of the taunt had roused her better half; and, finding that it had not been successful, proceeded to descend the stairs with sobs innumerable: when there came a loud double knock at the street door: whereupon she burst into an hysterical fit of weeping, accompanied with dismal moans, which was prolonged until the knock had been repeated six times, when, in an uncontrollable burst of mental agony, she threw down all the umbrellas, and disappeared into the back parlour, closing the door after her with an awful crash.

"Does Mr. Sawyer live here?" said Mr. Pickwick, when the door was opened.

"Yes," said the girl, "first floor. It's the door straight afore you, when you gets to the top of the stairs." Having given this instruction, the handmaid, who had been brought

39

up among the aboriginal inhabitants of Southwark, disappeared, with the candle in her hand, down the kitchen stairs : perfectly satisfied that she had done everything that could possibly be required of her under the circumstances.

Mr. Snodgrass, who entered last, secured the street door, after several ineffectual efforts, by putting up the chain ; and the friends stumbled up stairs, where they were received by Mr. Bob Sawyer, who had been afraid to go down, lest he should be waylaid by Mrs. Raddle.

"How are you ? " said the discomfited student. " Glad to see you,—take care of the glasses." This caution was addressed to Mr. Pickwick, who had put his hat in the tray.

"Dear me," said Mr. Pickwick, "I beg your pardon."

"Don't mention it, don't mention it," said Bob Sawyer. "I'm rather confined for room here, but you must put up with all that, when you come to see a young bachelor. Walk in. You've seen this gentleman before, I think ? " Mr. Pickwick shook hands with Mr. Benjamin Allen, and his friends followed his example. They had scarcely taken their seats when there was another double knock.

"I hope that's Jack Hopkins ! " said Mr. Bob Sawyer. "Hush. Yes, it is. Come up, Jack ; come up."

A heavy footstep was heard upon the stairs, and Jack Hopkins presented himself. He wore a black velvet waistcoat, with thunder-and-lightning buttons ; and a blue striped shirt, with a white false collar.

"You're late, Jack ? " said Mr. Benjamin Allen.

"Been detained at Bartholomew's," replied Hopkins.

"Anything new ? "

"No, nothing particular. Rather a good accident brought into the casualty ward."

"What was that, sir ? " inquired Mr. Pickwick.

"Only a man fallen out of a four pair of stairs' window ; —but it's a very fair case—very fair case indeed."

"Do you mean that the patient is in a fair way to recover ? " inquired Mr. Pickwick.

ANECDOTE OF A NECKLACE.

"No," replied Hopkins, carelessly. "No, I should rather say he wouldn't. There must be a splendid operation though, to-morrow—magnificent sight if Slasher does it."

"You consider Mr. Slasher a good operator?" said Mr. Pickwick.

"Best alive," replied Hopkins. "Took a boy's leg out of the socket last week—boy ate five apples and a gingerbread cake—exactly two minutes after it was all over, boy said he wouldn't lie there to be made game of, and he'd tell his mother if they didn't begin."

"Dear me!" said Mr. Pickwick, astonished.

"Pooh! That's nothing, that ain't," said Jack Hopkins. "Is it, Bob?"

"Nothing at all," replied Mr. Bob Sawyer.

"By the bye, Bob," said Hopkins, with a scarcely perceptible glance at Mr. Pickwick's attentive face, "we had a curious accident last night. A child was brought in, who had swallowed a necklace."

"Swallowed what, sir?" interrupted Mr. Pickwick.

"A necklace," replied Jack Hopkins. "Not all at once, you know, that would be too much—*you* couldn't swallow that, if the child did—eh, Mr. Pickwick, ha! ha!" Mr. Hopkins appeared highly gratified with his own pleasantry; and continued. "No, the way was this. Child's parents were poor people who lived in a court. Child's eldest sister bought a necklace; common necklace, made of large black wooden beads. Child, being fond of toys, cribbed the necklace, hid it, played with it, cut the string, and swallowed a bead. Child thought it capital fun, went back next day, and swallowed another bead."

"Bless my heart," said Mr. Pickwick, "what a dreadful thing! I beg your pardon, sir. Go on."

"Next day, child swallowed two beads; the day after that, he treated himself to three, and so on, till in a week's time he had got through the necklace—five-and-twenty beads in all. The sister, who was an industrious girl, and seldom

41

treated herself to a bit of finery, cried her eyes out, at the loss of the necklace; looked high and low for it; but, I needn't say, didn't find it. A few days afterwards, the family were at dinner—baked shoulder of mutton, and potatoes under it—the child, who wasn't hungry, was playing about the room, when suddenly there was heard a devil of a noise, like a small hail storm. 'Don't do that, my boy,' said the father. 'I ain't a doin' nothing,' said the child. 'Well, don't do it again,' said the father. There was a short silence, and then the noise began again, worse than ever. 'If you don't mind what I say, my boy,' said the father, 'you'll find yourself in bed, in something less than a pig's whisper.' He gave the child a shake to make him obedient, and such a rattling ensued as nobody ever heard before. 'Why, damme, it's *in* the child!' said the father, 'he's got the croup in the wrong place!' 'No I haven't, father,' said the child, beginning to cry, 'it's the necklace; I swallowed it, father.'—The father caught the child up, and ran with him to the hospital: the beads in the boy's stomach rattling all the way with the jolting; and the people looking up in the air, and down in the cellars, to see where the unusual sound came from. He's in the hospital now," said Jack Hopkins, "and he makes such a devil of a noise when he walks about, that they're obliged to muffle him in a watchman's coat, for fear he should wake the patients!"

"That's the most extraordinary case I ever heard of," said Mr. Pickwick, with an emphatic blow on the table.

"Oh, that's nothing," said Jack Hopkins; "is it, Bob?"

"Certainly not," replied Mr. Bob Sawyer.

"Very singular things occur in our profession, I can assure you, sir," said Hopkins.

"So I should be disposed to imagine," replied Mr. Pickwick.

Another knock at the door, announced a large-headed young man in a black wig, who brought with him a scorbutic youth in a long stock. The next comer was a gentleman in a shirt emblazoned with pink anchors, who was closely

PREPARATIONS FOR SUPPER.

followed by a pale youth with a plated watchguard. The
arrival of a prim personage in clean linen and cloth boots
rendered the party complete. The little table with the green
baize cover was wheeled out; the first instalment of punch
was brought in, in a white jug; and the succeeding three
hours were devoted to *vingt-et-un* at sixpence a dozen, which
was only once interrupted by a slight dispute between the
scorbutic youth and the gentleman with the pink anchors; in
the course of which, the scorbutic youth intimated a burning
desire to pull the nose of the gentleman with the emblems of
hope: in reply to which, that individual expressed his decided
unwillingness to accept of any "sauce" on gratuitous terms,
either from the irascible young gentleman with the scorbutic
countenance, or any other person who was ornamented with
a head.

When the last "natural" had been declared, and the profit
and loss account of fish and sixpences adjusted, to the satisfaction of all parties, Mr. Bob Sawyer rang for supper, and the
visitors squeezed themselves into corners while it was getting
ready.

It was not so easily got ready as some people may imagine.
First of all, it was necessary to awaken the girl, who had
fallen asleep with her face on the kitchen table; this took a
little time, and, even when she did answer the bell, another
quarter of an hour was consumed in fruitless endeavours to
impart to her a faint and distant glimmering of reason.
The man to whom the order for the oysters had been sent,
had not been told to open them; it is a very difficult thing
to open an oyster with a limp knife or a two-pronged fork;
and very little was done in this way. Very little of the beef
was done either; and the ham (which was also from the
German-sausage shop round the corner) was in a similar
predicament. However, there was plenty of porter in a tin
can; and the cheese went a great way, for it was very strong.
So upon the whole, perhaps, the supper was quite as good
as such matters usually are.

43

After supper, another jug of punch was put upon the table, together with a paper of cigars, and a couple of bottles of spirits. Then, there was an awful pause; and this awful pause was occasioned by a very common occurrence in this sort of places, but a very embarrassing one notwithstanding.

The fact is, the girl was washing the glasses. The establishment boasted four; we do not record the circumstance as at all derogatory to Mrs. Raddle, for there never was a lodging-house yet, that was not short of glasses. The landlady's glasses were little thin blown glass tumblers, and those which had been borrowed from the public-house were great, dropsical, bloated articles, each supported on a huge gouty leg. This would have been in itself sufficient to have possessed the company with the real state of affairs; but the young woman of all work had prevented the possibility of any misconception arising in the mind of any gentleman upon the subject, by forcibly dragging every man's glass away, long before he had finished his beer, and audibly stating, despite the winks and interruptions of Mr. Bob Sawyer, that it was to be conveyed down stairs, and washed forthwith.

It is a very ill wind that blows nobody any good. The prim man in the cloth boots, who had been unsuccessfully attempting to make a joke during the whole time the round game lasted, saw his opportunity, and availed himself of it. The instant the glasses disappeared, he commenced a long story about a great public character, whose name he had forgotten, making a particularly happy reply to another eminent and illustrious individual whom he had never been able to identify. He enlarged at some length and with great minuteness upon divers collateral circumstances, distantly connected with the anecdote in hand, but for the life of him he couldn't recollect at that precise moment what the anecdote was, although he had been in the habit of telling the story with great applause for the last ten years.

"Dear me," said the prim man in the cloth boots, "it is a very extraordinary circumstance."

"I am sorry you have forgotten it," said Mr. Bob Sawyer, glancing eagerly at the door, as he thought he heard the noise of glasses jingling; "very sorry."

"So am I," responded the prim man, "because I know it would have afforded so much amusement. Never mind; I dare say I shall manage to recollect it, in the course of half-an-hour or so."

The prim man arrived at this point, just as the glasses came back, when Mr. Bob Sawyer, who had been absorbed in attention during the whole time, said he should very much like to hear the end of it, for, so far as it went, it was, without exception, the very best story he had ever heard.

The sight of the tumblers restored Bob Sawyer to a degree of equanimity which he had not possessed since his interview with his landlady. His face brightened up, and he began to feel quite convivial.

"Now, Betsy," said Mr. Bob Sawyer, with great suavity, and dispersing, at the same time, the tumultuous little mob of glasses the girl had collected in the centre of the table: "now, Betsy, the warm water; be brisk, there's a good girl."

"You can't have no warm water," replied Betsy.

"No warm water!" exclaimed Mr. Bob Sawyer.

"No," said the girl, with a shake of the head which expressed a more decided negative than the most copious language could have conveyed. "Missis Raddle said you warn't to have none."

The surprise depicted on the countenances of his guests imparted new courage to the host.

"Bring up the warm water instantly—instantly!" said Mr. Bob Sawyer, with desperate sternness.

"No. I can't," replied the girl; "Missis Raddle raked out the kitchen fire afore she went to bed, and locked up the kittle."

"Oh, never mind; never mind. Pray don't disturb yourself about such a trifle," said Mr. Pickwick, observing the

45

conflict of Bob Sawyer's passions, as depicted in his countenance, "cold water will do very well."

"Oh, admirably," said Mr. Benjamin Allen.

"My landlady is subject to some slight attacks of mental
derangement," remarked Bob Sawyer with a ghastly smile;
"And I fear I must give her warning."

"No, don't," said Ben Allen.

"I fear I must," said Bob with heroic firmness. "I'll pay
her what I owe her, and give her warning to-morrow morning."
Poor fellow! how devoutly he wished he could!

Mr. Bob Sawyer's heart-sickening attempts to rally under
this last blow, communicated a dispiriting influence to the
company, the greater part of whom, with the view of raising
their spirits, attached themselves with extra cordiality to the
cold brandy and water, the first perceptible effects of which
were displayed in a renewal of hostilities between the scorbutic
youth and the gentleman in the shirt. The belligerents
vented their feelings of mutual contempt, for some time, in
a variety of frownings and snortings, until at last the scorbutic
youth felt it necessary to come to a more explicit understanding on the matter; when the following clear understanding
took place.

"Sawyer," said the scorbutic youth, in a loud voice.

"Well, Noddy," replied Mr. Bob Sawyer.

"I should be very sorry, Sawyer," said Mr. Noddy, "to
create any unpleasantness at any friend's table, and much less
at yours, Sawyer—very; but I must take this opportunity
of informing Mr. Gunter that he is no gentleman."

"And I should be very sorry, Sawyer, to create any disturbance in the street in which you reside," said Mr. Gunter,
"but I'm afraid I shall be under the necessity of alarming
the neighbours by throwing the person who has just spoken,
out o' window."

"What do you mean by that, sir?" inquired Mr. Noddy.

"What I say, sir," replied Mr. Gunter.

"I should like to see you do it, sir," said Mr. Noddy.

"You shall *feel* me do it in half a minute, sir," replied Mr. Gunter.

"I request that you'll favour me with your card, sir," said Mr. Noddy.

"I'll do nothing of the kind, sir," replied Mr. Gunter.

"Why not, sir?" inquired Mr. Noddy.

"Because you'll stick it up over your chimney-piece, and delude your visitors into the false belief that a gentleman has been to see you, sir," replied Mr. Gunter.

"Sir, a friend of mine shall wait on you in the morning," said Mr. Noddy.

"Sir, I'm very much obliged to you for the caution, and I'll leave particular directions with the servant to lock up the spoons," replied Mr. Gunter.

At this point the remainder of the guests interposed, and remonstrated with both parties on the impropriety of their conduct; on which Mr. Noddy begged to state that his father was quite as respectable as Mr. Gunter's father; to which Mr. Gunter replied that his father was to the full as respectable as Mr. Noddy's father, and that his father's son was as good a man as Mr. Noddy, any day in the week. As this announcement seemed the prelude to a recommencement of the dispute, there was another interference on the part of the company; and a vast quantity of talking and clamouring ensued, in the course of which Mr. Noddy gradually allowed his feelings to overpower him, and professed that he had ever entertained a devoted personal attachment towards Mr. Gunter. To this Mr. Gunter replied that, upon the whole, he rather preferred Mr. Noddy to his own brother; on hearing which admission, Mr. Noddy magnanimously rose from his seat, and proffered his hand to Mr. Gunter. Mr. Gunter grasped it with affecting fervour; and everybody said that the whole dispute had been conducted in a manner which was highly honourable to both parties concerned.

"Now," said Jack Hopkins, "just to set us going again, Bob, I don't mind singing a song." And Hopkins, incited thereto, by tumultuous applause, plunged himself at once into "The King, God bless him," which he sang as loud as he could, to a novel air, compounded of the "Bay of Biscay," and "A Frog he would." The chorus was the essence of the song; and, as each gentleman sang it to the tune he knew best, the effect was very striking indeed.

It was at the end of the chorus to the first verse, that Mr. Pickwick held up his hand in a listening attitude, and said, as soon as silence was restored:

"Hush! I beg your pardon. I thought I heard somebody calling from up stairs."

A profound silence immediately ensued; and Mr. Bob Sawyer was observed to turn pale.

"I think I hear it now," said Mr. Pickwick. "Have the goodness to open the door."

The door was no sooner opened than all doubt on the subject was removed.

"Mr. Sawyer! Mr. Sawyer!" screamed a voice from the two-pair landing.

"It's my landlady, said Bob Sawyer, looking round him with great dismay. "Yes, Mrs. Raddle."

"What do you mean by this, Mr. Sawyer?" replied the voice, with great shrillness and rapidity of utterance. "Ain't it enough to be swindled out of one's rent, and money lent out of pocket besides, and abused and insulted by your friends that dares to call themselves men: without having the house turned out of window, and noise enough made to bring the fire-engines here, at two o'clock in the morning?—Turn them wretches away."

"You ought to be ashamed of yourselves," said the voice of Mr. Raddle, which appeared to proceed from beneath some distant bed-clothes.

"Ashamed of themselves." said Mrs. Raddle. "Why don't you go down and knock 'em every one down stairs? You would if you was a man."

"I should if I was a dozen men, my dear," replied Mr.

Raddle, pacifically, "but they've the advantage of me in numbers, my dear."

"Ugh, you coward!" replied Mrs. Raddle, with supreme contempt. "*Do* you mean to turn them wretches out, or not, Mr. Sawyer?"

"They're going, Mrs. Raddle, they're going," said the miserable Bob. "I am afraid you'd better go," said Mr. Bob Sawyer to his friends. "I *thought* you were making too much noise."

"It's a very unfortunate thing," said the prim man. "Just as we were getting so comfortable too!" The prim man was just beginning to have a dawning recollection of the story he had forgotten.

"It's hardly to be borne," said the prim man, looking round. "Hardly to be borne, is it?"

"Not to be endured," replied Jack Hopkins; "let's have the other verse, Bob. Come, here goes!"

"No, no, Jack, don't," interposed Bob Sawyer; "it's a capital song, but I am afraid we had better not have the other verse. They are very violent people, the people of the house."

"Shall I step up stairs, and pitch into the landlord?" inquired Hopkins, "or keep on ringing the bell, or go and groan on the staircase? You may command me, Bob."

"I am very much indebted to you for your friendship and good nature, Hopkins," said the wretched Mr. Bob Sawyer, "but I think the best plan to avoid any further dispute is for us to break up at once."

"Now, Mr. Sawyer!" screamed the shrill voice of Mrs. Raddle, "*are* them brutes going?"

"They're only looking for their hats, Mrs. Raddle," said Bob; "they are going directly."

"Going!" said Mrs. Raddle, thrusting her night-cap over the banisters just as Mr. Pickwick, followed by Mr. Tupman, emerged from the sitting-room. "Going! what did they ever come for?"

"My dear ma'am," remonstrated Mr. Pickwick, looking up.

"Get along with you, you old wretch!" replied Mrs. Raddle, hastily withdrawing the night-cap. "Old enough to be his grandfather, you willin! You're worse than any of 'em."

Mr. Pickwick found it in vain to protest his innocence, so hurried down stairs into the street, whither he was closely followed by Mr. Tupman, Mr. Winkle, and Mr. Snodgrass. Mr. Ben Allen, who was dismally depressed with spirits and agitation, accompanied them as far as London Bridge, and in the course of the walk confided to Mr. Winkle, as an especially eligible person to intrust the secret to, that he was resolved to cut the throat of any gentleman except Mr. Bob Sawyer who should aspire to the affections of his sister Arabella. Having expressed his determination to perform this painful duty of a brother with proper firmness, he burst into tears, knocked his hat over his eyes, and, making the best of his way back, knocked double knocks at the door of the Borough Market office, and took short naps on the steps alternately, until daybreak, under the firm impression that he lived there, and had forgotten the key.

The visitors having all departed, in compliance with the rather pressing request of Mrs. Raddle, the luckless Mr. Bob Sawyer was left alone, to meditate on the probable events of to-morrow, and the pleasures of the evening.

CHAPTER XXXIII.

THE morning of the thirteenth of February, which the readers of this authentic narrative know, as well as we do, to have been the day immediately preceding that which was appointed for the trial of Mrs. Bardell's action, was a busy time for Mr. Samuel Weller, who was perpetually engaged in travelling from the George and Vulture to Mr. Perker's chambers and back again, from and between the hours of nine o'clock in the morning and two in the afternoon, both inclusive. Not that there was anything whatever to be done, for the consultation had taken place, and the course of proceeding to be adopted, had been finally determined on; but Mr. Pickwick being in a most extreme state of excitement, persevered in constantly sending small notes to his attorney, merely containing the inquiry, "Dear Perker. Is all going on well?" to which Mr. Perker invariably forwarded the reply, "Dear Pickwick. As well as possible;" the fact being, as we have already hinted, that there was nothing whatever to go on, either well or ill, until the sitting of the court on the following morning.

But people who go voluntarily to law, or are taken forcibly

there, for the first time, may be allowed to labour under some temporary irritation and anxiety: and Sam, with a due allowance for the frailties of human nature, obeyed all his master's behests with that imperturbable good humour and unruffable composure which formed one of his most striking and amiable characteristics.

Sam had solaced himself with a most agreeable little dinner, and was waiting at the bar for the glass of warm mixture in which Mr. Pickwick had requested him to drown the fatigues of his morning's walks, when a young boy of about three feet high, or thereabouts, in a hairy cap and fustian over-alls, whose garb bespoke a laudable ambition to attain in time the elevation of an hostler, entered the passage of the George and Vulture, and looked first up the stairs, and then along the passage, and then into the bar, as if in search of somebody to whom he bore a commission; whereupon the barmaid, conceiving it not improbable that the said commission might be directed to the tea or table spoons of the establishment, accosted the boy with

"Now, young man, what do *you* want?"

"Is there anybody here, named Sam?" inquired the youth, in a loud voice of treble quality.

"What's the t'other name?" said Sam Weller, looking round.

"How should I know?" briskly replied the young gentleman below the hairy cap.

"You're a sharp boy, you are," said Mr. Weller; "only I wouldn't show that wery fine edge too much, if I was you, in case anybody took it off. What do you mean by comin' to a hot-el, and asking arter Sam, vith as much politeness as a vild Indian?"

"'Cos an old gen'l'm'n told me to," replied the boy.

"What old gen'l'm'n?" inquired Sam, with deep disdain.

"Him as drives a Ipswich coach, and uses our parlour," rejoined the boy. "He told me yesterday mornin' to come to the George and Wultur this arternoon, and ask for Sam."

"It's my father, my dear," said Mr. Weller, turning with an explanatory air to the young lady in the bar; "blessed if I think he hardly knows wot my other name is. Vell, young brockiley sprout, wot then?"

"Why, then," said the boy, "you was to come to him at six o'clock to our 'ouse, 'cos he wants to see you—Blue Boar, Leaden'all Markit. Shall I say you're comin'?"

"You *may* wenture on that 'ere statement, sir," replied Sam. And thus empowered, the young gentleman walked away, awakening all the echoes in George Yard as he did so, with several chaste and extremely correct imitations of a drover's whistle, delivered in a tone of peculiar richness and volume.

Mr. Weller having obtained leave of absence from Mr. Pickwick, who, in his then state of excitement and worry was by no means displeased at being left alone, set forth, long before the appointed hour, and having plenty of time at his disposal, sauntered down as far as the Mansion House, where he paused and contemplated, with a face of great calmness and philosophy, the numerous cads and drivers of short stages who assemble near that famous place of resort, to the great terror and confusion of the old-lady population of these realms. Having loitered here, for half an hour or so, Mr. Weller turned, and began wending his way towards Leadenhall Market, through a variety of bye streets and courts. As he was sauntering away his spare time, and stopped to look at almost every object that met his gaze, it is by no means surprising that Mr. Weller should have paused before a small stationer's and print-seller's window; but without further explanation it does appear surprising that his eyes should have no sooner rested on certain pictures which were exposed for sale therein, than he gave a sudden start, smote his right leg with great vehemence, and exclaimed with energy, "If it hadn't been for this, I should ha' forgot all about it, till it was too late!"

The particular picture on which Sam Weller's eyes were

fixed, as he said this, was a highly coloured representation of a couple of human hearts skewered together with an arrow, cooking before a cheerful fire, while a male and female cannibal in modern attire: the gentleman being clad in a blue coat and white trousers, and the lady in a deep red pelisse with a parasol of the same: were approaching the meal with hungry eyes, up a serpentine gravel path leading thereunto. A decidedly indelicate young gentleman, in a pair of wings and nothing else, was depicted as superintending the cooking; a representation of the spire of the church in Langham Place, London, appeared in the distance; and the whole formed a "valentine," of which, as a written inscription in the window testified, there was a large assortment within, which the shopkeeper pledged himself to dispose of, to his countrymen generally, at the reduced rate of one and sixpence each.

"I should ha' forgot it; I should certainly ha' forgot it!" said Sam; so saying, he at once stepped into the stationer's shop, and requested to be served with a sheet of the best gilt-edged letter-paper, and a hard-nibbed pen which could be warranted not to splutter. These articles having been promptly supplied, he walked on direct towards Leadenhall Market at a good round pace, very different from his recent lingering one. Looking round him, he there beheld a sign-board on which the painter's art had delineated something remotely resembling a cerulean elephant with an aquiline nose in lieu of trunk. Rightly conjecturing that this was the Blue Boar himself, he stepped into the house, and inquired concerning his parent.

"He won't be here this three quarters of an hour or more," said the young lady who superintended the domestic arrangements of the Blue Boar.

"Wery good, my dear," replied Sam. "Let me have nine penn'orth o' brandy and water luke, and the inkstand, will you, miss?"

The brandy and water luke, and the inkstand, having been carried into the little parlour, and the young lady having

54

A VALENTINE.

carefully flattened down the coals to prevent their blazing, and carried away the poker to preclude the possibility of the fire being stirred, without the full privity and concurrence of the Blue Boar being first had and obtained, Sam Weller sat himself down in a box near the stove, and pulled out the sheet of gilt-edged letter-paper, and the hard-nibbed pen. Then looking carefully at the pen to see that there were no hairs in it, and dusting down the table, so that there might be no crumbs of bread under the paper, Sam tucked up the cuffs of his coat, squared his elbows, and composed himself to write.

To ladies and gentlemen who are not in the habit of devoting themselves practically to the science of penmanship, writing a letter is no very easy task; it being always considered necessary in such cases for the writer to recline his head on his left arm, so as to place his eyes as nearly as possible on a level with the paper, while glancing sideways at the letters he is constructing, to form with his tongue imaginary characters to correspond. These motions, although unquestionably of the greatest assistance to original composition, retard in some degree the progress of the writer; and Sam had unconsciously been a full hour and a half writing words in small text, smearing out wrong letters with his little finger, and putting in new ones which required going over very often to render them visible through the old blots, when he was roused by the opening of the door and the entrance of his parent.

"Vell, Sammy," said the father.

"Vell, my Prooshan Blue," responded the son, laying down his pen. "What's the last bulletin about mother-in-law?"

"Mrs. Veller passed a very good night, but is uncommon perwerse, and unpleasant this mornin'. Signed upon oath, S. Veller, Esquire, Senior. That's the last vun as was issued, Sammy," replied Mr. Weller, untying his shawl.

"No better yet?" inquired Sam.

"All the symptoms aggerawated," replied Mr. Weller, shaking his head. "But wot's that, you're a doin' of? Pursuit of knowledge under difficulties, Sammy?"

"I've done now," said Sam with slight embarrassment; "I've been a writin'."

"So I see," replied Mr. Weller. "Not to any young 'ooman, I hope, Sammy?"

'Why it's no use a sayin' it ain't," replied Sam, "It's a walentine."

"A what!" exclaimed Mr. Weller, apparently horror-stricken by the word.

"A walentine," replied Sam.

"Samivel, Samivel," said Mr. Weller, in reproachful accents, "I didn't think you'd ha' done it. Arter the warnin' you've had o' your father's wicious propensities; arter all I've said to you upon this here wery subject; arter activally seein' and bein' in the company o' your own mother-in-law, vich I should ha' thought wos a moral lesson as no man could never ha' forgotten to his dyin' day! I didn't think you'd ha' done it, Sammy, I didn't think you'd ha' done it!" These reflections were too much for the good old man. He raised Sam's tumbler to his lips and drank off its contents.

"Wot's the matter now?" said Sam.

"Nev'r mind, Sammy," replied Mr. Weller, "it'll be a wery agonizin' trial to me at my time of life, but I'm pretty tough, that's vun consolation, as the wery old turkey remarked wen the farmer said he wos afeerd he should be obliged to kill him for the London market."

"Wot'll be a trial?" inquired Sam.

"To see you married, Sammy—to see you a dilluded wictim, and thinkin' in your innocence that it's all wery capital," replied Mr. Weller. "It's a dreadful trial to a father's feelin's, that 'ere, Sammy."

"Nonsense," said Sam. "I ain't a goin' to get married, don't you fret yourself about that; I know you're a judge of these things. Order in your pipe, and I'll read you the letter. There!"

We cannot distinctly say whether it was the prospect of the pipe, or the consolatory reflection that a fatal disposition

The Valentine

to get married ran in the family and couldn't be helped, which calmed Mr. Weller's feelings, and caused his grief to subside. We should be rather disposed to say that the result was attained by combining the two sources of consolation, for he repeated the second in a low tone, very frequently; ringing the bell meanwhile, to order in the first. He then divested himself of his upper coat; and lighting the pipe and placing himself in front of the fire with his back towards it, so that he could feel its full heat, and recline against the mantelpiece at the same time, turned towards Sam, and, with a countenance greatly mollified by the softening influence of tobacco, requested him to "fire away."

Sam dipped his pen into the ink to be ready for any corrections, and began with a very theatrical air:

"'Lovely——.'"

"Stop," said Mr. Weller, ringing the bell. "A double glass o' the inwariable, my dear."

"Very well, sir," replied the girl; who with great quickness appeared, vanished, returned, and disappeared.

"They seem to know your ways here," observed Sam.

"Yes," replied his father, "I've been here before, in my time. Go on, Sammy."

"'Lovely creetur,'" repeated Sam.

"'Tain't in poetry, is it?" interposed his father.

"No, no," replied Sam.

"Werry glad to hear it," said Mr. Weller. "Poetry's unnat'ral; no man ever talked poetry 'cept a beadle on boxin' day, or Warren's blackin', or Rowland's oil, or some o' them low fellows; never you let yourself down to talk poetry, my boy. Begin agin, Sammy."

Mr. Weller resumed his pipe with critical solemnity, and Sam once more commenced, and read as follows:

"'Lovely creetur i feel myself a dammed'—."

"That ain't proper," said Mr. Weller, taking his pipe from his mouth.

"No; it ain't 'dammed'," observed Sam, holding the letter

57

up to the light, "it's 'shamed,' there's a blot there—'I feel myself ashamed.'"

"Werry good," said Mr. Weller. "Go on."

"'Feel myself ashamed, and completely cir—' I forget what this here word is," said Sam, scratching his head with the pen, in vain attempts to remember.

"Why don't you look at it, then?" inquired Mr. Weller.

"So I *am* a lookin' at it," replied Sam, "but there's another blot. Here's a 'c,' and a 'i,' and a 'd.'"

"Circumwented, p'haps," suggested Mr. Weller.

"No, it ain't that," said Sam, "circumscribed; that's it."

"That ain't as good a word as circumwented, Sammy," said Mr. Weller, gravely.

"Think not?" said Sam.

"Nothin' like it," replied his father.

"But don't you think it means more?" inquired Sam.

"Vell p'raps it is a more tenderer word," said Mr. Weller, after a few moments' reflection. "Go on, Sammy."

"'Feel myself ashamed and completely circumscribed in a dressin' of you, for you *are* a nice gal and nothin' but it.'"

"That's a werry pretty sentiment," said the elder Mr. Weller, removing his pipe to make way for the remark.

"Yes, I think it is rayther good," observed Sam, highly flattered.

"Wot I like in that 'ere style of writin'," said the elder Mr. Weller, "is, that there ain't no callin' names in it,—no Wenuses, nor nothin' o' that kind. Wot's the good o' callin' a young 'ooman a Wenus or a angel, Sammy?"

"Ah! what, indeed?" replied Sam.

"You might jist as well call her a griffin, or a unicorn, or a king's arms at once, which is werry well known to be a col-lection o' fabulous animals," added Mr. Weller.

"Just as well," replied Sam.

"Drive on, Sammy," said Mr. Weller.

Sam complied with the request, and proceeded as follows;

his father continuing to smoke, with a mixed expression of wisdom and complacency, which was particularly edifying.

"'Afore I see you, I thought all women was alike.'"

"So they are," observed the elder Mr. Weller, parenthetically.

"'But now,' continued Sam, 'now I find what a reg'lar soft-headed, inkred'lous turnip I must ha' been; for there ain't nobody like you, though *I* like you better than nothin' at all.' I thought it best to make that rayther strong," said Sam, looking up.

Mr. Weller nodded approvingly, and Sam resumed.

"'So I take the privilidge of the day, Mary, my dear—as the gen'l'm'n in difficulties did, ven he valked out of a Sunday, —to tell you that the first and only time I see you, your likeness was took on my hart in much quicker time and brighter colours than ever a likeness was took by the profeel macheen (wich p'raps you may have heerd on Mary my dear) altho it *does* finish a portrait and put the frame and glass on complete, with a hook at the end to hang it up by, and all in two minutes and a quarter.'"

"I am afeerd that werges on the poetical, Sammy," said Mr. Weller, dubiously.

"No it don't," replied Sam, reading on very quickly, to avoid contesting the point:

"'Except of me Mary my dear as your walentine and think over what I've said.—My dear Mary I will now conclude.' That's all," said Sam.

"That's rather a sudden pull up, ain't it, Sammy?" inquired Mr. Weller.

"Not a bit on it," said Sam; "she'll vish there wos more, and that's the great art o' letter writin'."

"Well," said Mr. Weller, "there's somethin' in that; and I wish your mother-in-law 'ud only conduct her conwersation on the same gen-teel principle. Ain't you a goin' to sign it?"

"That's the difficulty," said Sam; "I don't know what *to* sign it."

"Sign it, Veller," said the oldest surviving proprietor of that name.

"Won't do," said Sam. "Never sign a walentine with your own name."

"Sign it 'Pickvick,' then," said Mr. Weller; "it's a werry good name, and a easy one to spell."

"The wery thing," said Sam. "I *could* end with a werse; what do you think?"

"I don't like it, Sam," rejoined Mr. Weller. "I never know'd a respectable coachman as wrote poetry, 'cept one, as made an affectin' copy o' werses the night afore he wos hung for a highway robbery; and *he* wos only a Cambervell man, so even that's no rule."

But Sam was not to be dissuaded from the poetical idea that had occurred to him, so he signed the letter,

> "Your love-sick
> Pickwick."

And having folded it, in a very intricate manner, squeezed a down-hill direction in one corner: "To Mary, Housemaid, at Mr. Nupkins's Mayor's, Ipswich, Suffolk;" and put it into his pocket, wafered, and ready for the General Post. This important business having been transacted, Mr. Weller the elder proceeded to open that, on which he had summoned his son.

"The first matter relates to your governor, Sammy," said Mr. Weller. "He's a goin' to be tried to-morrow, ain't he?"

"The trial's a comin' on," replied Sam.

"Vell," said Mr. Weller, "Now I s'pose he'll want to call some witnesses to speak to his character, or p'haps to prove a alleybi. I've been a turnin' the bis'ness over in my mind, and he may make his-self easy, Sammy. I've got some friends as'll do either for him, but my adwice 'ud be this here—never mind the character, and stick to the alleybi. Nothing like a alleybi, Sammy, nothing." Mr. Weller looked very profound as he delivered this legal opinion; and burying his nose in his tumbler, winked over the top thereof, at his astonished son.

"Why, what do you mean?" said Sam; "you don't think he's a goin' to be tried at the Old Bailey, do you?"

"That ain't no part of the present con-sideration, Sammy," replied Mr. Weller. "Verever he's a goin' to be tried, my boy, a alleybi's the thing to get him off. Ve got Tom Vildspark off that 'ere manslaughter, with a alleybi, ven all the big vigs to a man said as nothing couldn't save him. And my 'pinion is, Sammy, that if your governor don't prove a alleybi, he'll be what the Italians call reg'larly flummoxed, and that's all about it."

As the elder Mr. Weller entertained a firm and unalterable conviction that the Old Bailey was the supreme court of judicature in this country, and that its rules and forms of proceeding regulated and controlled the practice of all other courts of justice whatsoever, he totally disregarded the assurances and arguments of his son, tending to show that the alibi was inadmissible; and vehemently protested that Mr. Pickwick was being "wictimised." Finding that it was of no use to discuss the matter further, Sam changed the subject, and inquired what the second topic was, on which his revered parent wished to consult him.

"That's a pint o' domestic policy, Sammy," said Mr. Weller. "This here Stiggins—"

"Red-nosed man?" inquired Sam.

"The wery same," replied Mr. Weller. "This here red-nosed man, Sammy, wisits your mother-in-law vith a kindness and constancy as I never see equalled. He's sitch a friend o' the family, Sammy, that wen he's avay from us, he can't be comfortable unless he has somethin' to remember us by."

"And I'd give him somethin' as 'ud turpentine and bees'-vax his memory for the next ten years or so, if I wos you," interposed Sam.

"Stop a minute," said Mr. Weller; "I wos a going to say, he always brings now, a flat bottle as holds about a

61

pint and a-half, and fills it vith the pine-apple rum afore he goes avay."

" And empties it afore he comes back, I s'pose ? " said Sam.

" Clean ! " replied Mr. Weller ; " never leaves nothin' in it but the cork and the smell ; trust him for that, Sammy. Now, these here fellows, my boy, are a goin' to-night to get up the monthly meetin' o' the Brick Lane Branch o' the United Grand Junction Ebenezer Temperance Association. Your mother-in-law *wos* a goin', Sammy, but she's got the rheumatics, and can't ; and I, Sammy—I've got the two tickets as wos sent her." Mr. Weller communicated this secret with great glee, and winked so indefatigably after doing so, that Sam began to think he must have got the *tic douloureux* in his right eye-lid.

" Well ? " said that young gentleman.

" Well," continued his progenitor, looking round him very cautiously, " you and I'll go, punctiwal to the time. The deputy shepherd won't, Sammy ; the deputy shepherd won't." Here Mr. Weller was seized with a paroxysm of chuckles, which gradually terminated in as near an approach to a choke as an elderly gentleman can, with safety, sustain.

" Well, I never see sitch an old ghost in all my born days," exclaimed Sam, rubbing the old gentleman's back, hard enough to set him on fire with the friction. " What are you a laughin' at, corpilence ? "

" Hush ! Sammy," said Mr. Weller, looking round him with increased caution, and speaking in a whisper : " Two friends o' mine, as works the Oxford Road, and is up to all kinds o' games, has got the deputy shepherd safe in tow, Sammy ; and ven he does come to the Ebenezer Junction, (vich he's sure to do : for they'll see him to the door, and shove him in if necessary) he'll be as far gone in rum and water as ever he wos at the Markis o' Granby, Dorkin', and that's not sayin' a little neither." And with this, Mr. Weller once more laughed immoderately, and once more relapsed into a state of partial suffocation, in consequence.

VISIT TO BRICK LANE.

Nothing could have been more in accordance with Sam Weller's feelings, than the projected exposure of the real propensities and qualities of the red-nosed man; and it being very near the appointed hour of meeting, the father and son took their way at once to Brick Lane: Sam not forgetting to drop his letter into a general post-office as they walked along.

The monthly meetings of the Brick Lane Branch of the United Grand Junction Ebenezer Temperance Association, were held in a large room, pleasantly and airily situated at the top of a safe and commodious ladder. The president was the straight-walking Mr. Anthony Humm, a converted fireman, now a schoolmaster, and occasionally an itinerant preacher; and the secretary was Mr. Jonas Mudge, chandler's shop-keeper, an enthusiastic and disinterested vessel, who sold tea to the members. Previous to the commencement of business, the ladies sat upon forms, and drank tea, till such time as they considered it expedient to leave off; and a large wooden money-box was conspicuously placed upon the green baize cloth of the business table, behind which the secretary stood, and acknowledged, with a gracious smile, every addition to the rich vein of copper which lay concealed within.

On this particular occasion the women drank tea to a most alarming extent; greatly to the horror of Mr. Weller senior, who, utterly regardless of all Sam's admonitory nudgings, stared about him in every direction with the most undisguised astonishment.

"Sammy," whispered Mr. Weller, "if some o' these here people don't want tappin' to-morrow mornin', I ain't your father, and that's wot it is. Why, this here old lady next me is a drowndin' herself in tea."

"Be quiet, can't you," murmured Sam.

"Sam," whispered Mr. Weller, a moment afterwards, in a tone of deep agitation, "mark my vords, my boy. If that 'ere secretary fellow keeps on for only five minutes more, he'll blow hisself up with toast and water."

63

"Well, let him, if he likes," replied Sam; "it ain't no bis'ness o' yourn."

"If this here lasts much longer, Sammy," said Mr. Weller, in the same low voice, "I shall feel it my duty, as a human bein', to rise and address the cheer. There's a young 'ooman on the next form but two, as has drunk nine breakfast cups and a half; and she's a swellin' wisibly before my wery eyes."

There is little doubt that Mr. Weller would have carried his benevolent intention into immediate execution, if a great noise, occasioned by putting up the cups and saucers, had not very fortunately announced that the tea-drinking was over. The crockery having been removed, the table with the green baize cover was carried out into the centre of the room, and the business of the evening was commenced by a little emphatic man, with a bald head, and drab shorts, who suddenly rushed up the ladder, at the imminent peril of snapping the two little legs encased in the drab shorts, and said:

"Ladies and gentlemen, I move our excellent brother, Mr. Anthony Humm, into the chair."

The ladies waved a choice collection of pocket-handkerchiefs at this proposition: and the impetuous little man literally moved Mr. Humm into the chair by taking him by the shoulders and thrusting him into a mahogany-frame which had once represented that article of furniture. The waving of handkerchiefs was renewed; and Mr. Humm, who was a sleek, white-faced man, in a perpetual perspiration, bowed meekly, to the great admiration of the females, and formally took his seat. Silence was then proclaimed by the little man in the drab shorts, and Mr. Humm rose and said—That, with the permission of his Brick Lane Branch brothers and sisters, then and there present, the secretary would read the report of the Brick Lane Branch committee; a proposition which was again received with a demonstration of pocket-handkerchiefs.

The secretary having sneezed in a very impressive manner, and the cough which always seizes an assembly, when anything particular is going to be done, having been duly performed, the following document was read:

"REPORT OF THE COMMITTEE OF THE BRICK LANE BRANCH OF THE UNITED GRAND JUNCTION EBENEZER TEMPERANCE ASSOCIATION.

"Your committee have pursued their grateful labours during the past month, and have the unspeakable pleasure of reporting the following additional cases of converts to Temperance.

"H. Walker, tailor, wife, and two children. When in better circumstances, owns to having been in the constant habit of drinking ale and beer; says he is not certain whether he did not twice a week, for twenty years, taste 'dog's nose,' which your committee find upon inquiry, to be compounded of warm porter, moist sugar, gin, and nutmeg (a groan, and 'So it is!' from an elderly female.) Is now out of work and pennyless; thinks it must be the porter (cheers) or the loss of the use of his right hand; is not certain which, but thinks it very likely that, if he had drank nothing but water all his life, his fellow work-man would never have stuck a rusty needle in him, and thereby occasioned his accident (tremendous cheering). Has nothing but cold water to drink, and never feels thirsty (great applause).

"Betsy Martin, widow, one child, and one eye. Goes out charing and washing, by the day; never had more than one eye, but knows her mother drank bottled stout, and shouldn't wonder if that caused it (immense cheering). Thinks it not impossible that if she had always abstained from spirits, she might have had two eyes by this time (tremendous applause). Used, at every place she went to, to have eighteen pence a day, a pint of porter, and a glass of spirits; but since she became a member of the Brick Lane Branch, has always demanded three and sixpence instead (the announcement of this most interesting fact was received with deafening enthusiasm).

"Henry Beller was for many years toast-master at various

65

corporation dinners, during which time he drank a great deal of foreign wine; may sometimes have carried a bottle or two home with him; is not quite certain of that, but is sure if he did, that he drank the contents. Feels very low and melancholy, is very feverish, and has a constant thirst upon him; thinks it must be the wine he used to drink (cheers). Is out of employ now: and never touches a drop of foreign wine by any chance (tremendous plaudits).

"Thomas Burton is purveyor of cat's meat to the Lord Mayor and Sheriffs, and several members of the Common Council (the announcement of this gentleman's name was received with breathless interest). Has a wooden leg; finds a wooden leg expensive, going over the stones; used to wear second-hand wooden legs, and drink a glass of hot gin and water regularly every night—sometimes two (deep sighs). Found the second-hand wooden legs split and rot very quickly; is firmly persuaded that their constitution was undermined by the gin and water (prolonged cheering). Buys new wooden legs now, and drinks nothing but water and weak tea. The new legs last twice as long as the others used to do, and he attributes this solely to his temperate habits (triumphant cheers)."

Anthony Humm now moved that the assembly do regale itself with a song. With a view to their rational and moral enjoyment, brother Mordlin had adapted the beautiful words of " Who hasn't heard of a Jolly Young Waterman?" to the tune of the Old Hundredth, which he would request them to join him in singing (great applause). He might take that opportunity of expressing his firm persuasion that the late Mr. Dibdin, seeing the errors of his former life, had written that song to show the advantages of abstinence. It was a temperance song (whirlwinds of cheers). The neatness of the young man's attire, the dexterity of his feathering, the enviable state of mind which enabled him in the beautiful words of the poet, to

" Row along, thinking of nothing at all,"

66

all combined to prove that he must have been a water-drinker
(cheers). Oh, what a state of virtuous jollity! (rapturous
cheering.) And what was the young man's reward? Let all
young men present mark this:

"The maidens all flock'd to his boat so readily."

(Loud cheers, in which the ladies joined.) What a bright
example! The sisterhood, the maidens, flocking round the
young waterman, and urging him along the stream of duty
and of temperance. But, was it the maidens of humble life
only, who soothed, consoled, and supported him? No!

"He was always first oars with the fine city ladies."

(Immense cheering.) The soft sex to a man—he begged
pardon, to a female—rallied round the young waterman, and
turned with disgust from the drinker of spirits (cheers). The
Brick Lane Branch brothers were watermen (cheers and
laughter). That room was their boat; that audience were
the maidens; and he (Mr. Anthony Humm), however un-
worthily, was "first oars" (unbounded applause).

"Wot does he mean by the soft sex, Sammy?" inquired
Mr. Weller, in a whisper.

"The womin," said Sam, in the same tone.

"He ain't far out there, Sammy," replied Mr. Weller;
"they *must* be a soft sex,—a wery soft sex, indeed—if they
let themselves be gammoned by such fellers as him."

Any further observations from the indignant old gentleman
were cut short by the announcement of the song, which Mr.
Anthony Humm gave out, two lines at a time, for the
information of such of his hearers as were unacquainted with
the legend. While it was being sung, the little man with
the drab shorts disappeared; he returned immediately on its
conclusion, and whispered Mr. Anthony Humm, with a face
of the deepest importance.

"My friends," said Mr. Humm, holding up his hand in a
deprecatory manner, to bespeak the silence of such of the
stout old ladies as were yet a line or two behind; "my friends,

a delegate from the Dorking branch of our society, Brother Stiggins, attends below."

Out came the pocket-handkerchiefs again, in greater force than ever; for Mr. Stiggins was excessively popular among the female constituency of Brick Lane.

"He may approach, I think," said Mr. Humm, looking round him, with a fat smile. "Brother Tadger, let him come forth and greet us."

The little man in the drab shorts who answered to the name of Brother Tadger, bustled down the ladder with great speed, and was immediately afterwards heard tumbling up with the reverend Mr. Stiggins.

"He's a comin', Sammy," whispered Mr. Weller, purple in the countenance with suppressed laughter.

"Don't say nothin' to me," replied Sam, "for I can't bear it. He's close to the door. I heard him a-knockin' his head again the lath and plaster now."

As Sam Weller spoke, the little door flew open, and brother Tadger appeared, closely followed by the reverend Mr. Stiggins, who no sooner entered, than there was a great clapping of hands, and stamping of feet, and flourishing of handkerchiefs; to all of which manifestations of delight, Brother Stiggins returned no other acknowledgment than staring with a wild eye, and a fixed smile, at the extreme top of the wick of the candle on the table: swaying his body to and fro, meanwhile, in a very unsteady and uncertain manner.

"Are you unwell, brother Stiggins?" whispered Mr. Anthony Humm.

"I am all right, sir," replied Mr. Stiggins, in a tone in which ferocity was blended with an extreme thickness of utterance; "I am all right, sir."

"Oh, very well," rejoined Mr. Anthony Humm, retreating a few paces.

"I believe no man here, has ventured to say that I am *not* all right, sir?" said Mr. Stiggins.

"Oh, certainly not," said Mr. Humm.

"I should advise him not to, sir; I should advise him not," said Mr. Stiggins.

By this time the audience were perfectly silent, and waited with some anxiety for the resumption of business.

"Will you address the meeting, brother?" said Mr. Humm, with a smile of invitation.

"No, sir," rejoined Mr. Stiggins; "No, sir. I will not, sir."

The meeting looked at each other with raised eye-lids; and a murmur of astonishment ran through the room.

"It's my opinion, sir," said Mr. Stiggins, unbuttoning his coat, and speaking very loudly; "it's my opinion, sir, that this meeting is drunk, sir. Brother Tadger, sir!" said Mr. Stiggins, suddenly increasing in ferocity, and turning sharp round on the little man in the drab shorts, "*you* are drunk, sir!" With this, Mr. Stiggins, entertaining a praiseworthy desire to promote the sobriety of the meeting, and to exclude therefrom all improper characters, hit brother Tadger on the summit of the nose with such unerring aim, that the drab shorts disappeared like a flash of lightning. Brother Tadger had been knocked, head first, down the ladder.

Upon this, the women set up a loud and dismal screaming; and rushing in small parties before their favourite brothers, flung their arms around them to preserve them from danger. An instance of affection, which had nearly proved fatal to Humm, who, being extremely popular, was all but suffocated, by the crowd of female devotees that hung about his neck, and heaped caresses upon him. The greater part of the lights were quickly put out, and nothing but noise and confusion resounded on all sides.

"Now, Sammy," said Mr. Weller, taking off his great coat with much deliberation, "just you step out, and fetch in a watchman."

"And wot are you a goin' to do, the while?" inquired Sam.

"Never you mind me, Sammy," replied the old gentleman; "I shall ockipy myself in havin' a small settlement with that 'ere Stiggins." Before Sam could interfere to prevent it, his heroic parent had penetrated into a remote corner of the room, and attacked the reverend Mr. Stiggins with manual dexterity.

"Come off!" said Sam.

"Come on!" cried Mr. Weller; and without further invitation he gave the reverend Mr. Stiggins a preliminary tap on the head, and began dancing round him in a buoyant and cork-like manner, which in a gentleman at his time of life was a perfect marvel to behold.

Finding all remonstrance unavailing, Sam pulled his hat firmly on, threw his father's coat over his arm, and taking the old man round the waist, forcibly dragged him down the ladder, and into the street; never releasing his hold, or permitting him to stop, until they reached the corner. As they gained it, they could hear the shouts of the populace, who were witnessing the removal of the reverend Mr. Stiggins to strong lodgings for the night: and could hear the noise occasioned by the dispersion in various directions of the members of the Brick Lane Branch of the United Grand Junction Ebenezer Temperance Association.

CHAPTER XXXIV.

IS WHOLLY DEVOTED TO A FULL AND FAITHFUL REPORT OF THE
MEMORABLE TRIAL OF BARDELL AGAINST PICKWICK.

"I WONDER what the foreman of the jury, whoever he'll be,
has got for breakfast," said Mr. Snodgrass, by way of keeping
up a conversation on the eventful morning of the fourteenth
of February.

"Ah!" said Perker, "I hope he's got a good one."

"Why so?" inquired Mr. Pickwick.

"Highly important; very important, my dear sir," replied
Perker. "A good, contented, well-breakfasted juryman, is
a capital thing to get hold of. Discontented or hungry
jurymen, my dear sir, always find for the plaintiff."

"Bless my heart," said Mr. Pickwick, looking very blank;
"what do they do that for?"

"Why, I don't know," replied the little man, coolly;
"saves time, I suppose. If it's near dinner-time, the foreman
takes out his watch when the jury has retired, and says,
'Dear me, gentlemen, ten minutes to five, I declare! I dine
at five, gentlemen.' 'So do I,' says every body else, except
two men who ought to have dined at three, and seem more
than half disposed to stand out in consequence. The foreman
smiles, and puts up his watch:—'Well, gentlemen, what do
we say, plaintiff or defendant, gentlemen? I rather think,
so far as I am concerned, gentlemen,—I say, I rather think,
—but don't let that influence you—I *rather* think the

71

plaintiff's the man.' Upon this, two or three other men are sure to say that they think so too—as of course they do; and then they get on very unanimously and comfortably. Ten minutes past nine!" said the little man, looking at his watch. "Time we were off, my dear sir; breach of promise trial—court is generally full in such cases. You had better ring for a coach, my dear sir, or we shall be rather late."

Mr. Pickwick immediately rang the bell; and a coach having been procured, the four Pickwickians and Mr. Perker ensconced themselves therein, and drove to Guildhall; Sam Weller, Mr. Lowten, and the blue bag, following in a cab.

"Lowten," said Perker, when they reached the outer hall of the court, "put Mr. Pickwick's friends in the students' box; Mr. Pickwick himself had better sit by me. This way, my dear sir, this way." Taking Mr. Pickwick by the coat-sleeve, the little man led him to the low seat just beneath the desks of the King's Counsel, which is constructed for the convenience of attorneys, who from that spot can whisper into the ear of the leading counsel in the case, any instructions that may be necessary during the progress of the trial. The occupants of this seat are invisible to the great body of spectators, inasmuch as they sit on a much lower level than either the barristers or the audience, whose seats are raised above the floor. Of course they have their backs to both, and their faces towards the judge.

"That's the witness-box, I suppose?" said Mr. Pickwick, pointing to a kind of pulpit, with a brass rail, on his left hand.

"That's the witness-box, my dear sir," replied Perker, disinterring a quantity of papers from the blue bag, which Lowten had just deposited at his feet.

"And that," said Mr. Pickwick, pointing to a couple of enclosed seats on his right, "that's where the jurymen sit, is it not?"

"The identical place, my dear sir," replied Perker, tapping the lid of his snuff-box.

Mr. Pickwick stood up in a state of great agitation, and

took a glance at the court. There were already a pretty large sprinkling of spectators in the gallery, and a numerous muster of gentlemen in wigs, in the barristers' seats: who presented, as a body, all that pleasing and extensive variety of nose and whisker for which the bar of England is so justly celebrated. Such of the gentlemen as had a brief to carry, carried it in as conspicuous a manner as possible, and occasionally scratched their noses therewith, to impress the fact more strongly on the observation of the spectators. Other gentlemen, who had no briefs to show, carried under their arms goodly octavos, with a red label behind, and that underdone-pie-crust-coloured cover, which is technically known as "law calf." Others, who had neither briefs nor books, thrust their hands into their pockets, and looked as wise as they conveniently could; others, again, moved here and there with great restlessness and earnestness of manner, content to awaken thereby the admiration and astonishment of the uninitiated strangers. The whole, to the great wonderment of Mr. Pickwick, were divided into little groups, who were chatting and discussing the news of the day in the most unfeeling manner possible,—just as if no trial at all were coming on.

A bow from Mr. Phunky, as he entered, and took his seat behind the row appropriated to the King's Counsel, attracted Mr. Pickwick's attention; and he had scarcely returned it, when Mr. Serjeant Snubbin appeared, followed by Mr. Mallard, who half hid the Serjeant behind a large crimson bag, which he placed on his table, and, after shaking hands with Perker, withdrew. Then there entered two or three more Serjeants; and among them, one with a fat body and a red face, who nodded in a friendly manner to Mr. Serjeant Snubbin, and said it was a fine morning.

"Who's that red-faced man, who said it was a fine morning, and nodded to our counsel?" whispered Mr. Pickwick.

"Mr. Serjeant Buzfuz," replied Perker. "He's opposed to us; he leads on the other side. That gentleman behind him is Mr. Skimpin, his junior."

THE PICKWICK CLUB.

Mr. Pickwick was on the point of inquiring, with great abhorrence of the man's cold-blooded villany, how Mr. Serjeant Buzfuz, who was counsel for the opposite party, dared to presume to tell Mr. Serjeant Snubbin, who was counsel for him, that it was a fine morning, when he was interrupted by a general rising of the barristers, and a loud cry of "Silence!" from the officers of the court. Looking round, he found that this was caused by the entrance of the judge.

Mr. Justice Stareleigh (who sat in the absence of the Chief Justice, occasioned by indisposition), was a most particularly short man, and so fat, that he seemed all face and waistcoat. He rolled in, upon two little turned legs, and having bobbed gravely to the bar, who bobbed gravely to him, put his little legs underneath his table, and his little three-cornered hat upon it; and when Mr. Justice Stareleigh had done this, all you could see of him was two queer little eyes, one broad pink face, and somewhere about half of a big and very comical-looking wig.

The judge had no sooner taken his seat, than the officer on the floor of the court called out "Silence!" in a commanding tone, upon which another officer in the gallery cried "Silence!" in an angry manner, whereupon three or four more ushers shouted "Silence!" in a voice of indignant remonstrance. This being done, a gentleman in black, who sat below the judge, proceeded to call over the names of the jury; and after a great deal of bawling, it was discovered that only ten special jurymen were present. Upon this, Mr. Serjeant Buzfuz prayed a *tales;* the gentleman in black then proceeded to press into the special jury, two of the common jurymen; and a green-grocer and a chemist were caught directly.

"Answer to your names, gentlemen, that you may be sworn," said the gentleman in black. "Richard Upwitch."

"Here," said the green-grocer.

"Thomas Groffin."

"Here," said the chemist.

THE CHEMIST SWORN ON THE JURY.

"Take the book, gentlemen. You shall well and truly try—"

"I beg this court's pardon," said the chemist, who was a tall, thin, yellow-visaged man, "but I hope this court will excuse my attendance."

"On what grounds, sir?" said Mr. Justice Stareleigh.

"I have no assistant, my Lord," said the chemist.

"I can't help that, sir," replied Mr. Justice Stareleigh. "You should hire one."

"I can't afford it, my Lord," rejoined the chemist.

"Then you ought to be able to afford it, sir," said the judge, reddening; for Mr. Justice Stareleigh's temper bordered on the irritable, and brooked not contradiction.

"I know I *ought* to do, if I got on as well as I deserved, but I don't, my Lord," answered the chemist.

"Swear the gentleman," said the judge, peremptorily.

The officer had got no further than the "You shall well and truly try," when he was again interrupted by the chemist.

"I am to be sworn, my Lord, am I?" said the chemist.

"Certainly, sir," replied the testy little judge.

"Very well, my Lord," replied the chemist, in a resigned manner. "Then there'll be murder before this trial's over; that's all. Swear me, if you please, sir;" and sworn the chemist was, before the judge could find words to utter.

"I merely wanted to observe, my Lord," said the chemist, taking his seat with great deliberation, "that I've left nobody but an errand-boy in my shop. He is a very nice boy, my Lord, but he is not acquainted with drugs; and I know that the prevailing impression on his mind is, that Epsom salts means oxalic acid; and syrup of senna, laudanum. That's all, my Lord." With this, the tall chemist composed himself into a comfortable attitude, and, assuming a pleasant expression of countenance, appeared to have prepared himself for the worst.

Mr. Pickwick was regarding the chemist with feelings of the deepest horror, when a slight sensation was perceptible

75

in the body of the court; and immediately afterwards Mrs. Bardell, supported by Mrs. Cluppins, was led in, and placed, in a drooping state, at the other end of the seat on which Mr. Pickwick sat. An extra sized umbrella was then handed in by Mr. Dodson, and a pair of pattens by Mr. Fogg, each of whom had prepared a most sympathising and melancholy face for the occasion. Mrs. Sanders then appeared, leading in Master Bardell. At sight of her child, Mrs. Bardell started; suddenly recollecting herself, she kissed him in a frantic manner; then relapsing into a state of hysterical imbecility, the good lady requested to be informed where she was. In reply to this, Mrs. Cluppins and Mrs. Sanders turned their heads away and wept, while Messrs. Dodson and Fogg intreated the plaintiff to compose herself. Serjeant Buzfuz rubbed his eyes very hard with a large white handkerchief, and gave an appealing look towards the jury, while the judge was visibly affected, and several of the beholders tried to cough down their emotions.

"Very good notion that, indeed," whispered Perker to Mr. Pickwick. "Capital fellows those Dodson and Fogg; excellent ideas of effect, my dear sir, excellent."

As Perker spoke, Mrs. Bardell began to recover by slow degrees, while Mrs. Cluppins, after a careful survey of Master Bardell's buttons and the button-holes to which they severally belonged, placed him on the floor of the court in front of his mother,—a commanding position in which he could not fail to awaken the full commiseration and sympathy of both judge and jury. This was not done without considerable opposition, and many tears, on the part of the young gentleman himself, who had certain inward misgivings that the placing him within the full glare of the judge's eye was only a formal prelude to his being immediately ordered away for instant execution, or for transportation beyond the seas, during the whole term of his natural life, at the very least.

"Bardell and Pickwick," cried the gentleman in black, calling on the case, which stood first on the list.

THE PLAINTIFF'S CASE OPENED.

"I am for the plaintiff, my Lord," said Mr. Serjeant Buzfuz.

"Who is with you, brother Buzfuz?" said the judge. Mr. Skimpin bowed, to intimate that he was.

"I appear for the defendant, my Lord," said Mr. Serjeant Snubbin.

"Anybody with you, brother Snubbin?" inquired the court.

"Mr. Phunky, my Lord," replied Serjeant Snubbin.

"Serjeant Buzfuz and Mr. Skimpin for the plaintiff," said the judge, writing down the names in his note-book, and reading as he wrote; "for the defendant, Serjeant Snubbin and Mr. Monkey."

"Beg your Lordship's pardon, Phunky."

"Oh, very good," said the judge; "I never had the pleasure of hearing the gentleman's name before." Here Mr. Phunky bowed and smiled, and the judge bowed and smiled too, and then Mr. Phunky, blushing into the very whites of his eyes, tried to look as if he didn't know that everybody was gazing at him: a thing which no man ever succeeded in doing yet, or in all reasonable probability, ever will.

"Go on," said the judge.

The ushers again called silence, and Mr. Skimpin proceeded to "open the case;" and the case appeared to have very little inside it when he had opened it, for he kept such particulars as he knew, completely to himself, and sat down, after a lapse of three minutes, leaving the jury in precisely the same advanced stage of wisdom as they were in before.

Serjeant Buzfuz then rose with all the majesty and dignity which the grave nature of the proceedings demanded, and having whispered to Dodson, and conferred briefly with Fogg, pulled his gown over his shoulders, settled his wig, and addressed the jury.

Serjeant Buzfuz began by saying, that never, in the whole course of his professional experience—never, from the very first moment of his applying himself to the study and practice of the law—had he approached a case with feelings of such deep emotion, or with such a heavy sense of the responsibility

77

imposed upon him—a responsibility, he would say, which he could never have supported, were he not buoyed up and sustained by a conviction so strong, that it amounted to positive certainty that the cause of truth and justice, or, in other words, the cause of his much-injured and most oppressed client, must prevail with the high-minded and intelligent dozen of men whom he now saw in that box before him.

Counsel usually begin in this way, because it puts the jury on the very best terms with themselves, and makes them think what sharp fellows they must be. A visible effect was produced immediately; several jurymen beginning to take voluminous notes with the utmost eagerness.

"You have heard from my learned friend, gentlemen," continued Serjeant Buzfuz, well knowing that, from the learned friend alluded to, the gentlemen of the jury had heard just nothing at all—"you have heard from my learned friend, gentlemen, that this is an action for a breach of promise of marriage, in which the damages are laid at £1,500. But you have not heard from my learned friend, inasmuch as it did not come within my learned friend's province to tell you, what are the facts and circumstances of the case. Those facts and circumstances, gentlemen, you shall hear detailed by me, and proved by the unimpeachable female whom I will place in that box before you."

Here Mr. Serjeant Buzfuz, with a tremendous emphasis on the word "box," smote his table with a mighty sound, and glanced at Dodson and Fogg, who nodded admiration of the serjeant, and indignant defiance of the defendant.

"The plaintiff, gentlemen," continued Serjeant Buzfuz, in a soft and melancholy voice, "the plaintiff is a widow; yes, gentlemen, a widow. The late Mr. Bardell, after enjoying, for many years, the esteem and confidence of his sovereign, as one of the guardians of his royal revenues, glided almost imperceptibly from the world, to seek elsewhere for that repose and peace which a custom-house can never afford."

At this pathetic description of the decease of Mr. Bardell,

who had been knocked on the head with a quart-pot in a public-house cellar, the learned serjeant's voice faltered, and he proceeded with emotion:

"Some time before his death, he had stamped his likeness upon a little boy. With this little boy, the only pledge of her departed exciseman, Mrs. Bardell shrunk from the world, and courted the retirement and tranquillity of Goswell Street; and here she placed in her front parlour-window a written placard, bearing this inscription—'Apartments furnished for a single gentleman. Inquire within.'" Here Serjeant Buzfuz paused, while several gentlemen of the jury took a note of the document.

"There is no date to that, is there, sir?" inquired a juror.

"There is no date, gentlemen," replied Serjeant Buzfuz; "but I am instructed to say that it was put in the plaintiff's parlour-window just this time three years. I intreat the attention of the jury to the wording of this document. 'Apartments furnished for a single gentleman'! Mrs. Bardell's opinions of the opposite sex, gentlemen, were derived from a long contemplation of the inestimable qualities of her lost husband. She had no fear, she had no distrust, she had no suspicion, all was confidence and reliance. 'Mr. Bardell,' said the widow; 'Mr. Bardell was a man of honour, Mr. Bardell was a man of his word, Mr. Bardell was no deceiver, Mr. Bardell was once a single gentleman himself; *to* single gentlemen I look for protection, for assistance, for comfort, and for consolation; *in* single gentlemen I shall perpetually see something to remind me of what Mr. Bardell was, when he first won my young and untried affections; to a single gentleman, then, shall my lodgings be let.' Actuated by this beautiful and touching impulse (among the best impulses of our imperfect nature, gentlemen,) the lonely and desolate widow dried her tears, furnished her first floor, caught the innocent boy to her maternal bosom, and put the bill up in her parlour-window. Did it remain there long? No. The serpent was on the watch, the train was laid, the mine was

preparing, the sapper and miner was at work. Before the
bill had been in the parlour-window three days—three days
—gentlemen—a Being, erect upon two legs, and bearing all
the outward semblance of a man, and not of a monster,
knocked at the door of Mrs. Bardell's house. He inquired
within; he took the lodgings; and on the very next day he
entered into possession of them. This man was Pickwick—
Pickwick, the defendant."

Serjeant Buzfuz, who had proceeded with such volubility
that his face was perfectly crimson, here paused for breath.
The silence awoke Mr. Justice Stareleigh, who immediately
wrote down something with a pen without any ink in it,
and looked unusually profound, to impress the jury with
the belief that he always thought most deeply with his eyes
shut. Serjeant Buzfuz proceeded.

"Of this man Pickwick I will say little; the subject
presents but few attractions; and I, gentlemen, am not the
man, nor are you, gentlemen, the men, to delight in the
contemplation of revolting heartlessness, and of systematic
villany."

Here Mr. Pickwick, who had been writhing in silence for
some time, gave a violent start, as if some vague idea of
assaulting Serjeant Buzfuz, in the august presence of justice
and law, suggested itself to his mind. An admonitory gesture
from Perker restrained him, and he listened to the learned
gentleman's continuation with a look of indignation, which
contrasted forcibly with the admiring faces of Mrs. Cluppins
and Mrs. Sanders.

"I say systematic villany, gentlemen," said Serjeant Buzfuz,
looking through Mr. Pickwick, and talking *at* him; "and
when I say systematic villany, let me tell the defendant Pickwick, if he be in court, as I am informed he is, that it would
have been more decent in him, more becoming, in better
judgment, and in better taste, if he had stopped away. Let
me tell him, gentlemen, that any gestures of dissent or disapprobation in which he may indulge in this court will not

go down with you; that you will know how to value and how to appreciate them; and let me tell him further, as my lord will tell you, gentlemen, that a counsel, in the discharge of his duty to his client, is neither to be intimidated nor bullied, nor put down; and that any attempt to do either the one or the other, or the first, or the last, will recoil on the head of the attempter, be he plaintiff or be he defendant, be his name Pickwick, or Noakes, or Stoakes, or Stiles, or Brown, or Thompson."

This little divergence from the subject in hand, had of course, the intended effect of turning all eyes to Mr. Pickwick. Sergeant Buzfuz, having partially recovered from the state of moral elevation into which he had lashed himself, resumed:

"I shall show you, gentlemen, that for two years Pickwick continued to reside constantly, and without interruption or intermission, at Mrs. Bardell's house. I shall show you that Mrs. Bardell, during the whole of that time waited on him, attended to his comforts, cooked his meals, looked out his linen for the washerwoman when it went abroad, darned, aired, and prepared it for wear, when it came home, and, in short, enjoyed his fullest trust and confidence. I shall show you that, on many occasions, he gave halfpence, and on some occasions even sixpences, to her little boy; and I shall prove to you, by a witness whose testimony it will be impossible for my learned friend to weaken or controvert, that on one occasion he patted the boy on the head, and, after inquiring whether he had won any *alley tors* or *commoneys* lately (both of which I understand to be a particular species of marbles much prized by the youth of this town), made use of this remarkable expression: 'How should you like to have another father?' I shall prove to you, gentlemen, that about a year ago, Pickwick suddenly began to absent himself from home, during long intervals, as if with the intention of gradually breaking off from my client; but I shall show you also, that his resolution was not at that time sufficiently strong, or that his better feelings conquered, if better feelings he has, or that the charms and accomplishments of my client prevailed against his unmanly intentions; by proving to you, that on one occasion, when he returned from the country, he distinctly and in terms, offered her marriage: previously however, taking special care that there should be no witness to their solemn contract; and I am in a situation to prove to you, on the testimony of three of his own friends, —most unwilling witnesses, gentlemen — most unwilling witnesses—that on that morning he was discovered by them holding the plaintiff in his arms, and soothing her agitation by his caresses and endearments."

A visible impression was produced upon the auditors by this part of the learned serjeant's address. Drawing forth two very small scraps of paper, he proceeded:

"And now, gentlemen, but one word more. Two letters have passed between these parties, letters which are admitted to be in the hand-writing of the defendant, and which speak volumes indeed. These letters, too, bespeak the character of the man. They are not open, fervent, eloquent epistles, breathing nothing but the language of affectionate attachment. They are covert, sly, underhanded communications, but, fortunately, far more conclusive than if couched in the most glowing language and the most poetic imagery—letters that must be viewed with a cautious and suspicious eye—letters that were evidently intended at the time, by Pickwick, to mislead and delude any third parties into whose hands they might fall. Let me read the first:—'Garraway's, twelve o'clock. Dear Mrs. B.—Chops and Tomata sauce. Yours, PICKWICK.' Gentlemen, what does this mean? Chops and Tomata sauce. Yours, Pickwick! Chops! Gracious heavens! and Tomata sauce! Gentlemen, is the happiness of a sensitive and confiding female to be trifled away, by such shallow artifices as these? The next has no date whatever, which is in itself suspicious. 'Dear Mrs. B., I shall not be at home till to-morrow. Slow coach.' And then follows this very

The Trial

remarkable expression. 'Don't trouble yourself about the warming-pan.' The warming pan! Why, gentlemen, who *does* trouble himself about a warming-pan? When was the peace of mind of man or woman broken or disturbed by a warming-pan, which is in itself a harmless, a useful, and I will add, gentlemen, a comforting article of domestic furniture? Why is Mrs. Bardell so earnestly entreated not to agitate herself about this warming-pan, unless (as is no doubt the case) it is a mere cover for hidden fire—a mere substitute for some endearing word or promise, agreeably to a preconcerted system of correspondence, artfully contrived by Pickwick with a view to his contemplated desertion, and which I am not in a condition to explain? And what does this allusion to the slow coach mean? For aught I know, it may be a reference to Pickwick himself, who has most unquestionably been a criminally slow coach during the whole of this transaction, but whose speed will now be very unexpectedly accelerated, and whose wheels, gentlemen, as he will find to his cost, will very soon be greased by you!"

Mr. Serjeant Buzfuz paused in this place, to see whether the jury smiled at his joke; but as nobody took it but the green-grocer, whose sensitiveness on the subject was very probably occasioned by his having subjected a chaise-cart to the process in question on that identical morning, the learned serjeant considered it advisable to undergo a slight relapse into the dismals before he concluded.

"But enough of this, gentlemen," said Mr. Serjeant Buzfuz, "it is difficult to smile with an aching heart; it is ill jesting when our deepest sympathies are awakened. My client's hopes and prospects are ruined, and it is no figure of speech to say that her occupation is gone indeed. The bill is down —but there is no tenant. Eligible single gentlemen pass and repass—but there is no invitation for them to inquire within or without. All is gloom and silence in the house; even the voice of the child is hushed; his infant sports are disregarded when his mother weeps; his 'alley tors' and his 'commoneys' are alike neglected; he forgets the long familiar cry of 'knuckle down,' and at tip-cheese, or odd and even, his hand is out. But Pickwick, gentlemen, Pickwick, the ruthless destroyer of this domestic oasis in the desert of Goswell Street—Pickwick, who has choked up the well, and thrown ashes on the sward—Pickwick, who comes before you to-day with his heartless Tomata sauce and warming-pans—Pickwick still rears his head with unblushing effrontery, and gazes without a sigh on the ruin he has made. Damages, gentlemen—heavy damages—is the only punishment with which you can visit him; the only recompence you can award to my client. And for those damages she now appeals to an enlightened, a high-minded, a right-feeling, a conscientious, a dispassionate, a sympathising, a contemplative jury of her civilised countrymen." With this beautiful peroration, Mr. Serjeant Buzfuz sat down, and Mr. Justice Stareleigh woke up.

"Call Elizabeth Cluppins," said Serjeant Buzfuz, rising a minute afterwards, with renewed vigour.

The nearest usher called for Elizabeth Tuppins; another one, at a little distance off, demanded Elizabeth Jupkins; and a third rushed in a breathless state into King Street, and screamed for Elizabeth Muffins till he was hoarse.

Meanwhile Mrs. Cluppins, with the combined assistance of Mrs. Bardell, Mrs. Sanders, Mr. Dodson, and Mr. Fogg, was hoisted into the witness-box; and when she was safely perched on the top step, Mrs. Bardell stood on the bottom one, with the pocket-handkerchief and pattens in one hand, and a glass bottle that might hold about a quarter of a pint of smelling salts in the other, ready for any emergency. Mrs. Sanders, whose eyes were intently fixed on the judge's face, planted herself close by, with the large umbrella: keeping her right thumb pressed on the spring with an earnest countenance, as if she were fully prepared to put it up at a moment's notice.

"Mrs. Cluppins," said Serjeant Buzfuz, "pray compose yourself, ma'am." Of course, directly Mrs. Cluppins was desired to compose herself she sobbed with increased vehemence, and gave divers alarming manifestations of an approaching fainting fit, or, as she afterwards said, of her feelings being too many for her.

"Do you recollect, Mrs. Cluppins?" said Serjeant Buzfuz, after a few unimportant questions, "do you recollect being in Mrs. Bardell's back one pair of stairs, on one particular morning in July last, when she was dusting Pickwick's apartment?"

"Yes, my Lord and Jury, I do," replied Mrs. Cluppins.

"Mr. Pickwick's sitting-room was the first-floor front, I believe?"

"Yes, it were, sir," replied Mrs. Cluppins.

"What were you doing in the back room, ma'am?" inquired the little judge.

"My Lord and Jury," said Mrs. Cluppins, with interesting agitation, "I will not deceive you."

"You had better not, ma'am," said the little judge.

"I was there," resumed Mrs. Cluppins, "unbeknown to Mrs. Bardell; I had been out with a little basket, gentlemen, to buy three pound of red kidney purtaties, which was three pound tuppense ha'penny, when I see Mrs. Bardell's street door on the jar."

"On the what?" exclaimed the little judge.

"Partly open, my Lord," said Serjeant Snubbin.

"She *said* on the jar," said the little judge, with a cunning look.

"It's all the same, my Lord," said Serjeant Snubbin. The little judge looked doubtful, and said he'd make a note of it. Mrs. Cluppins then resumed:

"I walked in, gentlemen, just to say good mornin', and went, in a permiscuous manner, up stairs, and into the back room. Gentlemen, there was the sound of voices in the front room, and——"

"And you listened, I believe, Mrs. Cluppins?" said Serjeant Buzfuz.

"Beggin' your pardon, sir," replied Mrs. Cluppins, in a

majestic manner, " I would scorn the haction. The voices was very loud, sir, and forced themselves upon my ear."

" Well, Mrs. Cluppins, you were not listening, but you heard the voices. Was one of those voices, Pickwick's?"

" Yes, it were, sir."

And Mrs. Cluppins, after distinctly stating that Mr. Pickwick addressed himself to Mrs. Bardell, repeated, by slow degrees, and by dint of many questions, the conversation with which our readers are already acquainted.

The jury looked suspicious, and Mr. Serjeant Buzfuz smiled and sat down. They looked positively awful when Serjeant Snubbin intimated that he should not cross-examine the witness, for Mr. Pickwick wished it to be distinctly stated that it was due to her to say, that her account was in substance correct.

Mrs. Cluppins having once broken the ice, thought it a favourable opportunity for entering into a short dissertation on her own domestic affairs; so, she straightway proceeded to inform the court that she was the mother of eight children at that present speaking, and that she entertained confident expectations of presenting Mr. Cluppins with a ninth, somewhere about that day six months. At this interesting point, the little judge interposed most irascibly; and the effect of the interposition was, that both the worthy lady and Mrs. Sanders were politely taken out of court, under the escort of Mr. Jackson, without further parley.

" Nathaniel Winkle!" said Mr. Skimpin.

" Here!" replied a feeble voice. Mr. Winkle entered the witness box, and having been duly sworn, bowed to the judge with considerable deference.

" Don't look at me, sir," said the judge, sharply, in acknowledgment of the salute; "look at the jury."

Mr. Winkle obeyed the mandate, and looked at the place where he thought it most probable the jury might be; for seeing anything in his then state of intellectual complication was wholly out of the question.

MR. WINKLE IN THE BOX.

Mr. Winkle was then examined by Mr. Skimpin, who, being a promising young man of two or three and forty, was of course anxious to confuse a witness who was notoriously predisposed in favour of the other side, as much as he could.

"Now, sir," said Mr. Skimpin, "have the goodness to let his Lordship and the jury know what your name is, will you?" and Mr. Skimpin inclined his head on one side to listen with great sharpness to the answer, and glanced at the jury meanwhile, as if to imply that he rather expected Mr. Winkle's natural taste for perjury would induce him to give some name which did not belong to him.

"Winkle," replied the witness.

"What's your Christian name, sir?" angrily inquired the little judge.

"Nathaniel, sir."

"Daniel,—any other name?"

"Nathaniel, sir—my Lord, I mean."

"Nathaniel Daniel, or Daniel Nathaniel?"

"No, my Lord, only Nathaniel; not Daniel at all."

"What did you tell me it was Daniel for, then, sir?" inquired the judge.

"I didn't, my Lord," replied Mr. Winkle.

"You did, sir," replied the judge, with a severe frown. "How could I have got Daniel on my notes, unless you told me so, sir?"

This argument, was, of course, unanswerable.

"Mr. Winkle has rather a short memory, my Lord," interposed Mr. Skimpin, with another glance at the jury. "We shall find means to refresh it before we have quite done with him, I dare say."

"You had better be careful, sir," said the little judge, with a sinister look at the witness.

Poor Mr. Winkle bowed, and endeavoured to feign an easiness of manner, which, in his then state of confusion, gave him rather the air of a disconcerted pickpocket.

"Now, Mr. Winkle," said Mr. Skimpin, "attend to me, if

you please, sir; and let me recommend you, for your own
sake, to bear in mind his Lordship's injunction to be careful.
I believe you are a particular friend of Pickwick, the defendant,
are you not?"

"I have known Mr. Pickwick now, as well as I recollect at
this moment, nearly——"

"Pray, Mr. Winkle, do not evade the question. Are you,
or are you not, a particular friend of the defendant's?"

"I was just about to say, that——"

"Will you, or will you not, answer my question, sir?"

"If you don't answer the question you'll be committed,
sir," interposed the little judge, looking over his note-book.

"Come, sir," said Mr. Skimpin, "yes or no, if you please."

"Yes, I am," replied Mr. Winkle.

"Yes, you are. And why couldn't you say that at once,
sir? Perhaps you know the plaintiff, too? Eh, Mr. Winkle?"

"I don't know her; I've seen her."

"Oh, you don't know her, but you've seen her? Now,
have the goodness to tell the gentlemen of the jury what you
mean by *that*, Mr. Winkle."

"I mean that I am not intimate with her, but I have
seen her when I went to call on Mr. Pickwick in Goswell
Street."

"How often have you seen her, sir?"

"How often?"

"Yes, Mr. Winkle, how often? I'll repeat the question
for you a dozen times, if you require it, sir." And the
learned gentleman, with a firm and steady frown, placed
his hands on his hips, and smiled suspiciously at the jury.

On this question there arose the edifying brow-beating,
customary on such points. First of all, Mr. Winkle said it
was quite impossible for him to say how many times he had
seen Mrs. Bardell. Then he was asked if he had seen her
twenty times, to which he replied, "Certainly,—more than
that." Then he was asked whether he hadn't seen her a
hundred times—whether he couldn't swear that he had seen

her more than fifty times—whether he didn't know that he had seen her at least seventy-five times—and so forth; the satisfactory conclusion which was arrived at, at last, being, that he had better take care of himself, and mind what he was about. The witness having been by these means reduced to the requisite ebb of nervous perplexity, the examination was continued as follows:

"Pray, Mr. Winkle, do you remember calling on the defendant Pickwick at these apartments in the plaintiff's house in Goswell Street, on one particular morning, in the month of July last?"

"Yes, I do."

"Were you accompanied on that occasion by a friend of the name of Tupman, and another of the name of Snodgrass?"

"Yes, I was."

"Are they here?"

"Yes, they are," replied Mr. Winkle, looking very earnestly towards the spot where his friends were stationed.

"Pray attend to me, Mr. Winkle, and never mind your friends," said Mr. Skimpin, with another expressive look at the jury. "They must tell their stories without any previous consultation with you, if none has yet taken place (another look at the jury). Now, sir, tell the gentlemen of the jury what you saw on entering the defendant's room, on this particular morning. Come; out with it, sir; we must have it, sooner or later."

"The defendant, Mr. Pickwick, was holding the plaintiff in his arms, with his hands clasping her waist," replied Mr. Winkle with natural hesitation, "and the plaintiff appeared to have fainted away."

"Did you hear the defendant say anything?"

"I heard him call Mrs. Bardell a good creature, and I heard him ask her to compose herself, for what a situation it was, if any body should come, or words to that effect."

"Now, Mr. Winkle, I have only one more question to ask you, and I beg you to bear in mind his lordship's caution.

Will you undertake to swear that Pickwick, the defendant, did not say on the occasion in question, 'My dear Mrs. Bardell, you're a good creature; compose yourself to this situation, for to this situation you must come,' or words to *that* effect?"

"I—I didn't understand him so, certainly," said Mr. Winkle, astounded at this ingenious dove-tailing of the few words he had heard. "I was on the staircase, and couldn't hear distinctly; the impression on my mind is—"

"The gentlemen of the jury want none of the impressions on your mind, Mr. Winkle, which I fear would be of little service to honest, straightforward men," interposed Mr. Skimpin. "You were on the staircase, and didn't distinctly hear; but you will not swear that Pickwick did not make use of the expressions I have quoted? Do I understand that?"

"No, I will not," replied Mr. Winkle; and down sat Mr. Skimpin with a triumphant countenance.

Mr. Pickwick's case had not gone off in so particularly happy a manner, up to this point, that it could very well afford to have any additional suspicion cast upon it. But as it could afford to be placed in a rather better light, if possible, Mr. Phunky rose for the purpose of getting something important out of Mr. Winkle in cross-examination. Whether he did get anything important out of him, will immediately appear.

"I believe, Mr. Winkle," said Mr. Phunky, "that Mr. Pickwick is not a young man?"

"Oh no," replied Mr. Winkle, "old enough to be my father."

"You have told my learned friend that you have known Mr. Pickwick a long time. Had you ever any reason to suppose or believe that he was about to be married?"

"Oh no; certainly not;" replied Mr. Winkle with so much eagerness, that Mr. Phunky ought to have got him out of the box with all possible dispatch. Lawyers hold that there are two kinds of particularly bad witnesses: a reluctant witness, and a too-willing witness; it was Mr. Winkle's fate to figure in both characters.

"I will even go further than this, Mr. Winkle," continued Mr. Phunky in a most smooth and complacent manner. "Did you ever see anything in Mr. Pickwick's manner and conduct towards the opposite sex, to induce you to believe that he ever contemplated matrimony of late years, in any case?"

"Oh no; certainly not," replied Mr. Winkle.

"Has his behaviour, when females have been in the case, always been that of a man, who, having attained a pretty advanced period of life, content with his own occupations and amusements, treats them only as a father might his daughters?"

"Not the least doubt of it," replied Mr. Winkle, in the fulness of his heart. "That is—yes—oh yes—certainly."

"You have never known anything in his behaviour towards Mrs. Bardell, or any other female, in the least degree suspicious?" said Mr. Phunky, preparing to sit down; for Serjeant Snubbin was winking at him.

"N—n—no," replied Mr. Winkle, "except on one trifling occasion, which, I have no doubt, might be easily explained."

Now, if the unfortunate Mr. Phunky had sat down when Serjeant Snubbin winked at him, or if Serjeant Buzfuz had stopped this irregular cross-examination at the outset (which he knew better than to do; observing Mr. Winkle's anxiety, and well knowing it would, in all probability, lead to something serviceable to him), this unfortunate admission would not have been elicited. The moment the words fell from Mr. Winkle's lips, Mr. Phunky sat down, and Serjeant Snubbin rather hastily told him he might leave the box, which Mr. Winkle prepared to do with great readiness, when Serjeant Buzfuz stopped him.

"Stay, Mr. Winkle, stay!" said Serjeant Buzfuz, "will your lordship have the goodness to ask him, what this one instance of suspicious behaviour towards females on the part of this gentleman, who is old enough to be his father, was?"

"You hear what the learned counsel says, sir," observed the judge, turning to the miserable and agonized Mr. Winkle. "Describe the occasion to which you refer."

"My lord," said Mr. Winkle, trembling with anxiety, "I—I'd rather not.'

"Perhaps so," said the little judge; "but you must."

Amid the profound silence of the whole court, Mr. Winkle faltered out, that the trifling circumstance of suspicion was Mr. Pickwick's being found in a lady's sleeping apartment at midnight; which had terminated, he believed, in the breaking off of the projected marriage of the lady in question, and had led, he knew, to the whole party being forcibly carried before George Nupkins, Esq., magistrate and justice of the peace, for the borough of Ipswich!

"You may leave the box, sir," said Serjeant Snubbin. Mr. Winkle *did* leave the box, and rushed with delirious haste to the George and Vulture, where he was discovered some hours after, by the waiter, groaning in a hollow and dismal manner, with his head buried beneath the sofa cushions.

Tracy Tupman, and Augustus Snodgrass, were severally called into the box; both corroborated the testimony of their unhappy friend; and each was driven to the verge of desperation by excessive badgering.

Susannah Sanders was then called, and examined by Serjeant Buzfuz, and cross-examined by Serjeant Snubbin. Had always said and believed that Pickwick would marry Mrs. Bardell; knew that Mrs. Bardell's being engaged to Pickwick was the current topic of conversation in the neighbourhood, after the fainting in July; had been told it herself by Mrs. Mudberry which kept a mangle, and Mrs. Bunkin which clear-starched, but did not see either Mrs. Mudberry or Mrs. Bunkin in court. Had heard Pickwick ask the little boy how he should like to have another father. Did not know that Mrs. Bardell was at that time keeping company with the baker, but did know that the baker was then a single man and is now married. Couldn't swear that Mrs. Bardell was not very fond of the baker, but should think that the baker was not very fond of Mrs. Bardell, or he wouldn't have married somebody else. Thought Mrs. Bardell fainted away on the morning in July, because Pickwick asked her to name the day; knew that she (witness) fainted away stone dead when Mr. Sanders asked *her* to name the day, and believed that everybody as called herself a lady would do the same, under similar circumstances. Heard Pickwick ask the boy the question about the marbles, but upon her oath did not know the difference between an alley tor and a commoney.

By the COURT.—During the period of her keeping company with Mr. Sanders, had received love letters, like other ladies. In the course of their correspondence Mr. Sanders had often called her a "duck," but never "chops," nor yet "tomata sauce." He was particularly fond of ducks. Perhaps if he had been as fond of chops and tomata sauce, he might have called her that, as a term of affection.

Serjeant Buzfuz now rose with more importance than he had yet exhibited, if that were possible, and vociferated: "Call Samuel Weller."

It was quite unnecessary to call Samuel Weller; for Samuel Weller stepped briskly into the box the instant his name was pronounced; and placing his hat on the floor, and his arms on the rail, took a bird's-eye view of the bar, and a comprehensive survey of the bench, with a remarkably cheerful and lively aspect.

"What's your name, sir?" inquired the judge.

"Sam Weller, my lord," replied that gentleman.

"Do you spell it with a 'V' or a 'W?'" inquired the judge.

"That depends upon the taste and fancy of the speller, my lord," replied Sam; "I never had occasion to spell it more than once or twice in my life, but I spells it with a 'V.'"

Here a voice in the gallery exclaimed aloud, "Quite right too, Samivel, quite right. Put it down a we, my lord, put it down a we."

"Who is that, who dares to address the court?" said the little judge, looking up. "Usher."

"Yes, my lord."

"Bring that person here instantly."

"Yes, my lord."

But as the usher didn't find the person, he didn't bring him; and, after a great commotion, all the people who had got up to look for the culprit, sat down again. The little judge turned to the witness as soon as his indignation would allow him to speak, and said,

"Do you know who that was, sir?"

"I rayther suspect it was my father, my lord," replied Sam.

"Do you see him here now?" said the judge.

"No, I don't, my lord," replied Sam, staring right up into the lantern in the roof of the court.

"If you could have pointed him out, I would have committed him instantly," said the judge.

Sam bowed his acknowledgments and turned, with unimpaired cheerfulness of countenance, towards Serjeant Buzfuz.

"Now, Mr. Weller," said Serjeant Buzfuz.

"Now, sir," replied Sam.

"I believe you are in the service of Mr. Pickwick, the defendant in this case. Speak up, if you please, Mr. Weller."

"I mean to speak up, sir," replied Sam; "I am in the service o' that 'ere gen'l'man, and a wery good service it is."

"Little to do, and plenty to get, I suppose?" said Serjeant Buzfuz, with jocularity.

"Oh, quite enough to get, sir, as the soldier said ven they ordered him three hundred and fifty lashes," replied Sam.

"You must not tell us what the soldier, or any other man, said, sir," interposed the judge; "it's not evidence."

"Wery good, my lord," replied Sam.

"Do you recollect anything particular happening on the morning when you were first engaged by the defendant; eh, Mr. Weller?" said Serjeant Buzfuz.

"Yes I do, sir," replied Sam.

94

ATTEMPT TO FRIGHTEN SAM.

"Have the goodness to tell the jury what it was."

"I had a reg'lar new fit out o' clothes that mornin', gen'l'-men of the jury," said Sam, "and that was a wery partickler and uncommon circumstance vith me in those days."

Hereupon there was a general laugh; and the little judge, looking with an angry countenance over his desk, said, "You had better be careful, sir."

"So Mr. Pickwick said at the time, my lord," replied Sam; "and I was wery careful o' that 'ere suit o' clothes; wery careful indeed, my lord."

The judge looked sternly at Sam for full two minutes, but Sam's features were so perfectly calm and serene that the judge said nothing, and motioned Serjeant Buzfuz to proceed.

"Do you mean to tell me, Mr. Weller," said Serjeant Buzfuz, folding his arms emphatically, and turning half-round to the jury, as if in mute assurance that he would bother the witness yet: "Do you mean to tell me, Mr. Weller, that you saw nothing of this fainting on the part of the plaintiff in the arms of the defendant, which you have heard described by the witnesses?"

"Certainly not," replied Sam. "I was in the passage 'till they called me up, and then the old lady was not there."

"Now, attend, Mr. Weller," said Serjeant Buzfuz, dipping a large pen into the inkstand before him, for the purpose of frightening Sam with a show of taking down his answer. "You were in the passage, and yet saw nothing of what was going forward. Have you a pair of eyes, Mr. Weller?"

"Yes, I have a pair of eyes," replied Sam, "and that's just it. If they wos a pair o' patent double million magnifyin' gas microscopes of hextra power, p'raps I might be able to see through a flight o' stairs and a deal door; but bein' only eyes, you see, my wision 's limited."

At this answer, which was delivered without the slightest appearance of irritation, and with the most complete simplicity and equanimity of manner, the spectators tittered, the little judge smiled, and Serjeant Buzfuz looked particularly foolish.

After a short consultation with Dodson and Fogg, the learned Serjeant again turned towards Sam, and said, with a painful effort to conceal his vexation, " Now, Mr. Weller, I'll ask you a question on another point, if you please."

" If you please, sir," rejoined Sam, with the utmost good-humour.

" Do you remember going up to Mrs. Bardell's house, one night in November last ? "

" Oh yes, wery well."

" Oh, you *do* remember that, Mr. Weller," said Serjeant Buzfuz, recovering his spirits; " I thought we should get at something at last."

" I rayther thought that, too, sir," replied Sam; and at this the spectators tittered again.

" Well; I suppose you went up to have a little talk about this trial—eh, Mr. Weller? " said Serjeant Buzfuz. looking knowingly at the jury.

" I went up to pay the rent; but we *did* get a talkin' about the trial," replied Sam.

" Oh, you did get a talking about the trial," said Serjeant Buzfuz, brightening up with the anticipation of some important discovery. " Now what passed about the trial; will you have the goodness to tell us, Mr. Weller? "

" Vith all the pleasure in life, sir," replied Sam. " Arter a few unimportant obserwations from the two wirtuous females as has been examined here to-day, the ladies gets into a very great state o' admiration at the honourable conduct of Mr. Dodson and Fogg—them two gen'l'men as is settin' near you now." This, of course, drew general attention to Dodson and Fogg, who looked as virtuous as possible.

" The attorneys for the plaintiff," said Mr. Serjeant Buzfuz. " Well! They spoke in high praise of the honourable conduct of Messrs. Dodson and Fogg, the attorneys for the plaintiff, did they? "

" Yes," said Sam. " they said what a wery gen'rous thing it was o' them to have taken up the case on spec, and to charge nothing at all for costs, unless they got 'em out of Mr. Pickwick."

At this very unexpected reply, the spectators tittered again, and Dodson and Fogg, turning very red, leant over to Serjeant Buzfuz, and in a hurried manner whispered something in his ear.

"You are quite right," said Serjeant Buzfuz aloud, with affected composure. "It's perfectly useless, my lord, attempting to get at any evidence through the impenetrable stupidity of this witness. I will not trouble the court by asking him any more questions. Stand down, sir."

"Would any other gen'l'man like to ask me anythin'?" inquired Sam, taking up his hat, and looking round most deliberately.

"Not I, Mr. Weller, thank you," said Serjeant Snubbin, laughing.

"You may go down, sir," said Serjeant Buzfuz, waving his hand impatiently. Sam went down accordingly, after doing Messrs. Dodson and Fogg's case as much harm as he conveniently could, and saying just as little respecting Mr. Pickwick as might be, which was precisely the object he had had in view all along.

"I have no objection to admit, my lord," said Serjeant Snubbin, "if it will save the examination of another witness, that Mr. Pickwick has retired from business, and is a gentleman of considerable independent property."

"Very well," said Serjeant Buzfuz, putting in the two letters to be read, "Then that's my case, my lord."

Serjeant Snubbin then addressed the jury on behalf of the defendant; and a very long and a very emphatic address he delivered, in which he bestowed the highest possible eulogiums on the conduct and character of Mr. Pickwick; but inasmuch as our readers are far better able to form a correct estimate of that gentleman's merits and deserts, than Serjeant Snubbin could possibly be, we do not feel called upon to enter at any length into the learned gentleman's observations. He

97

attempted to show that the letters which had been exhibited, merely related to Mr. Pickwick's dinner, or to the preparations for receiving him in his apartments on his return from some country excursion. It is sufficient to add in general terms, that he did the best he could for Mr. Pickwick; and the best, as every body knows, on the infallible authority of the old adage, could do no more.

Mr. Justice Stareleigh summed up, in the old-established and most approved form. He read as much of his notes to the jury as he could decipher on so short a notice, and made running comments on the evidence as he went along. If Mrs. Bardell were right, it was perfectly clear that Mr. Pickwick was wrong, and if they thought the evidence of Mrs. Cluppins worthy of credence they would believe it, and, if they didn't, why they wouldn't. If they were satisfied that a breach of promise of marriage had been committed, they would find for the plaintiff with such damages as they thought proper; and if, on the other hand, it appeared to them that no promise of marriage had ever been given, they would find for the defendant with no damages at all. The jury then retired to their private room to talk the matter over, and the judge retired to *his* private room, to refresh himself with a mutton chop and a glass of sherry.

An anxious quarter of an hour elapsed; the jury came back; the judge was fetched in. Mr. Pickwick put on his spectacles, and gazed at the foreman with an agitated countenance and a quickly beating heart.

"Gentlemen," said the individual in black, "are you all agreed upon your verdict?"

"We are," replied the foreman.

"Do you find for the plaintiff, gentlemen, or for the defendant?"

"For the plaintiff."

"With what damages, gentlemen?"

"Seven hundred and fifty pounds."

Mr. Pickwick took off his spectacles, carefully wiped the

glasses, folded them into their case, and put them in his pocket; then having drawn on his gloves with great nicety, and stared at the foreman all the while, he mechanically followed Mr. Perker and the blue bag out of court.

They stopped in a side room while Perker paid the court fees; and here, Mr. Pickwick was joined by his friends. Here, too, he encountered Messrs. Dodson and Fogg, rubbing their hands with every token of outward satisfaction.

" Well, gentlemen," said Mr. Pickwick.

" Well, sir," said Dodson: for self and partner.

" You imagine you'll get your costs, don't you, gentlemen ? " said Mr. Pickwick.

Fogg said they thought it rather probable. Dodson smiled, and said they'd try.

"You may try, and try, and try again, Messrs. Dodson and Fogg," said Mr. Pickwick vehemently, " but not one farthing of costs or damages do you ever get from me, if I spend the rest of my existence in a debtor's prison."

" Ha, ha ! " laughed Dodson. " You'll think better of that, before next term, Mr. Pickwick."

" He, he, he ! We'll soon see about that, Mr. Pickwick," grinned Fogg.

Speechless with indignation, Mr. Pickwick allowed himself to be led by his solicitor and friends to the door, and there assisted into a hackney-coach, which had been fetched for the purpose, by the ever watchful Sam Weller.

Sam had put up the steps, and was preparing to jump upon the box, when he felt himself gently touched on the shoulder; and looking round, his father stood before him. The old gentleman's countenance wore a mournful expression, as he shook his head gravely, and said, in warning accents:

" I know'd what 'ud come o' this here mode o' doin' bisness. Oh Sammy, Sammy, vy worn't there a alleybi ! "

CHAPTER XXXV.

" But surely, my dear sir," said little Perker, as he stood in
Mr. Pickwick's apartment on the morning after the trial:
" Surely you don't really mean—really and seriously now,
and irritation apart—that you won't pay these costs and
damages ? "

" Not one halfpenny," said Mr. Pickwick, firmly; " not
one halfpenny."

" Hooroar for the principle, as the money-lender said ven
he vouldn't renew the bill," observed Mr. Weller, who was
clearing away the breakfast things.

" Sam," said Mr. Pickwick, " have the goodness to step
down stairs."

" Cert'nly, sir," replied Mr. Weller; and acting on Mr.
Pickwick's gentle hint, Sam retired.

" No, Perker," said Mr. Pickwick, with great seriousness of
manner, " my friends here, have endeavoured to dissuade me
from this determination, but without avail. I shall employ
myself as usual, until the opposite party have the power of
issuing a legal process of execution against me; and if they
are vile enough to avail themselves of it, and to arrest my
person, I shall yield myself up with perfect cheerfulness and
content of heart. When can they do this ? "

" They can issue execution, my dear sir, for the amount

of the damages and taxed costs, next term," replied Perker, "just two months hence, my dear sir."

"Very good," said Mr. Pickwick. "Until that time, my dear fellow, let me hear no more of the matter. And now," continued Mr. Pickwick, looking round on his friends with a good-humoured smile, and a sparkle in the eye which no spectacles could dim or conceal, "the only question is, Where shall we go next?"

Mr. Tupman and Mr. Snodgrass were too much affected by their friend's heroism to offer any reply. Mr. Winkle had not yet sufficiently recovered the recollection of his evidence at the trial, to make any observation on any subject, so Mr. Pickwick paused in vain.

"Well," said that gentleman, "if you leave me to suggest our destination, I say Bath. I think none of us have ever been there."

Nobody had; and as the proposition was warmly seconded by Perker, who considered it extremely probable that if Mr. Pickwick saw a little change and gaiety he would be inclined to think better of his determination, and worse of a debtor's prison, it was carried unanimously: and Sam was at once dispatched to the White Horse Cellar, to take five places by the half-past seven o'clock coach, next morning.

There were just two places to be had inside, and just three to be had out; so Sam Weller booked for them all, and having exchanged a few compliments with the booking-office clerk on the subject of a pewter half-crown which was tendered him as a portion of his "change," walked back to the George and Vulture, where he was pretty busily employed until bedtime in reducing clothes and linen into the smallest possible compass, and exerting his mechanical genius in constructing a variety of ingenious devices for keeping the lids on boxes which had neither locks nor hinges.

The next was a very unpropitious morning for a journey—muggy, damp, and drizzly. The horses in the stages that were going out, and had come through the city, were smoking

101

THE PICKWICK CLUB.

so, that the outside passengers were invisible. The newspaper-
sellers looked moist, and smelt mouldy; the wet ran off the hats
of the orange-venders as they thrust their heads into the coach
windows, and diluted the insides in a refreshing manner. The
Jews with the fifty-bladed penknives shut them up in despair;
the men with the pocket-books made pocket-books of them.
Watch-guards and toasting-forks were alike at a discount, and
pencil-cases and sponge were a drug in the market.

Leaving Sam Weller to rescue the luggage from the seven
or eight porters who flung themselves savagely upon it, the
moment the coach stopped: and finding that they were about
twenty minutes too early, Mr. Pickwick and his friends went
for shelter into the travellers' room—the last resource of
human dejection.

The travellers' room at the White Horse Cellar is of course
uncomfortable; it would be no travellers' room if it were not.
It is the right-hand parlour, into which an aspiring kitchen
fire-place appears to have walked, accompanied by a rebellious
poker, tongs, and shovel. It is divided into boxes, for the
solitary confinement of travellers, and is furnished with a
clock, a looking-glass, and a live waiter: which latter article
is kept in a small kennel for washing glasses, in a corner of
the apartment.

One of these boxes was occupied, on this particular occasion,
by a stern-eyed man of about five-and-forty, who had a bald
and glossy forehead, with a good deal of black hair at the
sides and back of his head, and large black whiskers. He
was buttoned up to the chin in a brown coat; and had a
large seal-skin travelling cap, and a great-coat and cloak,
lying on the seat beside him. He looked up from his breakfast as Mr. Pickwick entered, with a fierce and peremptory
air, which was very dignified; and having scrutinised that
gentleman and his companions to his entire satisfaction,
hummed a tune, in a manner which seemed to say that he
rather suspected somebody wanted to take advantage of him,
but it wouldn't do.

"Waiter," said the gentleman with the whiskers.

"Sir?" replied a man with a dirty complexion, and a towel of the same, emerging from the kennel before mentioned.

"Some more toast."

"Yes, sir."

"Buttered toast, mind," said the gentleman, fiercely.

"D'rectly, sir," replied the waiter.

The gentleman with the whiskers hummed a tune in the same manner as before, and pending the arrival of the toast, advanced to the front of the fire, and, taking his coat tails under his arms, looked at his boots, and ruminated.

"I wonder whereabouts in Bath this coach puts up," said Mr. Pickwick, mildly addressing Mr. Winkle.

"Hum—eh—what's that?" said the strange man.

"I made an observation to my friend, sir," replied Mr. Pickwick, always ready to enter into conversation. "I wondered at what house the Bath coach put up. Perhaps you can inform me."

"Are you going to Bath?" said the strange man.

"I am, sir," replied Mr. Pickwick.

"And those other gentlemen?"

"They are going also," said Mr. Pickwick.

"Not inside—I'll be damned if you're going inside," said the strange man.

"Not all of us," said Mr. Pickwick.

"No, not all of you," said the strange man emphatically. "I've taken two places. If they try to squeeze six people into an infernal box that only holds four, I'll take a post-chaise and bring an action. I've paid my fare. It won't do; I told the clerk when I took my places that it wouldn't do. I know these things have been done. I know they are done every day; but *I* never was done, and I never will be. Those who know me best, best know it; crush me!" Here the fierce gentleman rang the bell with great violence, and told the waiter he'd better bring the toast in five seconds, or he'd know the reason why.

"My good sir," said Mr. Pickwick, "you will allow me to observe that this is a very unnecessary display of excitement. I have only taken places inside for two."

"I am glad to hear it," said the fierce man. "I withdraw my expressions. I tender an apology. There's my card. Give me your acquaintance."

"With great pleasure, sir," replied Mr. Pickwick. "We are to be fellow travellers, and I hope we shall find each other's society mutually agreeable."

"I hope we shall," said the fierce gentleman. "I know we shall. I like your looks; they please me. Gentlemen, your hands and names. Know me."

Of course, an interchange of friendly salutations followed this gracious speech; and the fierce gentleman immediately proceeded to inform the friends, in the same short, abrupt, jerking sentences, that his name was Dowler; that he was going to Bath on pleasure; that he was formerly in the army; that he had now set up in business as a gentleman; that he lived upon the profits; and that the individual for whom the second place was taken, was a personage no less illustrious than Mrs. Dowler his lady wife.

"She's a fine woman," said Mr. Dowler. "I am proud of her. I have reason."

"I hope I shall have the pleasure of judging," said Mr. Pickwick, with a smile.

"You shall," replied Dowler. "She shall know you. She shall esteem you. I courted her under singular circumstances. I won her through a rash vow. Thus. I saw her; I loved her; I proposed; she refused me.—'You love another?'— 'Spare my blushes.'—'I know him.'—'You do.'—'Very good; if he remains here, I'll skin him.'"

"Lord bless me!" exclaimed Mr. Pickwick, involuntarily.

"Did you skin the gentleman, sir?" inquired Mr. Winkle, with a very pale face.

"I wrote him a note. I said it was a painful thing. And so it was."

"Certainly," interposed Mr. Winkle.

"I said I had pledged my word as a gentleman to skin him. My character was at stake. I had no alternative. As an officer in His Majesty's service, I was bound to skin him. I regretted the necessity, but it must be done. He was open to conviction. He saw that the rules of the service were imperative. He fled. I married her. Here's the coach. That's her head."

As Mr. Dowler concluded, he pointed to a stage which had just driven up, from the open window of which a rather pretty face in a bright blue bonnet was looking among the crowd on the pavement: most probably for the rash man himself. Mr. Dowler paid his bill and hurried out with his travelling-cap, coat, and cloak; and Mr. Pickwick and his friends followed to secure their places.

Mr. Tupman and Mr. Snodgrass had seated themselves at the back part of the coach; Mr. Winkle had got inside; and Mr. Pickwick was preparing to follow him, when Sam Weller came up to his master, and whispering in his ear, begged to speak to him, with an air of the deepest mystery.

"Well, Sam," said Mr. Pickwick, "what's the matter now?"

"Here's rayther a rum go, sir," replied Sam.

"What?" inquired Mr. Pickwick.

"This here, sir," rejoined Sam. "I'm wery much afeerd, sir, that the proprieator o' this here coach is a playin' some imperence vith us."

"How is that, Sam?" said Mr. Pickwick; "aren't the names down on the way-bill?"

"The names is not only down on the vay-bill, sir," replied Sam, "but they've painted vun on 'em up, on the door o' the coach." As Sam spoke, he pointed to that part of the coach door on which the proprietor's name usually appears; and there, sure enough, in gilt letters of a goodly size, was the magic name of PICKWICK!

"Dear me," exclaimed Mr. Pickwick, quite staggered by the coincidence; "what a very extraordinary thing!"

"Yes, but that ain't all," said Sam, again directing his master's attention to the coach door; "not content vith writin' up Pickwick, they puts 'Moses' afore it, vich I call addin' insult to injury, as the parrot said ven they not only took him from his native land, but made him talk the English langwidge arterwards."

"It's odd enough certainly, Sam," said Mr. Pickwick; "but if we stand talking here, we shall lose our places."

"Wot, ain't nothin' to be done in consequence, sir?" exclaimed Sam, perfectly aghast at the coolness with which Mr. Pickwick appeared to ensconce himself inside.

"Done!" said Mr. Pickwick. "What should be done?"

"Ain't nobody to be whopped for takin' this here liberty, sir?" said Mr. Weller, who had expected that at least he would have been commissioned to challenge the guard and coachman to a pugilistic encounter on the spot.

"Certainly not," replied Mr. Pickwick eagerly; "not on any account. Jump up to your seat directly."

"I'm wery much afeerd," muttered Sam to himself, as he turned away, "that somethin' queer's come over the governor, or he'd never ha' stood this so quiet. I hope that 'ere trial hasn't broke his spirit, but it looks bad, wery bad." Mr. Weller shook his head gravely; and it is worthy of remark, as an illustration of the manner in which he took this circumstance to heart, that he did not speak another word until the coach reached the Kensington turnpike. Which was so long a time for him to remain taciturn, that the fact may be considered wholly unprecedented.

Nothing worthy of special mention occurred during the journey. Mr. Dowler related a variety of anecdotes, all illustrative of his own personal prowess and desperation, and appealed to Mrs. Dowler in corroboration thereof: when Mrs. Dowler invariably brought in, in the form of an appendix, some remarkable fact or circumstance which Mr. Dowler had forgotten, or had perhaps through modesty omitted: for the addenda in every instance went to show that Mr. Dowler was

106

even a more wonderful fellow than he made himself out to be. Mr. Pickwick and Mr. Winkle listened with great admiration, and at intervals conversed with Mrs. Dowler, who was a very agreeable and fascinating person. So, what between Mr. Dowler's stories, and Mrs. Dowler's charms, and Mr. Pickwick's good humour, and Mr. Winkle's good listening, the insides contrived to be very companionable all the way.

The outsides did as outsides always do. They were very cheerful and talkative at the beginning of every stage, and very dismal and sleepy in the middle, and very bright and wakeful again towards the end. There was one young gentleman in an India-rubber cloak, who smoked cigars all day; and there was another young gentleman in a parody upon a great coat, who lighted a good many, and feeling obviously unsettled after the second whiff, threw them away when he thought nobody was looking at him. There was a third young man on the box who wished to be learned in cattle; and an old one behind, who was familiar with farming. There was a constant succession of Christian names in smock frocks and white coats, who were invited to have a "lift" by the guard, and who knew every horse and hostler on the road and off it; and there was a dinner which would have been cheap at half-a-crown a mouth, if any moderate number of mouths could have eaten it in the time. And at seven o'clock P.M., Mr. Pickwick and his friends, and Mr. Dowler and his wife, respectively retired to their private sitting-rooms at the White Hart hotel, opposite the Great Pump Room, Bath, where the waiters, from their costume, might be mistaken for Westminster boys, only they destroy the illusion by behaving themselves much better.

Breakfast had scarcely been cleared away on the succeeding morning, when a waiter brought in Mr. Dowler's card, with a request to be allowed permission to introduce a friend. Mr. Dowler at once followed up the delivery of the card, by bringing himself and the friend also.

The friend was a charming young man of not much more

107

than fifty, dressed in a very bright blue coat with resplendent buttons, black trousers, and the thinnest possible pair of highly-polished boots. A gold eye-glass was suspended from his neck by a short broad black ribbon; a gold snuff-box was lightly clasped in his left hand; gold rings innumerable, glittered on his fingers; and a large diamond pin set in gold glistened in his shirt frill. He had a gold watch, and a gold curb chain with large gold seals; and he carried a pliant ebony cane with a heavy gold top. His linen was of the very whitest, finest, and stiffest; his wig of the glossiest, blackest, and curliest. His snuff was princes' mixture; his scent *bouquet du roi*. His features were contracted into a perpetual smile; and his teeth were in such perfect order that it was difficult at a small distance to tell the real from the false.

"Mr. Pickwick," said Mr. Dowler; "my friend, Angelo Cyrus Bantam, Esquire, M.C. Bantam; Mr. Pickwick. Know each other.'

"Welcome to Ba—ath, sir. This is indeed an acquisition. Most welcome to Ba—ath, sir. It is long—very long, Mr. Pickwick, since you drank the waters. It appears an age, Mr. Pickwick. Re—markable!"

Such were the expressions with which Angelo Cyrus Bantam, Esquire, M.C., took Mr. Pickwick's hand; retaining it in his, meantime, and shrugging up his shoulders with a constant succession of bows, as if he really could not make up his mind to the trial of letting it go again.

"It is a very long time since I drank the waters, certainly," replied Mr. Pickwick; "for to the best of my knowledge, I was never here before."

"Never in Ba—ath, Mr. Pickwick!" exclaimed the Grand Master, letting the hand fall in astonishment. "Never in Ba—ath! He! he! Mr. Pickwick, you are a wag. Not bad, not bad. Good, good. He! he! he! Re—markable!"

"To my shame, I must say that I am perfectly serious," rejoined Mr. Pickwick. "I really never was here before."

"Oh, I see," exclaimed the Grand Master, looking extremely

pleased; " Yes, yes—good, good—better and better. You
are the gentleman of whom we have heard. Yes; we know
you, Mr. Pickwick; we know you."

" The reports of the trial in those confounded papers,"
thought Mr. Pickwick. " They have heard all about me."

" You are the gentleman residing on Clapham Green,"
resumed Bantam, " who lost the use of his limbs from
imprudently taking cold after port wine; who could not be
moved in consequence of acute suffering, and who had the
water from the King's Bath bottled at one hundred and
three degrees, and sent by waggon to his bed-room in town,
where he bathed, sneezed, and same day recovered. Very
re-markable ! "

Mr. Pickwick acknowledged the compliment which the
supposition implied, but had the self-denial to repudiate it,
notwithstanding; and taking advantage of a moment's silence
on the part of the M.C., begged to introduce his friends, Mr.
Tupman, Mr. Winkle, and Mr. Snodgrass. An introduction
which overwhelmed the M.C. with delight and honour.

" Bantam," said Mr. Dowler, " Mr. Pickwick and his friends
are strangers. They must put their names down. Where's
the book ? "

" The register of the distinguished visitors in Ba—ath will
be at the Pump Room this morning at two o'clock," replied
the M.C. " Will you guide our friends to that splendid
building, and enable me to procure their autographs ? "

" I will," rejoined Dowler. " This is a long call. It's
time to go. I shall be here again in an hour. Come."

" This is a ball night," said the M.C., again taking Mr.
Pickwick's hand, as he rose to go. " The ball-nights in
Ba—ath are moments snatched from Paradise; rendered
bewitching by music, beauty, elegance, fashion, etiquette,
and—and—above all, by the absence of tradespeople, who
are quite inconsistent with Paradise; and who have an
amalgamation of themselves at the Guildhall every fortnight,
which is, to say the least, remarkable. Good bye, good

bye!" and protesting all the way down stairs that he was most satisfied, and most delighted, and most overpowered, and most flattered, Angelo Cyrus Bantam, Esquire, M.C., stepped into a very elegant chariot that waited at the door, and rattled off.

At the appointed hour, Mr. Pickwick and his friends, escorted by Dowler, repaired to the Assembly Rooms, and wrote their names down in a book. An instance of condescension at which Angelo Bantam was even more overpowered than before. Tickets of admission to that evening's assembly were to have been prepared for the whole party, but as they were not ready, Mr. Pickwick undertook, despite all the protestations to the contrary of Angelo Bantam, to send Sam for them at four o'clock in the afternoon, to the M.C.'s house in Queen Square. Having taken a short walk through the city, and arrived at the unanimous conclusion that Park Street was very much like the perpendicular street a man sees in a dream, which he cannot get up for the life of him, they returned to the White Hart, and despatched Sam on the errand to which his master had pledged him.

Sam Weller put on his hat in a very easy and graceful manner, and thrusting his hands in his waistcoat pockets, walked with great deliberation to Queen Square, whistling as he went along, several of the most popular airs of the day, as arranged with entirely new movements for that noble instrument the organ, either mouth or barrel. Arriving at the number in Queen Square to which he had been directed, he left off whistling, and gave a cheerful knock, which was instantaneously answered by a powdered-headed footman in gorgeous livery, and of symmetrical stature.

"Is this here Mr. Bantam's, old feller? inquired Sam Weller, nothing abashed by the blaze of splendour which burst upon his sight, in the person of the powdered-headed footman with the gorgeous livery.

"Why, young man?" was the haughty inquiry of the powdered-headed footman.

PLUSH AND POWDER.

"''Cos if it is, jist you step into him with that 'ere card, and say Mr. Veller's a waitin', will you?" said Sam. And saying it, he very coolly walked into the hall, and sat down.

The powdered-headed footman slammed the door very hard, and scowled very grandly; but both the slam and the scowl were lost upon Sam, who was regarding a mahogany umbrella stand with every outward token of critical approval.

Apparently, his master's reception of the card had impressed the powdered-headed footman in Sam's favour, for when he came back from delivering it, he smiled in a friendly manner, and said that the answer would be ready directly.

"Werry good," said Sam. "Tell the old gen'lm'n not to put himself in a perspiration. No hurry, six-foot. I've had my dinner."

"You dine early, sir," said the powdered-headed footman.

"I find I gets on better at supper when I does," replied Sam.

"Have you been long in Bath, sir?" inquired the powdered-headed footman. "I have not had the pleasure of hearing of you before."

"I haven't created any werry surprisin' sensation here, as yet," rejoined Sam, "for me and the other fash'nables only come last night."

"Nice place, sir," said the powdered-headed footman.

"Seems so," observed Sam.

"Pleasant society, sir," remarked the powdered-headed footman. "Very agreeable servants, sir."

"I should think they wos," replied Sam. "Affable, unaffected, say-nothin'-to-nobody sort o' fellers."

"Oh, very much so, indeed, sir," said the powdered-headed footman, taking Sam's remark as a high compliment. "Very much so indeed. Do you do anything in this way, sir?" inquired the tall footman, producing a small snuff-box with a fox's head on the top of it.

"Not without sneezing," replied Sam.

"Why, it *is* difficult, sir, I confess," said the tall footman.

111

"It may be done by degrees, sir. Coffee is the best practice. I carried coffee, sir, for a long time. It looks very like rappee, sir."

Here, a sharp pull at the bell, reduced the powdered-headed footman to the ignominious necessity of putting the fox's head in his pocket, and hastening with a humble countenance to Mr. Bantam's "study." By the by, who ever knew a man who never read or wrote either, who hadn't got some small back parlour which he *would* call a study!

"There is the answer, sir," said the powdered-headed footman. "I am afraid you'll find it inconveniently large."

"Don't mention it," said Sam, taking a letter with a small enclosure. "It's just possible as exhausted nature may manage to surwive it."

"I hope we shall meet again, sir," said the powdered-headed footman, rubbing his hands, and following Sam out to the door-step.

"You are wery obligin', sir," replied Sam. "Now, don't allow yourself to be fatigued beyond your powers; there's a amiable bein'. Consider what you owe to society, and don't let yourself be injured by too much work. For the sake o' your feller creeturs, keep your self as quiet as you can; only think what a loss you would be!" with these pathetic words, Sam Weller departed.

"A very singular young man that," said the powdered-headed footman, looking after Mr. Weller, with a countenance which clearly showed he could make nothing of him.

Sam said nothing at all. He winked, shook his head, smiled, winked again; and with an expression of countenance which seemed to denote that he was greatly amused with something or other, walked merrily away.

At precisely twenty minutes before eight o'clock that night, Angelo Cyrus Bantam, Esq., the Master of the Ceremonies, emerged from his chariot at the door of the Assembly Rooms in the same wig, the same teeth, the same eye-glass, the same watch and seals, the same rings, the same shirt-pin, and the

112

same cane. The only observable alterations in his appearance were, that he wore a brighter blue coat, with a white silk lining: black tights, black silk stockings, and pumps, and a white waistcoat, and was, if possible, just a thought more scented.

Thus attired, the Master of the Ceremonies, in strict discharge of the important duties of his all-important office, planted himself in the rooms to receive the company.

Bath being full, the company and the sixpences for tea, poured in, in shoals. In the ball-room, the long card-room, the octagonal card-room, the staircases, and the passages, the hum of many voices, and the sound of many feet, were perfectly bewildering. Dresses rustled, feathers waved, lights shone, and jewels sparkled. There was the music—not of the quadrille band, for it had not yet commenced; but the music of soft tiny footsteps, with now and then a clear merry laugh —low and gentle, but very pleasant to hear in a female voice, whether in Bath or elsewhere. Brilliant eyes, lighted up with pleasurable expectation, gleamed from every side; and look where you would, some exquisite form glided gracefully through the throng, and was no sooner lost, than it was replaced by another as dainty and bewitching.

In the tea-room, and hovering round the card-tables, were a vast number of queer old ladies and decrepid old gentlemen, discussing all the small talk and scandal of the day, with a relish and gusto which sufficiently bespoke the intensity of the pleasure they derived from the occupation. Mingled with these groups, were three or four matchmaking mammas, appearing to be wholly absorbed by the conversation in which they were taking part, but failing not from time to time to cast an anxious sidelong glance upon their daughters, who, remembering the maternal injunction to make the best use of their youth, had already commenced incipient flirtations in the mislaying of scarves, putting on gloves, setting down cups, and so forth; slight matters apparently, but which may be turned to surprisingly good account by expert practitioners.

Lounging near the doors, and in remote corners, were various knots of silly young men, displaying various varieties of puppyism and stupidity; amusing all sensible people near them with their folly and conceit; and happily thinking themselves the objects of general admiration. A wise and merciful dispensation which no good man will quarrel with.

And lastly, seated on some of the back benches, where they had already taken up their positions for the evening, were divers unmarried ladies past their grand climacteric, who, not dancing because there were no partners for them, and not playing cards lest they should be set down as irretrievably single, were in the favourable situation of being able to abuse everybody without reflecting on themselves. In short, they could abuse everybody, because everybody was there. It was a scene of gaiety, glitter, and show; of richly-dressed people, handsome mirrors, chalked floors, girandoles, and wax-candles; and in all parts of the scene, gliding from spot to spot in silent softness, bowing obsequiously to this party, nodding familiarly to that, and smiling complacently on all, was the sprucely attired person of Angelo Cyrus Bantam, Esquire, Master of the Ceremonies.

"Stop in the tea-room. Take your sixpenn'orth. They lay on hot water, and call it tea. Drink it," said Mr. Dowler, in a loud voice, directing Mr. Pickwick, who advanced at the head of the little party, with Mrs. Dowler on his arm. Into the tea-room Mr. Pickwick turned; and catching sight of him, Mr. Bantam corkscrewed his way through the crowd, and welcomed him with ecstasy.

"My dear sir, I am highly honoured. Ba—ath is favoured. Mrs. Dowler, you embellish the rooms. I congratulate you on your feathers. Re—markable!"

"Any body here?" inquired Dowler, suspiciously.

"Any body!" The *élite* of Ba—ath. Mr. Pickwick, do you see the lady in the gauze turban?"

"The fat old lady?" inquired Mr. Pickwick, innocently.

"Hush, my dear sir—nobody's fat or old in Ba—ath. That's the Dowager Lady Snuphanuph."

"Is it indeed?" said Mr. Pickwick.

"No less a person, I assure you," said the Master of the Ceremonies. "Hush. Draw a little nearer, Mr. Pickwick. You see the splendidly dressed young man coming this way?"

"The one with the long hair, and the particularly small forehead?" inquired Mr. Pickwick.

"The same. The richest young man in Ba—ath at this moment. Young Lord Mutanhed."

"You don't say so?" said Mr. Pickwick.

"Yes. You'll hear his voice in a moment, Mr. Pickwick. He'll speak to me. The other gentleman with him, in the red under waistcoat and dark moustache, is the Honourable Mr. Crushton, his bosom friend. How do you do, my lord?"

"Veway hot, Bantam," said his lordship.

"It *is* very warm, my lord," replied the M.C.

"Confounded," assented the Honourable Mr. Crushton.

"Have you seen his lordship's mail cart, Bantam?" inquired the Honourable Mr. Crushton, after a short pause, during which young Lord Mutanhed had been endeavouring to stare Mr. Pickwick out of countenance, and Mr. Crushton had been reflecting what subject his lordship could talk about best.

"Dear me, no," replied the M.C. "A mail cart! What an excellent idea. Re—markable!"

"Gwacious heavens!" said his lordship, "I thought evewebody had seen the new mail cart; it's the neatest, pwettiest, gwacefullest thing that ever wan upon wheels. Painted wed, with a cweam piebald."

"With a real box for the letters, and all complete," said the Honourable Mr. Crushton.

"And a little seat in fwont, with an iwon wail, for the dwiver," added his lordship. "I dwove it over to Bwistol the other morning, in a cwimson coat, with two servants widing a quarter of a mile behind; and confound me if the

115

people didn't wush out of their cottages, and awest my pwo-
gwess, to know if I wasn't the post. Glorwious, glorwious!"

At this anecdote his lordship laughed very heartily, as did
the listeners, of course. Then, drawing his arm through that
of the obsequious Mr. Crushton, Lord Mutanhed walked
away.

"Delightful young man, his lordship," said the Master of
the Ceremonies.

"So I should think," rejoined Mr. Pickwick, drily.

The dancing having commenced, the necessary introductions
having been made, and all preliminaries arranged, Angelo
Bantam rejoined Mr. Pickwick, and led him into the card-
room.

Just at the very moment of their entrance, the Dowager
Lady Snuphanuph and two other ladies of an ancient and
whist-like appearance, were hovering over an unoccupied card-
table; and they no sooner set eyes upon Mr. Pickwick under
the convoy of Angelo Bantam, than they exchanged glances
with each other, seeing that he was precisely the very person
they wanted, to make up the rubber.

"My dear Bantam," said the Dowager Lady Snuphanuph,
coaxingly, "find us some nice creature to make up this table;
there's a good soul." Mr. Pickwick happened to be looking
another way at the moment, so her ladyship nodded her head
towards him, and frowned expressively.

"My friend Mr. Pickwick, my lady, will be most happy, I
am sure, re—markably so," said the M.C., taking the hint.
"Mr. Pickwick, Lady Snuphanuph—Mrs. Colonel Wugsby—
Miss Bolo."

Mr. Pickwick bowed to each of the ladies, and, finding
escape impossible, cut. Mr. Pickwick and Miss Bolo against
Lady Snuphanuph and Mrs. Colonel Wugsby.

As the trump card was turned up, at the commencement of
the second deal, two young ladies hurried into the room, and
took their stations on either side of Mrs. Colonel Wugsby's
chair, where they waited patiently until the hand was over.

MR. PICKWICK PLAYS WHIST.

" Now, Jane," said Mrs. Colonel Wugsby, turning to one
of the girls, " what is it?"

" I came to ask, ma, whether I might dance with the
youngest Mr. Crawley," whispered the prettier and younger
of the two.

" Good God, Jane, how can you think of such things?"
replied the mamma, indignantly. " Haven't you repeatedly
heard that his father has eight hundred a-year, which dies
with him? I am ashamed of you. Not on any account."

" Ma," whispered the other, who was much older than her
sister, and very insipid and artificial, " Lord Mutanhed has
been introduced to me. I said I *thought* I wasn't engaged,
ma."

" You're a sweet pet, my love," replied Mrs. Colonel Wugsby,
tapping her daughter's cheek with her fan, " and are always
to be trusted. He's immensely rich, my dear. Bless you!"
With these words Mrs. Colonel Wugsby kissed her eldest
daughter most affectionately, and frowning in a warning
manner upon the other, sorted her cards.

Poor Mr. Pickwick! he had never played with three
thorough-paced female card-players before. They were so
desperately sharp, that they quite frightened him. If he
played a wrong card, Miss Bolo looked a small armoury of
daggers; if he stopped to consider which was the right one,
Lady Snuphanuph would throw herself back in her chair, and
smile with a mingled glance of impatience and pity to Mrs.
Colonel Wugsby; at which Mrs. Colonel Wugsby would shrug
up her shoulders, and cough, as much as to say she wondered
whether he ever would begin. Then, at the end of every
hand, Miss Bolo would inquire with a dismal countenance
and reproachful sigh, why Mr. Pickwick had not returned that
diamond, or led the club, or roughed the spade, or finessed
the heart, or led through the honour, or brought out the
ace, or played up to the king, or some such thing; and in
reply to all these grave charges, Mr. Pickwick would be wholly
unable to plead any justification whatever, having by this time

forgotten all about the game. People came and looked on, too, which made Mr. Pickwick nervous. Besides all this, there was a great deal of distracting conversation near the table, between Angelo Bantam and the two Miss Matinters, who, being single and singular, paid great court to the Master of the Ceremonies, in the hope of getting a stray partner now and then. All these things, combined with the noises and interruptions of constant comings in and goings out, made Mr. Pickwick play rather badly; the cards were against him, also; and when they left off at ten minutes past eleven, Miss Bolo rose from the table considerably agitated, and went straight home, in a flood of tears, and a sedan-chair.

Being joined by his friends, who one and all protested that they had scarcely ever spent a more pleasant evening, Mr. Pickwick accompanied them to the White Hart, and having soothed his feelings with something hot, went to bed, and to sleep, almost simultaneously.

The Card-Room at Bath

CHAPTER XXXVI.

As Mr. Pickwick contemplated a stay of at least two
months in Bath, he deemed it advisable to take private
lodgings for himself and friends for that period; and as a
favourable opportunity offered for their securing, on moderate
terms, the upper portion of a house in the Royal Crescent,
which was larger than they required, Mr. and Mrs. Dowler
offered to relieve them of a bed-room and sitting-room. This
proposition was at once accepted, and in three days' time they
were all located in their new abode, when Mr. Pickwick began
to drink the waters with the utmost assiduity. Mr. Pickwick
took them systematically. He drank a quarter of a pint before
breakfast, and then walked up a hill; and another quarter of
a pint after breakfast, and then walked down a hill; and after
every fresh quarter of a pint, Mr. Pickwick declared, in the
most solemn and emphatic terms, that he felt a great deal
better: whereat his friends were very much delighted, though
they had not been previously aware that there was anything
the matter with him.

The great pump-room is a spacious saloon, ornamented
with Corinthian pillars, and a music gallery, and a Tompion
clock, and a statue of Nash, and a golden inscription, to

which all the water-drinkers should attend, for it appeals
to them in the cause of a deserving charity. There is a
large bar with a marble vase, out of which the pumper
gets the water; and there are a number of yellow-looking
tumblers, out of which the company get it; and it is a
most edifying and satisfactory sight to behold the perseverance and gravity with which they swallow it. There are
baths near at hand, in which a part of the company wash
themselves; and a band plays afterwards, to congratulate the
remainder on their having done so. There is another pump-
room, into which infirm ladies and gentlemen are wheeled, in
such an astonishing variety of chairs and chaises, that any
adventurous individual who goes in with the regular number
of toes, is in imminent danger of coming out without them;
and there is a third, into which the quiet people go, for it
is less noisy than either. There is an immensity of promenading,
on crutches and off, with sticks and without, and a great
deal of conversation, and liveliness, and pleasantry.

Every morning, the regular water-drinkers, Mr. Pickwick
among the number, met each other in the pump-room, took
their quarter of a pint, and walked constitutionally. At the
afternoon's promenade, Lord Mutanhed, and the Honourable
Mr. Crushton, the Dowager Lady Snuphanuph, Mrs. Colonel
Wugsby, and all the great people, and all the morning water-
drinkers, met in grand assemblage. After this, they walked
out, or drove out, or were pushed out in bath chairs, and
met one another again. After this, the gentlemen went to
the reading-rooms and met divisions of the mass. After this,
they went home. If it were theatre night, perhaps they met
at the theatre; if it were assembly night, they met at the
rooms; and if it were neither, they met the next day. A very
pleasant routine, with perhaps a slight tinge of sameness.

Mr. Pickwick was sitting up by himself, after a day spent
in this manner, making entries in his journal: his friends having
retired to bed: when he was roused by a gentle tap at the
room door.

THE TRUE LEGEND OF PRINCE BLADUD.

"Beg your pardon, sir," said Mrs. Craddock, the landlady, peeping in; "but *did* you want anything more, sir?"

"Nothing more, ma'am," replied Mr. Pickwick.

"My young girl is gone to bed, sir," said Mrs. Craddock; "and Mr. Dowler is good enough to say that he'll sit up for Mrs. Dowler, as the party isn't expected to be over till late; so I was thinking if you wanted nothing more, Mr. Pickwick, I would go to bed."

"By all means, ma'am," replied Mr. Pickwick.

"Wish you good night, sir," said Mrs. Craddock.

"Good night, ma'am," rejoined Mr. Pickwick.

Mrs. Craddock closed the door, and Mr. Pickwick resumed his writing.

In half an hour's time the entries were concluded. Mr. Pickwick carefully rubbed the last page on the blotting-paper, shut up the book, wiped his pen on the bottom of the inside of his coat tail, and opened the drawer of the inkstand to put it carefully away. There were a couple of sheets of writing-paper, pretty closely written over, in the inkstand drawer, and they were folded so, that the title, which was in a good round hand, was fully disclosed to him. Seeing from this, that it was no private document: and as it seemed to relate to Bath, and was very short: Mr. Pickwick unfolded it, lighted his bed-room candle that it might burn up well by the time he finished; and drawing his chair nearer the fire, read as follows:

THE TRUE LEGEND OF PRINCE BLADUD.

"Less than two hundred years agone, on one of the public baths in this city, there appeared an inscription in honour of its mighty founder, the renowned Prince Bladud. That inscription is now erased.

"For many hundred years before that time, there had been handed down, from age to age, an old legend, that the illustrious Prince being afflicted with leprosy, on his return from reaping a rich harvest of knowledge in Athens, shunned the court of his royal father, and consorted moodily with husband-men and pigs. Among the herd (so said the legend) was a pig of grave and solemn countenance, with whom the Prince had a fellow feeling—for he too was wise—a pig of thoughtful and reserved demeanour; an animal superior to his fellows, whose grunt was terrible, and whose bite was sharp. The young Prince sighed deeply as he looked upon the countenance of the majestic swine; he thought of his royal father, and his eyes were bedewed with tears.

"This sagacious pig was fond of bathing in rich, moist mud. Not in summer, as common pigs do, now, to cool themselves, and did even in those distant ages (which is a proof that the light of civilisation had already begun to dawn, though feebly), but in the cold sharp days of winter. His coat was ever so sleek, and his complexion so clear, that the Prince resolved to essay the purifying qualities of the same water that his friend resorted to. He made the trial. Beneath that black mud, bubbled the hot springs of Bath. He washed, and was cured. Hastening to his father's court, he paid his best respects, and returning quickly hither, founded this city, and its famous baths.

"He sought the pig with all the ardour of their early friendship—but, alas! the waters had been his death. He had imprudently taken a bath at too high a temperature, and the natural philosopher was no more! He was succeeded by Pliny, who also fell a victim to his thirst for knowledge.

"This *was* the legend. Listen to the true one.

"A great many centuries since, there flourished, in great state, the famous and renowned Lud Hudibras, king of Britain. He was a mighty monarch. The earth shook when he walked: he was so very stout. His people basked in the light of his countenance: it was so red and glowing. He was, indeed, every inch a king. And there were a good many inches of him too, for although he was not very tall, he was a remarkable size round, and the inches that he wanted in height, he made up in circumference. If any degenerate monarch of modern

times could be in any way compared with him, I should say
the venerable King Cole would be that illustrious potentate.

"This good king had a queen, who eighteen years before,
had had a son, who was called Bladud. He was sent to a
preparatory seminary in his father's dominions until he was
ten years old, and was then dispatched, in charge of a trusty
messenger, to a finishing school at Athens; and as there was
no extra charge for remaining during the holidays, and no
notice required previous to the removal of a pupil, there he
remained for eight long years, at the expiration of which
time, the king his father sent the lord chamberlain over, to
settle the bill, and to bring him home; which, the lord
chamberlain doing, was received with shouts, and pensioned
immediately.

"When King Lud saw the Prince his son, and found he
had grown up such a fine young man, he perceived at once
what a grand thing it would be to have him married without
delay, so that his children might be the means of perpetuating
the glorious race of Lud, down to the very latest ages of
the world. With this view, he sent a special embassy,
composed of great noblemen who had nothing particular to do,
and wanted lucrative employment, to a neighbouring king,
and demanded his fair daughter in marriage for his son;
stating at the same time that he was anxious to be on the
most affectionate terms with his brother and friend, but that
if they couldn't agree in arranging this marriage, he should
be under the unpleasant necessity of invading his kingdom,
and putting his eyes out. To this, the other king (who was
the weaker of the two) replied, that he was very much obliged
to his friend and brother for all his goodness and magnanimity,
and that his daughter was quite ready to be married,
whenever Prince Bladud liked to come and fetch her.

"This answer no sooner reached Britain, than the whole
nation were transported with joy. Nothing was heard, on all
sides, but the sounds of feasting and revelry,—except the
chinking of money as it was paid in by the people to the

collector of the Royal Treasures, to defray the expenses of the happy ceremony. It was upon this occasion that King Lud, seated on the top of his throne in full council, rose, in the exuberance of his feelings, and commanded the lord chief justice to order in the richest wines and the court minstrels : an act of graciousness which has been, through the ignorance of traditionary historians, attributed to King Cole, in those celebrated lines in which his majesty is represented as

> Calling for his pipe, and calling for his pot,
> And calling for his fiddlers three.

Which is an obvious injustice to the memory of King Lud, and a dishonest exaltation of the virtues of King Cole.

"But, in the midst of all this festivity and rejoicing, there was one individual present, who tasted not when the sparkling wines were poured forth, and who danced not, when the minstrels played. This was no other than Prince Bladud himself, in honour of whose happiness a whole people were at that very moment, straining alike their throats and purse-strings. The truth was, that the Prince, forgetting the undoubted right of the minister for foreign affairs to fall in love on his behalf, had, contrary to every precedent of policy and diplomacy, already fallen in love on his own account, and privately contracted himself unto the fair daughter of a noble Athenian.

"Here we have a striking example of one of the manifold advantages of civilisation and refinement. If the Prince had lived in later days, he might at once have married the object of his father's choice, and then set himself seriously to work, to relieve himself of the burden which rested heavily upon him. He might have endeavoured to break her heart by a systematic course of insult and neglect; or, if the spirit of her sex, and a proud consciousness of her many wrongs had upheld her under this ill treatment, he might have sought to take her life, and so get rid of her effectually. But neither mode of relief suggested itself to Prince Bladud; so he solicited a private audience, and told his father.

124

KING LUD IS ENRAGED.

"It is an old prerogative of kings to govern everything but their passions. King Lud flew into a frightful rage, tossed his crown up to the ceiling, and caught it again—for in those days kings kept their crowns on their heads, and not in the Tower—stamped the ground, rapped his forehead, wondered why his own flesh and blood rebelled against him, and, finally, calling in his guards, ordered the Prince away to instant confinement in a lofty turret; a course of treatment which the kings of old very generally pursued towards their sons, when their matrimonial inclinations did not happen to point to the same quarter as their own.

"When Prince Bladud had been shut up in the lofty turret for the greater part of a year, with no better prospect before his bodily eyes than a stone wall, or before his mental vision than prolonged imprisonment, he naturally began to ruminate on a plan of escape, which, after months of preparation, he managed to accomplish; considerately leaving his dinner knife in the heart of his gaoler, lest the poor fellow (who had a family) should be considered privy to his flight, and punished accordingly by the infuriated king.

"The monarch was frantic at the loss of his son. He knew not on whom to vent his grief and wrath, until fortunately bethinking himself of the Lord Chamberlain who had brought him home, he struck off his pension and his head together.

"Meanwhile, the young Prince, effectually disguised, wandered on foot through his father's dominions, cheered and supported in all his hardships by sweet thoughts of the Athenian maid, who was the innocent cause of his weary trials. One day he stopped to rest in a country village; and seeing that there were gay dances going forward on the green, and gay faces passing to and fro, ventured to inquire of a reveller who stood near him, the reason for this rejoicing.

"'Know you not, O stranger,' was the reply, 'of the recent proclamation of our gracious king?'

"'Proclamation! No. What proclamation?' rejoined the Prince—for he had travelled along the bye and little-frequented ways, and knew nothing of what had passed upon the public roads, such as they were.

"'Why,' replied the peasant, 'the foreign lady that our Prince wished to wed, is married to a foreign noble of her own country; and the king proclaims the fact, and a great public festival besides; for now, of course, Prince Bladud will come back and marry the lady his father chose, who they say is as beautiful as the noonday sun. Your health, sir. God save the King!'

"The Prince remained to hear no more. He fled from the spot, and plunged into the thickest recesses of a neighbouring wood. On, on, he wandered, night and day: beneath the blazing sun, and the cold pale moon: through the dry heat of noon, and the damp cold of night: in the grey light of morn, and the red glare of eve. So heedless was he of time or object, that being bound for Athens, he wandered as far out of his way as Bath.

"There was no city where Bath stands, then. There was no vestige of human habitation, or sign of man's resort, to bear the name; but there was the same noble country, the same broad expanse of hill and dale, the same beautiful channel stealing on, far away: the same lofty mountains which, like the troubles of life, viewed at a distance, and partially obscured by the bright mist of its morning, lose their ruggedness and asperity, and seem all ease and softness. Moved by the gentle beauty of the scene, the Prince sank upon the green turf, and bathed his swollen feet in his tears.

"'Oh!' said the unhappy Bladud, clasping his hands, and mournfully raising his eyes towards the sky, 'would that my wanderings might end here! Would that these grateful tears with which I now mourn hope misplaced, and love despised, might flow in peace for ever!'

"The wish was heard. It was in the time of the heathen deities, who used occasionally to take people at their words, with a promptness, in some cases extremely awkward. The ground opened beneath the Prince's feet; he sunk into the chasm; and instantaneously it closed upon his head for ever, save where his hot tears welled up through the earth, and where they have continued to gush forth ever since.

" It is observable that, to this day, large numbers of elderly ladies and gentlemen who have been disappointed in procuring partners, and almost as many young ones who are anxious to obtain them, repair, annually, to Bath to drink the waters, from which they derive much strength and comfort. This is most complimentary to the virtue of Prince Bladud's tears, and strongly corroborative of the veracity of this legend."

Mr. Pickwick yawned several times, when he had arrived at the end of this little manuscript : carefully refolded, and replaced it in the inkstand drawer: and then, with a countenance expressive of the utmost weariness, lighted his chamber candle, and went up stairs to bed.

He stopped at Mr. Dowler's door, according to custom, and knocked to say good night.

"Ah!" said Dowler, "going to bed? I wish I was. Dismal night. Windy; isn't it?"

"Very," said Mr. Pickwick. "Good night."

"Good night."

Mr. Pickwick went to his bed-chamber, and Mr. Dowler resumed his seat before the fire, in fulfilment of his rash promise to sit up till his wife came home.

There are few things more worrying than sitting up for somebody, especially if that somebody be at a party. You cannot help thinking how quickly the time passes with them, which drags so heavily with you; and the more you think of this, the more your hopes of their speedy arrival decline. Clocks tick so loud, too, when you are sitting up alone, and you seem as if you had an under garment of cobwebs on. First, something tickles your right knee, and then the same sensation irritates your left. You have no sooner changed your position, than it comes again in the arms; when you have fidgeted your limbs into all sorts of odd shapes, you have a sudden relapse in the nose, which you rub as if to rub it off—as there is no doubt you would, if you could. Eyes, too, are mere personal inconveniences; and the wick of one candle gets an inch and a half long, while you are snuffing the other. These, and various other little nervous annoyances, render sitting up for a length of time after everybody else has gone to bed, anything but a cheerful amusement.

This was just Mr. Dowler's opinion, as he sat before the fire, and felt honestly indignant with all the inhuman people at the party who were keeping him up. He was not put into better humour either, by the reflection that he had taken it into his head, early in the evening, to think he had got an ache there, and so stopped at home. At length, after several droppings asleep, and fallings forward towards the bars, and catchings backward soon enough to prevent being branded in the face, Mr. Dowler made up his mind that he would throw himself on the bed in the back-room and *think*—not sleep, of course.

"I'm a heavy sleeper," said Mr. Dowler, as he flung himself on the bed. "I must keep awake. I suppose I shall hear a knock here. Yes. I thought so. I can hear the watchman. There he goes. Fainter now though. A little fainter. He's turning the corner. Ah!" When Mr. Dowler arrived at this point, *he* turned the corner at which he had been long hesitating, and fell fast asleep.

Just as the clock struck three, there was blown into the crescent a sedan-chair with Mrs. Dowler inside, borne by one short fat chairman, and one long thin one, who had had much ado to keep their bodies perpendicular: to say nothing of the chair. But on that high ground, and in the crescent, which the wind swept round and round as if it were going to tear the paving stones up, its fury was tremendous. They were very glad to set the chair down, and give a good round loud double-knock at the street door.

They waited some time, but nobody came.

"Servants is in the arms o' Porpus, I think," said the short chairman, warming his hands at the attendant link-boy's torch.

"I wish he'd give 'em a squeeze and wake 'em," observed the long one.

"Knock again, will you, if you please," cried Mrs. Dowler from the chair. "Knock two or three times, if you please."

The short man was quite willing to get the job over, as soon as possible; so he stood on the step, and gave four or five most startling double knocks, of eight or ten knocks a piece: while the long man went into the road, and looked up at the windows for a light.

Nobody came. It was all as silent and dark as ever.

"Dear me!" said Mrs. Dowler. "You must knock again, if you please."

"There ain't a bell, is there, ma'am?" said the short chairman.

"Yes, there is," interposed the link-boy, "I've been a ringing at it ever so long."

"It's only a handle," said Mrs. Dowler, "the wire's broken."

"I wish the servants' heads wos," growled the long man.

"I must trouble you to knock again, if you please," said Mrs. Dowler with the utmost politeness.

The short man did knock again several times, without producing the smallest effect. The tall man, growing very impatient, then relieved him, and kept on perpetually knocking double-knocks of two loud knocks each, like an insane postman.

At length Mr. Winkle began to dream that he was at a club, and that the members being very refractory, the chairman was obliged to hammer the table a good deal to preserve order; then, he had a confused notion of an auction room where there were no bidders, and the auctioneer was buying everything in; and ultimately he began to think it just within the bounds of possibility that somebody might be knocking at the street door. To make quite certain, however, he remained quiet in bed for ten minutes or so, and listened;

and when he had counted two or three and thirty knocks, he felt quite satisfied, and gave himself a great deal of credit for being so wakeful.

"Rap rap—rap rap—rap rap—ra, ra, ra, ra, ra, rap!" went the knocker.

Mr. Winkle jumped out of bed, wondering very much what could possibly be the matter, and hastily putting on his stockings and slippers, folded his dressing gown round him, lighted a flat candle from the rush-light that was burning in the fire-place, and hurried down stairs.

"Here's somebody comin' at last, ma'am," said the short chairman.

"I wish I wos behind him vith a bradawl," muttered the long one.

"Who's there?" cried Mr. Winkle, undoing the chain.

"Don't stop to ask questions, cast-iron head," replied the long man, with great disgust, taking it for granted that the inquirer was a footman; "but open the door."

"Come, look sharp, timber eye-lids," added the other encouragingly.

Mr. Winkle, being half asleep, obeyed the command mechanically, opened the door a little, and peeped out. The first thing he saw, was the red glare of the link-boy's torch. Startled by the sudden fear that the house might be on fire, he hastily threw the door wide open, and holding the candle above his head, stared eagerly before him, not quite certain whether what he saw was a sedan-chair or a fire engine. At this instant there came a violent gust of wind; the light was blown out; Mr. Winkle felt himself irresistibly impelled on to the steps; and the door blew to, with a loud crash.

"Well, young man, now you *have* done it!" said the short chairman.

Mr. Winkle, catching sight of a lady's face at the window of the sedan, turned hastily round, plied the knocker with all his might and main, and called frantically upon the chairman to take the chair away again.

"Take it away, take it away," cried Mr. Winkle. "Here's somebody coming out of another house; put me into the chair. Hide me! Do something with me!"

All this time he was shivering with cold; and every time he raised his hand to the knocker, the wind took the dressing gown in a most unpleasant manner.

"The people are coming down the Crescent now. There are ladies with 'em; cover me up with something. Stand before me!" roared Mr. Winkle. But the chairmen were too much exhausted with laughing to afford him the slightest assistance, and the ladies were every moment approaching nearer and nearer.

Mr. Winkle gave a last hopeless knock; the ladies were only a few doors off. He threw away the extinguished candle, which, all this time, he had held above his head, and fairly bolted into the sedan-chair where Mrs. Dowler was.

Now, Mrs. Craddock had heard the knocking and the voices at last; and, only waiting to put something smarter on her head than her night-cap, ran down into the front drawing-room to make sure that it was the right party. Throwing up the window-sash as Mr. Winkle was rushing into the chair, she no sooner caught sight of what was going forward below, than she raised a vehement and dismal shriek, and implored Mr. Dowler to get up directly, for his wife was running away with another gentleman.

Upon this Mr. Dowler bounced off the bed as abruptly as an India-rubber ball, and rushing into the front room, arrived at one window just as Mr. Pickwick threw up the other: when the first object that met the gaze of both, was Mr. Winkle bolting into the sedan-chair.

"Watchman," shouted Dowler furiously; "stop him—hold him—keep him tight—shut him in, till I come down. I'll cut his throat—give me a knife—from ear to ear, Mrs. Craddock—I will!" And breaking from the shrieking landlady, and from Mr. Pickwick, the indignant husband seized a small supper-knife, and tore into the street.

But Mr. Winkle didn't wait for him. He no sooner heard the horrible threat of the valorous Dowler, than he bounced out of the sedan, quite as quickly as he had bounced in, and throwing off his slippers into the road, took to his heels and tore round the Crescent, hotly pursued by Dowler and the watchman. He kept ahead; the door was open as he came round the second time; he rushed in, slammed it in Dowler's face, mounted to his bed-room, locked the door, piled a wash-hand-stand, chest of drawers, and table against it, and packed up a few necessaries ready for flight with the first ray of morning.

Dowler came up to the outside of the door; avowed, through the key-hole, his stedfast determination of cutting Mr. Winkle's throat next day; and, after a great confusion of voices in the drawing-room, amidst which that of Mr. Pickwick was distinctly heard endeavouring to make peace, the inmates dispersed to their several bed-chambers, and all was quiet once more.

It is not unlikely that the inquiry may be made, where Mr. Weller was, all this time? We will state where he was in the next chapter.

Mr. Winkle's Situation when the Door "blew to"

CHAPTER XXXVII.

" MR. WELLER," said Mrs. Craddock, upon the morning of
this very eventful day, "here's a letter for you."

" Wery odd that," said Sam, " I'm afeerd there must be
somethin' the matter, for I don't recollect any gen'lm'n in
my circle of acquaintance as is capable o' writin' one."

" Perhaps something uncommon has taken place," observed
Mrs. Craddock.

" It must be somethin' wery uncommon indeed, as could
produce a letter out o' any friend o' mine," replied Sam,
shaking his head dubiously; " nothin' less than a nat'ral
conwulsion, as the young gen'lm'n observed ven he wos took
with fits. It can't be from the gov'ner," said Sam, looking
at the direction. " He always prints, I know, 'cos he learnt
writin' from the large bills in the bookin' offices. It's a wery
strange thing now, where this here letter can ha' come from."

As Sam said this, he did what a great many people do when
they are uncertain about the writer of a note,—looked at the
seal, and then at the front, and then at the back, and then
at the sides, and then at the superscription; and, as a last
resource, thought perhaps he might as well look at the inside,
and try to find out, from that.

133

" It's wrote on gilt-edged paper," said Sam, as he unfolded it, " and sealed in bronze vax with the top of a door-key. Now for it." And, with a very grave face, Mr. Weller slowly read as follows :

" A select company of the Bath footmen presents their compliments to Mr. Weller, and requests the pleasure of his company this evening, to a friendly swarry, consisting of a boiled leg of mutton with the usual trimmings. The swarry to be on table at half-past nine o'clock punctually."

This was inclosed in another note, which ran thus—

" Mr. John Smauker, the gentleman who had the pleasure of meeting Mr. Weller at the house of their mutual acquaintance, Mr. Bantam, a few days since, begs to enclose Mr. Weller the herewith invitation. If Mr. Weller will call on Mr. John Smauker at nine o'clock, Mr. John Smauker will have the pleasure of introducing Mr. Weller.

(Signed)   " JOHN SMAUKER."

The envelope was directed to blank Weller, Esq., at Mr. Pickwick's ; and in a parenthesis, in the left hand corner, were the words " airy bell," as an instruction to the bearer.

" Vell," said Sam, " this is comin' it rayther powerful, this is. I never heerd a biled leg o' mutton called a swarry afore. I wonder wot they'd call a roast one."

However, without waiting to debate the point, Sam at once betook himself into the presence of Mr. Pickwick, and requested leave of absence for that evening, which was readily granted. With this permission, and the street-door key, Sam Weller issued forth a little before the appointed time, and strolled leisurely towards Queen Square, which he no sooner gained than he had the satisfaction of beholding Mr. John Smauker leaning his powdered head against a lamp post at a short distance off, smoking a cigar through an amber tube.

" How do you do, Mr. Weller?" said Mr. John Smauker, raising his hat gracefully with one hand, while he gently waved the other in a condescending manner. "How do you do, sir?"

"Why, reasonably convalessent," replied Sam. "How do *you* find yourself, my dear feller?"

"Only so so," said Mr. John Smauker.

"Ah, you've been a workin' too hard," observed Sam. "I was fearful you would; it won't do, you know; you must not give way to that 'ere uncompromisin' spirit o' your'n."

"It's not so much that, Mr. Weller," replied Mr. John Smauker, "as bad wine; I'm afraid I've been dissipating."

"Oh! that's it, is it?" said Sam; "that's a wery bad complaint, that."

"And yet the temptation, you see, Mr. Weller," observed Mr. John Smauker.

"Ah, to be sure," said Sam.

"Plunged into the very vortex of society, you know, Mr. Weller," said Mr. John Smauker with a sigh.

"Dreadful indeed!" rejoined Sam.

"But it's always the way," said Mr. John Smauker; "if your destiny leads you into public life, and public station, you must expect to be subjected to temptations which other people is free from, Mr. Weller."

"Precisely what my uncle said, ven *he* vent into the public line," remarked Sam, "and wery right the old gen'lm'n wos, for he drank hisself to death in somethin' less than a quarter."

Mr. John Smauker looked deeply indignant at any parallel being drawn between himself and the deceased gentleman in question; but as Sam's face was in the most immoveable state of calmness, he thought better of it, and looked affable again.

"Perhaps we had better be walking," said Mr. Smauker, consulting a copper time-piece which dwelt at the bottom of a deep watch-pocket, and was raised to the surface by means of a black string, with a copper key at the other end.

"P'raps we had," replied Sam, "or they'll overdo the swarry, and that'll spile it."

"Have you drank the waters, Mr. Weller?" inquired his companion, as they walked towards High Street.

"Once," replied Sam.

"What did you think of 'em, sir?"

"I thought they wos particklery unpleasant," replied Sam.

"Ah," said Mr. John Smauker, "you disliked the killibeate taste, perhaps?"

"I don't know much about that 'ere," said Sam. "I thought they'd a wery strong flavour o' warm flat irons."

"That *is* the killibeate, Mr. Weller," observed Mr. John Smauker, contemptuously.

"Well, if it is, it's a wery inexpressive word, that's all," said Sam. "It may be, but I ain't much in the chimical line myself, so I can't say." And here, to the great horror of Mr. John Smauker, Sam Weller began to whistle.

"I beg your pardon, Mr. Weller," said Mr. John Smauker, agonized at the exceedingly ungenteel sound, "Will you take my arm?"

"Thankee, you're wery good, but I won't deprive you of it," replied Sam. "I've rayther a way o' puttin' my hands in my pockets, if it's all the same to you." As Sam said this, he suited the action to the word, and whistled far louder than before.

"This way," said his new friend, apparently much relieved as they turned down a bye street; "we shall soon be there."

"Shall we?" said Sam, quite unmoved by the announcement of his close vicinity to the select footmen of Bath.

"Yes," said Mr. John Smauker. "Don't be alarmed, Mr. Weller."

"Oh no," said Sam.

"You'll see some very handsome uniforms, Mr. Weller," continued Mr. John Smauker; "and perhaps you'll find some of the gentlemen rather high at first, you know, but they'll soon come round."

"That's wery kind on 'em," replied Sam.

"And you know," resumed Mr. John Smauker, with an air

of sublime protection; "you know, as you're a stranger, perhaps they'll be rather hard upon you at first."

"They won't be wery cruel, though, will they?" inquired Sam.

"No, no," replied Mr. John Smauker, pulling forth the fox's head, and taking a gentlemanly pinch. "There are some funny dogs among us, and they will have their joke, you know; but you mustn't mind 'em, you mustn't mind 'em."

"I'll try and bear up agin such a reg'lar knock down o' talent," replied Sam.

"That's right," said Mr. John Smauker, putting up the fox's head, and elevating his own; "I'll stand by you."

By this time they had reached a small greengrocer's shop, which Mr. John Smauker entered, followed by Sam: who, the moment he got behind him, relapsed into a series of the very broadest and most unmitigated grins, and manifested other demonstrations of being in a highly enviable state of inward merriment.

Crossing the greengrocer's shop, and putting their hats on the stairs in the little passage behind it, they walked into a small parlour; and here the full splendour of the scene burst upon Mr. Weller's view.

A couple of tables were put together in the middle of the parlour, covered with three or four cloths of different ages and dates of washing, arranged to look as much like one as the circumstances of the case would allow. Upon these were laid knives and forks for six or eight people. Some of the knife handles were green, others red, and a few yellow; and as all the forks were black, the combination of colours was exceedingly striking. Plates for a corresponding number of guests were warming behind the fender; and the guests themselves were warming before it: the chief and most important of whom appeared to be a stoutish gentleman in a bright crimson coat with long tails, vividly red breeches, and a cocked hat, who was standing with his back to the fire, and had apparently just entered, for besides retaining his cocked

137

hat on his head, he carried in his hand a high stick, such as gentlemen of his profession usually elevate in a sloping position over the roofs of carriages.

"Smauker, my lad, your fin," said the gentleman with the cocked hat.

Mr. Smauker dovetailed the top joint of his right hand little finger into that of the gentleman with the cocked hat, and said he was charmed to see him looking so well.

"Well, they tell me I am looking pretty blooming," said the man with the cocked hat, "and it's a wonder, too. I've been following our old woman about, two hours a-day, for the last fortnight; and if a constant contemplation of the manner in which she hooks-and-eyes that infernal lavender coloured old gown of hers behind, isn't enough to throw any body into a low state of despondency for life, stop my quarter's salary."

At this, the assembled selections laughed very heartily; and one gentleman in a yellow waistcoat, with a coach trimming border, whispered a neighbour in green foil smalls, that Tuckle was in spirits to-night.

"By the bye," said Mr. Tuckle, "Smauker, my boy, you——" The remainder of the sentence was forwarded into Mr. John Smauker's ear, by whisper.

"Oh, dear me, I quite forgot," said Mr. John Smauker. "Gentlemen, my friend Mr. Weller."

"Sorry to keep the fire off you, Weller," said Mr. Tuckle, with a familiar nod. "Hope you're not cold, Weller."

"Not by no means, Blazes," replied Sam. "It 'ud be a wery chilly subject as felt cold wen you stood opposit. You'd save coals if they put you behind the fender in the waitin' room at a public office, you would."

As this retort appeared to convey rather a personal allusion to Mr. Tuckle's crimson livery, that gentleman looked majestic for a few seconds, but gradually edging away from the fire, broke into a forced smile, and said it wasn't bad.

"Wery much obliged for your good opinion, sir," replied

MR. TUCKLE IS INDIGNANT.

Sam. "We shall get on by degrees, I des-say. We'll try a better one, bye-and-bye."

At this point the conversation was interrupted by the arrival of a gentleman in orange-coloured plush, accompanied by another selection in purple cloth, with a great extent of stocking. The new comers having been welcomed by the old ones, Mr. Tuckle put the question that supper be ordered in, which was carried unanimously.

The greengrocer and his wife then arranged upon the table a boiled leg of mutton, hot, with caper sauce, turnips, and potatoes. Mr. Tuckle took the chair, and was supported at the other end of the board by the gentleman in orange plush. The greengrocer put on a pair of wash-leather gloves to hand the plates with, and stationed himself behind Mr. Tuckle's chair.

"Harris," said Mr. Tuckle, in a commanding tone.

"Sir," said the greengrocer.

"Have you got your gloves on?"

"Yes, sir."

"Then take the kiver off."

"Yes, sir."

The greengrocer did as he was told, with a show of great humility, and obsequiously handed Mr. Tuckle the carving knife; in doing which, he accidentally gaped.

"What do you mean by that, sir?" said Mr. Tuckle, with great asperity.

"I beg your pardon, sir," replied the crest-fallen greengrocer, "I didn't mean to do it, sir; I was up very late last night, sir."

"I tell you what my opinion of you is, Harris," said Mr. Tuckle with a most impressive air, "you're a wulgar beast."

"I hope, gentlemen," said Harris, "that you won't be severe with me, gentlemen. I'm very much obliged to you indeed, gentlemen, for your patronage, and also for your recommendations, gentlemen, whenever additional assistance in waiting is required. I hope, gentlemen, I give satisfaction."

" No, you don't, sir," said Mr. Tuckle. " Very far from it, sir."

" We consider you an inattentive reskel," said the gentleman in the orange plush.

" And a low thief," added the gentleman in the green-foil smalls.

" And an unreclaimable blaygaird," added the gentleman in purple.

The poor greengrocer bowed very humbly while these little epithets were bestowed upon him, in the true spirit of the very smallest tyranny; and when every body had said something to show his superiority, Mr. Tuckle proceeded to carve the leg of mutton, and to help the company.

This important business of the evening had hardly commenced, when the door was thrown briskly open, and another gentleman in a light-blue suit, and leaden buttons, made his appearance.

" Against the rules," said Mr. Tuckle. " Too late, too late."

" No, no; positively I couldn't help it," said the gentleman in blue. " I appeal to the company. An affair of gallantry now, an appointment at the theayter."

" Oh, that indeed," said the gentleman in the orange plush.

" Yes; raly now, honour bright," said the man in blue. " I made a promese to fetch our youngest daughter at half-past ten, and she is such an uncauminly fine gal, that I raly hadn't the art to disappint her. No offence to the present company, sir, but a petticut, sir, a petticut, sir, is irrevokeable."

" I begin to suspect there's something in that quarter," said Tuckle, as the new comer took his seat next Sam. " I've remarked, once or twice, that she leans very heavy on your shoulder when she gets in and out of the carriage."

" Oh raly, raly, Tuckle, you shouldn't," said the man in blue. " It's not fair. I may have said to one or two friends that she was a very divine creechure, and had refused one or two offers without any hobvus cause, but—no, no, no, indeed, Tuckle—before strangers, too—it's not right—you shouldn't. Delicacy, my dear friend, delicacy!" And the man in blue, pulling up his neckerchief, and adjusting his coat cuffs, nodded and frowned as if there were more behind, which he could say if he liked, but was bound in honour to suppress.

The man in blue being a light-haired, stiff-necked, free and easy sort of footman, with a swaggering air and pert face, had attracted Mr. Weller's especial attention at first, but when he began to come out in this way, Sam felt more than ever disposed to cultivate his acquaintance; so he launched himself into the conversation at once, with characteristic independence.

"Your health, sir," said Sam. "I like your conwersation much. I think it's wery pretty."

At this the man in blue smiled, as if it were a compliment he was well used to; but looked approvingly on Sam at the same time, and said he hoped he should be better acquainted with him, for without any flattery at all he seemed to have the makings of a very nice fellow about him, and to be just the man after his own heart.

"You're wery good, sir," said Sam. "What a lucky feller you are!"

"How do you mean?" inquired the gentleman in blue.

"That 'ere young lady," replied Sam. "She knows wot's wot, she does. Ah! I see." Mr. Weller closed one eye, and shook his head from side to side, in a manner which was highly gratifying to the personal vanity of the gentleman in blue.

"I'm afraid you're a cunning fellow, Mr. Weller," said that individual.

"No, no," said Sam. "I leave all that 'ere to you. It's a great deal more in your way than mine, as the gen'lm'n on the right side o' the garden vall said to the man on the wrong 'un, ven the mad bull wos a comin' up the lane."

"Well, well, Mr. Weller," said the gentleman in blue, "I think she has remarked my air and manner, Mr. Weller."

"I should think she couldn't wery well be off o' that," said Sam.

"Have you any little thing of that kind in hand, sir?" inquired the favoured gentleman in blue, drawing a toothpick from his waistcoat pocket.

"Not exactly," said Sam. "There's no daughters at my place, else o' course I should ha' made up to vun on 'em. As it is, I don't think I can do with any thin' under a female markis. I might take up with a young ooman o' large property as hadn't a title, if she made wery fierce love to me. Not else."

"Of course not, Mr. Weller," said the gentleman in blue, "one can't be troubled, you know; and we know, Mr. Weller—we, who are men of the world—that a good uniform must work its way with the women, sooner or later. In fact, that's the only thing, between you and me, that makes the service worth entering into."

"Just so," said Sam. "That's it, o' course."

When this confidential dialogue had gone thus far, glasses were placed round, and every gentleman ordered what he liked best, before the public-house shut up. The gentleman in blue, and the man in orange, who were the chief exquisites of the party, ordered "cold srub and water," but with the others, gin and water, sweet, appeared to be the favourite beverage. Sam called the greengrocer a "desp'rate willin'," and ordered a large bowl of punch; two circumstances which seemed to raise him very much in the opinion of the selections.

"Gentlemen," said the man in blue, with an air of the most consummate dandyism, "I'll give you the ladies; come."

"Hear, hear!" said Sam, "The young mississes."

Here there was a loud cry of "Order," and Mr. John Smauker, as the gentleman who had introduced Mr. Weller into that company, begged to inform him that the word he had just made use of, was unparliamentary.

"Which word was that 'ere, sir?" inquired Sam.

AN AFFLICTING CIRCUMSTANCE.

"Missises, sir," replied Mr. John Smauker, with an alarming frown. "We don't recognise such distinctions here."

"Oh, wery good," said Sam; "then I'll amend the observation, and call 'em the dear creeturs, if Blazes vill allow me."

Some doubt appeared to exist in the mind of the gentleman in the green-foil smalls, whether the chairman could be legally appealed to, as "Blazes," but as the company seemed more disposed to stand upon their own rights than his, the question was not raised. The man with the cocked hat, breathed short, and looked long at Sam, but apparently thought it as well to say nothing, in case he should get the worst of it.

After a short silence, a gentleman in an embroidered coat reaching down to his heels, and a waistcoat of the same which kept one half of his legs warm, stirred his gin and water with great energy, and putting himself upon his feet, all at once, by a violent effort, said he was desirous of offering a few remarks to the company: whereupon the person in the cocked hat, had no doubt that the company would be very happy to hear any remarks that the man in the long coat might wish to offer.

"I feel a great delicacy, gentlemen, in coming for'ard," said the man in the long coat, "having the misforchune to be a coachman, and being only admitted as a honorary member of these agreeable swarrys, but I do feel myself bound, gentlemen—drove into a corner, if I may use the expression—to make known an afflicting circumstance which has come to my knowledge; which has happened I may say within the soap of my every day contemplation. Gentlemen, our friend Mr. Whiffers (everybody looked at the individual in orange), our friend Mr. Whiffers has resigned."

Universal astonishment fell upon the hearers. Each gentleman looked in his neighbour's face, and then transferred his glance to the upstanding coachman.

"You may well be sapparised, gentlemen," said the coachman. "I will not wenchure to state the reasons of this irrepairabel loss to the service, but I will beg Mr. Whiffers to state them himself, for the improvement and imitation of his admiring friends."

The suggestion being loudly approved of, Mr. Whiffers explained. He said he certainly could have wished to have continued to hold the appointment he had just resigned. The uniform was extremely rich and expensive, the females of the family was most agreeable, and the duties of the situation was not, he was bound to say, too heavy; the principal service that was required of him, being, that he should look out of the hall window as much as possible, in company with another gentleman, who had also resigned. He could have wished to have spared that company the painful and disgusting detail on which he was about to enter, but as the explanation had been demanded of him, he had no alternative but to state, boldly and distinctly, that he had been required to eat cold meat.

It is impossible to conceive the disgust which this avowal awakened in the bosoms of the hearers. Loud cries of "Shame!" mingled with groans and hisses, prevailed for a quarter of an hour.

Mr. Whiffers then added that he feared a portion of this outrage might be traced to his own forbearing and accom- modating disposition. He had a distinct recollection of having once consented to eat salt butter, and he had, moreover, on an occasion of sudden sickness in the house, so far forgotten himself as to carry a coal scuttle up to the second floor. He trusted he had not lowered himself in the good opinion of his friends by this frank confession of his faults; and he hoped the promptness with which he had resented the last unmanly outrage on his feelings, to which he had referred, would reinstate him in their good opinion, if he had.

Mr. Whiffers' address was responded to, with a shout of admiration, and the health of the interesting martyr was drunk in a most enthusiastic manner; for this, the martyr returned thanks, and proposed their visitor, Mr. Weller; a gentleman whom he had not the pleasure of an intimate acquaintance with, but who was the friend of Mr. John Smauker, which was a sufficient letter of recommendation to any society of gentlemen whatever, or wherever. On this account, he should have been disposed to have given Mr. Weller's health with all the honours, if his friends had been drinking wine; but as they were taking spirits by way of a change, and as it might be inconvenient to empty a tumbler at every toast, he should propose that the honours be understood.

At the conclusion of this speech, everybody took a sip in honour of Sam; and Sam having ladled out, and drunk, two full glasses of punch in honour of himself, returned thanks in a neat speech.

"Wery much obliged to you, old fellers," said Sam, ladling away at the punch in the most unembarrassed manner possible, "for this here compliment; wich, comin' from sich a quarter, is wery overvelmin'. I've heerd a good deal on you as a body, but I will say, that I never thought you was sich uncommon nice men as I find you air. I only hope you'll take care o' yourselves, and not compromise nothin' o' your dignity, which is a wery charmin' thing to see, when one's out a walkin', and has always made me wery happy to look at, ever since I was a boy about half as high as the brass-headed stick o' my wery respectable friend, Blazes, there. As to the wictim of oppression in the suit o' brimstone, all I can say of him, is, that I hope he'll get jist as good a berth as he deserves: in vich case it's wery little cold swarry as ever he'll be troubled with agin."

Here Sam sat down with a pleasant smile, and his speech having been vociferously applauded, the company broke up.

"Why, you don't mean to say you're a goin', old feller?" said Sam Weller to his friend Mr. John Smauker.

"I must indeed," said Mr. Smauker; "I promised Bantam."

"Oh, wery well," said Sam; "that's another thing. P'raps *he'd* resign if you disappinted him. You ain't a goin', Blazes?"

145

"Yes, I am," said the man with the cocked hat.

"Wot, and leave three quarters of a bowl of punch behind you!" said Sam; "nonsense, set down agin."

Mr. Tuckle was not proof against this invitation. He laid aside the cocked hat and stick which he had just taken up, and said he would have one glass, for good fellowship's sake.

As the gentleman in blue went home the same way as Mr. Tuckle, he was prevailed upon to stop too. When the punch was about half gone, Sam ordered in some oysters from the greengrocer's shop; and the effect of both was so extremely exhilarating, that Mr. Tuckle, dressed out with the cocked hat and stick, danced the frog hornpipe among the shells on the table: while the gentleman in blue played an accompaniment upon an ingenious musical instrument formed of a hair comb and a curl-paper. At last, when the punch was all gone, and the night nearly so, they sallied forth to see each other home. Mr. Tuckle no sooner got into the open air, than he was seized with a sudden desire to lie on the curbstone; Sam thought it would be a pity to contradict him, and so let him have his own way. As the cocked hat would have been spoilt if left there, Sam very considerately flattened it down on the head of the gentleman in blue, and putting the big stick in his hand, propped him up against his own street-door, rang the bell, and walked quietly home.

At a much earlier hour next morning than his usual time of rising, Mr. Pickwick walked down stairs completely dressed, and rang the bell.

"Sam," said Mr. Pickwick, when Mr. Weller appeared in reply to the summons, "shut the door."

Mr. Weller did so.

"There was an unfortunate occurrence here, last night, Sam," said Mr. Pickwick, "which gave Mr. Winkle some cause to apprehend violence from Mr. Dowler."

"So I've heerd from the old lady down stairs, sir," replied Sam.

"And I'm sorry to say, Sam," continued Mr. Pickwick, with a most perplexed countenance, "that in dread of this violence, Mr. Winkle has gone away."

"Gone avay!" said Sam.

"Left the house early this morning, without the slightest previous communication with me," replied Mr. Pickwick. "And is gone, I know not where."

"He should ha' stopped and fought it out, sir," replied Sam, contemptuously. "It wouldn't take much to settle that 'ere Dowler, sir."

"Well, Sam," said Mr. Pickwick, "I may have my doubts of his great bravery and determination, also. But however that may be, Mr. Winkle is gone. He must be found, Sam. Found and brought back to me."

"And s'pose he won't come back, sir?" said Sam.

"He must be made, Sam," said Mr. Pickwick.

"Who's to do it, sir?" inquired Sam with a smile.

"You," replied Mr. Pickwick.

"Wery good, sir."

With these words Mr. Weller left the room, and immediately afterwards was heard to shut the street door. In two hours' time he returned with as much coolness as if he had been despatched on the most ordinary message possible, and brought the information that an individual, in every respect answering Mr. Winkle's description, had gone over to Bristol that morning, by the branch coach from the Royal Hotel.

"Sam," said Mr. Pickwick, grasping his hand, "you're a capital fellow; an invaluable fellow. You must follow him, Sam."

"Cert'nly, sir," replied Mr. Weller.

"The instant you discover him, write to me immediately, Sam," said Mr. Pickwick. "If he attempts to run away from you, knock him down, or lock him up. You have my full authority, Sam."

"I'll be wery careful, sir," rejoined Sam.

"You'll tell him," said Mr. Pickwick, "that I am highly

147

excited, highly displeased, and naturally indignant, at the very extraordinary course he has thought proper to pursue."

" I will, sir," replied Sam.

" You'll tell him," said Mr. Pickwick, " that if he does not come back to this very house, with you, he will come back with me, for I will come and fetch him."

" I'll mention that 'ere, sir," rejoined Sam.

" You think you can find him, Sam ?" said Mr. Pickwick, looking earnestly in his face.

" Oh, I'll find him if he's any vere," rejoined Sam, with great confidence.

" Very well," said Mr. Pickwick. " Then the sooner you go the better."

With these instructions, Mr. Pickwick placed a sum of money in the hands of his faithful servitor, and ordered him to start for Bristol immediately, in pursuit of the fugitive.

Sam put a few necessaries in a carpet bag, and was ready for starting. He stopped when he had got to the end of the passage, and walking quietly back, thrust his head in at the parlour door.

" Sir," whispered Sam.

" Well, Sam," said Mr. Pickwick.

" I fully understands my instructions, do I, sir ?" inquired Sam.

" I hope so," said Mr. Pickwick.

" It's reg'larly understood about the knockin' down, is it, sir ?" inquired Sam.

" Perfectly," replied Mr. Pickwick. " Thoroughly. Do what you think necessary. You have my orders."

Sam gave a nod of intelligence, and withdrawing his head from the door, set forth on his pilgrimage with a light heart.

CHAPTER XXXVIII.

THE ill-starred gentleman who had been the unfortunate cause of the unusual noise and disturbance which alarmed the inhabitants of the Royal Crescent in manner and form already described, after passing a night of great confusion and anxiety, left the roof beneath which his friends still slumbered, bound he knew not whither. The excellent and considerate feelings which prompted Mr. Winkle to take this step can never be too highly appreciated or too warmly extolled. " If," reasoned Mr. Winkle with himself, " if this Dowler attempts (as I have no doubt he will) to carry into execution his threat of personal violence against myself, it will be incumbent on me to call him out. He has a wife ; that wife is attached to, and dependent on him. Heavens ! If I should kill him in the blindness of my wrath, what would be my feelings ever afterwards ! " This painful consideration operated so powerfully on the feelings of the humane young man, as to cause his knees to knock together, and his countenance to exhibit alarming manifestations of inward emotion. Impelled by such reflections, he grasped his carpet-bag, and creeping stealthily down stairs, shut the detestable street-door with as little noise as possible, and walked off. Bending his steps towards the Royal Hotel, he found a coach on the point of starting for Bristol, and, thinking Bristol as good a place for his purpose as any other he could go to, he mounted the box, and reached his place of destination in such time as the pair of horses, who went the whole stage and back again twice a day or more, could be reasonably supposed to arrive there.

He took up his quarters at The Bush, and, designing to postpone any communication by letter with Mr. Pickwick until it was probable that Mr. Dowler's wrath might have in some degree evaporated, walked forth to view the city, which struck him as being a shade more dirty than any place he had ever seen. Having inspected the docks and shipping, and viewed the cathedral, he inquired his way to Clifton, and being directed thither, took the route which was pointed out to him. But, as the pavements of Bristol are not the widest or cleanest upon earth, so its streets are not altogether the straightest or least intricate; Mr. Winkle being greatly puzzled by their manifold windings and twistings, looked about him for a decent shop in which he could apply afresh, for counsel and instruction.

His eye fell upon a newly-painted tenement which had been recently converted into something between a shop and a private-house, and which a red lamp, projecting over the fan-light of the street-door, would have sufficiently announced as the residence of a medical practitioner, even if the word "Surgery" had not been inscribed in golden characters on a wainscot ground, above the window of what, in times bygone, had been the front parlour. Thinking this an eligible place wherein to make his inquiries, Mr. Winkle stepped into the little shop where the gilt-labelled drawers and bottles were; and finding nobody there, knocked with a half-crown on the counter, to attract the attention of anybody who might happen to be in the back parlour, which he judged to be the innermost and peculiar sanctum of the establishment, from the repetition of the word surgery on the door— painted in white letters this time, by way of taking off the monotony.

DISCOVERY OF A MEDICAL GENTLEMAN.

At the first knock, a sound, as of persons fencing with fire-irons, which had until now been very audible, suddenly ceased; at the second, a studious-looking young gentleman in green spectacles, with a very large book in his hand, glided quietly into the shop, and stepping behind the counter, requested to know the visitor's pleasure.

"I am sorry to trouble you, sir," said Mr. Winkle, "but will you have the goodness to direct me to——"

"Ha! ha! ha!" roared the studious young gentleman, throwing the large book up into the air, and catching it with great dexterity at the very moment when it threatened to smash to atoms all the bottles on the counter. "Here's a start!"

There was, without doubt; for Mr. Winkle was so very much astonished at the extraordinary behaviour of the medical gentleman, that he involuntarily retreated towards the door, and looked very much disturbed at his strange reception.

"What, don't you know me?" said the medical gentleman.

Mr. Winkle murmured, in reply, that he had not that pleasure.

"Why, then," said the medical gentleman, "there are hopes for me yet; I may attend half the old women in Bristol if I've decent luck. Get out, you mouldy old villain, get out!" With this adjuration, which was addressed to the large book, the medical gentleman kicked the volume with remark-able agility to the further end of the shop, and, pulling off his green spectacles, grinned the identical grin of Robert Sawyer, Esquire, formerly of Guy's Hospital in the Borough, with a private residence in Lant Street.

"You don't mean to say you weren't down upon me!" said Mr. Bob Sawyer, shaking Mr. Winkle's hand with friendly warmth.

"Upon my word I was not," replied Mr. Winkle, returning the pressure.

"I wonder you didn't see the name," said Bob Sawyer, calling his friend's attention to the outer door, on which, in

151

the same white paint, were traced the words "Sawyer, late Nockemorf."

"It never caught my eye," returned Mr. Winkle.

"Lord, if I had known who you were, I should have rushed out, and caught you in my arms," said Bob Sawyer; "but upon my life, I thought you were the King's-taxes."

"No!" said Mr. Winkle.

"I did, indeed," responded Bob Sawyer, "and I was just going to say that I wasn't at home, but if you'd leave a message I'd be sure to give it to myself; for he don't know me; no more does the Lighting and Paving. I think the Church-rates guesses who I am, and I know the Water-works does, because I drew a tooth of his when I first came down here. But come in, come in!" Chattering in this way, Mr. Bob Sawyer pushed Mr. Winkle into the back room, where, amusing himself by boring little circular caverns in the chimney-piece with a red-hot poker, sat no less a person than Mr. Benjamin Allen.

"Well!" said Mr. Winkle. "This is indeed a pleasure I did not expect. What a very nice place you have here!"

"Pretty well, pretty well," replied Bob Sawyer. "I *passed*, soon after that precious party, and my friends came down with the needful for this business; so I put on a black suit of clothes, and a pair of spectacles, and came here to look as solemn as I could."

"And a very snug little business you have, no doubt?" said Mr. Winkle, knowingly.

"Very," replied Bob Sawyer. "So snug, that at the end of a few years you might put all the profits in a wine glass, and cover 'em over with a gooseberry leaf."

"You cannot surely mean that?" said Mr. Winkle. "The stock itself—"

"Dummies, my dear boy," said Bob Sawyer; "half the drawers have nothing in 'em, and the other half don't open."

"Nonsense!" said Mr. Winkle.

"Fact—honor!" returned Bob Sawyer, stepping out into

the shop, and demonstrating the veracity of the assertion by divers hard pulls at the little gilt knobs on the counterfeit drawers. "Hardly anything real in the shop but the leeches, and *they* are second-hand."

"I shouldn't have thought it!" exclaimed Mr. Winkle, much surprised.

"I hope not," replied Bob Sawyer, "else where's the use of appearances, eh? But what will you take? Do as we do? That's right. Ben, my fine fellow, put your hand into the cupboard, and bring out the patent digester."

Mr. Benjamin Allen smiled his readiness, and produced from the closet at his elbow a black bottle half full of brandy.

"You don't take water, of course?" said Bob Sawyer.

"Thank you," replied Mr. Winkle. "It's *rather* early. I should like to qualify it, if you have no objection."

"None in the least, if you can reconcile it to your conscience," replied Bob Sawyer; tossing off, as he spoke, a glass of the liquor with great relish. "Ben, the pipkin!"

Mr. Benjamin Allen drew forth, from the same hiding-place, a small brass pipkin, which Bob Sawyer observed he prided himself upon, particularly because it looked so business-like. The water in the professional pipkin having been made to boil, in course of time, by various little shovelsfull of coal, which Mr. Bob Sawyer took out of a practicable window-seat, labelled "Soda Water," Mr. Winkle adulterated his brandy; and the conversation was becoming general, when it was interrupted by the entrance into the shop of a boy, in a sober grey livery and a gold-laced hat, with a small covered basket under his arm: whom Mr. Bob Sawyer immediately hailed with, "Tom, you vagabond, come here."

The boy presented himself accordingly.

"You've been stopping to over all the posts in Bristol, you idle young scamp!" said Mr. Bob Sawyer.

"No, sir, I haven't," replied the boy.

"You had better not!" said Mr. Bob Sawyer, with a

threatening aspect. "Who do you suppose will ever employ a professional man, when they see his boy playing at marbles in the gutter, or flying the garter in the horse-road? Have you no feeling for your profession, you groveller? Did you leave all the medicine?"

"Yes, sir."

"The powders for the child, at the large house with the new family, and the pills to be taken four times a day at the ill-tempered old gentleman's with the gouty leg?"

"Yes, sir."

"Then shut the door, and mind the shop."

"Come," said Mr. Winkle, as the boy retired, "things are not quite so bad as you would have me believe, either. There is *some* medicine to be sent out."

Mr. Bob Sawyer peeped into the shop to see that no stranger was within hearing, and leaning forward to Mr. Winkle, said, in a low tone:

"He leaves it all at the wrong houses."

Mr. Winkle looked perplexed, and Bob Sawyer and his friend laughed.

"Don't you see?" said Bob. "He goes up to a house, rings the area bell, pokes a packet of medicine without a direction into the servant's hand, and walks off. Servant takes it into the dining-parlour; master opens it, and reads the label: 'Draught to be taken at bed-time—pills as before —lotion as usual—*the* powder. From Sawyer's, late Nockemorf's. Physicians' prescriptions carefully prepared,' and all the rest of it. Shows it to his wife—*she* reads the label; it goes down to the servants—*they* read the label. Next day, boy calls: 'Very sorry—his mistake—immense business— great many parcels to deliver—Mr. Sawyer's compliments— late Nockemorf.' The name gets known, and that's the thing, my boy, in the medical way. Bless your heart, old fellow, it's better than all the advertising in the world. We have got one four-ounce bottle that's been to half the houses in Bristol, and hasn't done yet."

MR. BENJAMIN ALLEN.

"Dear me, I see," observed Mr. Winkle; "what an excellent plan!"

"Oh, Ben and I have hit upon a dozen such," replied Bob Sawyer, with great glee. "The lamplighter has eighteenpence a week to pull the night-bell for ten minutes every time he comes round; and my boy always rushes into church, just before the psalms, when the people have got nothing to do but look about 'em, and calls me out, with horror and dismay depicted on his countenance. 'Bless my soul,' everybody says, 'somebody taken suddenly ill! Sawyer, late Nockemorf, sent for. What a business that young man has!'"

At the termination of this disclosure of some of the mysteries of medicine, Mr. Bob Sawyer and his friend, Ben Allen, threw themselves back in their respective chairs, and laughed boisterously. When they had enjoyed the joke to their hearts' content, the discourse changed to topics in which Mr. Winkle was more immediately interested.

We think we have hinted elsewhere, that Mr. Benjamin Allen had a way of becoming sentimental after brandy. The case is not a peculiar one, as we ourselves can testify: having, on a few occasions, had to deal with patients who have been afflicted in a similar manner. At this precise period of his existence, Mr. Benjamin Allen had perhaps a greater predisposition to maudlinism than he had ever known before; the cause of which malady was briefly this. He had been staying nearly three weeks with Mr. Bob Sawyer; Mr. Bob Sawyer was not remarkable for temperance, nor was Mr. Benjamin Allen for the ownership of a very strong head; the consequence was, that, during the whole space of time just mentioned, Mr. Benjamin Allen had been wavering between intoxication partial, and intoxication complete.

"My dear friend," said Mr. Ben Allen, taking advantage of Mr. Bob Sawyer's temporary absence behind the counter, whither he had retired to dispense some of the second-hand leeches, previously referred to: "my dear friend, I am very miserable."

Mr. Winkle professed his heartfelt regret to hear it, and begged to know whether he could do anything to alleviate the sorrows of the suffering student.

"Nothing, my dear boy, nothing," said Ben. "You recollect Arabella, Winkle? My sister Arabella—a little girl, Winkle, with black eyes—when we were down at Wardle's? I don't know whether you happened to notice her, a nice little girl, Winkle. Perhaps my features may recal her countenance to your recollection?"

Mr. Winkle required nothing to recal the charming Arabella to his mind; and it was rather fortunate he did not, for the features of her brother Benjamin would unquestionably have proved but an indifferent refresher to his memory. He answered, with as much calmness as he could assume, that he perfectly remembered the young lady referred to, and sincerely trusted she was in good health.

"Our friend Bob is a delightful fellow, Winkle," was the only reply of Mr. Ben Allen.

"Very," said Mr. Winkle; not much relishing this close connexion of the two names.

"I designed 'em for each other; they were made for each other, sent into the world for each other, born for each other, Winkle," said Mr. Ben Allen, setting down his glass with emphasis. "There's a special destiny in the matter, my dear sir; there's only five years' difference between 'em, and both their birthdays are in August."

Mr. Winkle was too anxious to hear what was to follow, to express much wonderment at this extraordinary coincidence, marvellous as it was; so Mr. Ben Allen, after a tear or two, went on to say, that, notwithstanding all his esteem and respect and veneration for his friend, Arabella had unaccountably and undutifully evinced the most determined antipathy to his person.

"And I think," said Mr. Ben Allen, in conclusion, "*I* think there's a prior attachment."

A SUSPECTED PRIOR ATTACHMENT.

"Have you any idea who the object of it might be?" asked Mr. Winkle, with great trepidation.

Mr. Ben Allen seized the poker, flourished it in a warlike manner above his head, inflicted a savage blow on an imaginary skull, and wound up by saying, in a very expressive manner, that he only wished he could guess; that was all.

"I'd show him what I thought of him," said Mr. Ben Allen. And round went the poker again, more fiercely than before.

All this was, of course, very soothing to the feelings of Mr. Winkle, who remained silent for a few minutes; but at length mustered up resolution to inquire whether Miss Allen was in Kent.

"No, no," said Mr. Ben Allen, laying aside the poker, and looking very cunning; "I didn't think Wardle's exactly the place for a headstrong girl; so, as I am her natural protector and guardian, our parents being dead, I have brought her down into this part of the country to spend a few months at an old aunt's, in a nice dull close place. I think that will cure her, my boy. If it doesn't, I'll take her abroad for a little while, and see what that'll do."

"Oh, the aunt's is in Bristol, is it?" faltered Mr. Winkle.

"No, no, not in Bristol," replied Mr. Ben Allen, jerking his thumb over his right shoulder: "over that way; down there. But, hush, here's Bob. Not a word, my dear friend, not a word."

Short as this conversation was, it roused in Mr. Winkle the highest degree of excitement and anxiety. The suspected prior attachment rankled in his heart. Could he be the object of it? Could it be for him that the fair Arabella had looked scornfully on the sprightly Bob Sawyer, or had he a successful rival? He determined to see her, cost what it might; but here an insurmountable objection presented itself, for whether the explanatory "over that way," and "down there," of Mr. Ben Allen, meant three miles off, or thirty, or three hundred, he could in no wise guess.

But he had no opportunity of pondering over his love just

then, for Bob Sawyer's return was the immediate precursor of the arrival of a meat pie from the baker's, of which that gentleman insisted on his staying to partake. The cloth was laid by an occasional charwoman, who officiated in the capacity of Mr. Bob Sawyer's housekeeper; and a third knife and fork having been borrowed from the mother of the boy in the grey livery (for Mr. Sawyer's domestic arrangements were as yet conducted on a limited scale), they sat down to dinner; the beer being served up, as Mr. Sawyer remarked, "in its native pewter."

After dinner, Mr. Bob Sawyer ordered in the largest mortar in the shop, and proceeded to brew a reeking jorum of rum-punch therein: stirring up and amalgamating the materials with a pestle in a very creditable and apothecary-like manner. Mr. Sawyer, being a bachelor, had only one tumbler in the house, which was assigned to Mr. Winkle as a compliment to the visitor: Mr. Ben Allen being accommodated with a funnel with a cork in the narrow end: and Bob Sawyer contented himself with one of those wide-lipped crystal vessels inscribed with a variety of cabalistic characters, in which chemists are wont to measure out their liquid drugs in compounding prescriptions. These preliminaries adjusted, the punch was tasted, and pronounced excellent; and it having been arranged that Bob Sawyer and Ben Allen should be considered at liberty to fill twice to Mr. Winkle's once, they started fair, with great satisfaction and good-fellowship.

There was no singing, because Mr. Bob Sawyer said it wouldn't look professional; but to make amends for this deprivation there was so much talking and laughing that it might have been heard, and very likely was, at the end of the street. Which conversation materially lightened the hours and improved the mind of Mr. Bob Sawyer's boy, who, instead of devoting the evening to his ordinary occupation of writing his name on the counter, and rubbing it out again, peeped through the glass door, and thus listened and looked on at the same time.

Conviviality at Bob Sawyer's

THE REVELLERS HASTILY DISPERSED.

The mirth of Mr. Bob Sawyer was rapidly ripening into
the furious; Mr. Ben Allen was fast relapsing into the sentimental, and the punch had well-nigh disappeared altogether,
when the boy hastily running in, announced that a young
woman had just come over, to say that Sawyer late Nockemorf
was wanted directly, a couple of streets off. This broke up
the party. Mr. Bob Sawyer, understanding the message,
after some twenty repetitions, tied a wet cloth round his
head to sober himself, and, having partially succeeded, put on
his green spectacles and issued forth. Resisting all entreaties
to stay till he came back, and finding it quite impossible to
engage Mr. Ben Allen in any intelligible conversation on the
subject nearest his heart, or indeed on any other, Mr. Winkle
took his departure, and returned to the Bush.

The anxiety of his mind, and the numerous meditations
which Arabella had awakened, prevented his share of the
mortar of punch producing that effect upon him which it
would have had, under other circumstances. So, after taking
a glass of soda-water and brandy at the bar, he turned into
the coffee-room, dispirited rather than elevated by the occurrences of the evening.

Sitting in the front of the fire, with his back towards him,
was a tallish gentleman in a great-coat: the only other
occupant of the room. It was rather a cool evening for the
season of the year, and the gentleman drew his chair aside
to afford the new comer a sight of the fire. What were Mr.
Winkle's feelings when, in doing so, he disclosed to view the
face and figure of the vindictive and sanguinary Dowler!

Mr. Winkle's first impulse was to give a violent pull at
the nearest bell-handle, but that unfortunately happened to
be immediately behind Mr. Dowler's head. He had made
one step towards it, before he checked himself. As he did
so, Mr. Dowler very hastily drew back.

"Mr. Winkle, sir. Be calm. Don't strike me. I won't
bear it. A blow! Never!" said Mr. Dowler, looking meeker
than Mr. Winkle had expected in a gentleman of his ferocity.

"A blow, sir?" stammered Mr. Winkle.

"A blow, sir," replied Dowler. "Compose your feelings. Sit down. Hear me."

"Sir," said Mr. Winkle, trembling from head to foot, "before I consent to sit down beside, or opposite you, without the presence of a waiter, I must be secured by some further understanding. You used a threat against me last night, sir, a dreadful threat, sir." Here Mr. Winkle turned very pale indeed, and stopped short.

"I did," said Dowler, with a countenance almost as white as Mr. Winkle's. "Circumstances were suspicious. They have been explained. I respect your bravery. Your feeling is upright. Conscious innocence. There's my hand. Grasp it."

"Really, sir," said Mr. Winkle, hesitating whether to give his hand or not, and almost fearing that it was demanded in order that he might be taken at an advantage, "really, sir, I——"

"I know what you mean," interposed Dowler. "You feel aggrieved. Very natural. So should I. I was wrong. I beg your pardon. Be friendly. Forgive me." With this, Dowler fairly forced his hand upon Mr. Winkle, and shaking it with the utmost vehemence, declared he was a fellow of extreme spirit, and he had a higher opinion of him than ever.

"Now," said Dowler, "sit down. Relate it all. How did you find me? When did you follow? Be frank. Tell me."

"It's quite accidental," replied Mr. Winkle, greatly perplexed by the curious and unexpected nature of the interview, "Quite."

"Glad of it," said Dowler. "I woke this morning. I had forgotten my threat. I laughed at the accident. I felt friendly. I said so."

"To whom?" inquired Mr. Winkle.

"To Mrs. Dowler. 'You made a vow,' said she. 'I did,' said I. 'It was a rash one,' said she. 'It was,' said I. 'I'll apologise. Where is he?'"

"Who?" inquired Mr. Winkle.

Mr. Pickwick Sits for his Portrait

"You," replied Dowler. "I went down stairs. You were not to be found. Pickwick looked gloomy. Shook his head. Hoped no violence would be committed. I saw it all. You felt yourself insulted. You had gone, for a friend perhaps. Possibly for pistols. 'High spirit,' said I. 'I admire him.'"

Mr. Winkle coughed, and beginning to see how the land lay, assumed a look of importance.

"I left a note for you," resumed Dowler. "I said I was sorry. So I was. Pressing business called me here. You were not satisfied. You followed. You required a verbal explanation. You were right. It's all over now. My business is finished. I go back to-morrow. Join me."

As Dowler progressed in his explanation, Mr. Winkle's countenance grew more and more dignified. The mysterious nature of the commencement of their conversation was explained; Mr. Dowler had as great an objection to duelling as himself; in short, this blustering and awful personage was one of the most egregious cowards in existence, and interpreting Mr. Winkle's absence through the medium of his own fears, had taken the same step as himself, and prudently retired until all excitement of feeling should have subsided.

As the real state of the case dawned upon Mr. Winkle's mind, he looked very terrible, and said he was perfectly satisfied; but at the same time, said so, with an air that left Mr. Dowler no alternative but to infer that if he had not been, something most horrible and destructive must inevitably have occurred. Mr. Dowler appeared to be impressed with a becoming sense of Mr. Winkle's magnanimity and condescension; and the two belligerents parted for the night, with many protestations of eternal friendship.

About half-past twelve o'clock, when Mr. Winkle had been revelling some twenty minutes in the full luxury of his first sleep, he was suddenly awakened by a loud knocking at his chamber-door, which, being repeated with increased vehemence, caused him to start up in bed, and inquire who was there, and what the matter was.

"Please, sir, here's a young man which says he must see you directly," responded the voice of the chambermaid.

"A young man!" exclaimed Mr. Winkle.

"No mistake about that 'ere, sir," replied another voice through the keyhole; "and if that wery same interestin' young creetur ain't let in vithout delay, it's wery possible as his legs vill enter afore his countenance." The young man gave a gentle kick at one of the lower panels of the door, after he had given utterance to this hint, as if to add force and point to the remark.

"Is that you, Sam?" inquired Mr. Winkle, springing out of bed.

"Quite unpossible to identify any gen'l'm'n vith any degree o' mental satisfaction, vithout lookin' at him, sir," replied the voice, dogmatically.

Mr. Winkle, not much doubting who the young man was, unlocked the door; which he had no sooner done, than Mr. Samuel Weller entered with great precipitation, and carefully re-locking it on the inside, deliberately put the key in his waistcoat pocket: and, after surveying Mr. Winkle from head to foot, said:

"You're a wery humorous young gen'l'm'n, you air, sir!"

"What do you mean by this conduct, Sam?" inquired Mr. Winkle, indignantly. "Get out, sir, this instant. What do you mean, sir?"

"What do *I* mean," retorted Sam; "come, sir, this is rayther too rich, as the young lady said, wen she remonstrated with the pastry-cook, arter he'd sold her a pork-pie as had got nothin' but fat inside. What do *I* mean! Well, that ain't a bad 'un, that ain't."

"Unlock that door, and leave this room immediately, sir," said Mr. Winkle.

"I shall leave this here room, sir, just precisely at the wery same moment as you leaves it," responded Sam, speaking in a forcible manner, and seating himself with perfect gravity. "If I find it necessary to carry you away, pick-a-back, o' course I shall leave it the least bit o' time possible afore you; but allow me to express a hope as you won't reduce me to ex-tremities; in saying wich, I merely quote wot the nobleman said to the fractious pennywinkle, ven he vouldn't come out of his shell by means of a pin, and he conseqvently began to be afeered that he should be obliged to crack him in the parlour-door." At the end of this address, which was unusually lengthy for him, Mr. Weller planted his hands on his knees, and looked full in Mr. Winkle's face, with an expression of countenance which showed that he had not the remotest intention of being trifled with.

"You re a amiably-disposed young man, sir, I don't think," resumed Mr. Weller, in a tone of moral reproof, "to go inwolving our precious governor in all sorts o' fanteegs, wen he's made up his mind to go through every think for principle. You're far worse nor Dodson, sir; and as for Fogg, I consider him a born angel to you!" Mr. Weller having accompanied this last sentiment with an emphatic slap on each knee, folded his arms with a look of great disgust, and threw himself back in his chair, as if awaiting the criminal's defence.

"My good fellow," said Mr. Winkle, extending his hand; his teeth chattering all the time he spoke, for he had been standing, during the whole of Mr. Weller's lecture, in his night-gear; "My good fellow, I respect your attachment to my excellent friend, and I am very sorry indeed, to have added to his causes for disquiet. There, Sam, there!"

"Well," said Sam, rather sulkily, but giving the proffered hand a respectful shake at the same time: "Well, so you ought to be, and I am very glad to find you air; for, if I can help it, I won't have him put upon by nobody, and that's all about it."

"Certainly not, Sam," said Mr. Winkle. "There! Now go to bed, Sam, and we'll talk further about this, in the morning."

163

"I'm wery sorry," said Sam, "but I can't go to bed."

"Not go to bed!" repeated Mr. Winkle.

"No," said Sam, shaking his head. "Can't be done."

"You don't mean to say you're going back to-night, Sam?" urged Mr. Winkle, greatly surprised.

"Not unless you particklerly wish it," replied Sam; "but I musn't leave this here room. The governor's orders wos peremptory."

"Nonsense, Sam," said Mr. Winkle, "I must stop here two or three days; and more than that, Sam, you must stop here too, to assist me in gaining an interview with a young lady—Miss Allen, Sam; you remember her—whom I must and will see before I leave Bristol."

But in reply to each of these positions, Sam shook his head with great firmness, and energetically replied, "It can't be done."

After a great deal of argument and representation on the part of Mr. Winkle, however, and a full disclosure of what had passed in the interview with Dowler, Sam began to waver; and at length a compromise was effected, of which the following were the main and principal conditions:

That Sam should retire, and leave Mr. Winkle in the undisturbed possession of his apartment, on the condition that he had permission to lock the door on the outside, and carry off the key; provided always, that in the event of an alarm of fire, or other dangerous contingency, the door should be instantly unlocked. That a letter should be written to Mr. Pickwick early next morning, and forwarded per Dowler, requesting his consent to Sam and Mr. Winkle's remaining at Bristol, for the purpose, and with the object, already assigned, and begging an answer by the next coach; if favourable, the aforesaid parties to remain accordingly, and if not, to return to Bath immediately on the receipt thereof. And, lastly, that Mr. Winkle should be understood as distinctly pledging himself not to resort to the window, fire-place, or other surreptitious mode of escape, in the meanwhile.

These stipulations having been concluded, Sam locked the door and departed.

He had nearly got down stairs, when he stopped, and drew the key from his pocket.

" I quite forgot about the knockin' down," said Sam, half turning back. " The governor distinctly said it was to be done. Amazin' stupid o' me, that 'ere! Never mind," said Sam, brightening up, " it's easily done to-morrow, anyvays."

Apparently much consoled by this reflection, Mr. Weller once more deposited the key in his pocket, and descending the remainder of the stairs without any fresh visitations of conscience, was soon, in common with the other inmates of the house, buried in profound repose.

CHAPTER XXXIX.

MR. SAMUEL WELLER, BEING ENTRUSTED WITH A MISSION OF
LOVE, PROCEEDS TO EXECUTE IT; WITH WHAT SUCCESS WILL
HEREINAFTER APPEAR.

DURING the whole of next day, Sam kept Mr. Winkle
steadily in sight, fully determined not to take his eye off him
for one instant, until he should receive express instructions
from the fountain-head. However disagreeable Sam's very
close watch and great vigilance were to Mr. Winkle, he
thought it better to bear with them, than, by any act of
violent opposition, to hazard being carried away by force,
which Mr. Weller more than once strongly hinted was the
line of conduct that a strict sense of duty prompted him to
pursue. There is little reason to doubt that Sam would very
speedily have quieted his scruples, by bearing Mr. Winkle
back to Bath, bound hand and foot, had not Mr. Pickwick's
prompt attention to the note, which Dowler had undertaken
to deliver, forestalled any such proceeding. In short, at
eight o'clock in the evening, Mr. Pickwick himself walked into
the coffee-room of the Bush tavern, and told Sam with a smile,
to his very great relief, that he had done quite right, and it
was unnecessary for him to mount guard any longer.

"I thought it better to come myself," said Mr. Pickwick,
addressing Mr. Winkle, as Sam disencumbered him of his
great-coat and travelling shawl, "to ascertain, before I gave
my consent to Sam's employment in this matter, that you

166

are quite in earnest and serious, with respect to this young lady."

"Serious, from my heart—from my soul!" returned Mr. Winkle, with great energy.

"Remember," said Mr. Pickwick, with beaming eyes, "we met her at our excellent and hospitable friend's, Winkle. It would be an ill return to tamper lightly, and without due consideration with this young lady's affections. I'll not allow that, sir. I'll not allow it."

"I have no such intention, indeed," exclaimed Mr. Winkle, warmly. "I have considered the matter well, for a long time, and I feel that my happiness is bound up in her."

"That's wot we call tying it up in a small parcel, sir," interposed Mr. Weller, with an agreeable smile.

Mr. Winkle looked somewhat stern at this interruption, and Mr. Pickwick angrily requested his attendant not to jest with one of the best feelings of our nature; to which Sam replied, "That he wouldn't, if he was aware on it; but there were so many on 'em, that he hardly know'd which was the best ones wen he heerd 'em mentioned."

Mr. Winkle then recounted what had passed between himself and Mr. Ben Allen, relative to Arabella; stated that his object was to gain an interview with the young lady, and make a formal disclosure of his passion; and declared his conviction, founded on certain dark hints and mutterings of the aforesaid Ben, that, wherever she was at present immured, it was somewhere near the Downs. And this was his whole stock of knowledge or suspicion on the subject.

With this very slight clue to guide him, it was determined that Mr. Weller should start next morning on an expedition of discovery; it was also arranged that Mr. Pickwick and Mr. Winkle, who were less confident of their powers, should parade the town meanwhile, and accidentally drop in upon Mr. Bob Sawyer in the course of the day, in the hope of seeing or hearing something of the young lady's whereabout.

Accordingly, next morning, Sam Weller issued forth upon

his quest, in no way daunted by the very discouraging prospect before him; and away he walked, up one street and down another—we were going to say, up one hill and down another, only it's all uphill at Clifton—without meeting with anything or anybody that tended to throw the faintest light on the matter in hand. Many were the colloquies into which Sam entered with grooms who were airing horses on roads, and nursemaids who were airing children in lanes; but nothing could Sam elicit from either the first-mentioned or the last, which bore the slightest reference to the object of his artfully-prosecuted inquiries. There were a great many young ladies in a great many houses, the greater part whereof were shrewdly suspected by the male and female domestics to be deeply attached to somebody, or perfectly ready to become so, if opportunity offered. But as none among these young ladies was Miss Arabella Allen, the information left Sam at exactly the old point of wisdom at which he had stood before.

Sam struggled across the Downs against a good high wind, wondering whether it was always necessary to hold your hat on with both hands in that part of the country, and came to a shady by-place about which were sprinkled several little villas of quiet and secluded appearance. Outside a stable-door at the bottom of a long back lane without a thoroughfare, a groom in undress was idling about, apparently persuading himself that he was doing something with a spade and a wheelbarrow. We may remark, in this place, that we have scarcely ever seen a groom near a stable, in his lazy moments, who has not been, to a greater or less extent, the victim of this singular delusion.

Sam thought he might as well talk to this groom as to any one else, especially as he was very tired with walking, and there was a good large stone just opposite the wheelbarrow; so he strolled down the lane, and, seating himself on the stone, opened a conversation with the ease and freedom for which he was remarkable.

"Mornin', old friend," said Sam.

"Arternoon, you mean," replied the groom, casting a surly look at Sam.

"You're wery right, old friend," said Sam; "I *do* mean arternoon. How are you?"

"Why, I don't find myself much the better for seeing of you," replied the ill-tempered groom.

"That's wery odd—that is," said Sam, "for you look so uncommon cheerful, and seem altogether so lively, that it does vun's heart good to see you."

The surly groom looked surlier still at this, but not sufficiently so to produce any effect upon Sam, who immediately inquired, with a countenance of great anxiety, whether his master's name was not Walker.

"No, it ain't," said the groom.

"Nor Brown, I s'pose?" said Sam.

"No, it ain't."

"Nor Vilson?"

"No; nor that neither," said the groom.

"Vell," replied Sam, "then I'm mistaken, and he hasn't got the honor o' my acquaintance, which I thought he had. Don't wait here out o' compliment to me," said Sam, as the groom wheeled in the barrow, and prepared to shut the gate. "Ease afore ceremony, old boy; I'll excuse you."

"I'd knock your head off for half-a-crown," said the surly groom, bolting one half of the gate.

"Couldn't afford to have it done on those terms," rejoined Sam. "It 'ud be worth a life's board vages at least, to you, and 'ud be cheap at that. Make my compliments in doors. Tell 'em not to vait dinner for me, and say they needn't mind puttin' any by, for it'll be cold afore I come in."

In reply to this, the groom waxing very wrath, muttered a desire to damage somebody's person; but disappeared without carrying it into execution, slamming the door angrily after him, and wholly unheeding Sam's affectionate request, that he would leave him a lock of his hair before he went.

Sam continued to sit on the large stone, meditating upon

what was best to be done, and revolving in his mind a plan for knocking at all the doors within five miles of Bristol, taking them at a hundred and fifty or two hundred a day, and endeavouring to find Miss Arabella by that expedient, when accident all of a sudden threw in his way what he might have sat there for a twelvemonth and yet not found without it.

Into the lane where he sat, there opened three or four garden-gates, belonging to as many houses, which though detached from each other, were only separated by their gardens. As these were large and long, and well planted with trees, the houses were not only at some distance off, but the greater part of them were nearly concealed from view. Sam was sitting with his eyes fixed upon the dust-heap outside the next gate to that by which the groom had disappeared, profoundly turning over in his mind the difficulties of his present undertaking, when the gate opened, and a female servant came out into the lane to shake some bed-side carpets.

Sam was so very busy with his own thoughts, that it is probable he would have taken no more notice of the young woman than just raising his head and remarking that she had a very neat and pretty figure, if his feelings of gallantry had not been most strongly roused by observing that she had no one to help her, and that the carpets seemed too heavy for her single strength. Mr. Weller was a gentleman of great gallantry in his own way, and he no sooner remarked this circumstance than he hastily rose from the large stone, and advanced towards her.

"My dear," said Sam, sliding up with an air of great respect, "You'll spile that wery pretty figure out o' all perportion if you shake them carpets by yourself. Let me help you."

The young lady, who had been coyly affecting not to know that a gentleman was so near, turned round as Sam spoke—no doubt (indeed she said so, afterwards) to decline this offer from a perfect stranger—when instead of speaking, she started back, and uttered a half-suppressed scream. Sam was scarcely less stupefied, for in the countenance of the well-shaped female servant, he beheld the very eyes of his Valentine, the pretty housemaid from Mr. Nupkins's.

"Wy, Mary my dear!" said Sam.

"Lauk, Mr. Weller," said Mary, "how you do frighten one!"

Sam made no verbal answer to this complaint, nor can we precisely say what reply he *did* make. We merely know that after a short pause Mary said, "Lor, do adun, Mr. Weller!" and that his hat had fallen off a few moments before—from both of which tokens we should be disposed to infer that one kiss or more, had passed between the parties.

"Why, how did you come here?" said Mary, when the conversation to which this interruption had been offered, was resumed.

"O' course I came to look arter you, my darlin," replied Mr. Weller; for once permitting his passion to get the better of his veracity.

"And how did you know I was here?" inquired Mary. "Who could have told you that I took another service at Ipswich, and that they afterwards moved all the way here? Who *could* have told you that, Mr. Weller?"

"Ah to be sure," said Sam with a cunning look, "that's the pint. Who could ha' told me?"

"It wasn't Mr. Muzzle, was it?" inquired Mary.

"Oh, no," replied Sam, with a solemn shake of the head, "it warn't him."

"It must have been the cook," said Mary.

"O' course it must," said Sam.

"Well, I never heard the like of that!" exclaimed Mary.

"No more did I," said Sam. "But Mary, my dear:" here Sam's manner grew extremely affectionate: "Mary, my dear, I've got another affair in hand as is wery pressin'. There's one o' my governor's friends—Mr. Winkle, you remember him."

"Him in the green coat?" said Mary. "Oh, yes, I remember him."

" Well," said Sam, " he's in a horrid state o' love; reg'larly comfoozled, and done over with it."

" Lor!" interposed Mary.

" Yes," said Sam: " but that's nothin' if we could find out the young 'ooman;" and here Sam, with many digressions upon the personal beauty of Mary, and the unspeakable tortures he had experienced since he last saw her, gave a faithful account of Mr. Winkle's present predicament.

" Well," said Mary, " I never did!"

" O' course not," said Sam, " and nobody never did, nor never vill neither; and here am I a walkin' about like the wandering Jew—a sportin' character you have perhaps heerd on, Mary, my dear, as wos alvays doin' a match agin' time, and never vent to sleep—looking arter this here Miss Arabella Allen."

" Miss who?" said Mary, in great astonishment.

" Miss Arabella Allen," said Sam.

" Goodness gracious!" said Mary, pointing to the garden door which the sulky groom had locked after him. " Why, it's that very house; she's been living there these six weeks. Their upper housemaid, which is lady's maid too, told me all about it over the wash-house palin's before the family was out of bed, one mornin'."

" Wot, the wery next door to you?" said Sam.

" The very next," replied Mary.

Mr. Weller was so deeply overcome on receiving this intelligence that he found it absolutely necessary to cling to his fair informant for support; and divers little love passages had passed between them, before he was sufficiently collected to return to the subject.

" Vell," said Sam at length, " if this don't beat cock-fightin', nothin' never vill, as the Lord Mayor said, ven the chief secretary o' state proposed his missis's health arter dinner. That wery next house! Wy, I've got a message to her as I've been a tryin' all day to deliver."

" Ah," said Mary, " but you can't deliver it now, because

172

she only walks in the garden in the evening, and then only for a very little time; she never goes out, without the old lady."

Sam ruminated for a few moments, and finally hit upon the following plan of operations; that he should return just at dusk—the time at which Arabella invariably took her walk —and, being admitted by Mary into the garden of the house to which she belonged, would contrive to scramble up the wall, beneath the over-hanging boughs of a large pear-tree, which would effectually screen him from observation; would there deliver his message, and arrange, if possible, an interview on behalf of Mr. Winkle for the ensuing evening at the same hour. Having made this arrangement with great dispatch, he assisted Mary in the long-deferred occupation of shaking the carpets.

It is not half as innocent a thing as it looks, that shaking little pieces of carpet—at least, there may be no great harm in the shaking, but the folding is a very insidious process. So long as the shaking lasts, and the two parties are kept the carpet's length apart, it is as innocent an amusement as can well be devised; but when the folding begins, and the distance between them gets gradually lessened from one half its former length to a quarter, and then to an eighth, and then to a sixteenth, and then to a thirty-second, if the carpet be long enough: it becomes dangerous. We do not know, to a nicety, how many pieces of carpet were folded in this instance, but we can venture to state that as many pieces as there were, so many times did Sam kiss the pretty housemaid.

Mr. Weller regaled himself with moderation at the nearest tavern until it was nearly dusk, and then returned to the lane without the thoroughfare. Having been admitted into the garden by Mary, and having received from that lady sundry admonitions concerning the safety of his limbs and neck, Sam mounted into the pear-tree, to wait until Arabella should come in sight.

He waited so long without this anxiously expected event occurring, that he began to think it was not going to take place at all, when he heard light footsteps upon the gravel, and immediately afterwards beheld Arabella walking pensively down the garden. As soon as she came nearly below the tree, Sam began, by way of gently indicating his presence, to make sundry diabolical noises similar to those which would probably be natural to a person of middle age who had been afflicted with a combination of inflammatory sore throat, croup, and hooping-cough, from his earliest infancy.

Upon this, the young lady cast a hurried glance towards the spot from whence the dreadful sounds proceeded; and her previous alarm being not at all diminished when she saw a man among the branches, she would most certainly have decamped, and alarmed the house, had not fear fortunately deprived her of the power of moving, and caused her to sink down on a garden seat; which happened by good luck to be near at hand.

"She's a goin' off," soliloquised Sam in great perplexity. "Wot a thing it is, as these here young creeturs *will* go a faintin' avay just wen they oughtn't to. Here, young 'ooman, Miss Sawbones, Mrs. Vinkle, don't!"

Whether it was the magic of Mr. Winkle's name, or the coolness of the open air, or some recollection of Mr. Weller's voice, that revived Arabella, matters not. She raised her head and languidly inquired, "Who's that, and what do you want?"

"Hush," said Sam, swinging himself on to the wall, and crouching there in as small a compass as he could reduce himself to, "only me, miss, only me."

"Mr. Pickwick's servant;" said Arabella, earnestly.

"The wery same, miss," replied Sam. "Here's Mr. Vinkle reg'larly sewed up vith desperation, miss."

"Ah!" said Arabella, drawing nearer the wall.

"Ah indeed," said Sam. "Ve thought ve should ha' been obliged to straightveskit him last night; he's been a ravin' all

174

day; and he says if he can't see you afore to-morrow night's over, he vishes he may be somethin'-unpleasanted if he don't drownd hisself.'

"Oh no, no, Mr. Weller!" said Arabella, clasping her hands.

"That's wot he says, miss," replied Sam. "He's a man of his word, and it's my opinion he'll do it, miss. He's heerd all about you from the Sawbones in barnacles."

"From my brother!" said Arabella, having some faint recognition of Sam's description.

"I don't rightly know which is your brother, miss," replied Sam. "Is it the dirtiest vun o' the two?"

"Yes, yes, Mr. Weller," returned Arabella, "go on. Make haste, pray."

"Well, miss," said Sam, "he's heerd all about it from him; and it's the gov'nor's opinion that if you don't see him wery quick, the Sawbones as we've been a speaking on, 'ull get as much extra lead in his head as'll damage the dewelopment o' the orgins if they ever put it in spirits artervards."

"Oh, what can I do to prevent these dreadful quarrels!" exclaimed Arabella.

"It's the suspicion of a priory 'tachment as is the cause of it all," replied Sam. "You'd better see him, miss."

"But how?—where?" cried Arabella. "I dare not leave the house alone. My brother is so unkind, so unreasonable! I know how strange my talking thus to you must appear, Mr. Weller, but I am very, very unhappy—" and here poor Arabella wept so bitterly, that Sam grew chivalrous.

"It may seem very strange talkin' to me about these here affairs, miss," said Sam with great vehemence: "but all I can say is, that I'm not only ready but villin' to do anythin' as'll make matters agreeable; and if chuckin' either o' them Sawboneses out o' winder 'ull do it, I'm the man." As Sam Weller said this, he tucked up his wristbands, at the imminent hazard of falling off the wall in so doing, to intimate his readiness to set to work immediately.

175

Flattering as these professions of good feeling were, Arabella resolutely declined (most unaccountably as Sam thought,) to avail herself of them. For some time she strenuously refused to grant Mr. Winkle the interview Sam had so pathetically requested; but at length, when the conversation threatened to be interrupted by the unwelcome arrival of a third party, she hurriedly gave him to understand, with many professions of gratitude, that it was barely possible she might be in the garden an hour later, next evening. Sam understood this perfectly well; and Arabella bestowing upon him one of her sweetest smiles, tripped gracefully away, leaving Mr. Weller in a state of very great admiration of her charms, both personal and mental.

Having descended in safety from the wall, and not forgotten to devote a few moments to his own particular business in the same department, Mr. Weller then made the best of his way back to the Bush, where his prolonged absence had occasioned much speculation and some alarm.

"We must be careful," said Mr. Pickwick, after listening attentively to Sam's tale, "not for our own sakes, but for that of the young lady. We must be very cautious."

" *We!* " said Mr. Winkle, with marked emphasis.

Mr. Pickwick's momentary look of indignation at the tone of this remark, subsided into his characteristic expression of benevolence, as he replied :

" *We*, sir ! I shall accompany you."

"You!" said Mr. Winkle.

"I," replied Mr. Pickwick, mildly. "In affording you this interview, the young lady has taken a natural, perhaps, but still a very imprudent step. If I am present at the meeting, a mutual friend, who is old enough to be the father of both parties, the voice of calumny can never be raised against her hereafter."

Mr. Pickwick's eyes lightened with honest exultation at his own foresight, as he spoke thus. Mr. Winkle was touched by this little trait of his delicate respect for the young *protégée* of his friend, and took his hand with a feeling of regard, akin to veneration.

"You *shall* go," said Mr. Winkle.

"I will," said Mr. Pickwick. "Sam, have my great-coat and shawl ready, and order a conveyance to be at the door to-morrow evening, rather earlier than is absolutely necessary, in order that we may be in good time."

Mr. Weller touched his hat, as an earnest of his obedience, and withdrew to make all needful preparations for the expedition.

The coach was punctual to the time appointed; and Mr. Weller, after duly installing Mr. Pickwick and Mr. Winkle inside, took his seat on the box by the driver. They alighted, as had been agreed on, about a quarter of a mile from the place of rendezvous, and desiring the coachman to await their return, proceeded the remaining distance on foot.

It was at this stage of the undertaking that Mr. Pickwick, with many smiles and various other indications of great self satisfaction, produced from one of his coat pockets a dark lantern, with which he had specially provided himself for the occasion, and the great mechanical beauty of which, he proceeded to explain to Mr. Winkle as they walked along, to the no small surprise of the few stragglers they met.

"I should have been the better for something of this kind, in my last garden expedition at night; eh, Sam?" said Mr. Pickwick, looking good-humouredly round at his follower, who was trudging behind.

"Wery nice things, if they're managed properly, sir," replied Mr. Weller; "but when you don't want to be seen, I think they're more useful arter the candle's gone out, than wen it's alight."

Mr. Pickwick appeared struck by Sam's remarks, for he put the lantern into his pocket again, and they walked on in silence.

"Down here, sir," said Sam. "Let me lead the way. This is the lane, sir."

Down the lane they went, and dark enough it was. Mr. Pickwick brought out the lantern, once or twice, as they groped their way along, and threw a very brilliant little tunnel of light before them, about a foot in diameter. It was very pretty to look at, but seemed to have the effect of rendering surrounding objects rather darker than before.

At length they arrived at the large stone. Here Sam recommended his master and Mr. Winkle to seat themselves, while he reconnoitred, and ascertained whether Mary was yet in waiting.

After an absence of five or ten minutes, Sam returned, to say that the gate was opened, and all quiet. Following him with stealthy tread, Mr. Pickwick and Mr. Winkle soon found themselves in the garden. Here everybody said "Hush!" a good many times; and that being done, no one seemed to have any very distinct apprehension of what was to be done next.

"Is Miss Allen in the garden yet, Mary?" inquired Mr. Winkle, much agitated.

"I don't know, sir," replied the pretty housemaid. "The best thing to be done, sir, will be for Mr. Weller to give you a hoist up into the tree, and perhaps Mr. Pickwick will have the goodness to see that nobody comes up the lane, while I watch at the other end of the garden. Goodness gracious, what's that!"

"That 'ere blessed lantern 'ull be the death on us all," exclaimed Sam, peevishly. "Take care wot you're a doin' on, sir; you're a sendin' a blaze o' light, right into the back parlor winder."

"Dear me!" said Mr. Pickwick, turning hastily aside, "I didn't mean to do that."

"Now, it's in the next house, sir," remonstrated Sam.

"Bless my heart!" exclaimed Mr. Pickwick, turning round again.

"Now, it's in the stable, and they'll think the place is a' fire," said Sam. "Shut it up, sir, can't you?"

"It's the most extraordinary lantern I ever met with, in all my life!" exclaimed Mr. Pickwick, greatly bewildered by the effects he had so unintentionally produced. "I never saw such a powerful reflector."

"It'll be vun too powerful for us, if you keep blazin' away in that manner, sir," replied Sam, as Mr. Pickwick, after various unsuccessful efforts, managed to close the slide. "There's the young lady's footsteps. Now, Mr. Vinkle, sir, up vith you."

"Stop, stop!" said Mr. Pickwick, "I must speak to her first. Help me up, Sam."

"Gently, sir," said Sam, planting his head against the wall, and making a platform of his back. "Step a top o' that 'ere flower-pot, sir. Now then, up vith you."

"I'm afraid I shall hurt you, Sam," said Mr. Pickwick.

"Never mind me, sir," replied Sam. "Lend him a hand, Mr. Vinkle, sir. Steady, sir, steady! That's the time o' day!"

As Sam spoke, Mr. Pickwick, by exertions almost supernatural in a gentleman of his years and weight, contrived to get upon Sam's back; and Sam gently raising himself up, and Mr. Pickwick holding on fast by the top of the wall, while Mr. Winkle clasped him tight by the legs, they contrived by these means to bring his spectacles just above the level of the coping.

"My dear," said Mr. Pickwick, looking over the wall, and catching sight of Arabella, on the other side, "Don't be frightened, my dear, it's only me."

"Oh pray go away, Mr. Pickwick," said Arabella. "Tell them all to go away. I am so dreadfully frightened. Dear, dear Mr. Pickwick, don't stop there. You'll fall down and kill yourself, I know you will."

"Now, pray don't alarm yourself, my dear," said Mr. Pickwick, soothingly. "There is not the least cause for fear, I assure you. Stand firm, Sam," said Mr. Pickwick, looking down.

"All right, sir," replied Mr. Weller. "Don't be longer than you can conweniently help, sir. You're rayther heavy."

"Only another moment, Sam," replied Mr. Pickwick. "I merely wished you to know, my dear, that I should not have allowed my young friend to see you in this clandestine way, if the situation in which you are placed, had left him any alternative; and lest the impropriety of this step should cause you any uneasiness, my love, it may be a satisfaction to you, to know that I am present. That's all, my dear."

"Indeed, Mr. Pickwick, I am very much obliged to you for your kindness and consideration," replied Arabella, drying her tears with her handkerchief. She would probably have said much more, had not Mr. Pickwick's head disappeared with great swiftness, in consequence of a false step on Sam's shoulder, which brought him suddenly to the ground. He was up again in an instant, however, and bidding Mr. Winkle make haste and get the interview over, ran out into the lane to keep watch, with all the courage and ardour of youth. Mr. Winkle himself, inspired by the occasion, was on the wall in a moment, merely pausing to request Sam to be careful of his master.

"I'll take care on him, sir," replied Sam. "Leave him to me."

"Where is he? What's he doing, Sam?" inquired Mr. Winkle.

"Bless his old gaiters," rejoined Sam, looking out at the garden-door. "He's a keepin' guard in the lane vith that 'ere dark lantern, like a amiable Guy Fawkes! I never see such a fine creetur in my days. Blessed if I don't think his heart must ha' been born five-and-twenty year arter his body, at least!"

Mr. Winkle stayed not to hear the encomium upon his friend. He had dropped from the wall; thrown himself at Arabella's feet; and by this time was pleading the sincerity of his passion with an eloquence worthy even of Mr. Pickwick himself.

While these things were going on in the open air, an elderly gentleman of scientific attainments was seated in his library, two or three houses off, writing a philosophical treatise, and ever and anon moistening his clay and his labours with a glass of claret from a venerable-looking bottle which stood by his side. In the agonies of composition, the elderly gentleman looked sometimes at the carpet, sometimes at the ceiling, and sometimes at the wall; and when neither carpet, ceiling, nor wall, afforded the requisite degree of inspiration, he looked out of the window.

In one of these pauses of invention, the scientific gentleman was gazing abstractedly on the thick darkness outside, when he was very much surprised by observing a most brilliant light glide through the air, at a short distance above the ground, and almost instantaneously vanish. After a short time the phenomenon was repeated, not once or twice, but several times: at last the scientific gentleman, laying down his pen, began to consider to what natural causes these appearances were to be assigned.

They were not meteors; they were too low. They were not glow-worms; they were too high. They were not will-o'-the-wisps; they were not fire-flies; they were not fire-works. What could they be? Some extraordinary and wonderful phenomenon of nature, which no philosopher had ever seen before; something which it had been reserved for him alone to discover, and which he should immortalize his name by chronicling for the benefit of posterity. Full of this idea, the scientific gentleman seized his pen again, and committed to paper sundry notes of these unparalleled appearances, with the date, day, hour, minute, and precise second at which they were visible: all of which were to form the data of a voluminous treatise of great research and deep learning, which should astonish all the atmospherical sages that ever drew breath in any part of the civilised globe.

He threw himself back in his easy chair, wrapped in contemplations of his future greatness. The mysterious light appeared more brilliantly than before: dancing, to all appearance, up and down the lane, crossing from side to side, and moving in an orbit as eccentric as comets themselves.

The scientific gentleman was a bachelor. He had no wife to call in and astonish, so he rang the bell for his servant.

"Pruffle," said the scientific gentleman, "there is something very extraordinary in the air to-night. Did you see that?" said the scientific gentleman, pointing out of the window, as the light again became visible.

"Yes, I did, sir."

"What do you think of it, Pruffle?"

"Think of it, sir?"

"Yes. You have been bred up in this country. What should you say was the cause of those lights, now?"

The scientific gentleman smilingly anticipated Pruffle's reply that he could assign no cause for them at all. Pruffle meditated.

"I should say it was thieves, sir," said Pruffle at length.

"You're a fool, and may go down stairs," said the scientific gentleman.

"Thank you, sir," said Pruffle. And down he went.

But the scientific gentleman could not rest under the idea of the ingenious treatise he had projected being lost to the world, which must inevitably be the case if the speculation of the ingenious Mr. Pruffle were not stifled in its birth. He put on his hat and walked quickly down the garden, determined to investigate the matter to the very bottom.

Now, shortly before the scientific gentleman walked out into the garden, Mr. Pickwick had run down the lane as fast as he could, to convey a false alarm that somebody was coming that way; occasionally drawing back the slide of the dark lantern to keep himself from the ditch. The alarm was no sooner given, than Mr. Winkle scrambled back over the wall, and Arabella ran into the house; the garden-gate was shut, and the three adventurers were making the best of their way down the lane, when they were startled by the scientific gentleman unlocking his garden-gate.

MR. WELLER'S DEXTEROUS FEAT.

"Hold hard," whispered Sam, who was, of course, the first of the party. "Show a light for just vun second, sir."

Mr. Pickwick did as he was desired, and Sam, seeing a man's head peeping out very cautiously within half-a-yard of his own, gave it a gentle tap with his clenched fist, which knocked it, with a hollow sound, against the gate. Having performed this feat with great suddenness and dexterity, Mr. Weller caught Mr. Pickwick up on his back, and followed Mr. Winkle down the lane at a pace which, considering the burden he carried, was perfectly astonishing.

"Have you got your vind back agin, sir," inquired Sam, when they had reached the end.

"Quite. Quite, now," replied Mr. Pickwick.

"Then come along, sir," said Sam, setting his master on his feet again. "Come betveen us, sir. Not half a mile to run. Think you're vinnin a cup, sir. Now for it."

Thus encouraged, Mr. Pickwick made the very best use of his legs. It may be confidently stated that a pair of black gaiters never got over the ground in better style than did those of Mr. Pickwick on this memorable occasion.

The coach was waiting, the horses were fresh, the roads were good, and the driver was willing. The whole party arrived in safety at the Bush before Mr. Pickwick recovered his breath.

"In with you at once, sir," said Sam, as he helped his master out. "Don't stop a second in the street, arter that 'ere exercise. Beg your pardon, sir," continued Sam, touching his hat as Mr. Winkle descended. "Hope there warn't a priory 'tachment, sir?"

Mr. Winkle grasped his humble friend by the hand, and whispered in his ear, "It's all right, Sam; quite right." Upon which Mr. Weller struck three distinct blows upon his nose in token of intelligence, smiled, winked, and proceeded to put the steps up, with a countenance expressive of lively satisfaction.

As to the scientific gentleman, he demonstrated, in a

masterly treatise, that these wonderful lights were the effect
of electricity; and clearly proved the same by detailing how
a flash of fire danced before his eyes when he put his head
out of the gate, and how he received a shock which stunned
him for a quarter of an hour afterwards; which demonstration
delighted all the Scientific Associations beyond measure, and
caused him to be considered a light of science ever afterwards.

CHAPTER XL.

THE remainder of the period which Mr. Pickwick had
assigned as the duration of the stay at Bath, passed over
without the occurrence of anything material. Trinity Term
commenced. On the expiration of its first week, Mr. Pickwick
and his friends returned to London; and the former gentleman,
attended of course by Sam, straightway repaired to his old
quarters at the George and Vulture.

On the third morning after their arrival, just as all the
clocks in the city were striking nine individually, and somewhere about nine hundred and ninety-nine collectively, Sam
was taking the air in George Yard, when a queer sort of fresh
painted vehicle drove up, out of which there jumped with
great agility, throwing the reins to a stout man who sat
beside him, a queer sort of gentleman, who seemed made for
the vehicle, and the vehicle for him.

The vehicle was not exactly a gig, neither was it a stanhope.
It was not what is currently denominated a dog-cart, neither
was it a taxed-cart, nor a chaise-cart, nor a guillotined cabriolet; and yet it had something of the character of each and
every of these machines. It was painted a bright yellow, with
the shafts and wheels picked out in black; and the driver
sat, in the orthodox sporting style, on cushions piled about

185

two feet above the rail. The horse was a bay, a well-looking animal enough; but with something of a flash and dog-fighting air about him, nevertheless, which accorded both with the vehicle and his master.

The master himself was a man of about forty, with black hair, and carefully combed whiskers. He was dressed in a particularly gorgeous manner, with plenty of articles of jewellery about him—all about three sizes larger than those which are usually worn by gentlemen—and a rough great-coat to crown the whole. Into one pocket of this great-coat, he thrust his left hand the moment he dismounted, while from the other he drew forth, with his right, a very bright and glaring silk handkerchief, with which he whisked a speck or two of dust from his boots, and then, crumbling it in his hand, swaggered up the court.

It had not escaped Sam's attention that, when this person dismounted, a shabby-looking man in a brown great-coat shorn of divers buttons, who had been previously slinking about, on the opposite side of the way, crossed over, and remained stationary close by. Having something more than a suspicion of the object of the gentleman's visit, Sam preceded him to the George and Vulture, and, turning sharp round, planted himself in the centre of the doorway.

"Now, my fine fellow!" said the man in the rough coat, in an imperious tone, attempting at the same time to push his way past.

"Now, sir, wot's the matter!" replied Sam, returning the push with compound interest.

"Come, none of this, my man; this won't do with me," said the owner of the rough coat, raising his voice, and turning white. "Here, Smouch!"

"Well, wot's amiss here?" growled the man in the brown coat, who had been gradually sneaking up the court during this short dialogue.

"Only some insolence of this young man's," said the principal, giving Sam another push.

"Come, none o' this gammon," growled Smouch, giving him another, and a harder one.

This last push had the effect which it was intended by the experienced Mr. Smouch to produce; for while Sam, anxious to return the compliment, was grinding that gentleman's body against the doorpost, the principal crept past, and made his way to the bar: whither Sam, after bandying a few epithetical remarks with Mr. Smouch, followed at once.

"Good morning, my dear," said the principal, addressing the young lady at the bar, with Botany Bay ease, and New South Wales gentility; "which is Mr. Pickwick's room, my dear?"

"Show him up," said the bar-maid to a waiter, without deigning another look at the exquisite, in reply to his inquiry.

The waiter led the way up stairs as he was desired, and the man in the rough coat followed, with Sam behind him: who, in his progress up the staircase, indulged in sundry gestures indicative of supreme contempt and defiance: to the unspeakable gratification of the servants and other lookers-on. Mr. Smouch, who was troubled with a hoarse cough, remained below, and expectorated in the passage.

Mr. Pickwick was fast asleep in bed, when his early visitor, followed by Sam, entered the room. The noise they made in so doing, awoke him.

"Shaving water, Sam," said Mr. Pickwick, from within the curtains.

"Shave you directly, Mr. Pickwick," said the visitor, drawing one of them back from the bed's head. "I've got an execution against you, at the suit of Bardell.—Here's the warrant.—Common Pleas.—Here's my card. I suppose you'll come over to my house." Giving Mr. Pickwick a friendly tap on the shoulder, the sheriff's officer (for such he was) threw his card on the counterpane, and pulled a gold toothpick from his waistcoat pocket.

"Namby's the name," said the sheriff's deputy, as Mr. Pickwick took his spectacles from under the pillow, and put them on, to read the card. "Namby, Bell Alley, Coleman Street."

At this point, Sam Weller, who had had his eyes fixed hitherto on Mr. Namby's shining beaver, interfered:

"Are you a Quaker?" said Sam.

"I'll let you know who I am, before I've done with you," replied the indignant officer. "I'll teach you manners, my fine fellow, one of these fine mornings."

"Thankee," said Sam. "I'll do the same to you. Take your hat off." With this, Mr. Weller, in the most dexterous manner, knocked Mr. Namby's hat to the other side of the room with such violence, that he had very nearly caused him to swallow the gold tooth-pick into the bargain.

"Observe this, Mr. Pickwick," said the disconcerted officer, gasping for breath. "I've been assaulted in the execution of my dooty by your servant in your chamber. I'm in bodily fear. I call you to witness this."

"Don't witness nothin', sir," interposed Sam. "Shut your eyes up tight, sir. I'd pitch him out o' winder, only he couldn't fall far enough, 'cause o' the leads outside."

"Sam," said Mr. Pickwick in an angry voice, as his attendant made various demonstrations of hostilities, "if you say another word, or offer the slightest interference with this person, I discharge you that instant."

"But, sir!" said Sam.

"Hold your tongue," interposed Mr. Pickwick. "Take that hat up again."

But this Sam flatly and positively refused to do; and, after he had been severely reprimanded by his master, the officer, being in a hurry, condescended to pick it up himself: venting a great variety of threats against Sam meanwhile, which that gentleman received with perfect composure: merely observing that if Mr. Namby would have the goodness to put his hat on again, he would knock it into the latter end of next week. Mr. Namby, perhaps thinking that such a process might be productive of inconvenience to himself, declined to offer the temptation, and, soon after, called up Smouch. Having informed him that the capture was made, and that he was to wait for the prisoner until he should have finished dressing, Namby then swaggered out, and drove away. Smouch, requesting Mr. Pickwick in a surly manner "to be as alive as he could, for it was a busy time," drew up a chair by the door, and sat there, until he had finished dressing. Sam was then dispatched for a hackney coach, and in it the triumvirate proceeded to Coleman Street. It was fortunate the distance was short, for Mr. Smouch, besides possessing no very enchanting conversational powers, was rendered a decidedly unpleasant companion in a limited space, by the physical weakness to which we have elsewhere adverted.

The coach having turned into a very narrow and dark street, stopped before a house with iron bars to all the windows; the door-posts of which were graced by the name and title of "Namby, Officer to the Sheriffs of London:" the inner gate having been opened by a gentleman who might have passed for a neglected twin brother of Mr. Smouch, and who was endowed with a large key for the purpose, Mr. Pickwick was shown into the "coffee-room."

This coffee-room was a front parlour: the principal features of which were fresh sand and stale tobacco smoke. Mr. Pickwick bowed to the three persons who were seated in it when he entered; and having dispatched Sam for Perker, withdrew into an obscure corner, and from thence looked with some curiosity upon his new companions.

One of these was a mere boy of nineteen or twenty, who, though it was yet barely ten o'clock, was drinking gin and water, and smoking a cigar: amusements to which, judging from his inflamed countenance, he had devoted himself pretty constantly for the last year or two of his life. Opposite him, engaged in stirring the fire with the toe of his right boot, was a coarse vulgar young man of about thirty, with a sallow face and harsh voice: evidently possessed of that knowledge of the world, and captivating freedom of manner, which is to be acquired in public-house parlours, and at low billiard-tables. The third tenant of the apartment was a middle-aged man in a very old suit of black, who looked pale and haggard, and paced up and down the room incessantly; stopping, now and then, to look with great anxiety out of the window as if he expected somebody, and then resuming his walk.

"You'd better have the loan of my razor this morning, Mr. Ayresleigh," said the man who was stirring the fire, tipping the wink to his friend the boy.

"Thank you, no, I shan't want it; I expect I shall be out, in the course of an hour or so," replied the other in a hurried manner. Then, walking again up to the window, and once more returning disappointed, he sighed deeply, and left the room; upon which the other two burst into a loud laugh.

"Well, I never saw such a game as that," said the gentleman who had offered the razor, whose name appeared to be Price. "Never!" Mr. Price confirmed the assertion with an oath, and then laughed again, when of course the boy (who thought his companion one of the most dashing fellows alive) laughed also.

"You'd hardly think, would you now," said Price, turning towards Mr. Pickwick, "that that chap's been here a week yesterday, and never once shaved himself yet, because he feels so certain he's going out in half an hour's time, that he thinks he may as well put it off till he gets home?"

"Poor man!" said Mr. Pickwick. "Are his chances of getting out of his difficulties really so great?"

"Chances be d—d," replied Price; "he hasn't half the ghost of one. I wouldn't give *that* for his chance of walking about the streets this time ten years." With this Mr. Price snapped his fingers contemptuously, and rang the bell.

"Give me a sheet of paper, Crookey," said Mr. Price to the attendant, who in dress and general appearance looked something between a bankrupt grazier, and a drover in a state of insolvency; "and a glass of brandy and water, Crookey, d'ye hear? I'm going to write to my father, and I must have a stimulant, or I shan't be able to pitch it strong enough into the old boy." At this facetious speech, the young boy, it is almost needless to say, was fairly convulsed.

"That's right," said Mr. Price. "Never say die. All fun, ain't it?"

"Prime!" said the young gentleman.

"You've some spirit about you, you have," said Price. "You've seen something of life."

"I rather think I have!" replied the boy. He had looked at it through the dirty panes of glass in a bar door.

Mr. Pickwick feeling not a little disgusted with this dialogue, as well as with the air and manner of the two beings by whom it had been carried on, was about to inquire whether he could not be accommodated with a private sitting-room, when two or three strangers of genteel appearance entered, at sight of whom the boy threw his cigar into the fire, and whispering to Mr. Price that they had come to "make it all right" for him, joined them at a table in the further end of the room.

It would appear, however, that matters were not going to be made all right quite so speedily as the young gentleman anticipated; for a very long conversation ensued, of which Mr. Pickwick could not avoid hearing certain angry fragments regarding dissolute conduct, and repeated forgiveness. At last, there were very distinct allusions made by the oldest gentleman of the party to one Whitecross Street, at which the young gentleman, notwithstanding his primeness and his spirit and his knowledge of life into the bargain, reclined his head upon the table, and howled dismally.

Very much satisfied with this sudden bringing down of the youth's valour, and this effectual lowering of his tone, Mr. Pickwick rang the bell, and was shown, at his own request, into a private room furnished with a carpet, table, chairs, sideboard and sofa, and ornamented with a looking-glass, and various old prints. Here, he had the advantage of hearing Mrs. Namby's performance on a square piano over head, while the breakfast was getting ready; when it came, Mr. Perker came too.

"Aha, my dear sir," said the little man, "nailed at last, eh? Come, come, I'm not sorry for it either, because now you'll see the absurdity of this conduct. I've noted down the amount of the taxed costs and damages for which the ca-sa was issued, and we had better settle at once and lose no time. Namby is come home by this time, I dare say. What say you, my dear sir? Shall I draw a cheque, or will you?" The little man rubbed his hands with affected cheerfulness as he said this, but glancing at Mr. Pickwick's countenance, could not forbear at the same time casting a desponding look towards Sam Weller.

"Perker," said Mr. Pickwick, "let me hear no more of this, I beg. I see no advantage in staying here, so I shall go to prison to-night."

"You can't go to Whitecross Street, my dear sir," said Perker. "Impossible! There are sixty beds in a ward; and the bolt's on, sixteen hours out of the four-and-twenty."

"I would rather go to some other place of confinement if I can," said Mr. Pickwick. "If not, I must make the best I can of that."

"You can go to the Fleet, my dear sir, if you're determined to go somewhere," said Perker.

"That'll do," said Mr. Pickwick. "I'll go there directly I have finished my breakfast."

"Stop, stop, my dear sir; not the least occasion for being in such a violent hurry to get into a place that most other men are as eager to get out of," said the good-natured little attorney. "We must have a habeas corpus. There'll be no judge at chambers till four o'clock this afternoon. You must wait till then."

"Very good," said Mr. Pickwick, with unmoved patience. "Then we will have a chop, here, at two. See about it, Sam, and tell them to be punctual."

Mr. Pickwick remaining firm, despite all the remonstrances

and arguments of Perker, the chops appeared and disappeared in due course; he was then put into another hackney-coach, and carried off to Chancery Lane, after waiting half an hour or so for Mr. Namby, who had a select dinner-party and could on no account be disturbed before.

There were two judges in attendance at Sergeant's Inn—one King's Bench, and one Common Pleas—and a great deal of business appeared to be transacting before them, if the number of lawyer's clerks who were hurrying in and out with bundles of papers, afforded any test. When they reached the low archway which forms the entrance to the Inn, Perker was detained a few moments parleying with the coachman about the fare and the change; and Mr. Pickwick, stepping to one side to be out of the way of the stream of people that were pouring in and out, looked about him with some curiosity.

The people that attracted his attention most, were three or four men of shabby-genteel appearance, who touched their hats to many of the attorneys who passed, and seemed to have some business there, the nature of which Mr. Pickwick could not divine. They were curious-looking fellows. One, was a slim and rather lame man in rusty black, and a white neckerchief; another, was a stout burly person, dressed in the same apparel, with a great reddish-black cloth round his neck; a third, was a little weazen drunken-looking body, with a pimply face. They were loitering about, with their hands behind them, and now and then with an anxious countenance whispered something in the ear of some of the gentlemen with papers, as they hurried by. Mr. Pickwick remembered to have very often observed them lounging under the archway when he had been walking past; and his curiosity was quite excited to know to what branch of the profession these dingy-looking loungers could possibly belong.

He was about to propound the question to Namby, who kept close beside him, sucking a large gold ring on his little finger, when Perker bustled up, and observing that there was no time to lose, led the way into the Inn. As Mr. Pickwick followed, the lame man stepped up to him, and civilly touching his hat, held out a written card, which Mr. Pickwick, not wishing to hurt the man's feelings by refusing, courteously accepted and deposited in his waistcoat-pocket.

"Now," said Perker, turning round before he entered one of the offices, to see that his companions were close behind him. "In here, my dear sir. Hallo, what do *you* want?"

This last question was addressed to the lame man, who, unobserved by Mr. Pickwick, made one of the party. In reply to it, the lame man touched his hat again, with all imaginable politeness, and motioned towards Mr. Pickwick.

"No, no," said Perker with a smile. "We don't want you, my dear friend, we don't want you."

"I beg your pardon, sir," said the lame man. "The gentleman took my card. I hope you will employ me, sir. The gentleman nodded to me. I'll be judged by the gentleman himself. You nodded to me, sir?"

"Pooh, pooh, nonsense. You didn't nod to any body, Pickwick? A mistake, a mistake," said Perker.

"The gentleman handed me his card," replied Mr. Pickwick, producing it from his waistcoat-pocket. "I accepted it, as the gentleman seemed to wish it—in fact I had some curiosity to look at it when I should be at leisure. I——"

The little attorney burst into a loud laugh, and returning the card to the lame man, informing him it was all a mistake, whispered to Mr. Pickwick as the man turned away in dudgeon, that he was only a bail.

"A what!" exclaimed Mr. Pickwick.

"A bail!" replied Perker.

"A bail!"

"Yes, my dear sir—half a dozen of 'em here. Bail you to any amount, and only charge half-a-crown. Curious trade, isn't it?" said Perker, regaling himself with a pinch of snuff.

"What! Am I to understand that these men earn a livelihood by waiting about here, to perjure themselves before

194

the judges of the land, at the rate of half-a-crown a crime!"
exclaimed Mr. Pickwick, quite aghast at the disclosure.

"Why, I don't exactly know about perjury, my dear sir,"
replied the little gentleman. "Harsh word, my dear sir,
very harsh word indeed. It's a legal fiction, my dear sir,
nothing more." Saying which, the attorney shrugged his
shoulders, smiled, took a second pinch of snuff, and led the
way into the office of the judge's clerk.

This was a room of specially dirty appearance, with a very
low ceiling and old panelled walls; and so badly lighted, that
although it was broad day outside, great tallow candles were
burning on the desks. At one end, was a door leading to
the judge's private apartment, round which were congregated
a crowd of attorneys and managing clerks, who were called
in, in the order in which their respective appointments stood
upon the file. Every time this door was opened to let a party
out, the next party made a violent rush to get in; and, as
in addition to the numerous dialogues which passed between
the gentlemen who were waiting to see the judge, a variety
of personal squabbles ensued between the greater part of those
who had seen him, there was as much noise as could well be
raised in an apartment of such confined dimensions.

Nor were the conversations of these gentlemen the only
sounds that broke upon the ear. Standing on a box behind a
wooden bar at another end of the room, was a clerk in
spectacles, who was "taking the affidavits:" large batches of
which were, from time to time, carried into the private room
by another clerk for the judge's signature. There were a
large number of attorneys' clerks to be sworn, and it being a
moral impossibility to swear them all at once, the struggles
of these gentlemen to reach the clerk in spectacles, were like
those of a crowd to get in at the pit door of a theatre when
Gracious Majesty honours it with its presence. Another
functionary, from time to time, exercised his lungs in calling
over the names of those who had been sworn, for the purpose
of restoring to them their affidavits after they had been signed

by the judge: which gave rise to a few more scuffles; and all these things going on at the same time, occasioned as much bustle as the most active and excitable person could desire to behold. There were yet another class of persons—those who were waiting to attend summonses their employers had taken out, which it was optional to the attorney on the opposite side to attend or not—and whose business it was, from time to time, to cry out the opposite attorney's name, to make certain that he was not in attendance without their knowledge.

For example. Leaning against the wall, close beside the seat Mr. Pickwick had taken, was an office-lad of fourteen, with a tenor voice; near him, a common-law clerk with a bass one.

A clerk hurried in with a bundle of papers, and stared about him.

"Sniggle and Blink," cried the tenor.

"Porkin and Snob," growled the bass.

"Stumpy and Deacon," said the new comer.

Nobody answered; the next man who came in, was hailed by the whole three; and he in his turn shouted for another firm; and then somebody else roared in a loud voice for another; and so forth.

All this time, the man in the spectacles was hard at work, swearing the clerks: the oath being invariably administered, without any effort at punctuation, and usually in the following terms:

"Take the book in your right hand this is your name and hand-writing you swear that the contents of this your affidavit are true so help you God a shilling you must get change I haven't got it."

"Well, Sam," said Mr. Pickwick, "I suppose they are getting the *habeas corpus* ready."

"Yes," said Sam, "and I vish they'd bring out the have-his-carcase. It's wery unpleasant keepin' us vaitin' here. I'd ha' got half a dozen have-his-carcases ready, pack'd up and all, by this time."

What sort of cumbrous and unmanageable machine, Sam

196

Weller imagined a habeas corpus to be, does not appear; for Perker, at that moment, walked up, and took Mr. Pickwick away.

The usual forms having been gone through, the body of Samuel Pickwick was soon afterwards confided to the custody of the tipstaff, to be by him taken to the Warden of the Fleet Prison, and there detained until the amount of the damages and costs in the action of Bardell against Pickwick was fully paid and satisfied.

"And that," said Mr. Pickwick, laughing, "will be a very long time. Sam, call another hackney-coach. Perker, my dear friend, good bye."

"I shall go with you, and see you safe there," said Perker.

"Indeed," replied Mr. Pickwick, "I would rather go without any other attendant than Sam. As soon as I get settled, I will write and let you know, and I shall expect you immediately. Until then, good bye."

As Mr. Pickwick said this, he got into the coach which had by this time arrived: followed by the tipstaff. Sam having stationed himself on the box, it rolled away.

"A most extraordinary man that!" said Perker, as he stopped to pull on his gloves.

"What a bankrupt he'd make, sir," observed Mr. Lowten, who was standing near. "How he would bother the commissioners! He'd set 'em at defiance if they talked of committing him, sir."

The attorney did not appear very much delighted with his clerk's professional estimate of Mr. Pickwick's character, for he walked away without deigning any reply.

The hackney-coach jolted along Fleet Street, as hackney-coaches usually do. The horses "went better," the driver said, when they had anything before them, (they must have gone at a most extraordinary pace when there was nothing,) and so the vehicle kept behind a cart; when the cart stopped, it stopped; and when the cart went on again, it did the same. Mr. Pickwick sat opposite the tipstaff; and the tipstaff sat with his hat between his knees, whistling a tune, and looking out of the coach window.

Time performs wonders. By the powerful old gentleman's aid, even a hackney-coach gets over half a mile of ground. They stopped at length, and Mr. Pickwick alighted at the gate of the Fleet.

The tipstaff, looking over his shoulder to see that his charge was following close at his heels, preceded Mr. Pickwick into the prison; turning to the left, after they had entered, they passed through an open door into a lobby, from which a heavy gate: opposite to that by which they had entered, and which was guarded by a stout turnkey with the key in his hand: led at once into the interior of the prison.

Here they stopped, while the tipstaff delivered his papers; and here Mr. Pickwick was apprised that he would remain, until he had undergone the ceremony, known to the initiated as "sitting for your portrait."

"Sitting for my portrait!" said Mr. Pickwick.

"Having your likeness taken, sir," replied the stout turnkey. "We're capital hands at likenesses here. Take 'em in no time, and always exact. Walk in, sir, and make yourself at home."

Mr. Pickwick complied with the invitation, and sat himself down: when Mr. Weller, who stationed himself at the back of the chair, whispered that the sitting was merely another term for undergoing an inspection by the different turnkeys, in order that they might know prisoners from visitors.

"Well, Sam," said Mr. Pickwick, "then I wish the artists would come. This is rather a public place."

"They vont be long, sir, I des-say," replied Sam. "There's a Dutch clock, sir."

"So I see," observed Mr. Pickwick.

"And a bird-cage, sir," says Sam. "Veels vithin veels, a prison in a prison. Ain't it, sir?"

As Mr. Weller made this philosophical remark, Mr. Pickwick was aware that his sitting had commenced. The stout turnkey having been relieved from the lock, sat down, and looked at him carelessly, from time to time, while a long thin man who had relieved him, thrust his hands beneath his coat-tails, and planting himself opposite, took a good long view of him. A third rather surly-looking gentleman: who had apparently been disturbed at his tea, for he was disposing of the last remnant of a crust and butter when he came in: stationed himself close to Mr. Pickwick; and, resting his hands on his hips, inspected him narrowly; while two others mixed with the group, and studied his features with most intent and thoughtful faces. Mr. Pickwick winced a good deal under the operation, and appeared to sit very uneasily in his chair; but he made no remark to anybody while it was being performed, not even to Sam, who reclined upon the back of the chair, reflecting, partly on the situation of his master, and partly on the great satisfaction it would have afforded him to make a fierce assault upon all the turnkeys there assembled, one after the other, if it were lawful and peaceable so to do.

At length the likeness was completed, and Mr. Pickwick was informed, that he might now proceed into the prison.

"Where am I to sleep to-night?" inquired Mr. Pickwick.

"Why I don't rightly know about to-night," replied the stout turnkey. "You'll be chummed on somebody to-morrow, and then you'll be all snug and comfortable. The first night's generally rather unsettled, but you'll be set all squares to-morrow."

After some discussion, it was discovered that one of the turnkeys had a bed to let, which Mr. Pickwick could have for that night. He gladly agreed to hire it.

"If you'll come with me, I'll show it you at once," said the man. "It ain't a large 'un; but it's an out-and-outer to sleep in. This way, sir."

They passed through the inner gate, and descended a short flight of steps. The key was turned after them; and Mr. Pickwick found himself, for the first time in his life, within the walls of a debtor's prison.

CHAPTER XLI.

WHAT BEFEL MR. PICKWICK WHEN HE GOT INTO THE FLEET; WHAT PRISONERS HE SAW THERE; AND HOW HE PASSED THE NIGHT.

Mr. Tom Roker, the gentleman who had accompanied Mr. Pickwick into the prison, turned sharp round to the right when he got to the bottom of the little flight of steps, and led the way, through an iron gate which stood open, and up another short flight of steps, into a long narrow gallery, dirty and low, paved with stone, and very dimly lighted by a window at each remote end.

"This," said the gentleman, thrusting his hands into his pockets, and looking carelessly over his shoulder to Mr. Pickwick, "This here is the hall flight."

"Oh," replied Mr. Pickwick, looking down a dark and filthy staircase, which appeared to lead to a range of damp and gloomy stone vaults, beneath the ground, "and those, I suppose, are the little cellars where the prisoners keep their small quantities of coals. Unpleasant places to have to go down to; but very convenient, I dare say."

"Yes, I shouldn't wonder if they was convenient," replied the gentleman, "seeing that a few people live there, pretty snug. That's the Fair, that is."

"My friend," said Mr. Pickwick, "you don't really mean to say that human beings live down in those wretched dungeons?"

THE WAYS OF THE PLACE.

"Don't I?" replied Mr. Roker, with indignant astonishment; "why shouldn't I?"

"Live! Live down there!" exclaimed Mr. Pickwick.

"Live down there! Yes, and die down there, too, wery often!" replied Mr. Roker; "and what of that? Who's got to say anything agin it? Live down there! Yes, and a wery good place it is to live in, ain't it?"

As Roker turned somewhat fiercely upon Mr. Pickwick in saying this, and, moreover muttered in an excited fashion certain unpleasant invocations concerning his own eyes, limbs, and circulating fluids, the latter gentleman deemed it advisable to pursue the discourse no further. Mr. Roker then proceeded to mount another staircase, as dirty as that which led to the place which had just been the subject of discussion, in which ascent he was closely followed by Mr. Pickwick and Sam.

"There," said Mr. Roker, pausing for breath when they reached another gallery of the same dimensions as the one below, "this is the coffee-room flight; the one above's the third, and the one above that's the top; and the room where you're a-going to sleep to-night is the warden's room, and it's this way—come on." Having said all this in a breath, Mr. Roker mounted another flight of stairs, with Mr. Pickwick and Sam Weller following at his heels.

These staircases received light from sundry windows placed at some little distance above the floor, and looking into a gravelled area bounded by a high brick wall, with iron *chevaux-de-frise* at the top. This area, it appeared from Mr. Roker's statement, was the racket-ground; and it further appeared, on the testimony of the same gentleman, that there was a smaller area in that portion of the prison which was nearest Farringdon Street, denominated and called "the Painted Ground," from the fact of its walls having once displayed the semblances of various men-of-war in full sail, and other artistical effects achieved in bygone times by some imprisoned draughtsman in his leisure hours.

Having communicated this piece of information, apparently more for the purpose of discharging his bosom of an important fact, than with any specific view of enlightening Mr. Pickwick, the guide, having at length reached another gallery, led the way into a small passage at the extreme end: opened a door: and disclosed an apartment of an appearance by no means inviting, containing eight or nine iron bedsteads.

"There," said Mr. Roker, holding the door open, and looking triumphantly round at Mr. Pickwick, "there's a room!"

Mr. Pickwick's face, however, betokened such a very trifling portion of satisfaction at the appearance of his lodging, that Mr. Roker looked for a reciprocity of feeling into the countenance of Samuel Weller, who, until now, had observed a dignified silence.

"There's a room, young man," observed Mr. Roker.

"I see it," replied Sam, with a placid nod of the head.

"You wouldn't think to find such a room as this in the Farringdon Hotel, would you?" said Mr. Roker, with a complacent smile.

To this Mr. Weller replied with an easy and unstudied closing of one eye; which might be considered to mean, either that he would have thought it, or that he would not have thought it, or that he had never thought anything at all about it: as the observer's imagination suggested. Having executed this feat, and re-opened his eye, Mr. Weller proceeded to inquire which was the individual bedstead that Mr. Roker had so flatteringly described as an out-an-outer to sleep in.

"That's it," replied Mr. Roker, pointing to a very rusty one in a corner. "It would make any one go to sleep, that bedstead would, whether they wanted to or not."

"I should think," said Sam, eyeing the piece of furniture in question with a look of excessive disgust, "I should think poppies was nothing to it."

"Nothing at all," said Mr. Roker.

THE POPULATION OF THE PLACE.

"And I s'pose," said Sam, with a sidelong glance at his master, as if to see whether there were any symptoms of his determination being shaken by what passed, "I s'pose the other gen'l'men as sleeps here, *are* gen'l'men."

"Nothing but it," said Mr. Roker. "One of 'em takes his twelve pints of ale a-day, and never leaves off smoking even at his meals."

"He must be a first-rater," said Sam.

"A, 1," replied Mr. Roker.

Nothing daunted, even by this intelligence, Mr. Pickwick smilingly announced his determination to test the powers of the narcotic bedstead for that night; and Mr. Roker, after informing him that he could retire to rest at whatever hour he thought proper, without any further notice or formality, walked off, leaving him standing with Sam in the gallery.

It was getting dark; that is to say, a few gas jets were kindled in this place which was never light, by way of compliment to the evening, which had set in outside. As it was rather warm, some of the tenants of the numerous little rooms which opened into the gallery on either hand, had set their doors ajar. Mr. Pickwick peeped into them as he passed along, with great curiosity and interest. Here four or five great hulking fellows, just visible through a cloud of tobacco-smoke, were engaged in noisy and riotous conversation over half-emptied pots of beer, or playing at all-fours with a very greasy pack of cards. In the adjoining room, some solitary tenant might be seen, poring, by the light of a feeble tallow candle, over a bundle of soiled and tattered papers, yellow with dust and dropping to pieces from age: writing, for the hundredth time, some lengthened statement of his grievances, for the perusal of some great man whose eyes it would never reach, or whose heart it would never touch. In a third, a man, with his wife and a whole crowd of children, might be seen making up a scanty bed on the ground, or upon a few chairs, for the younger ones to pass the night in. And in a fourth, and a fifth, and a sixth, and a seventh, the noise, and the beer, and the tobacco-smoke, and the cards, all came over again in greater force than before.

In the galleries themselves, and more especially on the staircases, there lingered a great number of people, who came there, some because their rooms were empty and lonesome, others because their rooms were full and hot: the greater part because they were restless and uncomfortable, and not possessed of the secret of exactly knowing what to do with themselves. There were many classes of people here, from the labouring man in his fustian jacket, to the broken-down spendthrift in his shawl dressing-gown, most appropriately out at elbows; but there was the same air about them all—a listless jail-bird careless swagger, a vagabondish who's-afraid sort of bearing, which is wholly indescribable in words, but which any man can understand in one moment if he wish, by setting foot in the nearest debtor's prison, and looking at the very first group of people he sees there, with the same interest as Mr. Pickwick did.

"It strikes me, Sam," said Mr. Pickwick, leaning over the iron-rail at the stairhead, "It strikes me, Sam, that imprisonment for debt is scarcely any punishment at all."

"Think not, sir?" inquired Mr. Weller.

"You see how these fellows drink, and smoke, and roar," replied Mr. Pickwick. "It's quite impossible that they can mind it much."

"Ah, that's just the wery thing, sir," rejoined Sam, "*they* don't mind it; it's a regular holiday to them—all porter and skittles. It's the t'other vuns as gets done over, vith this sort o' thing: them down-hearted fellers as can't svig avay at the beer, nor play at skittles neither; them as vould pay if they could, and gets low by being boxed up. I'll tell you wot it is, sir; them as is always a idlin' in public houses it don't damage at all, and them as is alvays a workin' wen they can, it damages too much. 'It's unekal,' as my father used to say wen his grog worn't made half-and-half: 'It's unekal, and that's the fault on it.'"

THE STORY OF NUMBER TWENTY.

"I think you're right, Sam," said Mr. Pickwick, after a few moments' reflection, "quite right."

"P'raps, now and then, there's some honest people as likes it," observed Mr. Weller, in a ruminative tone, "but I never heerd o' one as I can call to mind, 'cept the little dirty-faced man in the brown coat; and that was force of habit."

"And who was he?" inquired Mr. Pickwick.

"Wy, that's just the wery point as nobody never know'd," replied Sam.

"But what did he do?"

"Wy he did wot many men as has been much better know'd has done in their time, sir," replied Sam, "he run a match agin the constable, and vun it."

"In other words, I suppose," said Mr. Pickwick, "he got into debt."

"Just that, sir," replied Sam, "and in course o' time he come here in consekens. It warn't much—execution for nine pound nothin', multiplied by five for costs; but hows'ever here he stopped for seventeen year. If he got any wrinkles in his face, they was stopped up vith the dirt, for both the dirty face and the brown coat wos just the same at the end o' that time as they wos at the beginnin'. He wos a wery peaceful inoffendin' little creetur, and wos alvays a bustlin' about for somebody, or playin' rackets and never vinnin'; till at last the turnkeys they got quite fond on him, and he wos in the lodge ev'ry night, a chattering vith 'em, and tellin' stories, and all that 'ere. Vun night he wos in there as usual, along vith a wery old friend of his, as wos on the lock, ven he says all of a sudden, 'I ain't seen the market outside, Bill,' he says (Fleet Market wos there at that time) —'I ain't seen the market outside, Bill,' he says, 'for seventeen year.' 'I know you ain't,' says the turnkey, smoking his pipe. 'I should like to see it for a minit, Bill,' he says. 'Wery probable,' says the turnkey, smoking his pipe wery fierce, and making believe he warn't up to wot the little man wanted. 'Bill,' says the little man, more abrupt than afore, 'I've got the fancy in my head. Let me see the public streets once more afore I die; and if I ain't struck with apoplexy, I'll be back in five minits by the clock.' 'And wot 'ud become o' me if you *wos* struck with apoplexy?' said the turnkey. 'Wy,' says the little creetur, 'whoever found me, 'ud bring me home, for I've got my card in my pocket, Bill,' he says, 'No. 20, Coffee-room Flight:' and that wos true, sure enough, for wen he wanted to make the acquaintance of any new comer, he used to pull out a little limp card vith them words on it and nothin' else; in consideration of vich, he wos alvays called Number Tventy. The turnkey takes a fixed look at him, and at last he says in a solemn manner, 'Tventy,' he says, 'I'll trust you; you won't get your old friend into trouble.' 'No, my boy; I hope I've somethin' better behind here,' says the little man; and as he said it he hit his little veskit wery hard, and then a tear started out o' each eye, which wos wery extraordinary, for it wos supposed as water never touched his face. He shook the turnkey by the hand; out he vent——"

"And never came back again," said Mr. Pickwick.

"Wrong for vunce, sir," replied Mr. Weller, "for back he come, two minits afore the time, a bilin' with rage: sayin' how he'd been nearly run over by a hackney-coach: that he warn't used to it: and he was blowed if he wouldn't write to the Lord Mayor. They got him pacified at last; and for five years arter that, he never even so much as peeped out o' the lodge-gate."

"At the expiration of that time he died, I suppose," said Mr. Pickwick.

"No he didn't, sir," replied Sam. "He got a curiosity to go and taste the beer at a new public-house over the way, and it wos such a wery nice parlour, that he took it into his head to go there every night, wich he did for a long time, always comin' back reg'lar about a quarter of an hour afore the gate shut, wich wos all wery snug and comfortable. At last he began to get so precious jolly, that he used to forget

how the time vent, or care nothin' at all about it, and he
vent on gettin' later and later, till vun night his old friend
wos just a shuttin' the gate—had turned the key in fact—
wen he come up. 'Hold hard, Bill,' he says. 'Wot, ain't
you come home yet, Tventy?' says the turnkey, 'I thought
you wos in, long ago.' 'No I wasn't,' says the little man,
vith a smile. 'Well then, I'll tell you wot it is, my friend,'
says the turnkey, openin' the gate wery slow and sulky, 'it's
my 'pinion as you've got into bad company o' late, which
I'm wery sorry to see. Now, I don't wish to do nothing
harsh,' he says, 'but if you can't confine yourself to steady
circles, and find your vay back at reg'lar hours, as sure as
you're a standin' there, I'll shut you out altogether!' The
little man was seized vith a wiolent fit o' tremblin', and never
vent outside the prison walls artervards!'"

As Sam concluded, Mr. Pickwick slowly retraced his steps
down stairs. After a few thoughtful turns in the Painted
Ground, which, as it was now dark, was nearly deserted, he
intimated to Mr. Weller that he thought it high time for
him to withdraw for the night; requesting him to seek a
bed in some adjacent public-house, and return early in the
morning, to make arrangements for the removal of his master's
wardrobe from the George and Vulture. This request Mr.
Samuel Weller prepared to obey, with as good a grace as
he could assume, but with a very considerable show of
reluctance nevertheless. He even went so far as to essay
sundry ineffectual hints regarding the expediency of stretching himself on the gravel for that night; but finding Mr.
Pickwick obstinately deaf to any such suggestions, finally
withdrew.

There is no disguising the fact that Mr. Pickwick felt
very low-spirited and uncomfortable; not for lack of society,
for the prison was very full, and a bottle of wine would at
once have purchased the utmost good-fellowship of a few
choice spirits, without any more formal ceremony of introduction; but he was alone in the coarse vulgar crowd, and felt

the depression of spirit and sinking of heart, naturally consequent on the reflection that he was cooped and caged up, without a prospect of liberation. As to the idea of releasing himself by ministering to the sharpness of Dodson and Fogg, it never for an instant entered his thoughts.

In this frame of mind he turned again into the coffee-room gallery, and walked slowly to and fro. The place was intolerably dirty, and the smell of tobacco-smoke perfectly suffocating. There was a perpetual slamming and banging of doors as the people went in and out; and the noise of their voices and footsteps echoed and re-echoed through the passages constantly. A young woman, with a child in her arms, who seemed scarcely able to crawl, from emaciation and misery, was walking up and down the passage in conversation with her husband, who had no other place to see her in. As they passed Mr. Pickwick, he could hear the female sob; and once she burst into such a passion of grief, that she was compelled to lean against the wall for support, while the man took the child in his arms, and tried to soothe her.

Mr. Pickwick's heart was really too full to bear it, and he went up stairs to bed.

Now, although the warden's room was a very uncomfortable one (being, in every point of decoration and convenience, several hundred degrees inferior to the common infirmary of a county gaol), it had at present the merit of being wholly deserted save by Mr. Pickwick himself. So, he sat down at the foot of his little iron bedstead, and began to wonder how much a year the warden made out of the dirty room. Having satisfied himself, by mathematical calculation, that the apartment was about equal in annual value to the freehold of a small street in the suburbs of London, he took to wondering what possible temptation could have induced a dingy-looking fly that was crawling over his pantaloons, to come into a close prison, when he had the choice of so many airy situations—a course of meditation which led him to the irresistible conclusion that the insect was mad. After settling this point,

The Warden's Room

he began to be conscious that he was getting sleepy; where-upon he took his nightcap out of the pocket in which he had had the precaution to stow it in the morning, and, leisurely undressing himself, got into bed, and fell asleep.

"Bravo! Heel over toe—cut and shuffle—pay away at it, Zephyr! I'm smothered if the Opera House isn't your proper hemisphere. Keep it up! Hooray!" These expressions, delivered in a most boisterous tone, and accompanied with loud peals of laughter, roused Mr. Pickwick from one of those sound slumbers which, lasting in reality some half hour, seem to the sleeper to have been protracted for three weeks or a month.

The voice had no sooner ceased than the room was shaken with such violence that the windows rattled in their frames, and the bedsteads trembled again. Mr. Pickwick started up, and remained for some minutes fixed in mute astonishment at the scene before him.

On the floor of the room, a man in a broad-skirted green coat, with corderoy knee smalls and grey cotton stockings, was performing the most popular steps of a hornpipe, with a slang and burlesque caricature of grace and lightness, which, combined with the very appropriate character of his costume, was inexpressibly absurd. Another man, evidently very drunk, who had probably been tumbled into bed by his companions, was sitting up between the sheets, warbling as much as he could recollect of a comic song, with the most intensely sentimental feeling and expression; while a third, seated on one of the bedsteads, was applauding both performers with the air of a profound connoisseur, and encouraging them by such ebullitions of feeling as had already roused Mr. Pickwick from his sleep.

This last man was an admirable specimen of a class of gentry which never can be seen in full perfection but in such places;—they may be met with, in an imperfect state, occasionally about stable-yards and public-houses; but they never attain their full bloom except in these hot-beds, which

THE PICKWICK CLUB.

would almost seem to be considerately provided by the Legislature for the sole purpose of rearing them.

He was a tall fellow, with an olive complexion, long dark hair, and very thick bushy whiskers meeting under his chin. He wore no neckerchief, as he had been playing rackets all day, and his open shirt collar displayed their full luxuriance. On his head he wore one of the common eighteenpenny French skull-caps, with a gawdy tassel dangling therefrom, very happily in keeping with a common fustian coat. His legs: which, being long, were afflicted with weakness: graced a pair of Oxford-mixture trousers, made to show the full symmetry of those limbs. Being somewhat negligently braced, however, and, moreover, but imperfectly buttoned, they fell in a series of not the most graceful folds over a pair of shoes sufficiently down at heel to display a pair of very soiled white stockings. There was a rakish, vagabond smartness, and a kind of boastful rascality, about the whole man, that was worth a mine of gold.

This figure was the first to perceive that Mr. Pickwick was looking on; upon which he winked to the Zephyr, and entreated him, with mock gravity, not to wake the gentleman.

"Why, bless the gentleman's honest heart and soul!" said the Zephyr, turning round and affecting the extremity of surprise; "the gentleman *is* awake. Hem, Shakespeare! How do you do, sir? How is Mary and Sarah, sir? and the dear old lady at home, sir? Will you have the kindness to put my compliments into the first little parcel you're sending that way, sir, and say that I would have sent 'em before, only I was afraid they might be broken in the waggon, sir?"

"Don't overwhelm the gentleman with ordinary civilities when you see he's anxious to have something to drink," said the gentleman with the whiskers, with a jocose air. "Why don't you ask the gentleman what he'll take?"

"Dear me, I quite forgot," replied the other. "What *will* you take, sir? Will you take port wine, sir, or sherry wine, sir? I can recommend the ale, sir; or perhaps you'd like to taste the porter, sir? Allow me to have the felicity of hanging up your nightcap, sir."

With this, the speaker snatched that article of dress from Mr. Pickwick's head, and fixed it in a twinkling on that of the drunken man, who, firmly impressed with the belief that he was delighting a numerous assembly, continued to hammer away at the comic song in the most melancholy strains imaginable.

Taking a man's nightcap from his brow by violent means, and adjusting it on the head of an unknown gentleman of dirty exterior, however ingenious a witticism in itself, is unquestionably one of those which come under the denomination of practical jokes. Viewing the matter precisely in this light, Mr. Pickwick, without the slightest intimation of his purpose, sprang vigorously out of bed, struck the Zephyr so smart a blow in the chest as to deprive him of a considerable portion of the commodity which sometimes bears his name, and then, recapturing his nightcap, boldly placed himself in an attitude of defence.

"Now," said Mr. Pickwick, gasping no less from excitement than from the expenditure of so much energy, "come on—both of you—both of you!" With this liberal invitation the worthy gentleman communicated a revolving motion to his clenched fists, by way of appalling his antagonists with a display of science.

It might have been Mr. Pickwick's very unexpected gallantry, or it might have been the complicated manner in which he had got himself out of bed, and fallen all in a mass upon the hornpipe man, that touched his adversaries. Touched they were; for, instead of then and there making an attempt to commit manslaughter, as Mr. Pickwick implicitly believed they would have done, they paused, stared at each other a short time, and finally laughed outright.

"Well; you're a trump, and I like you all the better for it," said the Zephyr. "Now jump into bed again, or you'll catch the rheumatics. No malice, I hope?" said the man, extending a hand the size of the yellow clump of fingers which sometimes swing over a glover's door.

"Certainly not," said Mr. Pickwick with great alacrity; for, now that the excitement was over, he began to feel rather cool about the legs.

"Allow me the *honour*," said the gentleman with the whiskers, presenting his dexter hand, and aspirating the h.

"With much pleasure, sir," said Mr. Pickwick; and having executed a very long and solemn shake, he got into bed again.

"My name is Smangle, sir," said the man with the whiskers.

"Oh," said Mr. Pickwick.

"Mine is Mivins," said the man in the stockings.

"I am delighted to hear it, sir," said Mr. Pickwick.

"Hem," coughed Mr. Smangle.

"Did you speak, sir?" said Mr. Pickwick.

"No, I did not, sir," said Mr. Smangle.

"I thought you did, sir," said Mr. Pickwick.

All this was very genteel and pleasant; and, to make matters still more comfortable, Mr. Smangle assured Mr. Pickwick a great many times that he entertained a very high respect for the feelings of a gentleman; which sentiment, indeed, did him infinite credit, as he could be in no wise supposed to understand them.

"Are you going through the Court, sir?" inquired Mr. Smangle.

"Through the what?" said Mr. Pickwick.

"Through the Court—Portugal Street—the Court for the Relief of——you know."

"Oh, no," replied Mr. Pickwick. "No, I am not."

"Going out, perhaps?" suggested Mivins.

"I fear not," replied Mr. Pickwick. "I refuse to pay some damages, and am here in consequence."

"Ah," said Mr. Smangle, "paper has been my ruin."

"A stationer, I presume, sir?" said Mr. Pickwick, innocently.

212

"Stationer! No, no; confound and curse me! Not so low as that. No trade. When I say paper, I mean bills."

"Oh, you use the word in that sense. I see," said Mr. Pickwick.

"Damme! A gentleman must expect reverses," said Smangle. "What of that? Here am I in the Fleet Prison. Well; good. What then? I'm none the worse for that, am I?"

"Not a bit," replied Mr. Mivins. And he was quite right; for, so far from Mr. Smangle being any the worse for it, he was something the better, inasmuch as to qualify himself for the place, he had attained gratuitous possession of certain articles of jewellery, which, long before that, had found their way to the pawnbroker's.

"Well; but come," said Mr. Smangle; "this is dry work. Let's rinse our mouths with a drop of burnt sherry; the last comer shall stand it, Mivins shall fetch it, and I'll help to drink it. That's a fair and gentlemanlike division of labour, any how. Curse me!"

Unwilling to hazard another quarrel, Mr. Pickwick gladly assented to the proposition, and consigned the money to Mr. Mivins, who, as it was nearly eleven o'clock, lost no time in repairing to the coffee-room on his errand.

"I say," whispered Smangle, the moment his friend had left the room; "what did you give him?"

"Half a sovereign," said Mr. Pickwick.

"He's a devilish pleasant gentlemanly dog," said Mr. Smangle;—"infernal pleasant. I don't know anybody more so; but—— " Here Mr. Smangle stopped short, and shook his head dubiously.

"You don't think there is any probability of his appropriating the money to his own use?" said Mr. Pickwick.

"Oh, no! Mind, I don't say that; I expressly say that he's a devilish gentlemanly fellow," said Mr. Smangle. "But I think, perhaps, if somebody went down, just to see that he didn't dip his beak into the jug by accident, or make

213

some confounded mistake in losing the money as he came up stairs, it would be as well. Here, you sir, just run down stairs, and look after that gentleman, will you?"

This request was addressed to a little timid-looking nervous man, whose appearance bespoke great poverty, and who had been crouching on his bedstead all this while, apparently stupified by the novelty of his situation.

"You know where the coffee-room is," said Smangle: "just run down, and tell that gentleman you've come to help him up with the jug. Or—stop—I'll tell you what— I'll tell you how we'll do him," said Smangle, with a cunning look.

"How?" said Mr. Pickwick.

"Send down word that he's to spend the change in cigars. Capital thought. Run and tell him that; d'ye hear? They shan't be wasted," continued Smangle, turning to Mr. Pickwick. "*I'll* smoke 'em."

This manœuvering was so exceedingly ingenious, and, withal, performed with such immovable composure and coolness, that Mr. Pickwick would have had no wish to disturb it, even if he had had the power. In a short time Mr. Mivins returned, bearing the sherry, which Mr. Smangle dispensed in two little cracked mugs: considerately remarking, with reference to himself, that a gentleman must not be particular under such circumstances, and that, for his part, he was not too proud to drink out of the jug. In which, to show his sincerity, he forthwith pledged the company in a draught which half emptied it.

An excellent understanding having been by these means promoted, Mr. Smangle proceeded to entertain his hearers with a relation of divers romantic adventures in which he had been from time to time engaged, involving various interesting anecdotes of a thorough-bred horse, and a magnificent Jewess, both of surpassing beauty, and much coveted by the nobility and gentry of these kingdoms.

Long before these elegant extracts from the biography of

a gentleman, were concluded, Mr. Mivins had betaken himself to bed, and had set in snoring for the night: leaving the timid stranger and Mr. Pickwick to the full benefit of Mr. Smangle's experiences.

Nor were the two last-named gentlemen as much edified as they might have been, by the moving passages narrated. Mr. Pickwick had been in a state of slumber for some time, when he had a faint perception of the drunken man bursting out afresh with the comic song, and receiving from Mr. Smangle a gentle intimation, through the medium of the water jug, that his audience were not musically disposed. Mr. Pickwick then once again dropped off to sleep, with a confused consciousness that Mr. Smangle was still engaged in relating a long story, the chief point of which appeared to be, that, on some occasion particularly stated and set forth, he had "done" a bill and a gentleman at the same time.

CHAPTER XLII.

ILLUSTRATIVE, LIKE THE PRECEDING ONE, OF THE OLD PROVERB,
THAT ADVERSITY BRINGS A MAN ACQUAINTED WITH STRANGE
BED-FELLOWS. LIKEWISE CONTAINING MR. PICKWICK'S EXTRA-
ORDINARY AND STARTLING ANNOUNCEMENT TO MR. SAMUEL
WELLER.

WHEN Mr. Pickwick opened his eyes next morning, the first
object upon which they rested, was Samuel Weller, seated
upon a small black portmanteau, intently regarding, apparently
in a condition of profound abstraction, the stately figure of
the dashing Mr. Smangle: while Mr. Smangle himself, who
was already partially dressed, was seated on his bedstead,
occupied in the desperately hopeless attempt of staring Mr.
Weller out of countenance. We say desperately hopeless,
because Sam, with a comprehensive gaze which took in Mr.
Smangle's cap, feet, head, face, legs, and whiskers, all at
the same time, continued to look steadily on, with every
demonstration of lively satisfaction, but with no more regard
to Mr. Smangle's personal sentiments on the subject than he
would have displayed had he been inspecting a wooden statue,
or a straw-embowelled Guy Faux.

"Well; will you know me again?" said Mr. Smangle,
with a frown.

"I'd svear to you anyveres, sir," replied Sam, cheerfully.

"Don't be impertinent to a gentleman, sir," said Mr.
Smangle.

CLEAN CLOTHES.

"Not on no account," replied Sam. "If you'll tell me wen he wakes, I'll be upon the wery best extra-super behaviour!" This observation, having a remote tendency to imply that Mr. Smangle was no gentleman, kindled his ire.

"Mivins!" said Mr. Smangle, with a passionate air.

"What's the office?" replied that gentleman from his couch.

"Who the devil is this fellow?"

"'Gad," said Mr. Mivins, looking lazily out from under the bed-clothes, "I ought to ask *you* that. Hasn't he any business here?"

"No," replied Mr. Smangle.

"Then knock him down stairs, and tell him not to presume to get up till I come and kick him," rejoined Mr. Mivins; with this prompt advice that excellent gentleman again betook himself to slumber.

The conversation exhibiting these unequivocal symptoms of verging on the personal, Mr. Pickwick deemed it a fit point at which to interpose.

"Sam," said Mr. Pickwick.

"Sir," rejoined that gentleman.

"Has anything new occurred since last night?"

"Nothin' partickler, sir," replied Sam, glancing at Mr. Smangle's whiskers; "the late prewailance of a close and confined atmosphere has been rayther favourable to the growth of veeds, of an alarmin' and sangvinary natur; but vith that 'ere exception things is quiet enough."

"I shall get up," said Mr. Pickwick; "give me some clean things."

Whatever hostile intentions Mr. Smangle might have entertained, his thoughts were speedily diverted by the unpacking of the portmanteau; the contents of which, appeared to impress him at once with a most favourable opinion, not only of Mr. Pickwick, but of Sam also, who, he took an early opportunity of declaring in a tone of voice loud enough for that eccentric personage to overhear, was a regular

THE PICKWICK CLUB.

thorough-bred original, and consequently the very man after his own heart. As to Mr. Pickwick, the affection he conceived for him knew no limits.

"Now is there anything I can do for you, my dear sir?" said Smangle.

"Nothing that I am aware of, I am obliged to you," replied Mr. Pickwick.

"No linen that you want sent to the washerwoman's? I know a delightful washerwoman outside, that comes for my things twice a week; and, by Jove!—how devilish lucky!— this is the day she calls. Shall I put any of those little things up with mine? Don't say anything about the trouble. Confound and curse it! if one gentleman under a cloud, is not to put himself a little out of the way to assist another gentleman in the same condition, what's human nature?"

Thus spake Mr. Smangle, edging himself meanwhile as near as possible to the portmanteau, and beaming forth looks of the most fervent and disinterested friendship.

"There's nothing you want to give out for the man to brush, my dear creature, is there?" resumed Smangle.

"Nothin' whatever, my fine feller," rejoined Sam, taking the reply into his own mouth. "P'raps if vun of us wos to brush, without troubling the man, it 'ud be more agreeable for all parties, as the schoolmaster said wen the young gentleman objected to being flogged by the butler."

"And there's nothing that I can send in my little box to the washerwoman's, is there?" said Smangle, turning from Sam to Mr. Pickwick, with an air of some discomfiture.

"Nothin' whatever, sir," retorted Sam; "I'm afeerd the little box must be chock full o' your own as it is."

This speech was accompanied with such a very expressive look at that particular portion of Mr. Smangle's attire, by the appearance of which the skill of laundresses in getting up gentlemen's linen is generally tested, that he was fain to turn upon his heel, and, for the present at any rate, to give up all design on Mr. Pickwick's purse and wardrobe. He accordingly retired in dudgeon to the racket-ground, where he made a light and wholesome breakfast on a couple of the cigars which had been purchased on the previous night.

Mr. Mivins, who was no smoker, and whose account for small articles of chandlery had also reached down to the bottom of the slate, and been "carried over" to the other side, remained in bed, and, in his own words, "took it out in sleep."

After breakfasting in a small closet attached to the coffee-room, which bore the imposing title of the Snuggery; the temporary inmate of which, in consideration of a small additional charge, had the unspeakable advantage of overhearing all the conversation in the coffee-room aforesaid; and after dispatching Mr. Weller on some necessary errands, Mr. Pickwick repaired to the Lodge, to consult Mr. Roker concerning his future accommodation.

"Accommodation, eh?" said that gentleman, consulting a large book. "Plenty of that, Mr. Pickvick. Your chummage ticket will be on twenty-seven, in the third."

"Oh," said Mr. Pickwick. "My what, did you say?"

"Your chummage ticket," replied Mr. Roker; "you're up to that?"

"Not quite," replied Mr. Pickwick, with a smile.

"Why," said Mr. Roker, "it's as plain as Salisbury. You'll have a chummage ticket upon twenty-seven in the third, and them as is in the room will be your chums."

"Are there many of them?" inquired Mr. Pickwick, dubiously.

"Three," replied Mr. Roker.

Mr. Pickwick coughed.

"One of 'em's parson," said Mr. Roker, filling up a little piece of paper as he spoke; "another's a butcher."

"Eh?" exclaimed Mr. Pickwick.

"A butcher," repeated Mr. Roker, giving the nib of his pen a tap on the desk to cure it of a disinclination to mark. "What a thorough-paced goer he used to be sure-ly! You remember Tom Martin, Neddy?" said Roker, appealing to another man in the lodge, who was paring the mud off his shoes with a five-and-twenty bladed pocket knife.

"*I* should think so," replied the party addressed, with a strong emphasis on the personal pronoun.

"Bless my dear eyes!" said Mr. Roker, shaking his head slowly from side to side, and gazing abstractedly out of the grated windows before him, as if he were fondly recalling some peaceful scene of his early youth; "it seems but yesterday that he whopped the coal-heaver down Fox-under-the-Hill by the wharf there. I think I can see him now, a coming up the Strand between the two street-keepers, a little sobered by the bruising, with a patch o' winegar and brown paper over his right eyelid, and that 'ere lovely bulldog, as pinned the little boy arterwards, a following at his heels. What a rum thing Time is, ain't it, Neddy?"

The gentleman to whom these observations were addressed, who appeared of a taciturn and thoughtful cast, merely echoed the inquiry; Mr. Roker, shaking off the poetical and gloomy train of thought into which he had been betrayed, descended to the common business of life, and resumed his pen.

"Do you know what the third gentleman is?" inquired Mr. Pickwick, not very much gratified by this description of his future associates.

"What is that Simpson, Neddy?" said Mr. Roker, turning to his companion.

"What Simpson?" said Neddy.

"Why him in twenty-seven in the third, that this gentleman's going to be chummed on."

"Oh, him!" replied Neddy: "he's nothing exactly. He *was* a horse chaunter: he's a leg now."

"Ah, so I thought," rejoined Mr. Roker, closing the book, and placing the small piece of paper in Mr. Pickwick's hands. "That's the ticket, sir."

Very much perplexed by this summary disposition of his person, Mr. Pickwick walked back into the prison, revolving in his mind what he had better do. Convinced, however, that before he took any other steps it would be advisable to see, and hold personal converse with, the three gentlemen with whom it was proposed to quarter him, he made the best of his way to the third flight.

After groping about in the gallery for some time, attempting in the dim light to decipher the numbers on the different doors, he at length appealed to a potboy, who happened to be pursuing his morning occupation of gleaning for pewter.

"Which is twenty-seven, my good fellow?" said Mr. Pickwick.

"Five doors further on," replied the potboy. "There's the likeness of a man being hung, and smoking a pipe the while, chalked outside the door."

Guided by this direction, Mr. Pickwick proceeded slowly along the gallery until he encountered the "portrait of a gentleman," above described, upon whose countenance he tapped, with the knuckle of his fore-finger — gently at first, and then audibly. After repeating this process several times without effect, he ventured to open the door and peep in.

There was only one man in the room, and he was leaning out of window as far as he could without overbalancing himself, endeavouring, with great perseverance, to spit upon the crown of the hat of a personal friend on the parade below. As neither speaking, coughing, sneezing, knocking, nor any other ordinary mode of attracting attention, made this person aware of the presence of a visitor, Mr. Pickwick, after some delay, stepped up to the window, and pulled him gently by the coat-tail. The individual brought in his head and shoulders with great swiftness, and surveying Mr. Pickwick from head to foot, demanded in a surly tone what the— something beginning with a capital H—he wanted.

"I believe," said Mr. Pickwick, consulting his ticket, " I believe this is twenty-seven in the third?"

"Well?" replied the gentleman.

"I have come here in consequence of receiving this bit of paper," rejoined Mr. Pickwick.

"Hand it over," said the gentleman.

Mr. Pickwick complied.

"I think Roker might have chummed you somewhere else," said Mr. Simpson (for it was the leg), after a very discontented sort of a pause.

Mr. Pickwick thought so also; but, under all the circumstances, he considered it a matter of sound policy to be silent.

Mr. Simpson mused for a few moments after this, and then, thrusting his head out of the window, gave a shrill whistle, and pronounced some word aloud, several times. What the word was, Mr. Pickwick could not distinguish; but he rather inferred that it must be some nickname which distinguished Mr. Martin: from the fact of a great number of gentlemen on the ground below, immediately proceeding to cry "Butcher!" in imitation of the tone in which that useful class of society are wont, diurnally, to make their presence known at area railings.

Subsequent occurrences confirmed the accuracy of Mr. Pickwick's impression; for, in a few seconds, a gentleman, prematurely broad for his years: clothed in a professional blue jean frock, and top-boots with circular toes: entered the room nearly out of breath, closely followed by another gentleman in very shabby black, and a seal-skin cap. The latter gentleman, who fastened his coat all the way up to his chin by means of a pin and a button alternately, had a very coarse red face, and looked like a drunken chaplain; which, indeed, he was.

These two gentlemen having by turns perused Mr. Pickwick's billet, the one expressed his opinion that it was "a rig," and the other his conviction that it was "a go." Having recorded their feelings in these very intelligible terms, they looked at Mr. Pickwick and each other in awkward silence.

"It's an aggravating thing, just as we got the beds so snug," said the chaplain, looking at three dirty mattresses, each rolled up in a blanket: which occupied one corner of the room during the day, and formed a kind of slab, on which were placed an old cracked basin, ewer, and soap-dish, of common yellow earthenware, with a blue flower: "Very aggravating."

Mr. Martin expressed the same opinion in rather stronger terms; Mr. Simpson, after having let a variety of expletive adjectives loose upon society without any substantive to accompany them, tucked up his sleeves, and began to wash the greens for dinner.

While this was going on, Mr. Pickwick had been eyeing the room, which was filthily dirty, and smelt intolerably close. There was no vestige of either carpet, curtain, or blind. There was not even a closet in it. Unquestionably there were but few things to put away, if there had been one; but, however few in number, or small in individual amount, still, remnants of loaves and pieces of cheese, and damp towels, and scrags of meat, and articles of wearing apparel, and mutilated crockery, and bellows without nozzles, and toasting-forks without prongs, *do* present somewhat of an uncomfortable appearance when they are scattered about the floor of a small apartment, which is the common sitting and sleeping room of three idle men.

"I suppose this can be managed somehow," said the butcher, after a pretty long silence. "What will you take to go out?"

"I beg your pardon," replied Mr. Pickwick. "What did you say? I hardly understand you."

"What will you take to be paid out?" said the butcher. "The regular chummage is two-and-six. Will you take three bob?"

"—And a bender," suggested the clerical gentleman.

"Well, I don't mind that; it's only twopence a-piece more," said Mr. Martin.

"What do you say, now? We'll pay you out for three-and-sixpence a week. Come!"

223

"And stand a gallon of beer down," chimed in Mr. Simpson. "There!"

"And drink it on the spot," said the chaplain. "Now!"

"I really am so wholly ignorant of the rules of this place," returned Mr. Pickwick, "that I do not yet comprehend you. *Can* I live anywhere else? I thought I could not."

At this inquiry Mr. Martin looked, with a countenance of excessive surprise, at his two friends, and then each gentleman pointed with his right thumb over his left shoulder. This action, imperfectly described in words by the very feeble term of "over the left," when performed by any number of ladies or gentlemen who are accustomed to act in unison, has a very graceful and airy effect; its expression is one of light and playful sarcasm.

"*Can* you!" repeated Mr. Martin, with a smile of pity.

"Well, if I knew as little of life as that, I'd eat my hat and swallow the buckle whole," said the clerical gentleman.

"So would I," added the sporting one, solemnly.

After this introductory preface, the three chums informed Mr. Pickwick, in a breath, that money was, in the Fleet, just what money was out of it; that it would instantly procure him almost anything he desired; and that, supposing he had it, and had no objection to spend it, if he only signified his wish to have a room to himself, he might take possession of one, furnished and fitted to boot, in half an hour's time.

With this, the parties separated, very much to their common satisfaction: Mr. Pickwick once more retracing his steps to the lodge: and the three companions adjourning to the coffee-room, there to spend the five shillings which the clerical gentleman had, with admirable prudence and foresight, borrowed of him for the purpose.

"I knowed it!" said Mr. Roker, with a chuckle, when Mr. Pickwick stated the object with which he had returned. "Didn't I say so, Neddy?"

LODGING FOUND AT LAST.

The philosophical owner of the universal penknife, growled an affirmative.

"I knowed you'd want a room for yourself, bless you!" said Mr. Roker. "Let me see. You'll want some furnitur. You'll hire that of me, I suppose? That's the reg'lar thing."

"With great pleasure," replied Mr. Pickwick.

"There's a capital room up in the coffee-room flight, that belongs to a Chancery prisoner," said Mr. Roker. "It'll stand you in a pound a-week. I suppose you don't mind that?"

"Not at all," said Mr. Pickwick.

"Just step there with me," said Roker, taking up his hat with great alacrity; "the matter's settled in five minutes. Lord! why didn't you say at first that you was willing to come down handsome?"

The matter was soon arranged, as the turnkey had foretold. The Chancery prisoner had been there long enough to have lost friends, fortune, home, and happiness, and to have acquired the right of having a room to himself. As he laboured, however, under the inconvenience of often wanting a morsel of bread, he eagerly listened to Mr. Pickwick's proposal to rent the apartment, and readily covenanted and agreed to yield him up the sole and undisturbed possession thereof, in consideration of the weekly payment of twenty shillings; from which fund he furthermore contracted to pay out any person or persons that might be chummed upon it.

As they struck the bargain, Mr. Pickwick surveyed him with a painful interest. He was a tall, gaunt, cadaverous man, in an old great-coat and slippers: with sunken cheeks, and a restless, eager eye. His lips were bloodless, and his bones sharp and thin. God help him! the iron teeth of confinement and privation had been slowly filing him down for twenty years.

"And where will you live meanwhile, sir?" said Mr. Pickwick, as he laid the amount of the first week's rent, in advance, on the tottering table.

The man gathered up the money with a trembling hand, and replied that he didn't know yet; he must go and see where he could move his bed to.

"I am afraid, sir," said Mr. Pickwick, laying his hand gently and compassionately on his arm; "I am afraid you will have to live in some noisy crowded place. Now, pray, consider this room your own when you want quiet, or when any of your friends come to see you."

"Friends!" interposed the man, in a voice which rattled in his throat. "If I lay dead at the bottom of the deepest mine in the world; tight screwed down and soldered in my coffin; rotting in the dark and filthy ditch that drags its slime along, beneath the foundations of this prison; I could not be more forgotten or unheeded than I am here. I am a dead man; dead to society, without the pity they bestow on those whose souls have passed to judgment. Friends to see *me*! My God! I have sunk, from the prime of life into old age, in this place, and there is not one to raise his hand above my bed when I lie dead upon it, and say, 'It is a blessing he is gone!'"

The excitement, which had cast an unwonted light over the man's face, while he spoke, subsided as he concluded; and, pressing his withered hands together in a hasty and disordered manner, he shuffled from the room.

"Rides rather rusty," said Mr. Roker, with a smile. "Ah! they're like the elephants. They feel it now and then, and it makes 'em wild!"

Having made this deeply-sympathising remark, Mr. Roker entered upon his arrangements with such expedition, that in a short time the room was furnished with a carpet, six chairs, a table, a sofa bedstead, a tea-kettle, and various small articles, on hire, at the very reasonable rate of seven-and-twenty shillings and sixpence per week.

"Now, is there anything more we can do for you?" inquired Mr. Roker, looking round with great satisfaction, and gaily chinking the first week's hire in his closed fist.

THE POOR SIDE.

"Why, yes," said Mr. Pickwick, who had been musing deeply for some time. "Are there any people here, who run on errands, and so forth?"

"Outside, do you mean?" inquired Mr. Roker.

"Yes. I mean who are able to go outside. Not prisoners."

"Yes, there is," said Roker. "There's an unfortunate devil, who has got a friend on the poor side, that's glad to do anything of that sort. He's been running odd jobs, and that, for the last two months. Shall I send him?"

"If you please," rejoined Mr. Pickwick. "Stay; no. The poor side, you say? I should like to see it. I'll go to him myself."

The poor side of a debtor's prison, is, as its name imports, that in which the most miserable and abject class of debtors are confined. A prisoner having declared upon the poor side, pays neither rent nor chummage. His fees, upon entering and leaving the gaol, are reduced in amount, and he becomes entitled to a share of some small quantities of food: to provide which, a few charitable persons have, from time to time, left trifling legacies in their wills. Most of our readers will remember, that, until within a very few years past, there was a kind of iron cage in the wall of the Fleet Prison, within which was posted some man of hungry looks, who, from time to time, rattled a money-box, and exclaimed in a mournful voice, "Pray, remember the poor debtors; pray, remember the poor debtors." The receipts of this box, when there were any, were divided among the poor prisoners; and the men on the poor side relieved each other in this degrading office.

Although this custom has been abolished, and the cage is now boarded up, the miserable and destitute condition of these unhappy persons remains the same. We no longer suffer them to appeal at the prison gates to the charity and compassion of the passers by; but we still leave unblotted in the leaves of our statute book, for the reverence and admiration

227

of succeeding ages, the just and wholesome law which declares that the sturdy felon shall be fed and clothed, and that the penniless debtor shall be left to die of starvation and nakedness. This is no fiction. Not a week passes over our heads, but, in every one of our prisons for debt, some of these men must inevitably expire in the slow agonies of want, if they were not relieved by their fellow-prisoners.

Turning these things in his mind, as he mounted the narrow staircase at the foot of which Roker had left him, Mr. Pickwick gradually worked himself to the boiling-over point; and so excited was he with his reflections on this subject, that he had burst into the room to which he had been directed, before he had any distinct recollection, either of the place in which he was, or of the object of his visit.

The general aspect of the room recalled him to himself at once; but he had no sooner cast his eyes on the figure of a man who was brooding over the dusty fire, than, letting his hat fall on the floor, he stood perfectly fixed, and immoveable, with astonishment.

Yes; in tattered garments, and without a coat; his common calico shirt, yellow and in rags; his hair hanging over his face; his features changed with suffering, and pinched with famine; there sat Mr. Alfred Jingle: his head resting on his hand, his eyes fixed upon the fire, and his whole appearance denoting misery and dejection!

Near him, leaning listlessly against the wall, stood a strong-built countryman, flicking with a worn-out hunting-whip the top-boot that adorned his right foot: his left being (for he dressed by easy stages) thrust into an old slipper. Horses, dogs, and drink, had brought him there, pell-mell. There was a rusty spur on the solitary boot, which he occasionally jerked into the empty air, at the same time giving the boot a smart blow, and muttering some of the sounds by which a sportsman encourages his horse. He was riding, in imagination, some desperate steeple-chase at that moment. Poor wretch! He never rode a match on the swiftest animal in his costly stud,

Discovery of Jingle in the Fleet

with half the speed at which he had torn along the course that ended in the Fleet.

On the opposite side of the room an old man was seated on a small wooden box, with his eyes rivetted on the floor, and his face settled into an expression of the deepest and most hopeless despair. A young girl—his little grand-daughter —was hanging about him : endeavouring, with a thousand childish devices, to engage his attention ; but the old man neither saw nor heard her. The voice that had been music to him, and the eyes that had been light, fell coldly on his senses. His limbs were shaking with disease, and the palsy had fastened on his mind.

There were two or three other men in the room, congregated in a little knot, and noisily talking among themselves. There was a lean and haggard woman, too—a prisoner's wife—who was watering, with great solicitude, the wretched stump of a dried-up, withered plant, which, it was plain to see, could never send forth a green leaf again ;—too true an emblem, perhaps, of the office she had come there to discharge.

Such were the objects which presented themselves to Mr. Pickwick's view, as he looked round him in amazement. The noise of some one stumbling hastily into the room, roused him. Turning his eyes towards the door, they encountered the new comer ; and in him, through his rags and dirt, he recognised the familiar features of Mr. Job Trotter.

" Mr. Pickwick ! " exclaimed Job aloud.

" Eh ? " said Jingle, starting from his seat. " Mr. ——— ! So it is—queer place—strange thing—serves me right—very." Mr. Jingle thrust his hands into the place where his trousers pockets used to be, and, dropping his chin upon his breast, sank back into his chair.

Mr. Pickwick was affected ; the two men looked so very miserable. The sharp involuntary glance Jingle had cast at a small piece of raw loin of mutton, which Job had brought in with him, said more of their reduced state than two hours' explanation could have done. Mr. Pickwick looked mildly at Jingle, and said:

"I should like to speak to you in private. Will you step out for an instant?"

"Certainly," said Jingle, rising hastily. "Can't step far—no danger of over-walking yourself here—Spike park—grounds pretty—romantic, but not extensive—open for public inspection—family always in town—housekeeper desperately careful —very."

"You have forgotten your coat," said Mr. Pickwick, as they walked out to the staircase, and closed the door after them.

"Eh?" said Jingle. "Spout—dear relation—uncle Tom —couldn't help it—must eat, you know. Wants of nature —and all that."

"What do you mean?"

"Gone, my dear sir—last coat—can't help it. Lived on a pair of boots—whole fortnight. Silk umbrella—ivory handle —week—fact—honour—ask Job—knows it."

"Lived for three weeks upon a pair of boots, and a silk umbrella with an ivory handle!" exclaimed Mr. Pickwick, who had only heard of such things in shipwrecks, or read of them in Constable's Miscellany.

"True," said Jingle, nodding his head. "Pawnbroker's shop—duplicates here—small sums—mere nothing—all rascals."

"Oh," said Mr. Pickwick, much relieved by this explanation; "I understand you. You have pawned your wardrobe."

"Everything—Job's too—all shirts gone—never mind— saves washing. Nothing soon—lie in bed—starve—die— Inquest—little bone-house—poor prisoner—common necessaries —hush it up—gentlemen of the jury—warden's tradesmen— keep it snug—natural death—coroner's order—workhouse funeral—serve him right—all over—drop the curtain."

Jingle delivered this singular summary of his prospects in life, with his accustomed volubility, and with various twitches of the countenance to counterfeit smiles. Mr. Pickwick easily perceived that his recklessness was assumed, and looking him full, but not unkindly, in the face, saw that his eyes were moist with tears.

" Good fellow," said Jingle, pressing his hand, and turning his head away. " Ungrateful dog—boyish to cry—can't help it—bad fever—weak—ill—hungry. Deserved it all—but suffered much—very." Wholly unable to keep up appearances any longer, and perhaps rendered worse by the effort he had made, the dejected stroller sat down on the stairs, and, covering his face with his hands, sobbed like a child.

" Come, come," said Mr. Pickwick, with considerable emotion, " we'll see what can be done, when I know all about the matter. Here, Job; where is that fellow ? "

" Here, sir," replied Job, presenting himself on the staircase. We have described him, by-the-bye, as having deeply-sunken eyes, in the best of times. In his present state of want and distress, he looked as if those features had gone out of town altogether.

" Here, sir," cried Job.

" Come here, sir," said Mr. Pickwick, trying to look stern, with four large tears running down his waistcoat. " Take that, sir."

Take what ? In the ordinary acceptation of such language, it should have been a blow. As the world runs, it ought to have been a sound, hearty cuff; for Mr. Pickwick had been duped, deceived, and wronged by the destitute outcast who was now wholly in his power. Must we tell the truth ? It was something from Mr. Pickwick's waistcoat-pocket, which chinked as it was given into Job's hand, and the giving of which, somehow or other imparted a sparkle to the eye, and a swelling to the heart, of our excellent old friend, as he hurried away.

Sam had returned when Mr. Pickwick reached his own room, and was inspecting the arrangements that had been made for his comfort, with a kind of grim satisfaction which was very pleasant to look upon. Having a decided objection to his master's being there at all, Mr. Weller appeared to consider it a high moral duty not to appear too much pleased with anything that was done, said, suggested, or proposed.

"Well, Sam," said Mr. Pickwick.

"Well, sir," replied Mr. Weller.

"Pretty comfortable now, eh, Sam?"

"Pretty vell, sir," responded Sam, looking round him in a disparaging manner.

"Have you seen Mr. Tupman and our other friends?"

"Yes, I *have* seen 'em, sir, and they're a comin' to-morrow, and wos wery much surprised to hear they warn't to come to-day," replied Sam.

"You have brought the things I wanted?"

Mr. Weller in reply pointed to various packages which he had arranged, as neatly as he could, in a corner of the room.

"Very well, Sam," said Mr. Pickwick, after a little hesitation; "listen to what I am going to say, Sam."

"Cert'nly, sir," rejoined Mr. Weller, "fire away, sir."

"I have felt from the first, Sam," said Mr. Pickwick, with much solemnity, "that this is not the place to bring a young man to."

"Nor an old 'un neither, sir," observed Mr. Weller.

"You're quite right, Sam," said Mr. Pickwick; "but old men may come here, through their own heedlessness and unsuspicion: and young men may be brought here by the selfishness of those they serve. It is better for those young men, in every point of view, that they should not remain here. Do you understand me, Sam?"

"Vy no, sir, I do NOT," replied Mr. Weller, doggedly.

"Try, Sam," said Mr. Pickwick.

"Vell, sir," rejoined Sam, after a short pause, "I think I see your drift; and if I do see your drift, it's my 'pinion that you 're a comin' it a great deal too strong, as the mail-coachman said to the snow-storm, ven it overtook him."

"I see you comprehend me, Sam," said Mr. Pickwick.

"Independently of my wish that you should not be idling about a place like this, for years to come, I feel that for a debtor in the Fleet to be attended by his man-servant is a monstrous absurdity. Sam," said Mr. Pickwick, "for a time, you must leave me."

"Oh, for a time, eh, sir?" rejoined Mr. Weller, rather sarcastically.

"Yes, for the time that I remain here," said Mr. Pickwick. "Your wages I shall continue to pay. Any one of my three friends will be happy to take you, were it only out of respect to me. And if I ever do leave this place, Sam," added Mr. Pickwick, with assumed cheerfulness: "if I do, I pledge you my word that you shall return to me instantly."

"Now I'll tell you wot it is, sir," said Mr. Weller, in a grave and solemn voice, "This here sort o' thing won't do at all, so don't let's hear no more about it."

"I am serious, and resolved, Sam," said Mr. Pickwick.

"You air, air you, sir?" inquired Mr. Weller, firmly. "Wery good, sir. Then so am I."

Thus speaking, Mr. Weller fixed his hat on his head with great precision, and abruptly left the room.

"Sam!" cried Mr. Pickwick, calling after him, "Sam! Here!"

But the long gallery ceased to re-echo the sound of footsteps. Sam Weller was gone.

233

CHAPTER XLIII.

In a lofty room, ill-lighted and worse ventilated, situate in Portugal Street, Lincoln's Inn Fields, there sit nearly the whole year round, one, two, three, or four gentlemen in wigs, as the case may be, with little writing desks before them, constructed after the fashion of those used by the judges of the land, barring the French polish. There is a box of barristers on their right hand; there is an inclosure of insolvent debtors on their left; and there is an inclined plane of most especially dirty faces in their front. These gentlemen are the Commissioners of the Insolvent Court, and the place in which they sit, is the Insolvent Court itself.

It is, and has been, time out of mind, the remarkable fate of this Court to be, somehow or other, held and understood, by the general consent of all the destitute shabby-genteel people in London, as their common resort, and place of daily refuge. It is always full. The steams of beer and spirits perpetually ascend to the ceiling, and, being condensed by the heat, roll down the walls like rain; there are more old suits of clothes in it at one time, than will be offered for sale in all Houndsditch in a twelvemonth; more unwashed skins and grizzly beards than all the pumps and shaving-shops between Tyburn and Whitechapel could render decent, between sunrise and sunset.

It must not be supposed that any of these people have the

least shadow of business in, or the remotest connection with, the place they so indefatigably attend. If they had, it would be no matter of surprise, and the singularity of the thing would cease. Some of them sleep during the greater part of the sitting; others carry small portable dinners wrapped in pocket-handkerchiefs or sticking out of their worn-out pockets, and munch and listen with equal relish; but no one among them was ever known to have the slightest personal interest in any case that was ever brought forward. Whatever they do, there they sit from the first moment to the last. When it is heavy rainy weather, they all come in, wet through; and at such times the vapours of the Court are like those of a fungus-pit.

A casual visitor might suppose this place to be a Temple dedicated to the Genius of Seediness. There is not a messenger or process-server attached to it, who wears a coat that was made for him; not a tolerably fresh, or wholesome-looking man in the whole establishment, except a little white-headed apple-faced tipstaff, and even he, like an ill-conditioned cherry preserved in brandy, seems to have artificially dried and withered up into a state of preservation to which he can lay no natural claim. The very barristers' wigs are ill-powdered, and their curls lack crispness.

But the attorneys, who sit at a large bare table below the Commissioners, are, after all, the greatest curiosities. The professional establishment of the more opulent of these gentlemen, consists of a blue bag and a boy: generally a youth of the Jewish persuasion. They have no fixed offices, their legal business being transacted in the parlours of public-houses, or the yards of prisons: whither they repair in crowds, and canvass for customers after the manner of omnibus cads. They are of a greasy and mildewed appearance; and if they can be said to have any vices at all, perhaps drinking and cheating are the most conspicuous among them. Their residences are usually on the outskirts of "the Rules," chiefly lying within a circle of one mile from the obelisk in St.

George's Fields. Their looks are not prepossessing, and their manners are peculiar.

Mr. Solomon Pell, one of this learned body, was a fat flabby pale man, in a surtout which looked green one minute and brown the next: with a velvet collar of the same cameleon tints. His forehead was narrow, his face wide, his head large, and his nose all on one side, as if Nature, indignant with the propensities she observed in him in his birth, had given it an angry tweak which it had never recovered. Being short-necked and asthmatic, however, he respired principally through this feature; so, perhaps, what it wanted in ornament, it made up in usefulness.

"I'm sure to bring him through it," said Mr. Pell.

"Are you though?" replied the person to whom the assurance was pledged.

"Certain sure," replied Pell; "but if he'd gone to any irregular practitioner, mind you, I wouldn't have answered for the consequences."

"Ah!" said the other, with open mouth.

"No, that I wouldn't," said Mr. Pell; and he pursed up his lips, frowned, and shook his head mysteriously.

Now, the place where this discourse occurred, was the public-house just opposite to the Insolvent Court; and the person with whom it was held, was no other than the elder Mr. Weller, who had come there, to comfort and console a friend, whose petition to be discharged under the act, was to be that day heard, and whose attorney he was at that moment consulting.

"And vere is George?" inquired the old gentleman.

Mr. Pell jerked his head in the direction of a back parlour: whither Mr. Weller at once repairing, was immediately greeted in the warmest and most flattering manner by some half-dozen of his professional brethren, in token of their gratification at his arrival. The insolvent gentleman, who had contracted a speculative but imprudent passion for horsing long stages, which had led to his present embarrassments, looked extremely well, and was soothing the excitement of his feelings with shrimps and porter.

The salutation between Mr. Weller and his friends was strictly confined to the freemasonry of the craft; consisting of a jerking round of the right wrist, and a tossing of the little finger into the air at the same time. We once knew two famous coachmen (they are dead now, poor fellows) who were twins, and between whom an unaffected and devoted attachment existed. They passed each other on the Dover road, every day, for twenty-four years, never exchanging any other greeting than this; and yet, when one died, the other pined away, and soon afterwards followed him!

"Vell, George," said Mr. Weller, senior, taking off his upper coat, and seating himself with his accustomed gravity. "How is it? All right behind, and full inside?"

"All right, old feller," replied the embarrassed gentleman.

"Is the grey mare made over to any body?" inquired Mr. Weller, anxiously.

George nodded in the affirmative.

"Vell, that's all right," said Mr. Weller. "Coach taken care on, also?"

"Con-signed in a safe quarter," replied George, wringing the heads off half-a-dozen shrimps, and swallowing them without any more ado.

"Wery good, wery good," said Mr. Weller. "Alvays see to the drag ven you go down hill. Is the vay-bill all clear and straight for'erd?"

"The schedule, sir," said Pell, guessing at Mr. Weller's meaning, "the schedule is as plain and satisfactory as pen and ink can make it."

Mr. Weller nodded in a manner which bespoke his inward approval of these arrangements; and then, turning to Mr. Pell, said, pointing to his friend George:

"Ven do you take his cloths off?"

"Why," replied Mr. Pell, "he stands third on the opposed list, and I should think it would be his turn in about half an hour. I told my clerk to come over and tell us when there was a chance."

Mr. Weller surveyed the attorney from head to foot with great admiration, and said emphatically:

" And what'll you take, sir ? "

" Why, really," replied Mr. Pell, " you're very——. Upon my word and honour, I'm not in the habit of——. It's so very early in the morning, that, actually, I am almost——. Well, you may bring me three penn'orth of rum, my dear."

The officiating damsel, who had anticipated the order before it was given, set the glass of spirits before Pell, and retired.

" Gentlemen," said Mr. Pell, looking round upon the company, " Success to your friend! I don't like to boast, gentlemen; it's not my way; but I can't help saying, that, if your friend hadn't been fortunate enough to fall into hands that——but I won't say what I was going to say. Gentlemen, my service to you." Having emptied the glass in a twinkling, Mr. Pell smacked his lips, and looked complacently round on the assembled coachmen, who evidently regarded him as a species of divinity.

" Let me see," said the legal authority. " What was I a-saying, gentlemen ? "

" I think you was remarkin' as you wouldn't have no objection to another o' the same, sir," said Mr. Weller, with grave facetiousness.

" Ha, ha ! " laughed Mr. Pell. " Not bad, not bad. A professional man, too! At this time of the morning, it would be rather too good a——. Well, I don't know, my dear— you *may* do that again, if you please. Hem ! "

This last sound was a solemn and dignified cough, in which Mr. Pell observing an indecent tendency to mirth in some of his auditors, considered it due to himself to indulge.

" The late Lord Chancellor, gentlemen, was very fond of me," said Mr. Pell.

" And wery creditable in him, too," interposed Mr. Weller.

"Hear, hear," assented Mr. Pell's client. "Why shouldn't he be?"

"Ah! Why, indeed!" said a very red-faced man, who had said nothing yet, and who looked extremely unlikely to say anything more. "Why shouldn't he?"

A murmur of assent ran through the company.

"I remember, gentlemen," said Mr. Pell, "dining with him on one occasion;—there was only us two, but every thing as splendid as if twenty people had been expected—the great seal on a dumb-waiter at his right hand, and a man in a bag-wig and suit of armour guarding the mace with a drawn sword and silk stockings—which is perpetually done, gentlemen, night and day; when he said, 'Pell,' he said, 'no false delicacy, Pell. You're a man of talent; you can get any body through the Insolvent Court, Pell; and your country should be proud of you.' Those were his very words. 'My Lord,' I said, 'you flatter me.'—'Pell,' he said, 'if I do, I'm damned.'"

"Did he say that?" inquired Mr. Weller.

"He did," replied Pell.

"Vell, then," said Mr. Weller, "I say Parliament ought to ha' took it up; and if he'd been a poor man, they *would* ha' done it."

"But, my dear friend," argued Mr. Pell, "it was in confidence."

"In what?" said Mr. Weller.

"In confidence."

"Oh! wery good," replied Mr. Weller, after a little reflection. "If he damned his-self in confidence, o' course that was another thing."

"Of course it was," said Mr. Pell. "The distinction's obvious, you will perceive."

"Alters the case entirely," said Mr. Weller. "Go on, sir."

"No, I will not go on, sir," said Mr. Pell, in a low and serious tone. "You have reminded me, sir, that this conversation was private—private and confidential, gentlemen. Gentlemen, I am a professional man. It may be that I am a good deal looked up to, in my profession—it may be that I am not. Most people know. I say nothing. Observations have already been made, in this room, injurious to the reputation of my noble friend. You will excuse me, gentlemen; I was imprudent. I feel that I have no right to mention this matter without his concurrence. Thank you, sir; thank you." Thus delivering himself, Mr. Pell thrust his hands into his pockets, and, frowning grimly around, rattled three-halfpence with terrible determination.

This virtuous resolution had scarcely been formed, when the boy and the blue bag, who were inseparable companions, rushed violently into the room, and said (at least the boy did, for the blue bag took no part in the announcement) that the case was coming on directly. The intelligence was no sooner received than the whole party hurried across the street, and began to fight their way into Court—a preparatory ceremony, which has been calculated to occupy, in ordinary cases, from twenty-five minutes to thirty.

Mr. Weller, being stout, cast himself at once into the crowd, with the desperate hope of ultimately turning up in some place which would suit him. His success was not quite equal to his expectations; for having neglected to take his hat off, it was knocked over his eyes by some unseen person, upon whose toes he had alighted with considerable force. Apparently, this individual regretted his impetuosity immediately afterwards; for, muttering an indistinct exclamation of surprise, he dragged the old man out into the hall, and, after a violent struggle, released his head and face.

"Samivel!" exclaimed Mr. Weller, when he was thus enabled to behold his rescuer.

Sam nodded.

"You're a dutiful and affectionate little boy, you are, ain't you?" said Mr. Weller, "to come a bonnetin' your father in his old age?"

"How should I know who you wos?" responded the son. "Do you s'pose I wos to tell you by the weight o' your foot?"

"Vell, that's wery true, Sammy," replied Mr. Weller, mollified at once; "but wot are you a doin' on here? Your gov'nor can't do no good here, Sammy. They won't pass that werdick, they won't pass it, Sammy." And Mr. Weller shook his head, with legal solemnity.

"Wot a perwerse old file it is!" exclaimed Sam, "alvays a goin' on about werdicks and alleybis, and that. Who said anything about the werdick?"

Mr. Weller made no reply, but once more shook his head most learnedly.

"Leave off rattlin' that 'ere nob o' yourn, if you don't want it to come off the springs altogether," said Sam impatiently, "and behave reasonable. I vent all the vay down to the Markis o' Granby, arter you, last night."

"Did you see the Marchioness o' Granby, Sammy?" inquired Mr. Weller, with a sigh.

"Yes, I did," replied Sam.

"How wos the dear creetur a lookin'?"

"Wery queer," said Sam. "I think she's a injurin' herself gradivally vith too much o' that 'ere pine-apple rum, and other strong medicines o' the same natur."

"You don't mean that, Sammy?" said the senior, earnestly.

"I do, indeed," replied the junior.

Mr. Weller seized his son's hand, clasped it, and let it fall. There was an expression on his countenance in doing so—not of dismay or apprehension, but partaking more of the sweet and gentle character of hope. A gleam of resignation, and even of cheerfulness, passed over his face too, as he slowly said, "I ain't quite certain, Sammy; I wouldn't like to say I wos altogether positive, in case of any subsekent disappintment, but I rayther think, my boy, I rayther think, that the shepherd's got the liver complaint!"

"Does he look bad?" inquired Sam.

"He's uncommon pale," replied his father, "'cept about the nose, wich is redder than ever. His appetite is wery so-so, but he imbibes wunderful."

Some thoughts of the rum appeared to obtrude themselves on Mr. Weller's mind, as he said this; for he looked gloomy and thoughtful; but he very shortly recovered, as was testified by a perfect alphabet of winks, in which he was only wont to indulge when particularly pleased.

"Vell, now," said Sam, "about my affair. Just open them ears o' yourn, and don't say nothin' till I've done." With this brief preface, Sam related, as succinctly as he could, the last memorable conversation he had had with Mr. Pickwick.

"Stop there by himself, poor creetur!" exclaimed the elder Mr. Weller, "without nobody to take his part! It can't be done, Samivel, it can't be done."

"O' course it can't," asserted Sam: "I know'd that, afore I came."

"Wy, they'll eat him up alive, Sammy," exclaimed Mr. Weller.

Sam nodded his concurrence in the opinion.

"He goes in rayther raw, Sammy," said Mr. Weller metaphorically, "and he'll come out, done so ex-ceedin' brown, that his most familiar friends won't know him. Roast pigeon's nothin' to it, Sammy."

Again Sam Weller nodded.

"It oughtn't to be, Samivel," said Mr. Weller, gravely.

"It mustn't be," said Sam.

"Cert'nly not," said Mr. Weller.

"Vell now," said Sam, "you've been a prophecyin' away, wery fine, like a red-faced Nixon as the sixpenny books gives picters on."

"Who wos he, Sammy?" inquired Mr. Weller.

"Never mind who he was," retorted Sam; "he warn't a coachman; that's enough for you."

"I know'd a ostler o' that name," said Mr. Weller, musing.

"It warn't him," said Sam. "This here gen'l'm'n was a prophet."

"Wot's a prophet?" inquired Mr. Weller, looking sternly on his son.

MR. WELLER BECOMES A BORROWER.

"Wy, a man as tells what's a goin' to happen," replied Sam.

"I wish I'd know'd him, Sammy," said Mr. Weller. "P'raps he might ha' throw'd a small light on that 'ere liver complaint as we wos a speakin' on, just now. Hows'ever, if he's dead, and ain't left the bisness to nobody, there's an end on it. Go on, Sammy," said Mr. Weller, with a sigh.

"Well," said Sam, "you've been a prophecyin' avay, about wot'll happen to the gov'nor if he's left alone. Don't you see any vay o' takin' care on him?"

"No, I don't, Sammy," said Mr. Weller, with a reflective visage.

"No vay at all?" inquired Sam.

"No vay," said Mr. Weller, "unless"—and a gleam of intelligence lighted up his countenance as he sunk his voice to a whisper, and applied his mouth to the ear of his offspring: "unless it is getting him out in a turn-up bedstead, unbeknown to the turnkeys, Sammy, or dressin' him up like a old 'ooman vith a green wail."

Sam Weller received both of these suggestions with unexpected contempt, and again propounded his question.

"No," said the old gentleman; "if he von't let you stop there, I see no vay at all. It's no thoroughfare, Sammy, no thoroughfare."

"Well, then, I'll tell you wot it is," said Sam, "I'll trouble you for the loan of five-and-twenty pound."

"Wot good 'ull that do?" inquired Mr. Weller.

"Never mind," replied Sam. "P'raps you may ask for it, five minits artervards; p'raps I may say I von't pay, and cut up rough. You von't think o' arrestin' your own son for the money, and sendin' him off to the Fleet, will you, you unnat'ral wagabone?"

At this reply of Sam's, the father and son exchanged a complete code of telegraphic nods and gestures, after which, the elder Mr. Weller sat himself down on a stone step, and laughed till he was purple.

"Wot a old image it is!" exclaimed Sam, indignant at this

loss of time. "What are you a settin' down there for con-wertin' your face into a street-door knocker, wen there's so much to be done. Where's the money?"

"In the boot, Sammy, in the boot," replied Mr. Weller, composing his features. "Hold my hat, Sammy."

Having divested himself of this incumbrance, Mr. Weller gave his body a sudden wrench to one side, and, by a dexterous twist, contrived to get his right hand into a most capacious pocket, from whence, after a great deal of panting and exertion, he extricated a pocket-book of the large octavo size, fastened by a huge leathern strap. From this ledger he drew forth a couple of whip-lashes, three or four buckles, a little sample-bag of corn, and finally a small roll of very dirty bank-notes: from which he selected the required amount, which he handed over to Sam.

"And now, Sammy," said the old gentleman, when the whip-lashes, and the buckles, and the samples, had been all put back, and the book once more deposited at the bottom of the same pocket, "Now, Sammy, I know a gen'l'm'n here, as'll do the rest o' the bisness for us, in no time—a limb o' the law, Sammy, as has got brains like the frogs, dispersed all over his body, and reachin' to the wery tips of his fingers; a friend of the Lord Chancellorship's, Sammy, who'd only have to tell him what he wanted, and he'd lock you up for life, if that wos all."

"I say," said Sam, "none o' that."

"None o' wot?" inquired Mr. Weller.

"Wy, none o' them unconstitootional ways o' doing it," retorted Sam. "The have-his-carcase, next to the perpetual motion, is vun of the blessedest things as wos ever made. I've read that 'ere in the newspapers, wery of'en."

"Well, wot's that got to do vith it?" inquired Mr. Weller.

"Just this here," said Sam, "that I'll patronise the inwention, and go in, that vay. No visperin's to the Chancellorship, I don't like the notion. It mayn't be altogether safe, vith reference to gettin' out agin."

AFFIDAVIT OF DEBT.

Deferring to his son's feeling upon this point, Mr. Weller at once sought the erudite Solomon Pell, and acquainted him with his desire to issue a writ, instantly, for the sum of twenty-five pounds, and costs of process; to be executed without delay upon the body of one Samuel Weller; the charges thereby incurred, to be paid in advance to Solomon Pell.

The attorney was in high glee, for the embarrassed coach-horser was ordered to be discharged forthwith. He highly approved of Sam's attachment to his master; declared that it strongly reminded him of his own feelings of devotion to his friend, the Chancellor; and at once led the elder Mr. Weller down to the Temple, to swear the affidavit of debt, which the boy, with the assistance of the blue bag, had drawn up on the spot.

Meanwhile, Sam, having been formally introduced to the whitewashed gentleman and his friends, as the offspring of Mr. Weller, of the Belle Savage, was treated with marked distinction, and invited to regale himself with them in honour of the occasion; an invitation which he was by no means backward in accepting.

The mirth of gentlemen of this class is of a grave and quiet character, usually; but the present instance was one of peculiar festivity, and they relaxed in proportion. After some rather tumultuous toasting of the Chief Commissioner and Mr. Solomon Pell, who had that day displayed such transcendent abilities, a mottled-faced gentleman in a blue shawl proposed that somebody should sing a song. The obvious suggestion was, that the mottled-faced gentleman, being anxious for a song, should sing it himself; but this the mottled-faced gentleman sturdily, and somewhat offensively, declined to do. Upon which, as is not unusual in such cases, a rather angry colloquy ensued.

"Gentlemen," said the coach-horser, "rather than disturb the harmony of this delightful occasion, perhaps Mr. Samuel Weller will oblige the company."

"Raly, gentlemen," said Sam, "I'm not wery much in the habit o' singin' without the instrument; but anythin' for a quiet life, as the man said wen he took the sitivation at the lighthouse."

With this prelude, Mr. Samuel Weller burst at once into the following wild and beautiful legend, which, under the impression that it is not generally known, we take the liberty of quoting. We would beg to call particular attention to the monosyllable at the end of the second and fourth lines, which not only enables the singer to take breath at those points, but greatly assists the metre.

ROMANCE.

I.

Bold Turpin vunce, on Hounslow Heath,
His bold mare Bess bestrode—er;
Ven there he see'd the Bishop's coach
A-coming along the road—er.
So he gallops close to the 'orse's legs,
And he claps his head vithin;
And the Bishop says, "Sure as eggs is eggs,
This here's the bold Turpin!"

CHORUS.

And the Bishop says, "Sure as eggs is eggs,
This here's the bold Turpin!"

II.

Says Turpin, "You shall eat your words,
With a sarse of leaden bul-let;"
So he puts a pistol to his mouth,
And he fires it down his gul-let.
The coachman he not likin' the job,
Set off at a full gal-lop,
But Dick put a couple of balls in his nob,
And perwailed on him to stop.

CHORUS (sarcastically).

But Dick put a couple of balls in his nob,
And perwailed on him to stop.

"I maintain that that 'ere song's personal to the cloth," said the mottled-faced gentleman, interrupting it at this point. "I demand the name o' that coachman."

"Nobody know'd," replied Sam. "He hadn't got his card in his pocket."

AN INEXORABLE CREDITOR.

"I object to the introduction o' politics," said the mottle-faced gentleman. "I submit that, in the present company, that 'ere song's political; and, wot's much the same, that it ain't true. I say that that coachman did *not* run away; but that he died game—game as pheasants; and I won't hear nothin' said to the contrairey."

As the mottle-faced gentleman spoke with great energy and determination : and as the opinions of the company seemed divided on the subject: it threatened to give rise to fresh altercation, when Mr. Weller and Mr. Pell most opportunely arrived.

"All right, Sammy," said Mr. Weller.

"The officer will be here at four o'clock," said Mr. Pell. "I suppose you won't run away meanwhile, eh? Ha! ha!"

"P'raps my cruel pa 'ull relent afore then," replied Sam, with a broad grin.

"Not I," said the elder Mr. Weller.

"Do," said Sam.

"Not on no account," replied the inexorable creditor.

"I'll give bills for the amount, at sixpence a month," said Sam.

"I won't take 'em," said Mr. Weller.

"Ha, ha, ha! very good, very good," said Mr. Solomon Pell, who was making out his little bill of costs; "a very amusing incident indeed! Benjamin, copy that." And Mr. Pell smiled again, as he called Mr. Weller's attention to the amount.

"Thank you, thank you," said the professional gentleman, taking up another of the greasy notes as Mr. Weller took it from the pocket-book. "Three ten and one ten is five. Much obliged to you, Mr. Weller. Your son is a most deserving young man, very much so indeed, sir. It's a very pleasant trait in a young man's character, very much so," added Mr. Pell, smiling smoothly round, as he buttoned up the money.

"Wot a game it is!" said the elder Mr. Weller, with a chuckle. "A reg'lar prodigy son!"

"Prodigal, prodigal son, sir," suggested Mr. Pell, mildly.

"Never mind, sir," said Mr. Weller, with dignity. "I know wot's o'clock, sir. Wen I don't, I'll ask you, sir."

By the time the officer arrived, Sam had made himself so extremely popular, that the congregated gentlemen determined to see him to prison in a body. So, off they set; the plaintiff and defendant walking arm-in-arm; the officer in front; and eight stout coachmen bringing up the rear. At Serjeant's Inn Coffee-house the whole party halted to refresh, and, the legal arrangements being completed, the procession moved on again.

Some little commotion was occasioned in Fleet Street, by the pleasantry of the eight gentlemen in the flank, who persevered in walking four abreast; it was also found necessary to leave the mottle-faced gentleman behind, to fight a ticket-porter, it being arranged that his friends should call for him as they came back. Nothing but these little incidents occurred on the way. When they reached the gate of the Fleet, the cavalcade, taking the time from the plaintiff, gave three tremendous cheers for the defendant, and, after having shaken hands all round, left him.

Sam, having been formally delivered into the warden's custody, to the intense astonishment of Roker, and to the evident emotion of even the phlegmatic Neddy, passed at once into the prison, walked straight to his master's room, and knocked at the door.

"Come in," said Mr. Pickwick.

Sam appeared, pulled off his hat, and smiled.

"Ah, Sam, my good lad!" said Mr. Pickwick, evidently delighted to see his humble friend again; "I had no intention of hurting your feelings yesterday, my faithful fellow, by what I said. Put down your hat, Sam, and let me explain my meaning, a little more at length."

"Won't presently do, sir?" inquired Sam.

"Certainly," said Mr. Pickwick; "but why not now?"

"I'd rayther not now, sir," rejoined Sam.

" Why ? " inquired Mr. Pickwick.

" 'Cause— " said Sam, hesitating.

" Because of what ? " inquired Mr. Pickwick, alarmed at his follower's manner. " Speak out, Sam."

" 'Cause," rejoined Sam ; " 'cause I've got a little bisness as I want to do."

" What business ? " inquired Mr. Pickwick, surprised at Sam's confused manner.

" Nothin' partickler, sir," replied Sam.

" Oh, if it's nothing particular," said Mr. Pickwick, with a smile, " you can speak with me first."

" I think I'd better see arter it at once," said Sam, still hesitating.

Mr. Pickwick looked amazed, but said nothing.

" The fact is," said Sam, stopping short.

" Well ! " said Mr. Pickwick. " Speak out, Sam."

" Why, the fact is," said Sam, with a desperate effort, " P'raps I'd better see arter my bed afore I do anythin' else."

" *Your bed!* " exclaimed Mr. Pickwick, in astonishment.

" Yes, my bed, sir," replied Sam. " I'm a pris'ner. I was arrested, this here wery arternoon, for debt."

" You arrested for debt ! " exclaimed Mr. Pickwick, sinking into a chair.

" Yes, for debt, sir," replied Sam. " And the man as puts me in, 'ull never let me out, till you go yourself."

" Bless my heart and soul ! " ejaculated Mr. Pickwick. " What do you mean ? "

" Wot I say, sir," rejoined Sam. " If it's forty year to come, I shall be a pris'ner, and I'm very glad on it, and if it had been Newgate, it would ha' been just the same. Now the murder's out, and, damme, there's an end on it ! "

With these words, which he repeated with great emphasis and violence, Sam Weller dashed his hat upon the ground, in a most unusual state of excitement ; and then, folding his arms, looked firmly and fixedly in his master's face.

CHAPTER XLIV.

Mr. Pickwick felt a great deal too much touched by the warmth of Sam's attachment, to be able to exhibit any manifestation of anger or displeasure at the precipitate course he had adopted, in voluntarily consigning himself to a debtors' prison, for an indefinite period. The only point on which he persevered in demanding any explanation, was, the name of Sam's detaining creditor; but this Mr. Weller as perseveringly withheld.

"It ain't o' no use, sir," said Sam, again and again. "He's a ma-licious, bad-disposed, vorldly-minded, spiteful, windictive creetur, with a hard heart as there ain't no soft'nin'. As the wirtuous clergyman remarked of the old gen'l'm'n with the dropsy, ven he said, that upon the whole he thought he'd rayther leave his property to his vife than build a chapel vith it."

"But consider, Sam," Mr. Pickwick remonstrated, "the sum is so small that it can very easily be paid; and having made up my mind that you shall stop with me, you should recollect how much more useful you would be, if you could go outside the walls."

DONE ON PRINCIPLE.

"Wery much obliged to you, sir," replied Mr. Weller gravely; "but I'd rayther not."

"Rather not do what, Sam?"

"Wy, I'd rayther not let myself down to ask a favour o' this here unremorseful enemy."

"But it is no favour asking him to take his money, Sam," reasoned Mr. Pickwick.

"Beg your pardon, sir," rejoined Sam; "but it 'ud be a wery great favour to pay it, and he don't deserve none; that's where it is, sir."

Here Mr. Pickwick, rubbing his nose with an air of some vexation, Mr. Weller thought it prudent to change the theme of the discourse.

"I takes my determination on principle, sir," remarked Sam, "and you takes yours on the same ground; wich puts me in mind o' the man as killed his-self on principle, wich o' course you've heerd on, sir." Mr. Weller paused when he arrived at this point, and cast a comical look at his master out of the corners of his eyes.

"There is no 'of course' in the case, Sam," said Mr. Pickwick, gradually breaking into a smile, in spite of the uneasiness which Sam's obstinacy had given him. "The fame of the gentleman in question, never reached my ears."

"No, sir!" exclaimed Mr. Weller. "You astonish me, sir; he wos a clerk in a gov'ment office, sir."

"Was he?" said Mr. Pickwick.

"Yes, he wos, sir," rejoined Mr. Weller; "and a wery pleasant gen'l'm'n too—one o' the precise and tidy sort, as puts their feet in little India-rubber fire-buckets wen its wet weather, and never has no other bosom friends but hare-skins; he saved up his money on principle, wore a clean shirt ev'ry day on principle; never spoke to none of his relations on principle, 'fear they shou'd want to borrow money of him; and wos altogether, in fact, an uncommon agreeable character. He had his hair cut on principle vunce a fortnight, and contracted for his clothes on the economic principle—three

251

suits a year, and send back the old uns. Being a wery reg'lar
gen'l'm'n, he din'd ev'ry day at the same place, where it wos
one and nine to cut off the joint, and a wery good one and
nine's worth he used to cut, as the landlord often said, with
the tears a tricklin' down his face: let alone the way he used
to poke the fire in the vinter time, which wos a dead loss o'
four-pence ha'penny a day: to say nothin' at all o' the
aggrawation o' seein' him do it. So uncommon grand with
it too! 'Post arter the next gen'lm'n', he sings out ev'ry
day ven he comes in. 'See arter the Times, Thomas; let me
look at the Mornin' Herald, wen it's out o' hand; don't
forget to bespeak the Chronicle; and just bring the 'Tizer,
vill you:' and then he'd set vith his eyes fixed on the clock,
and rush out, just a quarter of a minit afore the time,
to waylay the boy as wos a comin' in with the evenin' paper,
wich he'd read with sich intense interest and persewerance as
worked the other customers up to the wery confines o'
desperation and insanity, 'specially one i-rascible old gen'l'm'n
as the vaiter wos always obliged to keep a sharp eye on, at
sich times, fear he should be tempted to commit some rash
act with the carving knife. Vell, sir, here he'd stop, occupyin'
the best place for three hours, and never takin' nothin' arter
his dinner, but sleep, and then he'd go away to a coffee-house
a few streets off, and have a small pot o' coffee and four
crumpets, arter wich he'd walk home to Kensington and go
to bed. One night he wos took very ill; sends for a doctor;
doctor comes in a green fly, with a kind o' Robinson Crusoe
set o' steps, as he could let down wen he got out, and pull up
arter him wen he got in, to perwent the necessity o' the
coachman's gettin' down, and thereby undeceivin' the public
by lettin' 'em see that it wos only a livery coat as he'd
got on, and not the trousers to match. 'Wot's the matter?'
says the doctor. 'Wery ill,' says the patient. 'Wot have
you been a eatin' on?' says the doctor. 'Roast weal,' says
the patient. 'Wot's the last thing you dewoured?' says
the doctor. 'Crumpets,' says the patient. 'That's it!'

says the doctor. 'I'll send you a box of pills directly, and don't you never take no more of 'em,' he says. 'No more o' wot?' says the patient—'Pills?' 'No; crumpets,' says the doctor. 'Wy?' says the patient, starting up in bed; 'I've eat four crumpets, ev'ry night for fifteen year, on principle.' 'Well, then, you'd better leave 'em off, on principle,' says the doctor. 'Crumpets is wholesome, sir,' says the patient. 'Crumpets is *not* wholesome, sir,' says the doctor, wery fierce. 'But they're so cheap,' says the patient, comin' down a little, 'and so wery fillin' at the price.' 'They'd be dear to you, at any price; dear if you wos paid to eat 'em,' says the doctor. 'Four crumpets a night,' he says, 'vill do your business in six months!' The patient looks him full in the face, and turns it over in his mind for a long time, and at last he says, 'Are you sure o' that 'ere, sir?' 'I'll stake my professional reputation on it,' says the doctor. 'How many crumpets, at a sittin', do you think 'ud kill me off at once?' says the patient. 'I don't know,' says the doctor. 'Do you think half a crown's wurth 'ud do it?' says the patient. 'I think it might,' says the doctor. 'Three shillins' wurth 'ud be sure to do it, I s'pose?' says the patient. 'Certainly,' says the doctor. 'Wery good,' says the patient; 'good night.' Next mornin' he gets up, has a fire lit, orders in three shillins' wurth o' crumpets, toasts 'em all, eats 'em all, and blows his brains out."

"What did he do that for?" inquired Mr. Pickwick abruptly; for he was considerably startled by this tragical termination of the narrative.

"Wot did he do it for, sir?" reiterated Sam. "Wy in support of his great principle that crumpets wos wholesome, and to show that he wouldn't be put out of his way for nobody!"

With such like shiftings and changings of the discourse, did Mr. Weller meet his master's questioning on the night of his taking up his residence in the Fleet. Finding all gentle remonstrance useless, Mr. Pickwick at length yielded a reluctant consent to his taking lodgings by the week, of a bald-headed cobbler, who rented a small slip-room in one of the upper galleries. To this humble apartment Mr. Weller moved a mattress and bedding, which he hired of Mr. Roker; and, by the time he lay down upon it at night, was as much at home as if he had been bred in the prison, and his whole family had vegetated therein for three generations.

"Do you always smoke arter you goes to bed, old cock?" inquired Mr. Weller of his landlord, when they had both retired for the night.

"Yes, I does, young bantam," replied the cobbler.

"Will you allow me to in-quire wy you make up your bed under that 'ere deal table?" said Sam.

"'Cause I was always used to a four-poster afore I came here, and I find the legs of the table answer just as well," replied the cobbler.

"You're a character, sir," said Sam.

"I haven't got anything of the kind belonging to me," rejoined the cobbler, shaking his head; "and if you want to meet with a good one, I'm afraid you'll find some difficulty in suiting yourself at this register office."

The above short dialogue took place as Mr. Weller lay extended on his mattress at one end of the room, and the cobbler on his, at the other; the apartment being illumined by the light of a rush candle, and the cobbler's pipe, which was glowing below the table, like a red-hot coal. The conversation, brief as it was, predisposed Mr. Weller strongly in his landlord's favour; and raising himself on his elbow he took a more lengthened survey of his appearance than he had yet had either time or inclination to make.

He was a sallow man—all cobblers are; and had a strong bristly beard—all cobblers have. His face was a queer, good-tempered, crooked-featured piece of workmanship, ornamented with a couple of eyes that must have worn a very joyous expression at one time, for they sparkled yet. The man was sixty, by years, and Heaven knows how old by imprisonment, so that his having any look approaching to mirth or contentment, was singular enough. He was a little man, and, being half doubled up as he lay in bed, looked about as long as he ought to have been without his legs. He had a great red pipe in his mouth, and was smoking, and staring at the rush-light, in a state of enviable placidity.

"Have you been here long?" inquired Sam, breaking the silence which had lasted for some time.

"Twelve year," replied the cobbler, biting the end of his pipe as he spoke.

"Contempt?" inquired Sam.

The cobbler nodded.

"Well, then," said Sam, with some sternness, "wot do you persevere in bein' obstinit for, vastin' your precious life away in this here magnified pound? Wy don't you give in, and tell the Chancellorship that you're wery sorry for makin' his court contemptible, and you won't do so no more?"

The cobbler put his pipe in the corner of his mouth, while he smiled, and then brought it back to its old place again; but said nothing.

"Wy don't you?" said Sam, urging his question strenuously.

"Ah," said the cobbler, "you don't quite understand these matters. What do you suppose ruined me, now?"

"Wy," said Sam, trimming the rush-light, "I s'pose the beginnin' wos, that you got into debt, eh?"

"Never owed a farden," said the cobbler; "try again."

"Well, perhaps," said Sam, "you bought houses, wich is delicate English for goin' mad: or took to buildin', wich is a medical term for bein' incurable."

The cobbler shook his head and said, "Try again."

"You didn't go to law, I hope?" said Sam, suspiciously.

"Never in my life," replied the cobbler. "The fact is, I was ruined by having money left me."

"Come, come," said Sam, "that von't do. I wish some rich enemy 'ud try to vork *my* destruction in that 'ere vay. I'd let him."

"Oh, I dare say you don't believe it," said the cobbler, quietly smoking his pipe. "I wouldn't if I was you; but it's true for all that."

"How wos it?" inquired Sam, half induced to believe the fact already, by the look the cobbler gave him.

"Just this," replied the cobbler; "an old gentleman that I worked for, down in the country, and a humble relation of whose I married—she's dead, God bless her, and thank Him for it!—was seized with a fit and went off."

"Where?" inquired Sam, who was growing sleepy after the numerous events of the day.

"How should I know where he went?" said the cobbler, speaking through his nose in an intense enjoyment of his pipe. "He went off dead."

"Oh, that indeed," said Sam. "Well?"

"Well," said the cobbler, "he left five thousand pound behind him."

"And wery gen-teel in him so to do," said Sam.

"One of which," continued the cobbler, "he left to me, 'cause I'd married his relation, you see."

"Wery good," murmured Sam.

"And being surrounded by a great number of nieces and nevys, as was always a quarrelling and fighting among themselves for the property, he makes me his executor, and leaves the rest to me: in trust, to divide it among 'em as the will prowided."

"Wot do you mean by leavin' it on trust?" inquired Sam, waking up a little. "If it ain't ready money, where's the use on it?"

"It's a law term, that's all," said the cobbler.

"I don't think that," said Sam, shaking his head. "There's wery little trust at that shop. Hows'ever, go on."

"Well," said the cobbler: "when I was going to take out a probate of the will, the nieces and nevys, who was desperately disappointed at not getting all the money, enters a caveat against it."

THE COBBLER'S STORY.

"What's that?" inquired Sam.

"A legal instrument, which is as much as to say, it's no go," replied the cobbler.

"I see," said Sam, "a sort of brother-in-law o' the have-his-carcase. Well."

"But," continued the cobbler, "finding that they couldn't agree among themselves, and consequently couldn't get up a case against the will, they withdrew the caveat, and I paid all the legacies. I'd hardly done it, when one nevy brings an action to set the will aside. The case comes on, some months afterwards, afore a deaf old gentleman, in a back room somewhere down by Paul's Churchyard; and arter four counsels had taken a day a-piece to bother him regularly, he takes a week or two to consider, and read the evidence in six vollums, and then gives his judgment that how the testator was not quite right in his head, and I must pay all the money back again, and all the costs. I appealed; the case come on before three or four very sleepy gentlemen, who had heard it all before in the other court, where they're lawyers without work; the only difference being, that, there, they're called doctors, and in the other place delegates, if you understand that; and they very dutifully confirmed the decision of the old gentleman below. After that, we went into Chancery, where we are still, and where I shall always be. My lawyers have had all my thousand pound long ago; and what between the estate, as they call it, and the costs, I'm here for ten thousand, and shall stop here, till I die, mending shoes. Some gentlemen have talked of bringing it afore parliament, and I dare say would have done it, only they hadn't time to come to me, and I hadn't power to go to them, and they got tired of my long letters, and dropped the business. And this is God's truth, without one word of suppression or exaggeration, as fifty people, both in this place and out of it, very well know."

The cobbler paused to ascertain what effect his story had produced on Sam; but finding that he had dropped asleep, knocked the ashes out of his pipe, sighed, put it down, drew the bedclothes over his head, and went to sleep too.

Mr. Pickwick was sitting at breakfast, alone, next morning (Sam being busily engaged in the cobbler's room, polishing his master's shoes and brushing the black gaiters) when there came a knock at the door, which, before Mr. Pickwick could cry "Come in!" was followed by the appearance of a head of hair and a cotton-velvet cap, both of which articles of dress he had no difficulty in recognising as the personal property of Mr. Smangle.

"How are you?" said that worthy, accompanying the inquiry with a score or two of nods; "I say—do you expect anybody this morning? Three men—devilish gentlemanly fellows—have been asking after you down stairs, and knocking at every door on the Hall flight; for which they've been most infernally blown up by the collegians that had the trouble of opening 'em."

"Dear me! How very foolish of them," said Mr. Pickwick, rising. "Yes; I have no doubt they are some friends whom I rather expected to see, yesterday."

"Friends of yours!" exclaimed Smangle, seizing Mr. Pickwick by the hand. "Say no more. Curse me, they're friends of mine from this minute, and friends of Mivins's too. Infernal pleasant, gentlemanly dog, Mivins, isn't he?" said Smangle, with great feeling.

"I know so little of the gentleman," said Mr. Pickwick, hesitating, "that I——"

"I know you do," interposed Smangle, clasping Mr. Pickwick by the shoulder. "You shall know him better. You'll be delighted with him. That man, sir," said Smangle, with a solemn countenance, "has comic powers that would do honour to Drury Lane Theatre."

"Has he indeed?" said Mr. Pickwick.

"Ah, by Jove he has!" replied Smangle. "Hear him come the four cats in the wheelbarrow—four distinct cats, sir, I pledge you my honour. Now you know that's infernal

258

clever! Damme, you can't help liking a man, when you see these traits about him. He's only one fault—that little failing I mentioned to you, you know."

As Mr. Smangle shook his head in a confidential and sympathising manner at this juncture, Mr. Pickwick felt that he was expected to say something, so he said "Ah!" and looked restlessly at the door.

"Ah!" echoed Mr. Smangle, with a long-drawn sigh. "He's delightful company, that man is, sir. I don't know better company anywhere; but he has that one drawback. If the ghost of his grandfather, sir, was to rise before him this minute, he'd ask him for the loan of his acceptance on an eighteenpenny stamp."

"Dear me!" exclaimed Mr. Pickwick.

"Yes," added Mr. Smangle; "and if he'd the power of raising him again, he would, in two months and three days from this time, to renew the bill!"

"Those are very remarkable traits," said Mr. Pickwick; "but I'm afraid that while we are talking here, my friends may be in a state of great perplexity at not finding me."

"I'll show 'em the way," said Smangle, making for the door. "Good day. I won't disturb you while they're here, you know. By-the-bye——"

As Smangle pronounced the last three words, he stopped suddenly, re-closed the door which he had opened, and, walking softly back to Mr. Pickwick, stepped close up to him on tip-toe, and said in a very soft whisper:

"You couldn't make it convenient to lend me half-a-crown till the latter end of next week, could you?"

Mr. Pickwick could scarcely forbear smiling, but managing to preserve his gravity, he drew forth the coin, and placed it in Mr. Smangle's palm; upon which, that gentleman, with many nods and winks, implying profound mystery, disappeared in quest of the three strangers, with whom he presently returned; and having coughed thrice, and nodded as many times, as an assurance to Mr. Pickwick that he would not forget to pay, he shook hands all round, in an engaging manner, and at length took himself off.

"My dear friends," said Mr. Pickwick, shaking hands alternately with Mr. Tupman, Mr. Winkle, and Mr. Snodgrass, who were the three visitors in question, "I am delighted to see you."

The triumvirate were much affected. Mr. Tupman shook his head deploringly; Mr. Snodgrass drew forth his handkerchief, with undisguised emotion; and Mr. Winkle retired to the window, and sniffed aloud.

"Mornin', gen'l'm'n," said Sam, entering at the moment with the shoes and gaiters. "Avay vith melincholly, as the little boy said ven his school-missis died. Velcome to the College, gen'l'm'n."

"This foolish fellow," said Mr. Pickwick, tapping Sam on the head as he knelt down to button up his master's gaiters: "This foolish fellow has got himself arrested, in order to be near me."

"What!" exclaimed the three friends.

"Yes, gen'l'm'n," said Sam, "I'm a—stand steady, sir, if you please—I'm a pris'ner, gen'l'm'n. Con-fined, as the lady said."

"A prisoner!" exclaimed Mr. Winkle, with unaccountable vehemence.

"Hallo, sir!" responded Sam, looking up. "Wot's the matter, sir?"

"I had hoped, Sam, that——nothing, nothing," said Mr. Winkle, precipitately.

There was something so very abrupt and unsettled in Mr. Winkle's manner, that Mr. Pickwick involuntarily looked at his two friends, for an explanation.

"We don't know," said Mr. Tupman, answering this mute appeal aloud. "He has been much excited for two days past, and his whole demeanour very unlike what it usually is. We feared there must be something the matter, but he resolutely denies it."

260

"No, no," said Mr. Winkle, colouring beneath Mr. Pickwick's gaze; "there is really nothing. I assure you there is nothing, my dear sir. It will be necessary for me to leave town, for a short time, on private business, and I had hoped to have prevailed upon you to allow Sam to accompany me."

Mr. Pickwick looked more astonished than before.

"I think," faltered Mr. Winkle, "that Sam would have had no objection to do so; but, of course, his being a prisoner here, renders it impossible. So I must go alone."

As Mr. Winkle said these words, Mr. Pickwick felt, with some astonishment, that Sam's fingers were trembling at the gaiters, as if he were rather surprised or startled. Sam looked up at Mr. Winkle, too, when he had finished speaking; and though the glance they exchanged was instantaneous, they seemed to understand each other.

"Do you know anything of this, Sam?" said Mr. Pickwick, sharply.

"No, I don't, sir," replied Mr. Weller, beginning to button with extraordinary assiduity.

"Are you sure, Sam?" said Mr. Pickwick.

"Wy, sir," responded Mr. Weller; "I'm sure so far, that I've never heerd anythin' on the subject afore this moment. If I makes any guess about it," added Sam, looking at Mr. Winkle, "I haven't got any right to say wot it is, 'fear it should be a wrong 'un."

"I have no right to make any further inquiry into the private affairs of a friend, however intimate a friend," said Mr. Pickwick, after a short silence; "at present let me merely say, that I do not understand this at all. There. We have had quite enough of the subject."

Thus expressing himself, Mr. Pickwick led the conversation to different topics, and Mr. Winkle gradually appeared more at ease, though still very far from being completely so. They had all so much to converse about, that the morning very quickly passed away; and when, at three o'clock, Mr. Weller produced upon the little dining table, a roast leg of mutton and an enormous meat pie, with sundry dishes of vegetables, and pots of porter, which stood upon the chairs or the sofa-bedstead, or where they could, everybody felt disposed to do justice to the meal, notwithstanding that the meat had been purchased, and dressed, and the pie made, and baked, at the prison cookery hard by.

To these, succeeded a bottle or two of very good wine, for which a messenger was dispatched by Mr. Pickwick to the Horn Coffeehouse, in Doctors' Commons. The bottle or two, indeed, might be more properly described as a bottle or six, for by the time it was drunk, and tea over, the bell began to ring for strangers to withdraw.

But, if Mr. Winkle's behaviour had been unaccountable in the morning, it became perfectly unearthly and solemn when, under the influence of his feelings, and his share of the bottle or six, he prepared to take leave of his friend. He lingered behind, until Mr. Tupman and Mr. Snodgrass had disappeared, and then fervently clenched Mr. Pickwick's hand, with an expression of face in which deep and mighty resolve was fearfully blended with the very concentrated essence of gloom.

"Good night, my dear sir!" said Mr. Winkle between his set teeth.

"Bless you, my dear fellow!" replied the warm-hearted Mr. Pickwick, as he returned the pressure of his young friend's hand.

"Now then!" cried Mr. Tupman from the gallery.

"Yes, yes, directly," replied Mr. Winkle. "Good night!"

"Good night," said Mr. Pickwick.

There was another good night, and another, and half-a-dozen more after that, and still Mr. Winkle had fast hold of his friend's hand, and was looking into his face with the same strange expression.

"*Is* anything the matter?" said Mr. Pickwick at last, when his arm was quite sore with shaking.

"Nothing," said Mr. Winkle.

"Well then, good night," said Mr. Pickwick, attempting to disengage his hand.

"My friend, my benefactor, my honoured companion," murmured Mr. Winkle, catching at his wrist. "Do not judge me harshly; do not, when you hear that, driven to extremity by hopeless obstacles, I——"

"Now then," said Mr. Tupman, re-appearing at the door. "Are you coming, or are we to be locked in?"

"Yes, yes, I am ready," replied Mr. Winkle. And with a violent effort he tore himself away.

As Mr. Pickwick was gazing down the passage after them in silent astonishment, Sam Weller appeared at the stair-head, and whispered for one moment in Mr. Winkle's ear.

"Oh certainly, depend upon me," said that gentleman aloud.

"Thankee, sir. You won't forget, sir?" said Sam.

"Of course not," replied Mr. Winkle.

"Wish you luck, sir," said Sam, touching his hat. "I should very much like to ha' joined you, sir; but the gov'ner o' course is pairamount."

"It is very much to your credit that you remain here," said Mr. Winkle. With these words they disappeared down the stairs.

"Very extraordinary," said Mr. Pickwick, going back into his room, and seating himself at the table in a musing attitude. "What *can* that young man be going to do?"

He had sat ruminating about the matter for some time, when the voice of Roker, the turnkey, demanded whether he might come in.

"By all means," said Mr. Pickwick.

"I've brought you a softer pillow, sir," said Roker, "instead of the temporary one you had last night."

"Thank you," said Mr. Pickwick. "Will you take a glass of wine?"

"You're wery good, sir," replied Mr. Roker, accepting the proffered glass. "Yours, sir."

"Thank you," said Mr. Pickwick.

"I'm sorry to say that your landlord's wery bad to-night, sir," said Roker, setting down the glass, and inspecting the lining of his hat preparatory to putting it on again.

"What! The Chancery prisoner!" exclaimed Mr. Pickwick.

"He won't be a Chancery prisoner wery long, sir," replied Roker, turning his hat round, so as to get the maker's name right side upwards, as he looked into it.

"You make my blood run cold," said Mr. Pickwick. "What do you mean?"

"He's been consumptive for a long time past," said Mr. Roker, "and he's taken wery bad in the breath to-night. The doctor said, six months ago, that nothing but change of air could save him."

"Great Heaven!" exclaimed Mr. Pickwick; "has this man been slowly murdered by the law for six months?"

"I don't know about that," replied Roker, weighing the hat by the brims in both hands. "I suppose he'd have been took the same, wherever he was. He went into the infirmary, this morning; the doctor says his strength is to be kept up as much as possible; and the warden's sent him wine and broth and that, from his own house. It's not the warden's fault, you know, sir."

"Of course not," replied Mr. Pickwick hastily.

"I'm afraid, however," said Roker, shaking his head, "that it's all up with him. I offered Neddy two six penn'orths to one upon it just now, but he wouldn't take it, and quite right. Thankee, sir. Good night, sir."

"Stay," said Mr. Pickwick earnestly. "Where is this infirmary?"

"Just over where you slept, sir," replied Roker. "I'll show you, if you like to come." Mr. Pickwick snatched up his hat without speaking, and followed at once.

The turnkey led the way in silence; and gently raising the latch of the room-door, motioned Mr. Pickwick to enter. It was a large, bare, desolate room, with a number of stump bedsteads made of iron: on one of which lay stretched, the shadow of a man: wan, pale, and ghastly. His breathing was hard and thick, and he moaned painfully as it came and went. At the bedside, sat a short old man in a cobbler's apron, who, by the aid of a pair of horn spectacles, was reading from the Bible aloud. It was the fortunate legatee.

The sick man laid his hand upon his attendant's arm, and motioned him to stop. He closed the book, and laid it on the bed.

"Open the window," said the sick man.

He did so. The noise of carriages and carts, the rattle of wheels, the cries of men and boys, all the busy sounds of a mighty multitude instinct with life and occupation, blended into one deep murmur, floated into the room. Above the hoarse loud hum, arose from time to time a boisterous laugh; or a scrap of some jingling song, shouted forth by one of the giddy crowd, would strike upon the ear for an instant, and then be lost amidst the roar of voices and the tramp of footsteps; the breaking of the billows of the restless sea of life that rolled heavily on, without. Melancholy sounds to a quiet listener at any time; how melancholy to the watcher by the bed of death!

"There is no air here," said the sick man faintly. "The place pollutes it. It was fresh round about, when I walked there, years ago; but it grows hot and heavy in passing these walls. I cannot breathe it."

"We have breathed it together, for a long time," said the old man. "Come, come."

There was a short silence, during which the two spectators approached the bed. The sick man drew a hand of his old fellow prisoner towards him, and pressing it affectionately between both his own, retained it in his grasp.

"I hope," he gasped after a while: so faintly that they bent their ears close over the bed to catch the half-formed sounds his pale lips gave vent to: "I hope my merciful Judge will bear in mind my heavy punishment on earth. Twenty years, my friend, twenty years in this hideous grave! My heart broke when my child died, and I could not even kiss him in his little coffin. My loneliness since then, in all this noise and riot, has been very dreadful. May God forgive me! He has seen my solitary, lingering death."

He folded his hands, and murmuring something more they could not hear, fell into a sleep—only a sleep at first, for they saw him smile.

They whispered together for a little time, and the turnkey, stooping over the pillow, drew hastily back. "He has got his discharge, by G—!" said the man.

He had. But he had grown so like death in life, that they knew not when he died.

CHAPTER XLV.

A FEW mornings after his incarceration, Mr. Samuel Weller, having arranged his master's room with all possible care, and seen him comfortably seated over his books and papers, withdrew to employ himself for an hour or two to come, as he best could. It was a fine morning, and it occurred to Sam that a pint of porter in the open air would lighten his next quarter of an hour or so, as well as any little amusement in which he could indulge.

Having arrived at this conclusion, he betook himself to the tap. Having purchased the beer, and obtained, moreover, the day-but-one-before-yesterday's paper, he repaired to the skittle-ground, and seating himself on a bench, proceeded to enjoy himself in a very sedate and methodical manner.

First of all, he took a refreshing draught of the beer, and then he looked up at a window, and bestowed a Platonic wink on a young lady who was peeling potatoes thereat. Then he opened the paper, and folded it so as to get the police reports outwards; and this being a vexatious and difficult thing to do, when there is any wind stirring, he took another draught of the beer when he had accomplished it. Then, he read two lines of the paper, and stopped short, to look at a couple of men who were finishing a game at rackets, which being concluded, he cried out "wery good" in an approving manner, and looked round upon the spectators, to ascertain whether their sentiments coincided with his own. This involved the necessity of looking up at the windows also; and as the young lady was still there, it was an act of common politeness to wink again, and to drink to her good health in dumb show, in another draught of the beer, which Sam did; and having frowned hideously upon a small boy who had noted this latter proceeding with open eyes, he threw one leg over the other, and, holding the newspaper in both hands, began to read in real earnest.

He had hardly composed himself into the needful state of abstraction, when he thought he heard his own name proclaimed in some distant passage. Nor was he mistaken, for it quickly passed from mouth to mouth, and in a few seconds the air teemed with shouts of "Weller!"

"Here!" roared Sam, in a stentorian voice. "Wot's the matter? Who wants him? Has an express come to say that his country-house is a-fire?"

"Somebody wants you in the hall," said a man who was standing by.

"Just mind that 'ere paper and the pot, old feller, will you?" said Sam. "I'm a comin'. Blessed, if they was a callin' me to the bar, they couldn't make more noise about it!"

Accompanying these words with a gentle rap on the head of the young gentleman before noticed, who, unconscious of his close vicinity to the person in request, was screaming "Weller!" with all his might, Sam hastened across the ground, and ran up the steps into the hall. Here, the first object that met his eyes was his beloved father sitting on a bottom stair, with his hat in his hand, shouting out "Weller!" in his very loudest tone, at half-minute intervals.

"Wot are you a roarin' at?" said Sam impetuously, when the old gentleman had discharged himself of another shout;

268

"makin' yourself so precious hot that you looks like a aggra-wated glass-blower. Wot's the matter?"

"Aha!" replied the old gentleman, "I began to be afeerd that you'd gone for a walk round the Regency Park, Sammy."

"Come," said Sam, "none o' them taunts agin the wictim o' avarice, and come off that 'ere step. Wot are you a settin' down there for? I don't live there."

"I've got such a game for you, Sammy," said the elder Mr. Weller, rising.

"Stop a minit," said Sam, "you're all vite behind."

"That's right, Sammy, rub it off," said Mr. Weller, as his son dusted him. "It might look personal here, if a man walked about with whitevash on his clothes, eh, Sammy?"

As Mr. Weller exhibited in this place unequivocal symptoms of an approaching fit of chuckling, Sam interposed to stop it.

"Keep quiet, do," said Sam, "there never vos such a old picter-card born. Wot are you bustin' vith, now?"

"Sammy," said Mr. Weller, wiping his forehead, "I'm afeerd that vun o' these days I shall laugh myself into a appleplexy, my boy."

"Vell, then, wot do you do it for?" said Sam. "Now; wot have you got to say?"

"Who do you think's come here with me, Samivel?" said Mr. Weller, drawing back a pace or two, pursing up his mouth, and extending his eyebrows.

"Pell?" said Sam.

Mr. Weller shook his head, and his red cheek expanded with the laughter that was endeavouring to find a vent.

"Mottled-faced man, p'r'aps?" suggested Sam.

Again Mr. Weller shook his head.

"Who then?" asked Sam.

"Your mother-in-law," said Mr. Weller; and it was lucky he did say it, or his cheeks must inevitably have cracked, from their most unnatural distension.

"Your mother-in-law, Sammy," said Mr. Weller, "and the

269

red-nosed man, my boy; and the red-nosed man. Ho! ho! ho!"

With this, Mr. Weller launched into convulsions of laughter, while Sam regarded him with a broad grin gradually over-spreading his whole countenance.

"They've come to have a little serious talk with you, Samivel," said Mr. Weller, wiping his eyes. "Don't let out nothin' about the unnat'ral creditor, Sammy."

"Wot, don't they know who it is?" inquired Sam.

"Not a bit on it," replied his father.

"Vere are they?" said Sam, reciprocating all the old gentle-man's grins.

"In the snuggery," rejoined Mr. Weller. "Catch the red-nosed man a goin' any vere but vere the liquors is; not he, Samivel, not he. Ve'd a wery pleasant ride along the road from the Markis this mornin', Sammy," said Mr. Weller, when he felt himself equal to the task of speaking in an articulate manner. "I drove the old piebald in that 'ere little shay-cart as belonged to your mother-in-law's first wenter, into vich a harm-cheer wos lifted for the shepherd; and I'm blest," said Mr. Weller, with a look of deep scorn: "I'm blest if they didn't bring a portable flight o' steps out into the road a front o' our door, for him to get up by."

"You don't mean that?" said Sam.

"I *do* mean that, Sammy," replied his father, "and I vish you could ha' seen how tight he held on by the sides wen he did get up, as if he wos afeerd o' being precipitayted down full six foot, and dashed into a million o' hatoms. He tumbled in at last, however, and avay ve vent; and I rayther think, I say I rayther think, Samivel, that he found his-self a little jolted wen ve turned the corners."

"Wot, I s'pose you happened to drive up agin a post or two?" said Sam.

"I'm afeerd," replied Mr. Weller, in a rapture of winks, "I'm afeerd I took vun or two on 'em, Sammy; he wos a flyin' out o' the harm-cheer all the way."

Here the old gentleman shook his head from side to side, and was seized with a hoarse internal rumbling, accompanied with a violent swelling of the countenance, and a sudden increase in the breadth of all his features; symptoms which alarmed his son not a little.

"Don't be frightened, Sammy, don't be frightened," said the old gentleman, when, by dint of much struggling, and various convulsive stamps upon the ground, he had recovered his voice. "It's only a kind o' quiet laugh as I'm a tryin' to come, Sammy."

"Well, if that's wot it is," said Sam, "you'd better not try to come it agin. You'll find it rayther a dangerous inwention."

"Don't you like it, Sammy?" inquired the old gentleman.

"Not at all," replied Sam.

"Well," said Mr. Weller, with the tears still running down his cheeks, "it 'ud ha' been a wery great accommodation to me if I could ha' done it, and 'ud ha' saved a good many vords atween your mother-in-law and me, sometimes; but I am afeerd you're right, Sammy: it's too much in the apple-plexy line—a deal too much, Samivel."

This conversation brought them to the door of the snuggery, into which Sam—pausing for an instant to look over his shoulder, and cast a sly leer at his respected progenitor, who was still giggling behind—at once led the way.

"Mother-in-law," said Sam, politely saluting the lady, "wery much obliged to you for this here wisit. Shepherd, how air you?"

"Oh, Samuel!" said Mrs. Weller. "This is dreadful."

"Not a bit on it, mum," replied Sam. "Is it, shepherd?"

Mr. Stiggins raised his hands, and turned up his eyes, till the whites—or rather the yellows—were alone visible; but made no reply in words.

"Is this here gen'l'm'n troubled vith any painful complaint?" said Sam, looking to his mother-in-law for explanation.

271

"The good man is grieved to see you here, Samuel," replied Mrs. Weller.

"Oh, that's it, is it?" said Sam. "I was afeerd, from his manner, that he might ha' forgotten to take pepper vith that 'ere last cowcumber he eat. Set down, sir; ve make no extra charge for the settin' down, as the king remarked wen he blowed up his ministers."

"Young man," said Mr. Stiggins, ostentatiously, "I fear you are not softened by imprisonment."

"Beg your pardon, sir," replied Sam; "wot wos you graciously pleased to hobserve?"

"I apprehend, young man, that your nature is no softer for this chastening," said Mr. Stiggins, in a loud voice.

"Sir," replied Sam, "you're wery kind to say so. I hope my natur is *not* a soft vun, sir. Wery much obliged to you for your good opinion, sir."

At this point of the conversation, a sound, indecorously approaching to a laugh, was heard to proceed from the chair in which the elder Mr. Weller was seated; upon which Mrs. Weller, on a hasty consideration of all the circumstances of the case, considered it her bounden duty to become gradually hysterical.

"Weller," said Mrs. W. (the old gentleman was seated in a corner); "Weller! Come forth."

"Wery much obleeged to you, my dear," replied Mr. Weller; "but I'm quite comfortable vere I am."

Upon this, Mrs. Weller burst into tears.

"Wot's gone wrong, mum?" said Sam.

"Oh, Samuel!" replied Mrs. Weller, "your father makes me wretched. Will nothing do him good?"

"Do you hear this here?" said Sam. "Lady wants to know vether nothin' 'ull do you good."

"Wery much indebted to Mrs. Weller for her po-lite inquiries, Sammy," replied the old gentleman. "I think a pipe vould benefit me a good deal. Could I be accommodated, Sammy?"

Here Mrs. Weller let fall some more tears, and Mr. Stiggins groaned.

"Hallo! Here's this unfort'nate gen'l'm'n took ill agin," said Sam, looking round. "Were do you feel it now, sir?"

"In the same place, young man," rejoined Mr. Stiggins: "in the same place."

"Were may that be, sir?" inquired Sam, with great outward simplicity.

"In the buzzim, young man," replied Mr. Stiggins, placing his umbrella on his waistcoat.

At this affecting reply, Mrs. Weller, being wholly unable to suppress her feelings, sobbed aloud, and stated her conviction that the red-nosed man was a saint; whereupon Mr. Weller, senior, ventured to suggest, in an undertone, that he must be the representative of the united parishes of Saint Simon Without, and Saint Walker Within.

"I'm afeerd, mum," said Sam, "that this here gen'l'm'n, with the twist in his countenance, feels rayther thirsty, with the melancholy spectacle afore him. Is it the case, mum?"

The worthy lady looked at Mr. Stiggins for a reply; that gentleman, with many rollings of the eye, clenched his throat with his right hand, and mimicked the act of swallowing, to intimate that he was athirst.

"I am afraid, Samuel, that his feelings have made him so, indeed," said Mrs. Weller, mournfully.

"Wot's your usual tap, sir," replied Sam.

"Oh, my dear young friend," replied Mr. Stiggins, "all taps is vanities!"

"Too true, too true, indeed," said Mrs. Weller, murmuring a groan, and shaking her head assentingly.

"Well," said Sam, "I des-say they may be, sir; but which is your partickler wanity. Vich wanity do you like the flavour on best, sir?"

"Oh, my dear young friend," replied Mr. Stiggins, "I despise them all. If," said Mr. Stiggins, "if there is any one of them less odious than another, it is the liquor called rum.

273

Warm, my dear young friend, with three lumps of sugar to the tumbler."

"Wery sorry to say, sir," said Sam, "that they don't allow that particular wanity to be sold in this here establishment."

"Oh, the hardness of heart of these inveterate men!" ejaculated Mr. Stiggins. "Oh, the accursed cruelty of these inhuman persecutors!"

With these words, Mr. Stiggins again cast up his eyes, and rapped his breast with his umbrella; and it is but justice to the reverend gentleman to say, that his indignation appeared very real and unfeigned indeed.

After Mrs. Weller and the red-nosed gentleman had commented on this inhuman usage in a very forcible manner, and had vented a variety of pious and holy execrations against its authors, the latter recommended a bottle of port wine, warmed with a little water, spice, and sugar, as being grateful to the stomach, and savouring less of vanity than many other compounds. It was accordingly ordered to be prepared. Pending its preparation the red-nosed man and Mrs. Weller looked at the elder W. and groaned.

"Well, Sammy," said that gentleman, "I hope you'll find your spirits rose by this here lively wisit. Wery cheerful and improvin' conwersation, ain't it, Sammy?"

"You're a reprobate," replied Sam; "and I desire you won't address no more o' them ungraceful remarks to me."

So far from being edified by this very proper reply, the elder Mr. Weller at once relapsed into a broad grin; and this inexorable conduct causing the lady and Mr. Stiggins to close their eyes, and rock themselves to and fro on their chairs, in a troubled manner, he furthermore indulged in several acts of pantomime, indicative of a desire to pummel and wring the nose of the aforesaid Stiggins: the performance of which, appeared to afford him great mental relief. The old gentleman very narrowly escaped detection in one instance; for Mr. Stiggins happening to give a start on the arrival of

A DROP OF NEGUS.

the negus, brought his head in smart contact with the clenched
fist with which Mr. Weller had been describing imaginary
fireworks in the air, within two inches of his ear, for some
minutes.

"Wot are you a reachin' out your hand for the tumbler
in that 'ere sawage way for?" said Sam, with great promptitude. "Don't you see you've hit the gen'l'm'n?"

"I didn't go to do it, Sammy," said Mr. Weller, in some
degree abashed by the very unexpected occurrence of the
incident.

"Try an in'ard application, sir," said Sam, as the red-nosed
gentleman rubbed his head with a rueful visage. "Wot do
you think o' that, for a go o' wanity warm, sir?"

Mr. Stiggins made no verbal answer, but his manner was
expressive. He tasted the contents of the glass which Sam
had placed in his hand; put his umbrella on the floor, and
tasted it again: passing his hand placidly across his stomach
twice or thrice; he then drank the whole at a breath, and
smacking his lips, held out the tumbler for more.

Nor was Mrs. Weller behind-hand in doing justice to the
composition. The good lady began by protesting that she
couldn't touch a drop—then took a small drop—then a
large drop—then a great many drops; and her feelings being
of the nature of those substances which are powerfully affected
by the application of strong waters, she dropped a tear with
every drop of negus, and so got on, melting the feelings
down, until at length she had arrived at a very pathetic and
decent pitch of misery.

The elder Mr. Weller observed these signs and tokens with
many manifestations of disgust, and when, after a second jug
of the same, Mr. Stiggins began to sigh in a dismal manner,
he plainly evinced his disapprobation of the whole proceedings, by sundry incoherent ramblings of speech, among which
frequent angry repetitions of the word "gammon" were alone
distinguishable to the ear.

"I'll tell you wot it is, Samivel, my boy," whispered the

old gentleman into his son's ear, after a long and steadfast
contemplation of his lady and Mr. Stiggins: "I think there
must be somethin' wrong in your mother-in-law's inside,
as vell as in that o' the red-nosed man."

"Wot do you mean?" said Sam.

"I mean this here, Sammy," replied the old gentleman,
"that wot they drink, don't seem no nourishment to 'em;
it all turns to warm water, and comes a' pourin' out o' their
eyes. 'Pend upon it, Sammy, it's a constitootional infirmity."

Mr. Weller delivered this scientific opinion with many
confirmatory frowns and nods; which, Mrs. Weller remarking,
and concluding that they bore some disparaging reference
either to herself or to Mr. Stiggins, or to both, was on the
point of becoming infinitely worse, when Mr. Stiggins, getting
on his legs as well as he could, proceeded to deliver an
edifying discourse for the benefit of the company, but more
especially of Mr. Samuel, whom he adjured in moving terms
to be upon his guard in that sink of iniquity into which he
was cast; to abstain from all hypocrisy and pride of heart;
and to take in all things exact pattern and copy by him
(Stiggins), in which case he might calculate on arriving,
sooner or later at the comfortable conclusion, that, like him,
he was a most estimable and blameless character, and that all
his acquaintance and friends were hopelessly abandoned and
profligate wretches. Which consideration, he said, could not
but afford him the liveliest satisfaction.

He furthermore conjured him to avoid, above all things,
the vice of intoxication, which he likened unto the filthy
habits of swine, and to those poisonous and baleful drugs
which being chewed in the mouth, are said to filch away the
memory. At this point of his discourse, the reverend and
red-nosed gentleman became singularly incoherent, and staggering to and fro in the excitement of his eloquence, was
fain to catch at the back of a chair to preserve his perpendicular.

Mr. Stiggins did not desire his hearers to be upon their

The Red-Nosed Man Discourseth

AN EDIFYING DISCOURSE.

guard against those false prophets and wretched mockers of religion, who, without sense to expound its first doctrines, or hearts to feel its first principles, are more dangerous members of society than the common criminal; imposing, as they necessarily do, upon the weakest and worst informed, casting scorn and contempt on what should be held most sacred, and bringing into partial disrepute large bodies of virtuous and well-conducted persons of many excellent sects and persuasions. But as he leant over the back of the chair for a considerable time, and closing one eye, winked a good deal with the other, it is presumed that he thought all this, but kept it to himself.

During the delivery of the oration, Mrs. Weller sobbed and wept at the end of the paragraphs: while Sam, sitting cross-legged on a chair and resting his arms on the top-rail, regarded the speaker with great suavity and blandness of demeanour; occasionally bestowing a look of recognition on the old gentleman, who was delighted at the beginning, and went to sleep about half-way.

"Brayvo; wery pretty!" said Sam, when the red-nosed man having finished, pulled his worn gloves on: thereby thrusting his fingers through the broken tops till the knuckles were disclosed to view. "Wery pretty."

"I hope it may do you good, Samuel," said Mrs. Weller solemnly.

"I think it vill, mum," replied Sam.

"I wish I could hope that it would do your father good," said Mrs. Weller.

"Thankee, my dear," said Mr. Weller, senior. "How do *you* find yourself arter it, my love?"

"Scoffer!" exclaimed Mrs. Weller.

"Benighted man!" said the reverend Mr. Stiggins.

"If I don't get no better light than that 'ere moonshine o yourn, my worthy creetur," said the elder Mr. Weller, "it's wery likely as I shall continey to be a night coach till I'm took off the road altogether. Now, Mrs. We, if the piebald stands at livery much longer, he'll stand at nothin' as we go

277

back, and p'raps that 'ere harm cheer 'ull be tipped over into some hedge or another, with the shepherd in it."

At this supposition, the reverend Mr. Stiggins, in evident consternation, gathered up his hat and umbrella, and proposed an immediate departure, to which Mrs. Weller assented. Sam walked with them to the lodge-gate, and took a dutiful leave.

"A-do, Samivel," said the old gentleman.

"Wot's a-do?" inquired Sammy.

"Well, good-bye, then," said the old gentleman.

"Oh, that's wot you're a aimin' at, is it?" said Sam. "Good-bye!"

"Sammy," whispered Mr. Weller, looking cautiously round; "my duty to your gov'ner, and tell him if he thinks better o' this here bis'ness, to commoonicate vith me. Me and a cab'net-maker has dewised a plan for gettin' him out. A pianner, Samivel, a pianner!" said Mr. Weller, striking his son on the chest with the back of his hand, and falling back a step or two.

"Wot do you mean?" said Sam.

"A pianner forty, Samivel," rejoined Mr. Weller, in a still more mysterious manner, "as he can have on hire; vun as von't play, Sammy."

"And wot 'ud be the good o' that?" said Sam.

"Let him send to my friend, the cab'net-maker, to fetch it back, Sammy," replied Mr. Weller. "Are you avake, now?"

"No," rejoined Sam.

"There ain't no vurks in it," whispered his father. "It 'ull hold him easy, vith his hat and shoes on, and breathe through the legs, vich his holler. Have a passage ready taken for 'Merriker. The 'Merrikin gov'ment will never give him up, ven they find as he's got money to spend, Sammy. Let the gov'ner stop there, till Mrs. Bardell's dead, or Mr. Dodson and Fogg's hung (wich last ewent I think is the most likely to happen first, Sammy), and then let him come back and write a book about the 'Merrikins as'll pay all his expenses and more, if he blows 'em up enough."

Mr. Weller delivered this hurried abstract of his plot with great vehemence of whisper; then, as if fearful of weakening the effect of the tremendous communication, by any further dialogue, he gave the coachman's salute, and vanished.

Sam had scarcely recovered his usual composure of countenance, which had been greatly disturbed by the secret communication of his respected relative, when Mr. Pickwick accosted him.

"Sam," said that gentleman.

"Sir," replied Mr. Weller.

"I am going for a walk round the prison, and I wish you to attend me. I see a prisoner we know coming this way, Sam," said Mr. Pickwick, smiling.

"Wich, sir?" inquired Mr. Weller; "the gen'l'm'n vith the head o' hair, or the interestin' captive in the stockin's?"

"Neither," rejoined Mr. Pickwick. "He is an older friend of yours, Sam."

"O' mine, sir?" exclaimed Mr. Weller.

"You recollect the gentleman very well, I dare say, Sam," replied Mr. Pickwick, "or else you are more unmindful of your old acquaintances than I think you are. Hush! not a word, Sam; not a syllable. Here he is."

As Mr. Pickwick spoke, Jingle walked up. He looked less miserable than before, being clad in a half-worn suit of clothes, which, with Mr. Pickwick's assistance, had been released from the pawnbroker's. He wore clean linen too, and had had his hair cut. He was very pale and thin, however; and as he crept slowly up, leaning on a stick, it was easy to see that he had suffered severely from illness and want, and was still very weak. He took off his hat as Mr. Pickwick saluted him, and seemed much humbled and abashed at sight of Sam Weller.

Following close at his heels, came Mr. Job Trotter, in the catalogue of whose vices, want of faith and attachment to his companion could at all events find no place. He was still ragged and squalid, but his face was not quite so hollow as on his first meeting with Mr. Pickwick, a few days before. As he took off his hat to our benevolent old friend, he murmured some broken expressions of gratitude, and muttered something about having been saved from starving.

"Well, well," said Mr. Pickwick, impatiently interrupting him, "you can follow with Sam. I want to speak to you, Mr. Jingle. Can you walk without his arm?"

"Certainly, sir—all ready—not too fast—legs shaky—head queer—round and round—earthquaky sort of feeling—very."

"Here, give me your arm," said Mr. Pickwick.

"No, no," replied Jingle; "won't indeed—rather not."

"Nonsense," said Mr. Pickwick, "lean upon me, I desire, sir."

Seeing that he was confused and agitated, and uncertain what to do, Mr. Pickwick cut the matter short by drawing the invalided stroller's arm through his, and leading him away, without saying another word about it.

During the whole of this time, the countenance of Mr. Samuel Weller had exhibited an expression of the most overwhelming and absorbing astonishment that the imagination can portray. After looking from Job to Jingle, and from Jingle to Job in profound silence, he softly ejaculated the words, "Well, I *am* damn'd!" Which he repeated at least a score of times: after which exertion, he appeared wholly bereft of speech, and again cast his eyes, first upon the one and then upon the other, in mute perplexity and bewilderment.

"Now, Sam!" said Mr. Pickwick, looking back.

"I'm a comin', sir," replied Mr. Weller, mechanically following his master; and still he lifted not his eyes from Mr. Job Trotter, who walked at his side, in silence.

Job kept his eyes fixed on the ground for some time. Sam, with his glued to Job's countenance, ran up against the people

who were walking about, and fell over little children, and
stumbled against steps and railings, without appearing at all
sensible of it, until Job, looking stealthily up, said:

"How do you do, Mr. Weller?"

"It *is* him!" exclaimed Sam: and having established Job's
identity beyond all doubt, he smote his leg, and vented his
feelings in a long shrill whistle.

"Things has altered with me, sir," said Job.

"I should think they had," exclaimed Mr. Weller, surveying his companion's rags with undisguised wonder. "This is
rayther a change for the worse, Mr. Trotter, as the gen'l'm'n
said, wen he got two doubtful shillin's and sixpenn'orth o'
pocket pieces for a good half-crown."

"It is, indeed," replied Job, shaking his head. "There
is no deception now, Mr. Weller. Tears," said Job, with a
look of momentary slyness, "tears are not the only proofs
of distress, nor the best ones."

"No, they ain't," replied Sam, expressively.

"They may be put on, Mr. Weller," said Job.

"I know they may," said Sam; "some people, indeed,
has 'em always ready laid on, and can pull out the plug
wenever they likes."

"Yes," replied Job; "but *these* sort of things are not so
easily counterfeited, Mr. Weller, and it is a more painful
process to get them up." As he spoke, he pointed to his
sallow sunken cheeks, and, drawing up his coat sleeves, disclosed an arm which looked as if the bone could be broken
at a touch: so sharp and brittle did it appear, beneath its
thin covering of flesh.

"Wot have you been a doin' to yourself?" said Sam,
recoiling.

"Nothing," replied Job.

"Nothin'!" echoed Sam.

"I have been doin' nothing for many weeks past," said
Job; "and eating and drinking almost as little."

Sam took one comprehensive glance at Mr. Trotter's thin

face and wretched apparel; and then, seizing him by the arm, commenced dragging him away with great violence.

"Where are you going, Mr. Weller?" said Job, vainly struggling in the powerful grasp of his old enemy.

"Come on," said Sam; "come on!" He deigned no further explanation until they reached the tap; and then called for a pot of porter, which was speedily produced.

"Now," said Sam, "drink that up, ev'ry drop on it, and then turn the pot upside down, to let me see as you've took the med'cine."

"But, my dear Mr. Weller," remonstrated Job.

"Down vith it!" said Sam, peremptorily.

Thus admonished, Mr. Trotter raised the pot to his lips, and, by gentle and almost imperceptible degrees, tilted it into the air. He paused once, and only once, to draw a long breath, but without raising his face from the vessel, which, in a few moments thereafter, he held out at arm's length, bottom upward. Nothing fell upon the ground but a few particles of froth, which slowly detached themselves from the rim, and trickled lazily down.

"Well done!" said Sam. "How do you find yourself arter it?"

"Better, sir. I think I am better," responded Job.

"O' course you air," said Sam, argumentatively. "It's like puttin' gas in a balloon. I can see with the naked eye that you gets stouter under the operation. Wot do you say to another o' the same di-mensions?"

"I would rather not, I am much obliged to you, sir," replied Job, "much rather not."

"Vell, then, wot do you say to some wittles?" inquired Sam.

"Thanks to your worthy governor, sir," said Mr. Trotter, "we have half a leg of mutton, baked, at a quarter before three, with the potatoes under it to save boiling."

"Wot! Has *he* been a purwidin' for you?" asked Sam, emphatically.

MR. WELLER CONFIDES A SECRET.

"He has, sir," replied Job. "More than that, Mr. Weller; my master being very ill, he got us a room—we were in a kennel before—and paid for it, sir; and come to look at us, at night, when nobody should know. Mr. Weller," said Job, with real tears in his eyes, for once, "I could serve that gentleman till I fell down dead at his feet."

"I say!" said Sam, "I'll trouble you, my friend! None o' that!"

Job Trotter looked amazed.

"None o' that, I say, young feller," repeated Sam, firmly. "No man serves him but me. And now we're upon it, I'll let you into another secret besides that," said Sam, as he paid for the beer. "I never heerd, mind you, nor read of in story-books, nor see in picters, any angel in tights and gaiters—not even in spectacles, as I remember, though that may ha' been done for anythin' I know to the contrairey— but mark my vords, Job Trotter, he's a reg'lar thorough-bred angel for all that; and let me see the man as wenturs to tell me he knows a better vun." With this defiance, Mr. Weller buttoned up his change in a side pocket, and, with many confirmatory nods and gestures by the way, proceeded in search of the subject of discourse.

They found Mr. Pickwick, in company with Jingle, talking very earnestly, and not bestowing a look on the groups who were congregated on the racket-ground; they were very motley groups too, and worth the looking at, if it were only in idle curiosity.

"Well," said Mr. Pickwick, as Sam and his companion drew nigh, "you will see how your health becomes, and think about it meanwhile. Make the statement out for me when you feel yourself equal to the task, and I will discuss the subject with you when I have considered it. Now, go to your room. You are tired, and not strong enough to be out long."

Mr. Alfred Jingle, without one spark of his old animation —with nothing even of the dismal gaiety which he had assumed when Mr. Pickwick first stumbled on him in his misery—bowed low without speaking, and, motioning to Job not to follow him just yet, crept slowly away.

"Curious scene this, is it not, Sam?" said Mr. Pickwick, looking good-humouredly round.

"Wery much so, sir," replied Sam. "Wonders 'ull never cease," added Sam, speaking to himself. "I'm wery much mistaken if that 'ere Jingle worn't a doin' somethin' in the water-cart way!"

The area formed by the wall in that part of the Fleet in which Mr. Pickwick stood, was just wide enough to make a good racket court; one side being formed, of course, by the wall itself and the other by that portion of the prison which looked (or rather would have looked, but for the wall) towards St. Paul's Cathedral. Sauntering or sitting about, in every possible attitude of listless idleness, were a great number of debtors, the major part of whom were waiting in prison until their day of "going up" before the Insolvent Court should arrive; while others had been remanded for various terms, which they were idling away, as they best could. Some were shabby, some were smart, many dirty, a few clean; but there they all lounged, and loitered, and slunk about, with as little spirit or purpose as the beasts in a menagerie.

Lolling from the windows which commanded a view of this promenade, were a number of persons, some in noisy conversation with their acquaintance below, others playing at ball with some adventurous throwers outside, others looking on at the racket-players, or watching the boys as they cried the game. Dirty slipshod women passed and re-passed, on their way to the cooking-house in one corner of the yard; children screamed, and fought, and played together, in another; the tumbling of the skittles, and the shouts of the players, mingled perpetually with these and a hundred other sounds; and all was noise and tumult—save in a little miserable shed a few yards off, where lay, all quiet and ghastly, the body of the Chancery prisoner who had died the night before, awaiting the mockery of an inquest. The body! It is the lawyer's term for the restless whirling mass of cares and anxieties, affections, hopes, and griefs, that make up the living man. The law *had* his body; and there it lay, clothed in grave clothes, an awful witness to its tender mercy.

"Would you like to see a whistling-shop, sir?" inquired Job Trotter.

"What do you mean?" was Mr. Pickwick's counter inquiry.

"A vistlin' shop, sir," interposed Mr. Weller.

"What is that, Sam? A bird-fancier's?" inquired Mr. Pickwick.

"Bless your heart, no, sir," replied Job; "a whistling-shop, sir, is where they sell spirits." Mr. Job Trotter briefly explained here, that all persons, being prohibited under heavy penalties from conveying spirits into debtors' prisons, and such commodities being highly prized by the ladies and gentlemen confined therein, it had occurred to some speculative turnkey to connive, for certain lucrative considerations, at two or three prisoners retailing the favourite article of gin, for their own profit and advantage.

"This plan, you see, sir, has been gradually introduced into all the prisons for debt," said Mr. Trotter.

"And it has this wery great advantage," said Sam, "that the turnkeys takes wery good care to seize hold o' ev'ry body but them as pays 'em, that attempts the willainy, and wen it gets in the papers they're applauded for their wigilance; so it cuts two ways—frightens other people from the trade, and elewates their own characters."

"Exactly so, Mr. Weller," observed Job.

"Well, but are these rooms never searched, to ascertain whether any spirits are concealed in them?" said Mr. Pickwick.

"Cert'nly they are, sir," replied Sam; "but the turnkeys knows beforehand, and gives the word to the wistlers, and you *may* wistle for it wen you go to look."

By this time, Job had tapped at a door, which was opened by a gentleman with an uncombed head, who bolted it after them when they had walked in, and grinned; upon which Job grinned, and Sam also; whereupon Mr. Pickwick, thinking it might be expected of him, kept on smiling to the end of the interview.

The gentleman with the uncombed head appeared quite satisfied with this mute announcement of their business, and, producing a flat stone bottle, which might hold about a couple of quarts, from beneath his bedstead, filled out three glasses of gin, which Job Trotter and Sam disposed of in a most workmanlike manner.

"Any more?" said the whistling gentleman.

"No more," replied Job Trotter.

Mr. Pickwick paid, the door was unbolted, and out they came; the uncombed gentleman bestowing a friendly nod upon Mr. Roker, who happened to be passing at the moment.

From this spot, Mr. Pickwick wandered along all the galleries, up and down all the staircases, and once again round the whole area of the yard. The great body of the prison population appeared to be Mivins, and Smangle, and the parson, and the butcher, and the leg, over and over, and over again. There were the same squalor, the same turmoil and noise, the same general characteristics, in every corner; in the best and the worst alike. The whole place seemed restless and troubled; and the people were crowding and flitting to and fro, like the shadows in an uneasy dream.

"I have seen enough," said Mr. Pickwick, as he threw himself into a chair in his little apartment. "My head aches with these scenes, and my heart too. Henceforth I will be a prisoner in my own room."

And Mr. Pickwick steadfastly adhered to this determination. For three long months he remained shut up, all day; only stealing out at night to breathe the air when the

MR. PICKWICK'S RESOLUTION.

greater part of his fellow prisoners were in bed or carousing in their rooms.   His health was beginning to suffer from the closeness of the confinement, but neither the often-repeated entreaties of Perker and his friends, nor the still more frequently-repeated warnings and admonitions of Mr. Samuel Weller, could induce him to alter one jot of his inflexible resolution.

CHAPTER XLVI.

It was within a week of the close of the month of July, that a hackney cabriolet, number unrecorded, was seen to proceed at a rapid pace up Goswell Street; three people were squeezed into it besides the driver, who sat in his own particular little dickey at the side; over the apron were hung two shawls, belonging to two small vixenish-looking ladies under the apron; between whom, compressed into a very small compass, was stowed away, a gentleman of heavy and subdued demeanour, who, whenever he ventured to make an observation, was snapped up short by one of the vixenish ladies before-mentioned. Lastly, the two vixenish ladies and the heavy gentleman were giving the driver contradictory directions, all tending to the one point that he should stop at Mrs. Bardell's door; which the heavy gentleman, in direct opposition to, and defiance of, the vixenish ladies, contended was a green door and not a yellow one.

"Stop at the house with the green door, driver," said the heavy gentleman.

"Oh! You perwerse creetur!" exclaimed one of the vixenish ladies. "Drive to the ouse with the yellow door, cabmin."

Upon this, the cabman, who in a sudden effort to pull up

at the house with the green door, had pulled the horse up so high that he nearly pulled him backward into the cabriolet, let the animal's fore legs down to the ground again, and paused.

"Now vere am I to pull up?" inquired the driver. "Settle it among yourselves. All I ask is, vere?"

Here the contest was renewed with increased violence; and the horse being troubled with a fly on his nose, the cabman humanely employed his leisure in lashing him about the head, on the counter-irritation principle.

"Most wotes carries the day!" said one of the vixenish ladies at length. "The ouse with the yellow door, cabmin."

But after the cabriolet had dashed up, in splendid style, to the house with the yellow door: "making," as one of the vixenish ladies triumphantly said, "acterrally more noise than if one had come in one's own carriage"—and after the driver had dismounted to assist the ladies in getting out— the small round head of Master Thomas Bardell was thrust out of the one pair window of a house with a red door, a few numbers off.

"Aggrawatin' thing!" said the vixenish lady last mentioned, darting a withering glance at the heavy gentleman.

"My dear, it's not my fault," said the gentleman.

"Don't talk to me, you creetur, don't," retorted the lady. "The house with the red door, cabmin. Oh! If ever a woman was troubled with a ruffinly creetur, that takes a pride and a pleasure in disgracing his wife on every possible occasion afore strangers, I am that woman!"

"You ought to be ashamed of yourself, Raddle," said the other little woman, who was no other than Mrs. Cluppins.

"What have I been a doing of?" asked Mr. Raddle.

"Don't talk to me, don't, you brute, for fear I should be perwoked to forgit my sect and strike you!" said Mrs. Raddle.

While this dialogue was going on, the driver was most ignominiously leading the horse, by the bridle, up to the house with the red door, which Master Bardell had already opened. Here was a mean and low way of arriving at a friend's house! No dashing up, with all the fire and fury of the animal; no jumping down of the driver; no loud knocking at the door; no opening of the apron with a crash at the very last moment, for fear of the ladies sitting in a draught and then the man handing the shawls out, afterwards, as if he were a private coachman! The whole edge of the thing had been taken off; it was flatter than walking.

"Well, Tommy," said Mrs. Cluppins, "How's your poor dear mother?"

"Oh, she's very well," replied Master Bardell. "She's in the front parlour, all ready. I'm ready too, I am." Here Master Bardell put his hands in his pockets, and jumped off and on the bottom step of the door.

"Is anybody else a goin', Tommy?" said Mrs. Cluppins, arranging her pelerine.

"Mrs. Sanders is going, she is," replied Tommy, "I'm going too, I am."

"Drat the boy," said little Mrs. Cluppins. "He thinks of nobody but himself. Here, Tommy, dear."

"Well," said Master Bardell.

"Who else is a goin', lovey?" said Mrs. Cluppins in an insinuating manner.

"Oh! Mrs. Rogers is a goin'," replied Master Bardell, opening his eyes very wide as he delivered the intelligence.

"What! The lady as has taken the lodgings!" ejaculated Mrs. Cluppins.

Master Bardell put his hands deeper down into his pockets, and nodded exactly thirty-five times, to imply that it was the lady lodger, and no other.

"Bless us!" said Mrs. Cluppins. "It's quite a party!"

"Ah, if you knew what was in the cupboard, you'd say so," replied Master Bardell.

"What is there, Tommy?" said Mrs. Cluppins, coaxingly. "You'll tell *me*, Tommy, I know."

"No, I won't," replied Master Bardell, shaking his head, and applying himself to the bottom step again.

"Drat the child!" muttered Mrs. Cluppins. "What a prowokin' little wretch it is! Come, Tommy, tell your dear Cluppy."

"Mother said I wasn't to," rejoined Master Bardell, "I'm a goin' to have some, I am." Cheered by this prospect, the precocious boy applied himself to his infantile treadmill, with increased vigour.

The above examination of a child of tender years, took place while Mr. and Mrs. Raddle and the cab-driver were having an altercation concerning the fare: which, terminating at this point in favour of the cabman, Mrs. Raddle came up tottering.

"Lauk, Mary Ann! what's the matter?" said Mrs. Cluppins.

"It's put me all over in such a tremble, Betsy," replied Mrs. Raddle. "Raddle ain't like a man; he leaves everythink to me."

This was scarcely fair upon the unfortunate Mr. Raddle, who had been thrust aside by his good lady in the commencement of the dispute, and peremptorily commanded to hold his tongue. He had no opportunity of defending himself, however, for Mrs. Raddle gave unequivocal signs of fainting; which, being perceived from the parlour window, Mrs. Bardell, Mrs. Sanders, the lodger, and the lodger's servant, darted precipitately out, and conveyed her into the house: all talking at the same time, and giving utterance to various expressions of pity and condolence, as if she were one of the most suffering mortals on earth. Being conveyed into the front parlour, she was there deposited on a sofa; and the lady from the first floor running up *to* the first floor, returned with a bottle of sal volatile, which, holding Mrs. Raddle tight round the neck, she applied in all womanly kindness and pity to her nose, until that lady with many plunges and struggles was fain to declare herself decidedly better.

"Ah, poor thing!" said Mrs. Rogers, "I know what her feelin's is, too well."

"Ah, poor thing! so do I," said Mrs. Sanders: and then all the ladies moaned in unison, and said *they* knew what it was, and they pitied her from their hearts, they did. Even the lodger's little servant, who was thirteen years old, and three feet high, murmured her sympathy.

"But what's been the matter?" said Mrs. Bardell.

"Ah, what has decomposed you, ma'am?" inquired Mrs. Rogers.

"I have been a good deal flurried," replied Mrs. Raddle, in a reproachful manner. Thereupon the ladies cast indignant looks at Mr. Raddle.

"Why, the fact is," said that unhappy gentleman, stepping forward, "when we alighted at this door, a dispute arose with the driver of the cabrioily——" A loud scream from his wife, at the mention of this word, rendered all further explanation inaudible.

"You'd better leave us to bring her round, Raddle," said Mrs. Cluppins. "She'll never get better as long as you're here."

All the ladies concurred in this opinion; so Mr. Raddle was pushed out of the room, and requested to give himself an airing in the back yard. Which he did for about a quarter of an hour, when Mrs. Bardell announced to him with a solemn face that he might come in now, but that he must be very careful how he behaved towards his wife. She knew he didn't mean to be unkind; but Mary Ann was very far from strong, and, if he didn't take care, he might lose her when he least expected it, which would be a very dreadful reflection for him afterwards; and so on. All this, Mr. Raddle heard with great submission, and presently returned to the parlour in a most lamb-like manner.

"Why, Mrs. Rogers, ma'am," said Mrs. Bardell, "you've never been introduced, I declare! Mr. Raddle, ma'am; Mrs. Cluppins, ma'am; Mrs. Raddle, ma'am."

INTRODUCTION OF MRS. ROGERS.

——"Which is Mrs. Cluppins's sister," suggested Mrs. Sanders.

"Oh, indeed!" said Mrs. Rogers, graciously; for she was the lodger, and her servant was in waiting, so she was more gracious than intimate, in right of her position. "Oh, indeed!"

Mrs. Raddle smiled sweetly, Mr. Raddle bowed, and Mrs. Cluppins said "she was sure she was very happy to have a opportunity of being known to a lady which she had heerd so much in favour of, as Mrs. Rogers." A compliment which the last-named lady acknowledged with graceful condescension.

"Well, Mr. Raddle," said Mrs. Bardell; "I'm sure you ought to feel very much honoured at you and Tommy being the only gentlemen to escort so many ladies all the way to the Spaniards, at Hampstead. Don't you think he ought, Mrs. Rogers, ma'am?"

"Oh, certainly, ma'am," replied Mrs. Rogers; after whom all the other ladies responded "Oh, certainly."

"Of course I feel it, ma'am," said Mr. Raddle, rubbing his hands, and evincing a slight tendency to brighten up a little. "Indeed, to tell you the truth, I said, as we was a coming along in the cabrioily——"

At the recapitulation of the word which awakened so many painful recollections, Mrs. Raddle applied her handkerchief to her eyes again, and uttered a half-suppressed scream; so Mrs. Bardell frowned upon Mr. Raddle, to intimate that he had better not say anything more, and desired Mrs. Rogers's servant, with an air, to "put the wine on."

This was the signal for displaying the hidden treasures of the closet, which comprised sundry plates of oranges and biscuits, and a bottle of old crusted port—that at one and nine—with another of the celebrated East India sherry at fourteenpence, which were all produced in honour of the lodger, and afforded unlimited satisfaction to everybody. After great consternation had been excited in the mind of Mrs. Cluppins,

THE PICKWICK CLUB.

by an attempt on the part of Tommy to recount how he had been cross-examined regarding the cupboard then in action, (which was fortunately nipped in the bud by his imbibing half a glass of the old crusted "the wrong way," and thereby endangering his life for some seconds,) the party walked forth, in quest of a Hampstead stage. This was soon found, and in a couple of hours they all arrived safely in the Spaniards Tea-gardens, where the luckless Mr. Raddle's very first act nearly occasioned his good lady a relapse; it being neither more nor less than to order tea for seven, whereas (as the ladies one and all remarked), what could have been easier than for Tommy to have drank out of anybody's cup—or everybody's, if that was all—when the waiter wasn't looking : which would have saved one head of tea, and the tea just as good !

However, there was no help for it, and the tea-tray came, with seven cups and saucers, and bread and butter on the same scale. Mrs. Bardell was unanimously voted into the chair, and Mrs. Rogers being stationed on her right hand, and Mrs. Raddle on her left, the meal proceeded with great merriment and success.

"How sweet the country is, to-be-sure!" sighed Mrs. Rogers ; "I almost wish I lived in it always."

"Oh, you wouldn't like that, ma'am," replied Mrs. Bardell, rather hastily; for it was not at all advisable, with reference to the lodgings, to encourage such notions ; "you wouldn't like it, ma'am."

"Oh! I should think you was a deal too lively and sought-after, to be content with the country, ma'am," said little Mrs. Cluppins.

"Perhaps I am, ma'am. Perhaps I am," sighed the first-floor lodger.

"For lone people as have got nobody to care for them, or take care of them, or as have been hurt in their mind, or that kind of thing," observed Mr. Raddle, plucking up a little cheerfulness, and looking round, "the country is all very well. The country for a wounded spirit, they say."

UNMANLY CONDUCT OF MR. RADDLE.

Now, of all things in the world that the unfortunate man could have said, any would have been preferable to this. Of course Mrs. Bardell burst into tears, and requested to be led from the table instantly; upon which the affectionate child began to cry too, most dismally.

"Would anybody believe, ma'am," exclaimed Mrs. Raddle, turning fiercely to the first-floor lodger, "that a woman could be married to such a unmanly creetur, which can tamper with a woman's feelings as he does, every hour in the day, ma'am?"

"My dear," remonstrated Mr. Raddle, "I didn't mean anything, my dear."

"You didn't mean!" repeated Mrs. Raddle, with great scorn and contempt. "Go away. I can't bear the sight on you, you brute."

"You must *not* flurry yourself, Mary Ann," interposed Mrs. Cluppins. "You really must consider yourself, my dear, which you never do. Now go away, Raddle, there's a good soul, or you'll only aggravate her."

"You had better take your tea by yourself, sir, indeed," said Mrs. Rogers, again applying the smelling-bottle.

Mrs. Sanders, who according to custom was very busy with the bread and butter, expressed the same opinion, and Mr. Raddle quietly retired.

After this, there was a great hoisting up of Master Bardell, who was rather a large size for hugging, into his mother's arms: in which operation he got his boots in the tea-board, and occasioned some confusion among the cups and saucers. But that description of fainting fits, which is contagious among ladies, seldom lasts long; so when he had been well kissed, and a little cried over, Mrs. Bardell recovered, set him down again, wondered how she could have been so foolish, and poured out some more tea.

It was at this moment, that the sound of approaching wheels was heard, and that the ladies, looking up, saw a hackney-coach stop at the garden-gate.

"More company!" said Mrs. Sanders.

"It's a gentleman," said Mrs. Raddle.

"Well, if it ain't Mr. Jackson, the young man from Dodson and Fogg's!" cried Mrs. Bardell. "Why, gracious! Surely Mr. Pickwick can't have paid the damages."

"Or hoffered marriage!" said Mrs. Cluppins.

"Dear me, how slow the gentleman is," exclaimed Mrs. Rogers: "Why doesn't he make haste?"

As the lady spoke these words, Mr. Jackson turned from the coach where he had been addressing some observations to a shabby man in black leggings, who had just emerged from the vehicle with a thick ash stick in his hand, and made his way to the place where the ladies were seated; winding his hair round the brim of his hat as he came along.

"Is anything the matter? Has anything taken place, Mr. Jackson?" said Mrs. Bardell, eagerly.

"Nothing whatever, ma'am," replied Mr. Jackson. "How de do, ladies? I have to ask pardon, ladies, for intruding— but the law, ladies—the law." With this apology Mr. Jackson smiled, made a comprehensive bow, and gave his hair another wind. Mrs. Rogers whispered Mrs. Raddle that he was really a elegant young man.

"I called in Goswell Street," resumed Jackson, "and hearing that you were here, from the slavey, took a coach and came on. Our people want you down in the city directly, Mrs. Bardell."

"Lor!" ejaculated that lady, starting at the sudden nature of the communication.

"Yes," said Jackson, biting his lip. "It's very important and pressing business, which can't be postponed on any account. Indeed, Dodson expressly said so to me, and so did Fogg. I've kept the coach on purpose for you to go back in."

"How very strange!" exclaimed Mrs. Bardell.

The ladies agreed that it *was* very strange, but were unanimously of opinion that it must be very important, or Dodson and Fogg would never have sent; and further, that the business being urgent, she ought to repair to Dodson and Fogg's without any delay.

There was a certain degree of pride and importance about being wanted by one's lawyers in such a monstrous hurry, that was by no means displeasing to Mrs. Bardell, especially as it might be reasonably supposed to enhance her consequence in the eyes of the first-floor lodger. She simpered a little, affected extreme vexation and hesitation, and at last arrived at the conclusion that she supposed she must go.

"But won't you refresh yourself after your walk, Mr. Jackson?" said Mrs. Bardell, persuasively.

"Why, really there ain't much time to lose," replied Jackson; "and I've got a friend here," he continued, looking towards the man with the ash stick.

"Oh, ask your friend to come here, sir," said Mrs. Bardell. "Pray ask your friend here, sir."

"Why, thankee, I'd rather not," said Mr. Jackson, with some embarrassment of manner. "He's not much used to ladies' society, and it makes him bashful. If you'll order the waiter to deliver him anything short, he won't drink it off at once, won't he!—only try him!" Mr. Jackson's fingers wandered playfully round his nose, at this portion of his discourse, to warn his hearers that he was speaking ironically.

The waiter was at once despatched to the bashful gentleman, and the bashful gentleman took something; Mr. Jackson also took something, and the ladies took something, for hospitality's sake. Mr. Jackson then said he was afraid it was time to go; upon which, Mrs. Sanders, Mrs. Cluppins, and Tommy (who it was arranged should accompany Mrs. Bardell: leaving the others to Mr. Raddle's protection), got into the coach.

"Isaac," said Jackson, as Mrs. Bardell prepared to get in: looking up at the man with the ash stick, who was seated on the box, smoking a cigar.

" Well ? "

" *This* is Mrs. Bardell."

" Oh, I know'd that, long ago," said the man.

Mrs. Bardell got in, Mr. Jackson got in after her, and away they drove. Mrs. Bardell could not help ruminating on what Mr. Jackson's friend had said. Shrewd creatures, those lawyers. Lord bless us, how they find people out!

" Sad thing about these costs of our people's, ain't it ? " said Jackson, when Mrs. Cluppins and Mrs. Sanders had fallen asleep; " your bill of costs, I mean."

" I'm very sorry they can't get them," replied Mrs. Bardell. " But if you law-gentlemen do these things on speculation, why you must get a loss now and then, you know."

" You gave them a *cognovit* for the amount of your costs, after the trial, I'm told ? " said Jackson.

" Yes. Just as a matter of form," replied Mrs. Bardell.

" Certainly," replied Jackson, drily. " Quite a matter of form. Quite."

On they drove, and Mrs. Bardell fell asleep. She was awakened, after some time, by the stopping of the coach.

" Bless us! " said the lady. " Are we at Freeman's Court ? "

" We're not going quite so far," replied Jackson. " Have the goodness to step out."

Mrs. Bardell, not yet thoroughly awake, complied. It was a curious place: a large wall, with a gate in the middle, and a gas-light burning inside.

" Now, ladies," cried the man with the ash stick, looking into the coach, and shaking Mrs. Sanders to wake her, " Come! " Rousing her friend, Mrs. Sanders alighted. Mrs. Bardell, leaning on Jackson's arm, and leading Tommy by the hand, had already entered the porch. They followed.

The room they turned into, was even more odd-looking than the porch. Such a number of men standing about! And they stared so!

" What place is this ? " inquired Mrs. Bardell, pausing.

"Only one of our public offices," replied Jackson, hurrying her through a door, and looking round to see that the other women were following. "Look sharp, Isaac!"

"Safe and sound," replied the man with the ash stick. The door swung heavily after them, and they descended a small flight of steps.

"Here we are, at last. All right and tight, Mrs. Bardell!" said Jackson, looking exultingly round.

"What do you mean?" said Mrs. Bardell, with a palpitating heart.

"Just this," replied Jackson, drawing her a little on one side; "don't be frightened, Mrs. Bardell. There never was a more delicate man than Dodson, ma'am, or a more humane man than Fogg. It was their duty, in the way of business, to take you in execution for them costs; but they were anxious to spare your feelings as much as they could. What a comfort it must be, to you, to think how it's been done! This is the Fleet, ma'am. Wish you good night, Mrs. Bardell. Good night, Tommy!"

As Jackson hurried away in company with the man with the ash stick, another man with a key in his hand, who had been looking on, led the bewildered female to a second short flight of steps leading to a doorway. Mrs. Bardell screamed violently; Tommy roared; Mrs. Cluppins shrunk within herself; and Mrs. Sanders made off without more ado. For, there, stood the injured Mr. Pickwick, taking his nightly allowance of air; and beside him leant Samuel Weller, who, seeing Mrs. Bardell, took his hat off with mock reverence, while his master turned indignantly on his heel.

"Don't bother the woman," said the turnkey to Weller: "she's just come in."

"A pris'ner!" said Sam, quickly replacing his hat. "Who's the plaintives? What for? Speak up, old feller."

"Dodson and Fogg," replied the man; "execution on cognovit for costs."

"Here Job, Job!" shouted Sam, dashing into the passage.

"Run to Mr. Perker's, Job. *I* want him directly. I see some good in this. Here's a game. Hooray! were's the gov'nor?"

But there was no reply to these inquiries, for Job had started furiously off, the instant he received his commission, and Mrs. Bardell had fainted in real downright earnest.

Mrs. Bardell Encounters Mr. Pickwick in the Prison

CHAPTER XLVII.

IS CHIEFLY DEVOTED TO MATTERS OF BUSINESS, AND THE TEM-
PORAL ADVANTAGE OF DODSON AND FOGG.   MR. WINKLE
RE-APPEARS UNDER EXTRAORDINARY CIRCUMSTANCES.   MR.
PICKWICK'S BENEVOLENCE PROVES STRONGER THAN HIS
OBSTINACY.

JOB TROTTER, abating nothing of his speed, ran up Holborn;
sometimes in the middle of the road, sometimes on the
pavement, sometimes in the gutter, as the chances of getting
along varied with the press of men, women, children, and
coaches in each division of the thoroughfare; regardless of
all obstacles, he stopped not for an instant until he reached
the gate of Gray's Inn.   Notwithstanding all the expedition
he had used, however, the gate had been closed a good
half hour when he reached it, and by the time he had
discovered Mr. Perker's laundress, who lived with a married
daughter, who had bestowed her hand upon a non-resident
waiter, who occupied the one-pair of some number in some
street closely adjoining to some brewery somewhere behind
Gray's Inn Lane, it was within fifteen minutes of closing
the prison for the night.   Mr. Lowten had still to be ferreted
out from the back parlour of the Magpie and Stump; and
Job had scarcely accomplished this object, and communicated
Sam Weller's message, when the clock struck ten.

"There," said Lowten, "it's too late now.   You can't get
in to-night; you've got the key of the street, my friend."

"Never mind me," replied Job. "I can sleep anywhere. But won't it be better to see Mr. Perker to-night, so that we may be there, the first thing in the morning?"

"Why," responded Lowten, after a little consideration. "if it was in anybody else's case, Perker wouldn't be best pleased at my going up to his house; but as it's Mr. Pickwick's, I think I may venture to take a cab and charge it to the office." Deciding on this line of conduct, Mr. Lowten took up his hat, and begging the assembled company to appoint a deputy chairman during his temporary absence, led the way to the nearest coach-stand. Summoning the cab of most promising appearance, he directed the driver to repair to Montague Place, Russell Square.

Mr. Perker had had a dinner party that day, as was testified by the appearance of lights in the drawing-room windows, the sound of an improved grand piano, and an improvable cabinet voice issuing therefrom, and a rather overpowering smell of meat which pervaded the steps and entry. In fact a couple of very good country agencies happening to come up to town, at the same time, an agreeable little party had been got together to meet them: comprising Mr. Snicks the Life Office Secretary, Mr. Prosee the eminent counsel, three solicitors, one commissioner of bankrupts, a special pleader from the Temple, a small-eyed peremptory young gentleman, his pupil, who had written a lively book about the law of demises, with a vast quantity of marginal notes and references; and several other eminent and distinguished personages. From this society, little Mr. Perker detached himself, on his clerk being announced in a whisper; and repairing to the dining-room, there found Mr. Lowten and Job Trotter looking very dim and shadowy by the light of a kitchen candle, which the gentleman who condescended to appear in plush shorts and cottons for a quarterly stipend, had, with a becoming contempt for the clerk and all things appertaining to " the office," placed upon the table.

"Now, Lowten," said little Mr. Perker, shutting the door,

"what's the matter? No important letter come in a parcel, is there?"

"No, sir," replied Lowten. "This is a messenger from Mr. Pickwick, sir."

"From Pickwick, eh?" said the little man, turning quickly to Job. "Well, what is it?"

"Dodson and Fogg have taken Mrs. Bardell in execution for her costs, sir," said Job.

"No!" exclaimed Perker, putting his hands in his pockets, and reclining against the sideboard.

"Yes," said Job. "It seems they got a cognovit out of her, for the amount of 'em, directly after the trial."

"By Jove!" said Perker, taking both hands out of his pockets, and striking the knuckles of his right against the palm of his left, emphatically, "those are the cleverest scamps I ever had anything to do with!"

"The sharpest practitioners *I* ever knew, sir," observed Lowten.

"Sharp!" echoed Perker. "There's no knowing where to have them."

"Very true, sir, there is not," replied Lowten; and then, both master and man pondered for a few seconds, with animated countenances, as if they were reflecting upon one of the most beautiful and ingenious discoveries that the intellect of man had ever made. When they had in some measure recovered from their trance of admiration, Job Trotter discharged himself of the rest of his commission. Perker nodded his head thoughtfully, and pulled out his watch.

"At ten precisely, I will be there," said the little man. "Sam is quite right. Tell him so. Will you take a glass of wine, Lowten?"

"No, thank you, sir."

"You mean yes, I think," said the little man, turning to the sideboard for a decanter and glasses.

As Lowten *did* mean yes, he said no more on the subject,

but inquired of Job, in an audible whisper, whether the portrait of Perker, which hung opposite the fire-place, wasn't a wonderful likeness, to which, Job of course replied that it was. The wine being by this time poured out, Lowten drank to Mrs. Perker and the children, and Job to Perker. The gentleman in the plush shorts and cottons considering it no part of his duty to show the people from the office out, consistently declined to answer the bell, and they showed themselves out. The attorney betook himself to his drawing-room, the clerk to the Magpie and Stump, and Job to Covent Garden Market to spend the night in a vegetable basket.

Punctually at the appointed hour next morning, the good-humoured little attorney tapped at Mr. Pickwick's door, which was opened with great alacrity by Sam Weller.

"Mr. Perker, sir," said Sam, announcing the visitor to Mr. Pickwick, who was sitting at the window in a thoughtful attitude. "Wery glad you've looked in accidentally, sir. I rather think the gov'nor wants to have a word and a half with you, sir."

Perker bestowed a look of intelligence on Sam, intimating that he understood he was not to say he had been sent for: and beckoning him to approach, whispered briefly in his ear.

"You don't mean that 'ere, sir?" said Sam, starting back in excessive surprise.

Perker nodded and smiled.

Mr. Samuel Weller looked at the little lawyer, then at Mr. Pickwick, then at the ceiling, then at Perker again; grinned, laughed outright, and finally, catching up his hat from the carpet, without further explanation, disappeared.

"What does this mean?" inquired Mr. Pickwick, looking at Perker with astonishment. "What has put Sam into this most extraordinary state?"

"Oh, nothing, nothing," replied Perker. "Come, my dear

304

sir, draw up your chair to the table. I have a good deal to say to you."

"What papers are those?" inquired Mr. Pickwick, as the little man deposited on the table a small bundle of documents tied with red tape.

"The papers in Bardell and Pickwick," replied Perker, undoing the knot with his teeth.

Mr. Pickwick grated the legs of his chair against the ground; and throwing himself into it, folded his hands and looked sternly—if Mr. Pickwick ever could look sternly—at his legal friend.

"You don't like to hear the name of the cause?" said the little man, still busying himself with the knot.

"No, I do not indeed," replied Mr. Pickwick.

"Sorry for that," resumed Perker, "because it will form the subject of our conversation."

"I would rather that the subject should be never mentioned between us, Perker," interposed Mr. Pickwick, hastily.

"Pooh, pooh, my dear sir," said the little man, untying the bundle, and glancing eagerly at Mr. Pickwick out of the corners of his eyes. "It must be mentioned. I have come here on purpose. Now, are you ready to hear what I have to say, my dear sir? No hurry; if you are not, I can wait. I have this morning's paper here. Your time shall be mine. There!" Hereupon, the little man threw one leg over the other, and made a show of beginning to read with great composure and application.

"Well, well," said Mr. Pickwick, with a sigh, but softening into a smile at the same time. "Say what you have to say; it's the old story, I suppose?"

"With a difference, my dear sir; with a difference," rejoined Perker, deliberately folding up the paper and putting it into his pocket again. "Mrs. Bardell, the plaintiff in the action, is within these walls, sir."

"I know it," was Mr. Pickwick's reply.

"Very good," retorted Perker. "And you know how she

305

comes here, I suppose; I mean on what grounds, and at whose suit?"

"Yes; at least I have heard Sam's account of the matter," said Mr. Pickwick, with affected carelessness.

"Sam's account of the matter," replied Perker, "is, I will venture to say, a perfectly correct one. Well now, my dear sir, the first question I have to ask, is, whether this woman is to remain here?"

"To remain here!" echoed Mr. Pickwick.

"To remain here, my dear sir," rejoined Perker, leaning back in his chair and looking steadily at his client.

"How can you ask me?" said that gentleman. "It rests with Dodson and Fogg; you know that, very well."

"I know nothing of the kind," retorted Perker, firmly. "It does *not* rest with Dodson and Fogg; you know the men, my dear sir, as well as I do. It rests solely, wholly, and entirely with you."

"With me!" ejaculated Mr. Pickwick, rising nervously from his chair, and reseating himself directly afterwards.

The little man gave a double knock on the lid of his snuff-box, opened it, took a great pinch, shut it up again, and repeated the words, "With you."

"I say, my dear sir," resumed the little man, who seemed to gather confidence from the snuff; "I say, that her speedy liberation or perpetual imprisonment rests with you, and with you alone. Hear me out, my dear sir, if you please, and do not be so very energetic, for it will only put you into a perspiration and do no good whatever. I say," continued Perker, checking off each position on a different finger, as he laid it down; "I say that nobody but you can rescue her from this den of wretchedness; and that you can only do that, by paying the costs of this suit—both of plaintiff and defendant—into the hands of these Freeman's Court sharks. Now pray be quiet, my dear sir."

Mr. Pickwick, whose face had been undergoing most surprising changes during this speech, and who was evidently on the verge of a strong burst of indignation, calmed his wrath as well as he could. Perker, strengthening his argumentative powers with another pinch of snuff, proceeded.

"I have seen the woman, this morning. By paying the costs, you can obtain a full release and discharge from the damages ; and further—this I know is a far greater object of consideration with you, my dear sir—a voluntary statement, under her hand, in the form of a letter to me, that this business was, from the very first, fomented, and encouraged, and brought about, by these men, Dodson and Fogg; that she deeply regrets ever having been the instrument of annoyance or injury to you; and that she entreats me to intercede with you, and implore your pardon."

"If I pay her costs for her," said Mr. Pickwick, indignantly. "A valuable document, indeed!"

"No 'if' in the case, my dear sir," said Perker, triumphantly. "There is the very letter I speak of. Brought to my office by another woman at nine o'clock this morning, before I had set foot in this place, or held any communication with Mrs. Bardell, upon my honour." Selecting the letter from the bundle, the little lawyer laid it at Mr. Pickwick's elbow, and took snuff for two consecutive minutes, without winking.

"Is this all you have to say to me?" inquired Mr. Pickwick, mildly.

"Not quite," replied Perker. "I cannot undertake to say, at this moment, whether the wording of the cognovit, the nature of the ostensible consideration, and the proof we can get together about the whole conduct of the suit, will be sufficient to justify an indictment for conspiracy. I fear not, my dear sir; they are too clever for that, I doubt. I do mean to say, however, that the whole facts, taken together, will be sufficient to justify you, in the minds of all reasonable men. And now, my dear sir, I put it to you. This one hundred and fifty pounds, or whatever it may be—take it in round numbers—is nothing to you. A jury has decided against you; well, their verdict is wrong, but still they decided as they thought right, and it *is* against you. You have now an opportunity, on easy terms, of placing yourself in a much higher position than you ever could, by remaining here; which would only be imputed, by people who didn't know you, to sheer dogged, wrongheaded, brutal obstinacy: nothing else, my dear sir, believe me. Can you hesitate to avail yourself of it, when it restores you to your friends, your old pursuits, your health and amusements; when it liberates your faithful and attached servant, whom you otherwise doom to imprisonment for the whole of your life; and above all, when it enables you to take the very magnanimous revenge—which I know, my dear sir, is one after your own heart—of releasing this woman from a scene of misery and debauchery, to which no man should ever be consigned, if I had my will, but the infliction of which on any woman, is even more frightful and barbarous. Now I ask you, my dear sir, not only as your legal adviser, but as your very true friend, will you let slip the occasion of attaining all these objects, and doing all this good, for the paltry consideration of a few pounds finding their way into the pockets of a couple of rascals, to whom it makes no manner of difference, except that the more they gain, the more they'll seek, and so the sooner be led into some piece of knavery that must end in a crash? I have put these considerations to you, my dear sir, very feebly and imperfectly, but I ask you to think of them. Turn them over in your mind as long as you please. I wait here most patiently for your answer."

Before Mr. Pickwick could reply; before Mr. Perker had taken one twentieth part of the snuff with which so unusually long an address imperatively required to be followed up; there was a low murmuring of voices outside, and then a hesitating knock at the door.

"Dear, dear," exclaimed Mr. Pickwick, who had been evidently roused by his friend's appeal; "what an annoyance that door is! Who is that?"

"Me, sir," replied Sam Weller, putting in his head.

A PLEASANT SURPRISE.

"I can't speak to you just now, Sam," said Mr. Pickwick. "I am engaged, at this moment, Sam."

"Beg your pardon, sir," rejoined Mr. Weller. "But here's a lady here, sir, as says she's somethin' wery partickler to disclose."

"I can't see any lady," replied Mr. Pickwick, whose mind was filled with visions of Mrs. Bardell.

"I vouldn't make too sure o' that, sir," urged Mr. Weller, shaking his head. "If you know'd who was near, sir, I rayther think you'd change your note. As the hawk remarked to himself with a cheerful laugh, ven he heerd the robin redbreast a singin' round the corner."

"Who is it?" inquired Mr. Pickwick.

"Will you see her, sir?" asked Mr. Weller, holding the door in his hand as if he had some curious live animal on the other side.

"I suppose I must," said Mr. Pickwick, looking at Perker.

"Well then, all in to begin!" cried Sam. "Sound the gong, draw up the curtain, and enter the two con-spiraytors."

As Sam Weller spoke, he threw the door open, and there rushed tumultuously into the room, Mr. Nathaniel Winkle: leading after him by the hand, the identical young lady who at Dingley Dell had worn the boots with the fur round the tops, and who, now a very pleasing compound of blushes and confusion and lilac silk and a smart bonnet and a rich lace veil, looked prettier than ever.

"Miss Arabella Allen!" exclaimed Mr. Pickwick, rising from his chair.

"No," replied Mr. Winkle, dropping on his knees, "Mrs. Winkle. Pardon, my dear friend, pardon?"

Mr. Pickwick could scarcely believe the evidence of his senses, and perhaps would not have done so, but for the corroborative testimony afforded by the smiling countenance of Perker, and the bodily presence, in the background, of Sam and the pretty housemaid; who appeared to contemplate the proceedings with the liveliest satisfaction.

"Oh, Mr. Pickwick!" said Arabella, in a low voice, as if alarmed at the silence. "Can you forgive my imprudence?"

Mr. Pickwick returned no verbal response to this appeal; but he took off his spectacles in great haste, and seizing both the young lady's hands in his, kissed her a great number of times—perhaps a greater number than was absolutely necessary —and then, still retaining one of her hands, told Mr. Winkle he was an audacious young dog, and bade him get up. This, Mr. Winkle, who had been for some seconds scratching his nose with the brim of his hat, in a penitent manner, did; whereupon Mr. Pickwick slapped him on the back several times, and then shook hands heartily with Perker, who, not to be behind-hand in the compliments of the occasion, saluted both the bride and the pretty housemaid with right good will, and, having wrung Mr. Winkle's hand most cordially, wound up his demonstrations of joy by taking snuff enough to set any half dozen men with ordinarily constructed noses, a sneezing for life.

"Why, my dear girl," said Mr. Pickwick, "how has all this come about? Come! Sit down, and let me hear it all. How well she looks, doesn't she, Perker?" added Mr. Pickwick, surveying Arabella's face with a look of as much pride and exultation, as if she had been his daughter.

"Delightful, my dear sir," replied the little man. "If I were not a married man myself, I should be disposed to envy you, you dog." Thus expressing himself, the little lawyer gave Mr. Winkle a poke in the chest, which that gentleman reciprocated; after which they both laughed very loudly, but not so loudly as Mr. Samuel Weller. Who had just relieved his feelings by kissing the pretty housemaid, under cover of the cupboard-door.

"I can never be grateful enough to you, Sam, I am sure," said Arabella, with the sweetest smile imaginable. "I shall not forget your exertions in the garden at Clifton."

"Don't say nothin' wotever about it, ma'm," replied Sam.

Mr. Winkle Returns under Extraordinary Circumstances

"I only assisted natur', ma'm; as the doctor said to the boy's mother, arter he'd bled him to death."

"Mary, my dear, sit down," said Mr. Pickwick, cutting short these compliments. "Now then; how long have you been married, eh?"

Arabella looked bashfully at her lord and master, who replied, "Only three days."

"Only three days, eh?" said Mr. Pickwick. "Why, what have you been doing these three months?"

"Ah, to be sure!" interposed Perker; "come! Account for this idleness. You see Pickwick's only astonishment is, that it wasn't all over, months ago."

"Why, the fact is," replied Mr. Winkle, looking at his blushing young wife, "that I could not persuade Bella to run away, for a long time. And when I had persuaded her, it was a long time more, before we could find an opportunity. Mary had to give a month's warning, too, before she could leave her place next door, and we couldn't possibly have done it without her assistance."

"Upon my word," exclaimed Mr. Pickwick, who by this time had resumed his spectacles, and was looking from Arabella to Winkle, and from Winkle to Arabella, with as much delight depicted in his countenance as warm-heartedness and kindly feeling can communicate to the human face: "upon my word! you seem to have been very systematic in your proceedings. And is your brother acquainted with all this, my dear?"

"Oh, no, no," replied Arabella, changing colour. "Dear Mr. Pickwick, he must only know it from you—from your lips alone. He is so violent, so prejudiced, and has been so —so anxious in behalf of his friend, Mr. Sawyer," added Arabella, looking down, "that I fear the consequences dreadfully."

"Ah, to be sure," said Perker gravely. "You must take this matter in hand for them, my dear sir. These young men will respect you, when they would listen to nobody else.

311

THE PICKWICK CLUB.

You must prevent mischief, my dear sir. Hot blood, hot blood." And the little man took a warning pinch, and shook his head doubtfully.

"You forget, my love," said Mr. Pickwick, gently, "you forget that I am a prisoner."

"No, indeed I do not, my dear sir," replied Arabella. "I never have forgotten it. I have never ceased to think how great your sufferings must have been in this shocking place. But I hoped that what no consideration for yourself would induce you to do, a regard to our happiness, might. If my brother hears of this, first, from you, I feel certain we shall be reconciled. He is my only relation in the world, Mr. Pickwick, and unless you plead for me, I fear I have lost even him. I have done wrong, very, very wrong, I know." Here poor Arabella hid her face in her handkerchief, and wept bitterly.

Mr. Pickwick's nature was a good deal worked upon, by these same tears; but when Mrs. Winkle, drying her eyes, took to coaxing and entreating in the sweetest tones of a very sweet voice, he became particularly restless, and evidently undecided how to act. As was evinced by sundry nervous rubbings of his spectacle-glasses, nose, tights, head, and gaiters.

Taking advantage of these symptoms of indecision, Mr. Perker (to whom, it appeared, the young couple had driven straight that morning) urged with legal point and shrewdness that Mr. Winkle, senior, was still unacquainted with the important rise in life's flight of steps which his son had taken; that the future expectations of the said son depended entirely upon the said Winkle, senior, continuing to regard him with undiminished feelings of affection and attachment, which it was very unlikely he would, if this great event were long kept a secret from him; that Mr. Pickwick, repairing to Bristol to seek Mr. Allen, might, with equal reason, repair to Birmingham to seek Mr. Winkle, senior; lastly, that Mr. Winkle, senior, had good right and title to consider Mr. Pickwick as in some degree the guardian and adviser of his son, and that it consequently behoved that gentleman, and was indeed due to his personal character, to acquaint the aforesaid Winkle, senior, personally, and by word of mouth, with the whole circumstances of the case, and with the share he had taken in the transaction.

Mr. Tupman and Mr. Snodgrass arrived, most opportunely, in this stage of the pleadings, and as it was necessary to explain to them all that had occurred, together with the various reasons pro and con, the whole of the arguments were gone over again, after which everybody urged every argument in his own way, and at his own length. And, at last, Mr. Pickwick, fairly argued and remonstrated out of all his resolutions, and being in imminent danger of being argued and remonstrated out of his wits, caught Arabella in his arms, and declaring that she was a very amiable creature, and that he didn't know how it was, but he had always been very fond of her from the first, said he could never find it in his heart to stand in the way of young people's happiness, and they might do with him as they pleased.

Mr. Weller's first act, on hearing this concession, was to despatch Job Trotter to the illustrious Mr. Pell, with an authority to deliver to the bearer the formal discharge which his prudent parent had had the foresight to leave in the hands of that learned gentleman, in case it should be, at any time, required on an emergency; his next proceeding was, to invest his whole stock of ready money, in the purchase of five-and-twenty gallons of mild porter: which he himself dispensed on the racket ground to everybody who would partake of it; this done, he hurra'd in divers parts of the building until he lost his voice, and then quietly relapsed into his usual collected and philosophical condition.

At three o'clock that afternoon, Mr. Pickwick took a last look at his little room, and made his way, as well as he could, through the throng of debtors who pressed eagerly forward to shake him by the hand, until he reached the lodge steps. He turned here, to look about him, and his eye lightened as he did so. In all the crowd of wan, emaciated faces, he saw not one which was not the happier for his sympathy and charity.

"Perker," said Mr. Pickwick, beckoning one young man towards him, "this is Mr. Jingle, whom I spoke to you about."

"Very good, my dear sir," replied Perker, looking hard at Jingle. "You will see me again, young man, to-morrow. I hope you may live to remember and feel deeply, what I shall have to communicate, sir."

Jingle bowed respectfully, trembled very much as he took Mr. Pickwick's proffered hand, and withdrew.

"Job you know, I think?" said Mr. Pickwick, presenting that gentleman.

"I know the rascal," replied Perker, good-humouredly. "See after your friend, and be in the way to-morrow at one. Do you hear? Now, is there anything more?"

"Nothing," rejoined Mr. Pickwick. "You have delivered the little parcel I gave you for your old landlord, Sam?"

"I have, sir," replied Sam. "He bust out a cryin', sir, and said you wos wery gen'rous and thoughtful, and he only wished you could have him innokilated for a gallopin' consumption, for his old friend as had lived here so long, wos dead, and he'd noweres to look for another."

"Poor fellow, poor fellow!" said Mr. Pickwick. "God bless you, my friends!"

As Mr. Pickwick uttered this adieu, the crowd raised a loud shout. Many among them were pressing forward to shake him by the hand, again, when he drew his arm through Perker's, and hurried from the prison: far more sad and melancholy, for the moment, than when he had first entered it. Alas! how many sad and unhappy beings had he left behind!

A happy evening was that, for, at least, one party in the George and Vulture; and light and cheerful were two of the hearts that emerged from its hospitable door next morning. The owners thereof were Mr. Pickwick and Sam Weller, the former of whom was speedily deposited inside a comfortable post coach, with a little dickey behind, in which the latter mounted with great agility.

"Sir," called out Mr. Weller to his master.

"Well, Sam," replied Mr. Pickwick, thrusting his head out of the window.

"I wish them horses had been three months and better in the Fleet, sir."

"Why, Sam?" inquired Mr. Pickwick.

"Wy, sir," exclaimed Mr. Weller, rubbing his hands, "how they would go if they had been!"

CHAPTER XLVIII.

RELATES HOW MR. PICKWICK, WITH THE ASSISTANCE OF SAMUEL
WELLER, ESSAYED TO SOFTEN THE HEART OF MR. BENJAMIN
ALLEN, AND TO MOLLIFY THE WRATH OF MR. ROBERT
SAWYER.

MR. BEN ALLEN and Mr. Bob Sawyer sat together in the
little surgery behind the shop, discussing minced veal and
future prospects, when the discourse, not unnaturally, turned
upon the practice acquired by Bob the aforesaid, and his
present chances of deriving a competent independence from
the honourable profession to which he had devoted himself.

"—Which, I think," observed Mr. Bob Sawyer, pursuing
the thread of the subject, "which, I think, Ben, are rather
dubious."

"What's rather dubious?" inquired Mr. Ben Allen, at the
same time sharpening his intellects with a draught of beer.
"What's dubious?"

"Why, the chances," responded Mr. Bob Sawyer.

"I forgot," said Mr. Ben Allen. "The beer has reminded
me that I forgot, Bob—yes; they *are* dubious."

"It's wonderful how the poor people patronise me," said
Mr. Bob Sawyer, reflectively. "They knock me up, at all
hours of the night; they take medicine to an extent which
I should have conceived impossible; they put on blisters and
leeches with a perseverance worthy of a better cause; they
make additions to their families, in a manner which is quite

316

awful. Six of those last-named little promissory notes, all due on the same day, Ben, and all intrusted to me!"

"It's very gratifying, isn't it?" said Mr. Ben Allen, holding his plate for some more minced veal.

"Oh, very," replied Bob; "only not quite so much so, as the confidence of patients with a shilling or two to spare, would be. This business was capitally described in the advertisement, Ben. It is a practice, a very extensive practice —and that's all."

"Bob," said Mr. Ben Allen, laying down his knife and fork, and fixing his eyes on the visage of his friend: "Bob, I'll tell you what it is."

"What is it?" inquired Mr. Bob Sawyer.

"You must make yourself, with as little delay as possible, master of Arabella's one thousand pounds."

"Three per cent. consolidated Bank annuities, now standing in her name in the book or books of the Governor and Company of the Bank of England," added Bob Sawyer, in legal phraseology.

"Exactly so," said Ben. "She has it when she comes of age, or marries. She wants a year of coming of age, and if you plucked up a spirit she needn't want a month of being married."

"She's a very charming and delightful creature," quoth Mr. Robert Sawyer, in reply; "and has only one fault that I know of, Ben. It happens, unfortunately, that that single blemish is a want of taste. She don't like me."

"It's my opinion that she don't know what she does like," said Mr. Ben Allen, contemptuously.

"Perhaps not," remarked Mr. Bob Sawyer. "But it's my opinion that she does know what she doesn't like, and that's of more importance."

"I wish," said Mr. Ben Allen, setting his teeth together, and speaking more like a savage warrior who fed on raw wolf's flesh which he carved with his fingers, than a peaceable young gentleman who ate minced veal with a knife and fork,

"I wish I knew whether any rascal really has been tampering with her, and attempting to engage her affections. I think I should assassinate him, Bob."

"I'd put a bullet in him, if I found him out," said Mr. Sawyer, stopping in the course of a long draught of beer, and looking malignantly out of the porter pot. "If that didn't do his business, I'd extract it afterwards, and kill him that way."

Mr. Benjamin Allen gazed abstractedly on his friend for some minutes in silence, and then said:

"You have never proposed to her, point-blank, Bob?"

"No. Because I saw it would be of no use," replied Mr. Robert Sawyer.

"You shall do it, before you are twenty-four hours older," retorted Ben, with desperate calmness. "She *shall* have you, or I'll know the reason why. I'll exert my authority."

"Well," said Mr. Bob Sawyer, "we shall see."

"We *shall* see, my friend," replied Mr. Ben Allen, fiercely. He paused for a few seconds, and added in a voice broken by emotion, "You have loved her from a child, my friend. You loved her when we were boys at school together, and, even then, she was wayward, and slighted your young feelings. Do you recollect, with all the eagerness of a child's love, one day pressing upon her acceptance, two small caraway-seed biscuits and one sweet apple, neatly folded into a circular parcel with the leaf of a copybook?"

"I do," replied Bob Sawyer.

"She slighted that, I think?" said Ben Allen.

"She did," rejoined Bob. "She said I had kept the parcel so long in the pockets of my corduroys, that the apple was unpleasantly warm."

"I remember," said Mr. Allen, gloomily. "Upon which we ate it ourselves, in alternate bites."

Bob Sawyer intimated his recollection of the circumstance last alluded to, by a melancholy frown; and the two friends remained for some time absorbed, each in his own meditations.

ARRIVAL OF A FLY.

While these observations were being exchanged between Mr. Bob Sawyer and Mr. Benjamin Allen; and while the boy in the grey livery, marvelling at the unwonted prolongation of the dinner, cast an anxious look, from time to time, towards the glass door, distracted by inward misgivings regarding the amount of minced veal which would be ultimately reserved for his individual cravings; there rolled soberly on through the streets of Bristol, a private fly, painted of a sad green colour, drawn by a chubby sort of brown horse, and driven by a surly-looking man with his legs dressed like the legs of a groom, and his body attired in the coat of a coachman. Such appearances are common to many vehicles belonging to, and maintained by, old ladies of economic habits; and in this vehicle, sat an old lady who was its mistress and proprietor.

"Martin!" said the old lady, calling to the surly man, out of the front window.

"Well?" said the surly man, touching his hat to the old lady.

"Mr. Sawyer's," said the old lady.

"I was going there," said the surly man.

The old lady nodded the satisfaction which this proof of the surly man's foresight imparted to her feelings; and the surly man giving a smart lash to the chubby horse, they all repaired to Mr. Bob Sawyer's together.

"Martin!" said the old lady, when the fly stopped at the door of Mr. Robert Sawyer late Nockemorf.

"Well?" said Martin.

"Ask the lad to step out, and mind the horse."

"I'm going to mind the horse myself," said Martin, laying his whip on the roof of the fly.

"I can't permit it, on any account," said the old lady; "your testimony will be very important, and I must take you into the house with me. You must not stir from my side during the whole interview. Do you hear?"

"I hear," replied Martin.

" Well ; what are you stopping for ? "

"Nothing," replied Martin. So saying, the surly man leisurely descended from the wheel, on which he had been poising himself on the tops of the toes of his right foot, and having summoned the boy in the grey livery, opened the coach-door, flung down the steps, and thrusting in a hand enveloped in a dark wash-leather glove, pulled out the old lady with as much unconcern in his manner as if she were a bandbox.

"Dear me ! " exclaimed the old lady. " I am so flurried, now I have got here, Martin, that I'm all in a tremble."

Mr. Martin coughed behind the dark wash-leather glove, but expressed no sympathy ; so the old lady, composing herself, trotted up Mr. Bob Sawyer's steps, and Mr. Martin followed. Immediately on the old lady's entering the shop, Mr. Benjamin Allen and Mr. Bob Sawyer, who had been putting the spirits and water out of sight, and upsetting nauseous drugs to take off the smell of the tobacco-smoke, issued hastily forth in a transport of pleasure and affection.

"My dear aunt," exclaimed Mr. Ben Allen, "how kind of you to look in upon us ! Mr. Sawyer, aunt ; my friend Mr. Bob Sawyer whom I have spoken to you about, regarding—you know, aunt." And here Mr. Ben Allen, who was not at the moment extraordinarily sober, added the word "Arabella," in what was meant to be a whisper, but which was an especially audible and distinct tone of speech, which nobody could avoid hearing, if anybody were so disposed.

"My dear Benjamin," said the old lady, struggling with a great shortness of breath, and trembling from head to foot : "don't be alarmed, my dear, but I think I had better speak to Mr. Sawyer, alone, for a moment. Only for one moment."

"Bob," said Mr. Ben Allen, "will you take my aunt into the surgery ? "

"Certainly," responded Bob, in a most professional voice. "Step this way, my dear ma'am. Don't be frightened, ma'am. We shall be able to set you to rights in a very short time,

A MISUNDERSTANDING.

I have no doubt, ma'am. Here, my dear ma'am. Now then!"
With this, Mr. Bob Sawyer having handed the old lady
to a chair, shut the door, drew another chair close to her,
and waited to hear detailed the symptoms of some disorder
from which he saw in perspective a long train of profits and
advantages.

The first thing the old lady did, was to shake her head a
great many times, and begin to cry.

"Nervous," said Bob Sawyer complacently. "Camphor-
julep and water three times a-day, and composing draught
at night."

"I don't know how to begin, Mr. Sawyer," said the old
lady. "It is so very painful and distressing."

"You need not begin, ma'am," rejoined Mr. Bob Sawyer.
"I can anticipate all you would say. The head is in fault."

"I should be very sorry to think it was the heart," said
the old lady, with a slight groan.

"Not the slightest danger of that, ma'am," replied Bob
Sawyer. "The stomach is the primary cause."

"Mr. Sawyer!" exclaimed the old lady, starting.

"Not the least doubt of it, ma'am," rejoined Bob, looking
wondrous wise. "Medicine, in time, my dear ma'am, would
have prevented it all."

"Mr. Sawyer," said the old lady, more flurried than before,
"this conduct is either great impertinence to one in my
situation, sir, or it arises from your not understanding the
object of my visit. If it had been in the power of medicine,
or any foresight I could have used, to prevent what has
occurred, I should certainly have done so. I had better see
my nephew at once," said the old lady, twirling her reticule
indignantly, and rising as she spoke.

"Stop a moment, ma'am," said Bob Sawyer; "I'm afraid
I have not understood you. What *is* the matter, ma'am?"

"My niece, Mr. Sawyer," said the old lady; "your friend's
sister."

"Yes, ma'am," said Bob, all impatience; for the old lady,

321

although much agitated, spoke with the most tantalising deliberation, as old ladies often do. "Yes, ma'am."

"Left my home, Mr. Sawyer, three days ago, on a pretended visit to my sister, another aunt of hers, who keeps the large boarding-school just beyond the third mile-stone where there is a very large laburnum tree and an oak gate," said the old lady, stopping in this place to dry her eyes.

"Oh, devil take the laburnum tree! ma'am," said Bob, quite forgetting his professional dignity in his anxiety. "Get on a little faster; put a little more steam on, ma'am, pray."

"This morning," said the old lady, slowly, "this morning, she——"

"She came back, ma'am, I suppose," said Bob, with great animation. "Did she come back?"

"No, she did not; she wrote," replied the old lady.

"What did she say?" inquired Bob, eagerly.

"She said, Mr. Sawyer," replied the old lady—"and it is this, I want you to prepare Benjamin's mind for, gently and by degrees; she said that she was—I have got the letter in my pocket, Mr. Sawyer, but my glasses are in the carriage, and I should only waste your time if I attempted to point out the passage to you, without them; she said, in short, Mr. Sawyer, that she was married."

"What!" said, or rather shouted, Mr. Bob Sawyer.

"Married," repeated the old lady.

Mr. Bob Sawyer stopped to hear no more; but darting from the surgery into the outer shop, cried in a stentorian voice, "Ben, my boy, she's bolted!"

Mr. Ben Allen, who had been slumbering behind the counter, with his head half a foot or so below his knees, no sooner heard this appalling communication, than he made a precipitate rush at Mr. Martin, and, twisting his hand in the neckcloth of that taciturn servitor, expressed an intention of choking him where he stood. This intention, with a promptitude often the effect of desperation, he at once commenced carrying into execution, with much vigour and surgical skill.

322

AN EXCITING SCENE.

Mr. Martin, who was a man of few words and possessed but little power of eloquence or persuasion, submitted to this operation with a very calm and agreeable expression of countenance, for some seconds; finding, however, that it threatened speedily to lead to a result which would place it beyond his power to claim any wages, board or otherwise, in all time to come, he muttered an inarticulate remonstrance and felled Mr. Benjamin Allen to the ground. As that gentleman had his hands entangled in his cravat, he had no alternative but to follow him to the floor. There they both lay struggling, when the shop door opened, and the party was increased by the arrival of two most unexpected visitors: to wit, Mr. Pickwick, and Mr. Samuel Weller.

The impression at once produced on Mr. Weller's mind by what he saw, was, that Mr. Martin was hired by the establishment of Sawyer late Nockemorf, to take strong medicine, or to go into fits and be experimentalised upon, or to swallow poison now and then with the view of testing the efficacy of some new antidotes, or to do something or other to promote the great science of medicine, and gratify the ardent spirit of inquiry burning in the bosoms of its two young professors. So, without presuming to interfere, Sam stood perfectly still, and looked on, as if he were mightily interested in the result of the then pending experiment. Not so, Mr. Pickwick. He at once threw himself on the astonished combatants, with his accustomed energy, and loudly called upon the by-standers to interpose.

This roused Mr. Bob Sawyer, who had been hitherto quite paralysed by the frenzy of his companion. With that gentleman's assistance, Mr. Pickwick raised Ben Allen to his feet. Mr. Martin finding himself alone on the floor, got up, and looked about him.

"Mr. Allen," said Mr. Pickwick, "what is the matter, sir?"

"Never mind, sir!" replied Mr. Allen, with haughty defiance.

"What is it?" inquired Mr. Pickwick, looking at Bob Sawyer. "Is he unwell?"

Before Bob could reply, Mr. Ben Allen seized Mr. Pickwick by the hand, and murmured, in sorrowful accents, "My sister, my dear sir; my sister."

"Oh, is that all!" said Mr. Pickwick. "We shall easily arrange that matter, I hope. Your sister is safe and well, and I am here, my dear sir, to——"

"Sorry to do anythin' as may cause an interruption to such wery pleasant proceedin's, as the king said wen he dissolved the parliament," interposed Mr. Weller, who had been peeping through the glass door; "but there's another experiment here, sir. Here's a wenerable old lady a lyin' on the carpet waitin' for dissection, or galwinism, or some other rewivin' and scientific inwention."

"I forgot," exclaimed Mr. Ben Allen. "It is my aunt."

"Dear me!" said Mr. Pickwick. "Poor lady! Gently, Sam, gently."

"Strange sitivation for one o' the family," observed Sam Weller, hoisting the aunt into a chair. "Now, depitty Sawbones, bring out the wollatilly!"

The latter observation was addressed to the boy in grey, who, having handed over the fly to the care of the street-keeper, had come back to see what all the noise was about. Between the boy in grey, and Mr. Bob Sawyer, and Mr. Benjamin Allen (who having frightened his aunt into a fainting fit, was affectionately solicitous for her recovery) the old lady was, at length, restored to consciousness; then Mr. Ben Allen, turning with a puzzled countenance to Mr. Pickwick, asked him what he was about to say, when he had been so alarmingly interrrupted.

"We are all friends here, I presume?" said Mr. Pickwick, clearing his voice, and looking towards the man of few words with the surly countenance, who drove the fly with the chubby horse.

This reminded Mr. Bob Sawyer that the boy in grey was

looking on, with eyes wide open, and greedy ears. The incipient chemist having been lifted up by his coat collar, and dropped outside the door, Bob Sawyer assured Mr. Pickwick that he might speak without reserve.

"Your sister, my dear sir," said Mr. Pickwick, turning to Benjamin Allen, "is in London; well and happy."

"Her happiness is no object to me, sir," said Mr. Benjamin Allen, with a flourish of the hand.

"Her husband *is* an object to *me*, sir," said Bob Sawyer. "He shall be an object to me, sir, at twelve paces, and a very pretty object I'll make of him, sir—a mean-spirited scoundrel!" This, as it stood, was a very pretty denunciation, and magnanimous withal; but Mr. Bob Sawyer rather weakened its effect, by winding up with some general observations concerning the punching of heads and knocking out of eyes, which were commonplace by comparison.

"Stay, sir," said Mr. Pickwick; "before you apply those epithets to the gentleman in question, consider, dispassionately, the extent of his fault, and above all remember that he is a friend of mine."

"What!" said Mr. Bob Sawyer.

"His name!" cried Ben Allen. "His name!"

"Mr. Nathaniel Winkle," said Mr. Pickwick.

Mr. Benjamin Allen deliberately crushed his spectacles beneath the heel of his boot, and having picked up the pieces, and put them into three separate pockets, folded his arms, bit his lips, and looked in a threatening manner at the bland features of Mr. Pickwick.

"Then it's you, is it, sir, who have encouraged and brought about this match?" inquired Mr. Benjamin Allen at length.

"And it's this gentleman's servant, I suppose," interrupted the old lady, "who has been skulking about my house, and endeavouring to entrap my servants to conspire against their mistress. Martin!"

"Well?" said the surly man, coming forward.

"Is that the young man you saw in the lane, whom you told me about, this morning?"

Mr. Martin, who, as it has already appeared, was a man of few words, looked at Sam Weller, nodded his head, and growled forth, "That's the man!" Mr. Weller, who was never proud, gave a smile of friendly recognition as his eyes encountered those of the surly groom, and admitted, in courteous terms, that he had "knowed him afore."

"And this is the faithful creature," exclaimed Mr. Ben Allen, "whom I had nearly suffocated! Mr. Pickwick, how dare you allow your fellow to be employed in the abduction of my sister? I demand that you explain this matter, sir."

"Explain it, sir!" cried Bob Sawyer, fiercely.

"It's a conspiracy," said Ben Allen.

"A regular plant," added Mr. Bob Sawyer.

"A disgraceful imposition," observed the old lady.

"Nothing but a do," remarked Martin.

"Pray hear me," urged Mr. Pickwick, as Mr. Ben Allen fell into a chair that patients were bled in, and gave way to his pocket-handkerchief. "I have rendered no assistance in this matter, beyond that of being present at one interview between the young people, which I could not prevent, and from which I conceived my presence would remove any slight colouring of impropriety that it might otherwise have had; this is the whole share I have taken in the transaction, and I had no suspicion that an immediate marriage was even contemplated. Though, mind," added Mr. Pickwick, hastily checking himself, "mind, I do not say I should have prevented it, if I *had* known that it was intended."

"You hear that, all of you; you hear that?" said Mr. Benjamin Allen.

"I hope they do," mildly observed Mr. Pickwick, looking round, "and," added that gentleman: his colour mounting as he spoke: "I hope they hear this, sir, also. That from what has been stated to me, sir, I assert that you were by no means justified in attempting to force your sister's inclinations as you did, and that you should rather have endeavoured by your kindness and forbearance to have supplied the place of other nearer relations whom she has never known, from a child. As regards my young friend, I must beg to add, that in every point of worldly advantage, he is, at least, on an equal footing with yourself, if not on a much better one, and that unless I hear this question discussed with becoming temper and moderation, I decline hearing any more said upon the subject."

"I wish to make a wery few remarks in addition to wot has been put forard by the honorable gen'l'm'n as has jist give over," said Mr. Weller, stepping forth, "wich is this here : a indiwidual in company has called me a feller."

"That has nothing whatever to do with the matter, Sam," interposed Mr. Pickwick. "Pray hold your tongue."

"I ain't a goin' to say nothin' on that ere pint, sir," replied Sam, "but merely this here. P'raps that gen'l'm'n may think as there wos a priory 'tachment ; but there worn't nothin' o' the sort, for the young lady said, in the wery beginnin' o' the keepin' company, that she couldn't abide him. Nobody's cut him out, and it 'ud ha' been jist the wery same for him if the young lady had never seen Mr. Vinkle. That's wot I wished to say, sir, and I hope I've now made that 'ere gen'l'm'n's mind easy."

A short pause followed these consolatory remarks of Mr. Weller. Then Mr. Ben Allen rising from his chair, protested that he would never see Arabella's face again : while Mr. Bob Sawyer, despite Sam's flattering assurance, vowed dreadful vengeance on the happy bridegroom.

But, just when matters were at their height, and threatening to remain so, Mr. Pickwick found a powerful assistant in the old lady, who, evidently much struck by the mode in which he had advocated her niece's cause, ventured to approach Mr. Benjamin Allen with a few comforting reflections, of which the chief were, that after all, perhaps, it was well it was no worse ; the least said the soonest mended, and upon her word she did not know that it was so very bad after all; what was over couldn't be begun, and what couldn't be cured must be endured : with various other assurances of the like novel and strengthening description. To all of these, Mr. Benjamin Allen replied that he meant no disrespect to his aunt, or anybody there, but if it were all the same to them, and they would allow him to have his own way, he would rather have the pleasure of hating his sister till death, and after it.

At length, when this determination had been announced half a hundred times, the old lady suddenly bridling up and looking very majestic, wished to know what she had done that no respect was to be paid to her years or station, and that she should be obliged to beg and pray, in that way, of her own nephew, whom she remembered about five-and-twenty years before he was born, and whom she had known, personally, when he hadn't a tooth in his head? To say nothing of her presence on the first occasion of his having his hair cut, and assistance at numerous other times and ceremonies during his babyhood, of sufficient importance to found a claim upon his affection, obedience, and sympathies, for ever.

While the good lady was bestowing this objurgation on Mr. Ben Allen, Bob Sawyer and Mr. Pickwick had retired in close conversation to the inner room, where Mr. Sawyer was observed to apply himself several times to the mouth of a black bottle, under the influence of which, his features gradually assumed a cheerful and even jovial expression. And at last he emerged from the room, bottle in hand, and, remarking that he was very sorry to say he had been making a fool of himself, begged to propose the health and happiness of Mr. and Mrs. Winkle, whose felicity, so far from envying, he would be the first to congratulate them upon. Hearing this, Mr. Ben Allen suddenly arose from his chair, and, seizing the black bottle, drank the toast so heartily, that, the liquor being strong, he became nearly as black in the face as the bottle. Finally, the black bottle went round till it was empty, and there was so much shaking of hands and inter-changing of compliments, that even the metal-visaged Mr. Martin condescended to smile.

"And now," said Bob Sawyer, rubbing his hands, "we'll have a jolly night."

"I am sorry," said Mr. Pickwick, "that I must return to my inn. I have not been accustomed to fatigue lately, and my journey has tired me exceedingly."

"You'll take some tea, Mr. Pickwick?" said the old lady, with irresistible sweetness.

"Thank you, I would rather not," replied that gentleman. The truth is, that the old lady's evidently increasing admiration, was Mr. Pickwick's principal inducement for going away. He thought of Mrs. Bardell; and every glance of the old lady's eyes threw him into a cold perspiration.

As Mr. Pickwick could by no means be prevailed upon to stay, it was arranged at once, on his own proposition, that Mr. Benjamin Allen should accompany him on his journey to the elder Mr. Winkle's, and that the coach should be at the door, at nine o'clock next morning. He then took his leave, and, followed by Samuel Weller, repaired to the Bush. It is worthy of remark, that Mr. Martin's face was horribly convulsed as he shook hands with Sam at parting, and that he gave vent to a smile and an oath simultaneously: from which tokens it has been inferred by those who were best acquainted with that gentleman's peculiarities, that he expressed himself much pleased with Mr. Weller's society, and requested the honour of his further acquaintance.

"Shall I order a private room, sir?" inquired Sam, when they reached the Bush.

"Why, no, Sam," replied Mr. Pickwick; "as I dined in the coffee room, and shall go to bed soon, it is hardly worth while. See who there is in the travellers' room, Sam."

Mr. Weller departed on his errand, and presently returned to say, that there was only a gentleman with one eye; and that he and the landlord were drinking a bowl of bishop together.

"I will join them," said Mr. Pickwick.

"He's a queer customer, the vun-eyed vun, sir," observed Mr. Weller, as he led the way. "He's a gammonin' that 'ere landlord, he is, sir, till he don't rightly know wether he's a standing on the soles of his boots or the crown of his hat."

The individual to whom this observation referred, was sitting at the upper end of the room when Mr. Pickwick entered, and was smoking a large Dutch pipe, with his eye intently fixed on the round face of the landlord: a jolly looking old personage, to whom he had recently been relating some tale of wonder, as was testified by sundry disjointed exclamations of, "Well, I wouldn't have believed it! The strangest thing I ever heard! Couldn't have supposed it possible!" and other expressions of astonishment which burst spontaneously from his lips, as he returned the fixed gaze of the one-eyed man.

"Servant, sir," said the one-eyed man to Mr. Pickwick. "Fine night, sir."

"Very much so indeed," replied Mr. Pickwick, as the waiter placed a small decanter of brandy, and some hot water before him.

While Mr. Pickwick was mixing his brandy and water, the one-eyed man looked round at him earnestly, from time to time, and at length said:

"I think I've seen you before."

"I don't recollect you," rejoined Mr. Pickwick.

"I dare say not," said the one-eyed man. "You didn't know me, but I knew two friends of yours that were stopping at the Peacock at Eatanswill, at the time of the Election."

"Oh, indeed!" exclaimed Mr. Pickwick.

"Yes," rejoined the one-eyed man. "I mentioned a little circumstance to them about a friend of mine of the name of Tom Smart. Perhaps you've heard them speak of it."

330

THE ONE-EYED BAGMAN.

"Often," rejoined Mr. Pickwick, smiling. "He was your uncle, I think?"

"No, no; only a friend of my uncle's," replied the one-eyed man.

"He was a wonderful man, that uncle of yours, though," remarked the landlord, shaking his head.

"Well, I think he was, I think I may say he was," answered the one-eyed man. "I could tell you a story about that same uncle, gentlemen, that would rather surprise you."

"Could you?" said Mr. Pickwick. "Let us hear it, by all means."

The one-eyed Bagman ladled out a glass of negus from the bowl, and drank it; smoked a long whiff out of the Dutch pipe; and then, calling to Sam Weller who was lingering near the door, that he needn't go away unless he wanted to, because the story was no secret, fixed his eye upon the landlord's and proceeded, in the words of the next chapter.

CHAPTER XLIX.

"My uncle, gentlemen," said the bagman, "was one of the merriest, pleasantest, cleverest fellows that ever lived. I wish you had known him, gentlemen. On second thoughts, gentlemen, I *don't* wish you had known him, for if you had, you would have been all, by this time, in the ordinary course of nature, if not dead, at all events so near it, as to have taken to stopping at home and giving up company: which would have deprived me of the inestimable pleasure of addressing you at this moment. Gentlemen, I wish your fathers and mothers had known my uncle. They would have been amazingly fond of him, especially your respectable mothers; I know they would. If any two of his numerous virtues predominated over the many that adorned his character, I should say they were his mixed punch and his after supper song. Excuse my dwelling on these melancholy recollections of departed worth; you won't see a man like my uncle every day in the week.

"I have always considered it a great point in my uncle's character, gentlemen, that he was the intimate friend and companion of Tom Smart, of the great house of Bilson and Slum, Cateaton Street, City. My uncle collected for Tiggin and Welps, but for a long time he went pretty near the same journey as Tom; and the very first night they met, my uncle took a fancy for Tom, and Tom took a fancy for my uncle. They made a bet of a new hat before they had known each

332

other half an hour, who should brew the best quart of punch and drink it the quickest. My uncle was judged to have won the making, but Tom Smart beat him in the drinking by about half a salt-spoon-full. They took another quart a-piece to drink each other's health in, and were staunch friends ever afterwards. There's a destiny in these things, gentlemen; we can't help it.

"In personal appearance, my uncle was a trifle shorter than the middle size; he was a thought stouter too, than the ordinary run of people, and perhaps his face might be a shade redder. He had the jolliest face you ever saw, gentlemen: something like Punch, with a handsomer nose and chin; his eyes were always twinkling and sparkling with good humour; and a smile—not one of your unmeaning wooden grins, but a real, merry, hearty, good-tempered smile—was perpetually on his countenance. He was pitched out of his gig once, and knocked, head first, against a mile-stone. There he lay, stunned, and so cut about the face with some gravel which had been heaped up alongside it, that, to use my uncle's own strong expression, if his mother could have revisited the earth, she wouldn't have known him. Indeed, when I come to think of the matter, gentlemen, I feel pretty sure she wouldn't, for she died when my uncle was two years and seven months old, and I think it's very likely that, even without the gravel, his top-boots would have puzzled the good lady not a little: to say nothing of his jolly red face. However, there he lay, and I have heard my uncle say, many a time, that the man said who picked him up that he was smiling as merrily as if he had tumbled out for a treat, and that after they had bled him, the first faint glimmerings of returning animation, were, his jumping up in bed, bursting out into a loud laugh, kissing the young woman who held the basin, and demanding a mutton chop and a pickled walnut. He was very fond of pickled walnuts, gentlemen. He said he always found that, taken without vinegar, they relished the beer.

"My uncle's great journey was in the fall of the leaf, at

333

which time he collected debts, and took orders, in the north : going from London to Edinburgh, from Edinburgh to Glasgow, from Glasgow back to Edinburgh, and thence to London by the smack. You are to understand that his second visit to Edinburgh was for his own pleasure. He used to go back for a week, just to look up his old friends ; and what with breakfasting with this one, lunching with that, dining with a third, and supping with another, a pretty tight week he used to make of it. I don't know whether any of you, gentlemen, ever partook of a real substantial hospitable Scotch breakfast, and then went out to a slight lunch of a bushel of oysters, a dozen or so of bottled ale, and a noggin or two of whiskey to close up with. If you ever did, you will agree with me that it requires a pretty strong head to go out to dinner and supper afterwards.

"But, bless your hearts and eye-brows, all this sort of thing was nothing to my uncle! He was so well seasoned, that it was mere child's play. I have heard him say that he could see the Dundee people out, any day, and walk home afterwards without staggering ; and yet the Dundee people have as strong heads and as strong punch, gentlemen, as you are likely to meet with, between the poles. I have heard of a Glasgow man and a Dundee man drinking against each other for fifteen hours at a sitting. They were both suffocated, as nearly as could be ascertained, at the same moment, but with this trifling exception, gentlemen, they were not a bit the worse for it.

"One night, within four-and-twenty hours of the time when he had settled to take shipping for London, my uncle supped at the house of a very old friend of his, a Baillie Mac something and four syllables after it, who lived in the old town of Edinburgh. There were the baillie's wife, and the baillie's three daughters, and the baillie's grown-up son, and three or four stout, bushy eye-browed, canny old Scotch fellows, that the baillie had got together to do honour to my uncle, and help to make merry. It was a glorious supper. There were

334

WHISKEY TODDY.

kippered salmon, and Finnan haddocks, and a lamb's head, and a haggis—a celebrated Scotch dish, gentlemen, which my uncle used to say always looked to him, when it came to table, very much like a cupid's stomach—and a great many other things besides, that I forget the names of, but very good things notwithstanding. The lassies were pretty and agreeable; the baillie's wife was one of the best creatures that ever lived; and my uncle was in thoroughly good cue. The consequence of which was, that the young ladies tittered and giggled, and the old lady laughed out loud, and the baillie and the other old fellows roared till they were red in the face, the whole mortal time. I don't quite recollect how many tumblers of whiskey toddy each man drank after supper; but this I know, that about one o'clock in the morning, the baillie's grown-up son became insensible while attempting the first verse of ' Willie brewed a peck o' maut;' and he having been, for half an hour before, the only other man visible above the mahogany, it occurred to my uncle that it was almost time to think about going: especially as drinking had set in at seven o'clock, in order that he might get home at a decent hour. But, thinking it might not be quite polite to go just then, my uncle voted himself into the chair, mixed another glass, rose to propose his own health, addressed himself in a neat and complimentary speech, and drank the toast with great enthusiasm. Still nobody woke; so my uncle took a little drop more—neat this time, to prevent the toddy from disagreeing with him—and, laying violent hands on his hat, sallied forth into the street.

"It was a wild gusty night when my uncle closed the baillie's door, and settling his hat firmly on his head, to prevent the wind from taking it, thrust his hands into his pockets, and looking upward, took a short survey of the state of the weather. The clouds were drifting over the moon at their giddiest speed: at one time wholly obscuring her: at another, suffering her to burst forth in full splendour and shed her light on all the objects around: anon, driving over her again, with increased velocity, and shrouding everything in darkness. 'Really, this won't do,' said my uncle, addressing himself to the weather, as if he felt himself personally offended. 'This is not at all the kind of thing for my voyage. It will not do, at any price,' said my uncle very impressively. Having repeated this, several times, he recovered his balance with some difficulty—for he was rather giddy with looking up into the sky so long—and walked merrily on.

"The baillie's house was in the Canongate, and my uncle was going to the other end of Leith Walk, rather better than a mile's journey. On either side of him, there shot up against the dark sky, tall gaunt straggling houses, with time-stained fronts, and windows that seemed to have shared the lot of eyes in mortals, and to have grown dim and sunken with age. Six, seven, eight stories high, were the houses; story piled above story, as children build with cards—throwing their dark shadows over the roughly paved road, and making the dark night darker. A few oil lamps were scattered at long distances, but they only served to mark the dirty entrance to some narrow close, or to show where a common stair communicated, by steep and intricate windings, with the various flats above. Glancing at all these things with the air of a man who had seen them too often before, to think them worthy of much notice now, my uncle walked up the middle of the street, with a thumb in each waistcoat pocket, indulging from time to time in various snatches of song, chaunted forth with such good will and spirit, that the quiet honest folk started from their first sleep and lay trembling in bed till the sound died away in the distance; when, satisfying themselves that it was only some drunken ne'er-do-weel finding his way home, they covered themselves up warm and fell asleep again.

"I am particular in describing how my uncle walked up the middle of the street, with his thumbs in his waistcoat pockets, gentlemen, because, as he often used to say (and with great reason too) there is nothing at all extraordinary in this story, unless you distinctly understand at the beginning that he was not by any means of a marvellous or romantic turn.

"Gentlemen, my uncle walked on with his thumbs in his waistcoat pockets, taking the middle of the street to himself, and singing, now a verse of a love song, and then a verse of a drinking one, and when he was tired of both, whistling melodiously, until he reached the North Bridge, which, at this point, connects the old and new towns of Edinburgh. Here he stopped for a minute, to look at the strange irregular clusters of lights piled one above the other, and twinkling afar off so high, that they looked like stars, gleaming from the castle walls on the one side and the Calton Hill on the other, as if they illuminated veritable castles in the air; while the old picturesque town slept heavily on, in gloom and darkness below: its palace and chapel of Holyrood, guarded day and night, as a friend of my uncle's used to say, by old Arthur's Seat, towering, surly and dark, like some gruff genius, over the ancient city he has watched so long. I say, gentlemen, my uncle stopped here, for a minute, to look about him; and then, paying a compliment to the weather which had a little cleared up, though the moon was sinking, walked on again, as royally as before; keeping the middle of the road with great dignity, and looking as if he would very much like to meet with somebody who would dispute possession of it with him. There was nobody at all disposed to contest the point, as it happened; and so, on he went, with his thumbs in his waistcoat pockets, like a lamb.

"When my uncle reached the end of Leith Walk, he had to cross a pretty large piece of waste ground which separated him from a short street which he had to turn down, to go direct to his lodging. Now, in this piece of waste ground, there was, at that time, an enclosure belonging to some wheelwright who contracted with the Post-office for the purchase of old worn-out mail coaches; and my uncle, being very fond of coaches, old, young, or middle-aged, all at once took it into his head to step out of his road for no other purpose than to peep between the palings at these mails—about a dozen of which, he remembered to have seen, crowded together in a very forlorn and dismantled state, inside. My uncle was a very enthusiastic, emphatic sort of person, gentlemen; so, finding that he could not obtain a good peep between the palings, he got over them, and sitting himself quietly down on an old axletree, began to contemplate the mail coaches with a deal of gravity.

"There might be a dozen of them, or there might be more—my uncle was never quite certain on this point, and being a man of very scrupulous veracity about numbers, didn't like to say—but there they stood, all huddled together in the most desolate condition imaginable. The doors had been torn from their hinges and removed; the linings had been stripped off: only a shred hanging here and there by a rusty nail; the lamps were gone, the poles had long since vanished, the iron-work was rusty, the paint was worn away; the wind whistled through the chinks in the bare wood work; and the rain, which had collected on the roofs, fell, drop by drop, into the insides with a hollow and melancholy sound. They were the decaying skeletons of departed mails, and in that lonely place, at that time of night, they looked chill and dismal.

"My uncle rested his head upon his hands, and thought of the busy bustling people who had rattled about, years before, in the old coaches, and were now as silent and changed; he thought of the numbers of people to whom one of those crazy mouldering vehicles had borne, night after night, for many years, and through all weathers, the anxiously expected intelligence, the eagerly looked-for remittance, the promised assurance of health and safety, the sudden announcement of sickness and death. The merchant, the lover, the wife, the widow, the mother, the schoolboy, the very child who tottered to the door at the postman's knock—how had they all looked forward to the arrival of the old coach. And where were they all now!

OLD MAIL COACHES.

"Gentlemen, my uncle used to *say* that he thought all this at the time, but I rather suspect he learnt it out of some book afterwards, for he distinctly stated that he fell into a kind of doze, as he sat on the old axletree looking at the decayed mail coaches, and that he was suddenly awakened by some deep church-bell striking two. Now, my uncle was never a fast thinker, and if he had thought all these things, I am quite certain it would have taken him till full half-past two o'clock, at the very least. I am, therefore, decidedly of opinion, gentlemen, that my uncle fell into the kind of doze, without having thought about any thing at all.

"Be this, as it may, a church bell struck two. My uncle woke, rubbed his eyes, and jumped up in astonishment.

"In one instant after the clock struck two, the whole of this deserted and quiet spot had become a scene of most extraordinary life and animation. The mail coach doors were on their hinges, the lining was replaced, the iron-work was as good as new, the paint was restored, the lamps were alight, cushions and great coats were on every coach box, porters were thrusting parcels into every boot, guards were stowing away letter-bags, hostlers were dashing pails of water against the renovated wheels; numbers of men were rushing about, fixing poles into every coach; passengers arrived, portmanteaus were handed up, horses were put to; in short, it was perfectly clear that every mail there was to be off directly. Gentlemen, my uncle opened his eyes so wide at all this, that, to the very last moment of his life, he used to wonder how it fell out that he had ever been able to shut 'em again.

"'Now then!' said a voice, as my uncle felt a hand on his shoulder, 'You're booked for one inside. You'd better get in.'

"'*I* booked!' said my uncle, turning round.

"'Yes, certainly.'

"My uncle, gentlemen, could say nothing; he was so very much astonished. The queerest thing of all, was, that although there was such a crowd of persons, and although fresh faces were pouring in, every moment, there was no telling where they came from. They seemed to start up, in some strange manner, from the ground, or the air, and disappear in the same way. When a porter had put his luggage in the coach, and received his fare, he turned round and was gone; and before my uncle had well begun to wonder what had become of him, half-a-dozen fresh ones started up, and staggered along under the weight of parcels which seemed big enough to crush them. The passengers were all dressed so oddly too! Large, broad-skirted laced coats with great cuffs and no collars; and wigs, gentlemen,—great formal wigs with a tie behind. My uncle could make nothing of it.

" 'Now, *are* you going to get in?' said the person who had addressed my uncle before. He was dressed as a mail guard, with a wig on his head and most enormous cuffs to his coat, and had a lantern in one hand, and a huge blunderbuss in the other, which he was going to stow away in his little arm-chest. '*Are* you going to get in, Jack Martin?' said the guard, holding the lantern to my uncle's face.

" 'Hallo!' said my uncle, falling back a step or two. 'That's familiar!'

" 'It's so on the way-bill,' replied the guard.

" 'Isn't there a "Mister" before it?' said my uncle. For he felt, gentlemen, that for a guard he didn't know, to call him Jack Martin, was a liberty which the Post-office wouldn't have sanctioned if they had known it.

" 'No, there is not,' rejoined the guard coolly.

" 'Is the fare paid?' inquired my uncle.

" 'Of course it is,' rejoined the guard.

" 'It is, is it?' said my uncle. 'Then here goes! Which coach?'

" 'This,' said the guard, pointing to an old-fashioned Edinburgh and London Mail, which had the steps down, and the door open. 'Stop! Here are the other passengers. Let them get in first.'

" As the guard spoke, there all at once appeared, right in

front of my uncle, a young gentleman in a powdered wig, and a sky-blue coat trimmed with silver, made very full and broad in the skirts, which were lined with buckram. Tiggin and Welps were in the printed calico and waistcoat piece line, gentlemen, so my uncle knew all the materials at once. He wore knee breeches, and a kind of leggings rolled up over his silk stockings, and shoes with buckles; he had ruffles at his wrists, a three-cornered hat on his head, and a long taper sword by his side. The flaps of his waistcoat came half way down his thighs, and the ends of his cravat reached to his waist. He stalked gravely to the coach-door, pulled off his hat, and held it above his head at arm's length : cocking his little finger in the air at the same time, as some affected people do, when they take a cup of tea. Then he drew his feet together, and made a low grave bow, and then put out his left hand. My uncle was just going to step forward, and shake it heartily, when he perceived that these attentions were directed, not towards him, but to a young lady who just then appeared at the foot of the steps, attired in an old-fashioned green velvet dress with a long waist and stomacher. She had no bonnet on her head, gentlemen, which was muffled in a black silk hood, but she looked round for an instant as she prepared to get into the coach, and such a beautiful face as she disclosed, my uncle had never seen—not even in a picture. She got into the coach, holding up her dress with one hand ; and, as my uncle always said with a round oath, when he told the story, he wouldn't have believed it possible that legs and feet could have been brought to such a state of perfection unless he had seen them with his own eyes.

"But, in this one glimpse of the beautiful face, my uncle saw that the young lady cast an imploring look upon him, and that she appeared terrified and distressed. He noticed, too, that the young fellow in the powdered wig, notwithstanding his show of gallantry, which was all very fine and grand, clasped her tight by the wrist when she got in, and followed himself immediately afterwards. An uncommonly ill-looking fellow, in a close brown wig and a plum-coloured suit, wearing a very large sword, and boots up to his hips, belonged to the party; and when he sat himself down next to the young lady, who shrunk into a corner at his approach, my uncle was confirmed in his original impression that something dark and mysterious was going forward, or, as he always said himself, that 'there was a screw loose somewhere.' It's quite surprising how quickly he made up his mind to help the lady at any peril, if she needed help.

"'Death and lightning!' exclaimed the young gentleman, laying his hand upon his sword as my uncle entered the coach.

"'Blood and thunder!' roared the other gentleman. With this, he whipped his sword out, and made a lunge at my uncle without further ceremony. My uncle had no weapon about him, but with great dexterity he snatched the ill-looking gentleman's three-cornered hat from his head, and, receiving the point of his sword right through the crown, squeezed the sides together, and held it tight.

"'Pink him behind!' cried the ill-looking gentleman to his companion, as he struggled to regain his sword.

"'He had better not,' cried my uncle, displaying the heel of one of his shoes, in a threatening manner. 'I'll kick his brains out, if he has any, or fracture his skull if he hasn't.' Exerting all his strength, at this moment, my uncle wrenched the ill-looking man's sword from his grasp, and flung it clean out of the coach-window : upon which the younger gentleman vociferated 'Death and lightning!' again, and laid his hand upon the hilt of his sword, in a very fierce manner, but didn't draw it. Perhaps, gentlemen, as my uncle used to say with a smile, perhaps he was afraid of alarming the lady.

"'Now, gentlemen,' said my uncle, taking his seat deliberately, 'I don't want to have any death, with or without lightning, in a lady's presence, and we have had quite blood and thundering enough for one journey; so, if you please, we'll sit in our places like quiet insides. Here, guard, pick up that gentleman's carving-knife.'

The Ghostly Passengers in the Ghost of a Mail

" As quickly as my uncle said the words, the guard appeared at the coach-window, with the gentleman's sword in his hand. He held up his lantern, and looked earnestly in my uncle's face, as he handed it in : when, by its light, my uncle saw, to his great surprise, that an immense crowd of mail-coach guards swarmed round the window, every one of whom had his eyes earnestly fixed upon him too. He had never seen such a sea of white faces, red bodies, and earnest eyes, in all his born days.

" 'This is the strangest sort of thing I ever had anything to do with,' thought my uncle ; ' allow me to return you your hat, sir.'

" The ill-looking gentleman received his three-cornered hat in silence, looked at the hole in the middle with an inquiring air, and finally stuck it on the top of his wig with a solemnity the effect of which was a trifle impaired by his sneezing violently at the moment, and jerking it off again.

" ' All right ! ' cried the guard with the lantern, mounting into his little seat behind. Away they went. My uncle peeped out of the coach-window as they emerged from the yard, and observed that the other mails, with coachmen, guards, horses, and passengers, complete, were driving round and round in circles, at a slow trot of about five miles an hour. My uncle burnt with indignation, gentlemen. As a commercial man, he felt that the mail bags were not to be trifled with, and he resolved to memorialise the Post-office on the subject, the very instant he reached London.

" At present, however, his thoughts were occupied with the young lady who sat in the farthest corner of the coach, with her face muffled closely in her hood ; the gentleman with the sky-blue coat sitting opposite to her ; the other man in the plum-coloured suit, by her side, and both watching her intently. If she so much as rustled the folds of her hood, he could hear the ill-looking man clap his hand upon his sword, and could tell by the other's breathing (it was so dark he couldn't see his face) that he was looking as big as if he were going to devour her at a mouthful. This roused my uncle more and

more, and he resolved, come what come might, to see the end
of it. He had a great admiration for bright eyes, and sweet
faces, and pretty legs and feet; in short, he was fond of the
whole sex. It runs in our family, gentlemen—so am I.

"Many were the devices which my uncle practised, to attract
the lady's attention, or at all events, to engage the mysterious
gentlemen in conversation. They were all in vain; the
gentlemen wouldn't talk, and the lady didn't dare. He thrust
his head out of the coach-window at intervals, and bawled out
to know why they didn't go faster? But he called till he
was hoarse; nobody paid the least attention to him. He
leant back in the coach, and thought of the beautiful face,
and the feet and legs. This answered better; it whiled away
the time, and kept him from wondering where he was going,
and how it was that he found himself in such an odd situation.
Not that this would have worried him much, any way—he
was a mighty free and easy, roving, devil-may-care sort of
person, was my uncle, gentlemen.

"All of a sudden the coach stopped. 'Hallo!' said my
uncle, 'What's in the wind now?'

"'Alight here,' said the guard, letting down the steps.

"'Here!' cried my uncle.

"'Here,' rejoined the guard.

"'I'll do nothing of the sort,' said my uncle.

"'Very well, then stop where you are,' said the guard.

"'I will,' said my uncle.

"'Do,' said the guard.

"The other passengers had regarded this colloquy with
great attention, and, finding that my uncle was determined
not to alight, the younger man squeezed past him, to hand
the lady out. At this moment, the ill-looking man was
inspecting the hole in the crown of his three-cornered hat.
As the young lady brushed past, she dropped one of her
gloves into my uncle's hand, and softly whispered, with her
lips so close to his face that he felt her warm breath on his
nose, the single word 'Help!' Gentlemen, my uncle leaped

out of the coach at once, with such violence that it rocked on the springs again.

"'Oh! You've thought better of it, have you?' said the guard when he saw my uncle standing on the ground.

"My uncle looked at the guard for a few seconds, in some doubt whether it wouldn't be better to wrench his blunderbuss from him, fire it in the face of the man with the big sword, knock the rest of the company over the head with the stock, snatch up the young lady, and go off in the smoke. On second thoughts, however, he abandoned this plan, as being a shade too melodramatic in the execution, and followed the two mysterious men, who, keeping the lady between them, were now entering an old house in front of which the coach had stopped. They turned into the passage, and my uncle followed.

"Of all the ruinous and desolate places my uncle had ever beheld, this was the most so. It looked as if it had once been a large house of entertainment; but the roof had fallen in, in many places, and the stairs were steep, rugged, and broken. There was a huge fire-place in the room into which they walked, and the chimney was blackened with smoke; but no warm blaze lighted it up now. The white feathery dust of burnt wood was still strewed over the hearth, but the stove was cold, and all was dark and gloomy.

"'Well,' said my uncle, as he looked about him, 'A mail travelling at the rate of six miles and a half an hour, and stopping for an indefinite time at such a hole as this, is rather an irregular sort of proceeding, I fancy. This shall be made known. I'll write to the papers.'

"My uncle said this in a pretty loud voice, and in an open unreserved sort of manner, with the view of engaging the two strangers in conversation if he could. But, neither of them took any more notice of him than whispering to each other, and scowling at him as they did so. The lady was at the farther end of the room, and once she ventured to wave her hand, as if beseeching my uncle's assistance.

"At length the two strangers advanced a little, and the conversation began in earnest.

"'You don't know this is a private room, I suppose, fellow?' said the gentleman in sky-blue.

"'No, I do not, fellow,' rejoined my uncle. 'Only if this is a private room specially ordered for the occasion, I should think the public room must be a *very* comfortable one;' with this my uncle sat himself down in a high-backed chair, and took such an accurate measure of the gentleman, with his eyes, that Tiggin and Welps could have supplied him with printed calico for a suit, and not an inch too much or too little, from that estimate alone.

"'Quit this room,' said both the men together, grasping their swords.

"'Eh?' said my uncle, not at all appearing to comprehend their meaning.

"'Quit the room, or you are a dead man,' said the ill-looking fellow with the large sword, drawing it at the same time and flourishing it in the air.

"'Down with him!' cried the gentleman in sky-blue, drawing his sword also, and falling back two or three yards. 'Down with him!' The lady gave a loud scream.

"Now, my uncle was always remarkable for great boldness, and great presence of mind. All the time that he had appeared so indifferent to what was going on, he had been looking slyly about, for some missile or weapon of defence, and at the very instant when the swords were drawn, he espied, standing in the chimney corner, an old basket-hilted rapier in a rusty scabbard. At one bound, my uncle caught it in his hand, drew it, flourished it gallantly above his head, called aloud to the lady to keep out of the way, hurled the chair at the man in sky-blue, and the scabbard at the man in plum-colour, and taking advantage of the confusion, fell upon them both, pell-mell

"Gentlemen, there is an old story—none the worse for being true—regarding a fine young Irish gentleman, who being asked if he could play the fiddle, replied he had no doubt he could, but he couldn't exactly say, for certain, because he had never tried. This is not inapplicable to my uncle and his fencing. He had never had a sword in his hand before, except once when he played Richard the Third at a private theatre: upon which occasion it was arranged with Richmond that he was to be run through, from behind, without showing fight at all. But here he was, cutting and slashing with two experienced swordsmen: thrusting and guarding and poking and slicing, and acquitting himself in the most manful and dexterous manner possible, although up to that time he had never been aware that he had the least notion of the science. It only shows how true the old saying is, that a man never knows what he can do, till he tries, gentlemen.

"The noise of the combat was terrific; each of the three combatants swearing like troopers, and their swords clashing with as much noise as if all the knives and steels in Newport market were rattling together, at the same time. When it was at its very height, the lady (to encourage my uncle most probably) withdrew her hood entirely from her face, and disclosed a countenance of such dazzling beauty, that he would have fought against fifty men, to win one smile from it, and die. He had done wonders before, but now he began to powder away like a raving mad giant.

"At this very moment, the gentleman in sky-blue turning round, and seeing the young lady with her face uncovered, vented an exclamation of rage and jealousy, and, turning his weapon against her beautiful bosom, pointed a thrust at her heart, which caused my uncle to utter a cry of apprehension that made the building ring. The lady stepped lightly aside, and snatching the young man's sword from his hand, before he had recovered his balance, drove him to the wall, and running it through him, and the panelling, up to the very hilt, pinned him there, hard and fast. It was a splendid example. My uncle, with a loud shout of triumph, and a strength that was irresistible, made his adversary retreat in the same direction, and plunging the old rapier into the very centre of a large red flower in the pattern of his waistcoat, nailed him beside his friend; there they both stood, gentlemen, jerking their arms and legs about, in agony, like the toy-shop figures that are moved by a piece of packthread. My uncle always said, afterwards, that this was one of the surest means he knew of, for disposing of an enemy; but it was liable to one objection on the ground of expense, inasmuch as it involved the loss of a sword for every man disabled.

"'The mail, the mail!' cried the lady, running up to my uncle and throwing her beautiful arms round his neck; 'we may yet escape.'

"'*May!*' cried my uncle; 'why, my dear, there's nobody else to kill, is there?' My uncle was rather disappointed, gentlemen, for he thought a little quiet bit of love-making would be agreeable after the slaughtering, if it were only to change the subject.

"'We have not an instant to lose here,' said the young lady. 'He (pointing to the young gentleman in sky-blue) is the only son of the powerful Marquess of Filletoville.'

"'Well, then, my dear, I'm afraid he'll never come to the title,' said my uncle, looking coolly at the young gentleman as he stood fixed up against the wall, in the cockchafer fashion I have described. 'You have cut off the entail, my love.'

"'I have been torn from my home and friends by these villains,' said the young lady, her features glowing with indignation. 'That wretch would have married me by violence in another hour.'

"'Confound his impudence!' said my uncle, bestowing a very contemptuous look on the dying heir of Filletoville.

"'As you may guess from what you have seen,' said the young lady, 'the party were prepared to murder me if I appealed to any one for assistance. If their accomplices find us here, we are lost. Two minutes hence may be too late. The mail!' With these words, overpowered by her feelings, and the exertion of sticking the young Marquess of Filletoville, she sunk into my uncle's arms. My uncle caught her up, and bore her to the house-door. There stood the mail, with four long-tailed, flowing-maned, black horses, ready harnessed; but no coachman, no guard, no hostler even, at the horses' heads.

"Gentlemen, I hope I do no injustice to my uncle's memory, when I express my opinion, that although he was a bachelor, he *had* held some ladies in his arms, before this time; I believe indeed, that he had rather a habit of kissing barmaids; and I know, that in one or two instances, he had been seen by credible witnesses, to hug a landlady in a very perceptible manner. I mention the circumstance, to show what a very uncommon sort of person this beautiful young lady must have been, to have affected my uncle in the way she did; he used to say, that as her long dark hair trailed over his arm, and her beautiful dark eyes fixed themselves upon his face when she recovered, he felt so strange and nervous that his legs trembled beneath him. But, who can look in a sweet soft pair of dark eyes, without feeling queer? *I* can't, gentlemen. I am afraid to look at some eyes I know, and that's the truth of it.

"'You will never leave me,' murmured the young lady.

"'Never,' said my uncle. And he meant it too.

"'My dear preserver!' exclaimed the young lady. 'My dear, kind, brave preserver!'

"'Don't,' said my uncle, interrupting her.

"'Why?' inquired the young lady.

"'Because your mouth looks so beautiful when you speak,' rejoined my uncle, 'that I'm afraid I shall be rude enough to kiss it.'

"The young lady put up her hand as if to caution my uncle not to do so, and said—no, she didn't say anything—she smiled. When you are looking at a pair of the most delicious lips in the world, and see them gently break into a roguish smile—if you are very near them, and nobody else by—you cannot better testify your admiration of their beautiful form and colour than by kissing them at once. My uncle did so, and I honour him for it.

"'Hark!' cried the young lady, starting. 'The noise of wheels and horses!'

"'So it is,' said my uncle, listening. He had a good ear for wheels, and the trampling of hoofs; but there appeared to be so many horses and carriages rattling towards them, from a distance, that it was impossible to form a guess at their number. The sound was like that of fifty breaks, with six blood cattle in each.

"'We are pursued!' cried the young lady, clasping her hands. 'We are pursued. I have no hope but in you!'

"There was such an expression of terror in her beautiful face, that my uncle made up his mind at once. He lifted her into the coach, told her not to be frightened, pressed his lips to hers once more, and then advising her to draw up the window to keep the cold air out, mounted to the box.

"'Stay, love,' cried the young lady.

"'What's the matter?' said my uncle, from the coach-box.

"'I want to speak to you,' said the young lady; 'only a word. Only one word, dearest.'

"'Must I get down?' inquired my uncle. The lady made no answer, but she smiled again. Such a smile, gentlemen! It beat the other one, all to nothing. My uncle descended from his perch in a twinkling.

"'What is it, my dear?' said my uncle, looking in at the coach window. The lady happened to bend forward at the same time, and my uncle thought she looked more beautiful than she had done yet. He was very close to her just then, gentlemen, so he really ought to know.

"'What is it, my dear?' said my uncle.

"'Will you never love any one but me; never marry any one beside?' said the young lady.

"My uncle swore a great oath that he never would marry any body else, and the young lady drew in her head, and pulled up the window. He jumped upon the box, squared his elbows, adjusted the ribands, seized the whip which lay on the roof, gave one flick to the off leader, and away went the four long-tailed flowing-maned black horses, at fifteen good English miles an hour, with the old mail coach behind them. Whew! How they tore along!

"The noise behind grew louder. The faster the old mail went, the faster came the pursuers—men, horses, dogs, were leagued in the pursuit. The noise was frightful, but, above all, rose the voice of the young lady, urging my uncle on, and shrieking, 'Faster! Faster!'

"They whirled past the dark trees, as feathers would be swept before a hurricane. Houses, gates, churches, haystacks, objects of every kind they shot by, with a velocity and noise like roaring waters suddenly let loose. Still the noise of pursuit grew louder, and still my uncle could hear the young lady wildly screaming, 'Faster! Faster!'

"My uncle plied whip and rein, and the horses flew onward till they were white with foam; and yet the noise behind increased; and yet the young lady cried 'Faster! Faster!' My uncle gave a loud stamp on the boot in the energy of the moment, and—found that it was grey morning, and he was sitting in the wheelwright's yard, on the box of an old Edinburgh mail, shivering with the cold and wet and stamping his feet to warm them! He got down, and looked eagerly inside for the beautiful young lady. Alas! There was neither door nor seat to the coach. It was a mere shell.

"Of course, my uncle knew very well that there was some mystery in the matter, and that everything had passed exactly as he used to relate it. He remained staunch to the great oath he had sworn to the beautiful young lady: refusing several eligible landladies on her account, and dying a bachelor at last. He always said, what a curious thing it was that he should have found out, by such a mere accident as his clambering over the palings, that the ghosts of mail-coaches and horses, guards, coachmen, and passengers, were in the habit of making journeys regularly every night. He used to add, that he believed he was the only living person who had ever been taken as a passenger on one of these excursions. And I think he was right, gentlemen—at least I never heard of any other."

"I wonder what these ghosts of mail-coaches carry in their bags," said the landlord, who had listened to the whole story with profound attention.

"The dead letters, of course," said the Bagman.

"Oh, ah! To be sure," rejoined the landlord. "I never thought of that."

CHAPTER L.

HOW MR. PICKWICK SPED UPON HIS MISSION, AND HOW HE WAS REINFORCED IN THE OUTSET BY A MOST UNEXPECTED AUXILIARY.

THE horses were put to, punctually at a quarter before nine next morning, and Mr. Pickwick and Sam Weller having each taken his seat, the one inside and the other out, the postillion was duly directed to repair in the first instance to Mr. Bob Sawyer's house, for the purpose of taking up Mr. Benjamin Allen.

It was with feelings of no small astonishment, when the carriage drew up before the door with the red lamp, and the very legible inscription of "Sawyer, late Nockemorf," that Mr. Pickwick saw, on popping his head out of the coach-window, the boy in the grey livery very busily employed in putting up the shutters: the which, being an unusual and an un-business-like proceeding at that hour of the morning, at once suggested to his mind, two inferences; the one, that some good friend and patient of Mr. Bob Sawyer's was dead; the other, that Mr. Bob Sawyer himself was bankrupt.

"What is the matter?" said Mr. Pickwick to the boy.

"Nothing's the matter, sir," replied the boy, expanding his mouth to the whole breadth of his countenance.

"All right, all right!" cried Bob Sawyer suddenly appearing at the door, with a small leathern knapsack, limp and dirty, in one hand, and a rough coat and shawl thrown over the other arm. "I'm going, old fellow."

"You !" exclaimed Mr. Pickwick.

"Yes," replied Bob Sawyer, "and a regular expedition we'll make of it. Here, Sam! Look out!" Thus briefly bespeaking Mr. Weller's attention, Mr. Bob Sawyer jerked the leathern knapsack into the dickey, where it was immediately stowed away, under the seat, by Sam, who regarded the proceeding with great admiration. This done, Mr. Bob Sawyer, with the assistance of the boy, forcibly worked himself into the rough coat, which was a few sizes too small for him, and then advancing to the coach window, thrust in his head, and laughed boisterously.

"What a start it is, isn't it!" cried Bob, wiping the tears out of his eyes, with one of the cuffs of the rough coat.

"My dear sir," said Mr. Pickwick, with some embarrassment, "I had no idea of your accompanying us."

"No, that's just the very thing," replied Bob, seizing Mr. Pickwick by the lappel of his coat. "That's the joke."

"Oh, that's the joke?" said Mr. Pickwick.

"Of course," replied Bob. "It's the whole point of the thing, you know—that, and leaving the business to take care of itself, as it seems to have made up its mind not to take care of me." With this explanation of the phenomenon of the shutters, Mr. Bob Sawyer pointed to the shop, and relapsed into an ecstasy of mirth.

"Bless me, you are surely not mad enough to think of leaving your patients without anybody to attend them!" remonstrated Mr. Pickwick in a very serious tone.

"Why not?" asked Bob, in reply. "I shall save by it, you know. None of them ever pay. Besides," said Bob, lowering his voice to a confidential whisper, "they will be all the better for it; for, being nearly out of drugs, and not able to increase my account just now, I should have been obliged to give them calomel all round, and it would have been certain to have disagreed with some of them. So it's all for the best.

There was a philosophy, and a strength of reasoning, about this reply, which Mr. Pickwick was not prepared for. He paused a few moments, and added, less firmly than before:

"But this chaise, my young friend, will only hold two; and I am pledged to Mr. Allen."

"Don't think of me for a minute," replied Bob. "I've arranged it all; Sam and I will share the dickey between us. Look here. This little bill is to be wafered on the shop door: 'Sawyer, late Nockemorf. Enquire of Mrs. Cripps over the way.' Mrs. Cripps is my boy's mother. 'Mr. Sawyer's very sorry,' says Mrs. Cripps, 'couldn't help it—fetched away early this morning to a consultation of the very first surgeons in the country—couldn't do without him—would have him at any price—tremendous operation.' The fact is," said Bob in conclusion, "it'll do me more good than otherwise, I expect. If it gets into one of the local papers, it will be the making of me. Here's Ben; now then, jump in!"

With these hurried words, Mr. Bob Sawyer pushed the post-boy on one side, jerked his friend into the vehicle, slammed the door, put up the steps, wafered the bill on the street door, locked it, put the key in his pocket, jumped into the dickey, gave the word for starting, and did the whole with such extraordinary precipitation, that before Mr. Pickwick had well began to consider whether Mr. Bob Sawyer ought to go or not, they were rolling away, with Mr. Bob Sawyer thoroughly established as part and parcel of the equipage.

So long as their progress was confined to the streets of Bristol, the facetious Bob kept his professional green spectacles on, and conducted himself with becoming steadiness and gravity of demeanour; merely giving utterance to divers verbal witticisms for the exclusive behoof and entertainment of Mr. Samuel Weller. But when they emerged on the open road, he threw off his green spectacles and his gravity together, and performed a great variety of practical jokes, which were calculated to attract the attention of the passers-by, and to render the carriage and those it contained, objects of more than ordinary curiosity ; the least conspicuous among these feats, being, a most vociferous imitation of a key-bugle, and the ostentatious display of a crimson silk pocket-handkerchief attached to a walking-stick, which was occasionally waved in the air with various gestures indicative of supremacy and defiance.

" I wonder," said Mr. Pickwick, stopping in the midst of a most sedate conversation with Ben Allen, bearing reference to the numerous good qualities of Mr. Winkle and his sister : " I wonder what all the people we pass, can see in us to make them stare so."

" It's a neat turn-out," replied Ben Allen, with something of pride in his tone. " They're not used to see this sort of thing, every day, I dare say."

" Possibly," replied Mr. Pickwick. " It may be so. Perhaps it is."

Mr. Pickwick might very probably have reasoned himself into the belief that it really was : had he not, just then happening to look out of the coach window, observed that the looks of the passengers betokened anything but respectful astonishment, and that various telegraphic communications appeared to be passing between them and some persons outside the vehicle : whereupon it occurred to him that these demonstrations might be, in some remote degree, referable to the humorous deportment of Mr. Robert Sawyer.

" I hope," said Mr. Pickwick, " that our volatile friend is committing no absurdities in that dickey behind."

" Oh dear, no," replied Ben Allen. " Except when he's elevated, Bob's the quietest creature breathing."

Here a prolonged imitation of a key-bugle broke upon the ear, succeeded by cheers and screams, all of which evidently proceeded from the throat and lungs of the quietest creature breathing, or in plainer designation, of Mr. Bob Sawyer himself.

Mr. Pickwick and Mr. Ben Allen looked expressively at each other, and the former gentleman taking off his hat, and leaning out of the coach-window until nearly the whole of his waistcoat was outside it, was at length enabled to catch a glimpse of his facetious friend.

Mr. Bob Sawyer was seated: not in the dickey, but on the roof of the chaise, with his legs as far asunder as they would conveniently go, wearing Mr. Samuel Weller's hat on one side of his head, and bearing, in one hand, a most enormous sandwich, while, in the other, he supported a goodly-sized case bottle, to both of which he applied himself with intense relish: varying the monotony of the occupation by an occasional howl, or the interchange of some lively *badinage* with any passing stranger. The crimson flag was carefully tied in an erect position to the rail of the dickey; and Mr. Samuel Weller, decorated with Bob Sawyer's hat, was seated in the centre thereof, discussing a twin sandwich, with an animated countenance, the expression of which betokened his entire and perfect approval of the whole arrangement.

This was enough to irritate a gentleman with Mr. Pickwick's sense of propriety, but it was not the whole extent of the aggravation, for a stage-coach full, inside and out, was meeting them at the moment, and the astonishment of the passengers was very palpably evinced. The congratulations of an Irish family, too, who were keeping up with the chaise, and begging all the time, were of rather a boisterous description; especially those of its male head, who appeared to consider the display as part and parcel of some political, or other procession of triumph.

"Mr. Sawyer!" cried Mr. Pickwick, in a state of great excitement. "Mr. Sawyer, sir!"

"Hallo!" responded that gentleman, looking over the side of the chaise with all the coolness in life.

"Are you mad, sir?" demanded Mr. Pickwick.

"Not a bit of it," replied Bob; "only cheerful."

"Cheerful, sir!" ejaculated Mr. Pickwick. "Take down that scandalous red handkerchief, I beg. I insist, sir. Sam, take it down."

Before Sam could interpose, Mr. Bob Sawyer gracefully struck his colours, and having put them in his pocket, nodded in a courteous manner to Mr. Pickwick, wiped the mouth of the case-bottle, and applied it to his own; thereby informing him, without any unnecessary waste of words, that he devoted that draught to wishing him all manner of happiness and prosperity. Having done this, Bob replaced the cork with great care, and looking benignantly down on Mr. Pickwick, took a large bite out of the sandwich, and smiled.

"Come," said Mr. Pickwick, whose momentary anger was not quite proof against Bob's immovable self-possession, "pray let us have no more of this absurdity."

"No, no," replied Bob, once more exchanging hats with Mr. Weller; "I didn't mean to do it, only I got so enlivened with the ride that I couldn't help it."

"Think of the look of the thing," expostulated Mr. Pickwick; "have some regard to appearances."

"Oh, certainly," said Bob, "it's not the sort of thing at all. All over, governor."

Satisfied with this assurance, Mr. Pickwick once more drew his head into the chaise and pulled up the glass; but he had scarcely resumed the conversation which Mr. Bob Sawyer had interrupted, when he was somewhat startled by the apparition of a small dark body, of an oblong form, on the outside of the window, which gave sundry taps against it, as if impatient of admission.

"What's this?" exclaimed Mr. Pickwick.

"It looks like a case-bottle;" remarked Ben Allen, eyeing the object in question through his spectacles with some interest; "I rather think it belongs to Bob."

The impression was perfectly accurate; for Mr. Bob Sawyer having attached the case-bottle to the end of the walking-stick, was battering the window with it, in token of his wish that his friends inside would partake of its contents, in all good fellowship and harmony.

"What's to be done?" said Mr. Pickwick, looking at

358

Mr. Bob Sawyer's Mode of Travelling

the bottle. "This proceeding is more absurd than the other."

"I think it would be best to take it in," replied Mr. Ben Allen; "it would serve him right to take it in and keep it, wouldn't it?"

"It would," said Mr. Pickwick: "shall I?"

"I think it the most proper course we could possibly adopt," replied Ben.

This advice quite coinciding with his own opinion, Mr. Pickwick gently let down the window and disengaged the bottle from the stick: upon which the latter was drawn up, and Mr. Bob Sawyer was heard to laugh heartily.

"What a merry dog it is!" said Mr. Pickwick, looking round at his companion with the bottle in his hand.

"He is," said Mr. Allen.

"You cannot possibly be angry with him," remarked Mr. Pickwick.

"Quite out of the question," observed Benjamin Allen.

During this short interchange of sentiments, Mr. Pickwick had, in an abstracted mood, uncorked the bottle.

"What is it?" inquired Ben Allen, carelessly.

"I don't know," replied Mr. Pickwick, with equal carelessness. "It smells, I think, like milk-punch."

"Oh, indeed?" said Ben.

"I *think* so," rejoined Mr. Pickwick, very properly guarding himself against the possibility of stating an untruth: "mind, I could not undertake to say certainly, without tasting it."

"You had better do so," said Ben; "we may as well know what it is."

"Do you think so?" replied Mr. Pickwick. "Well; if you are curious to know, of course I have no objection."

Ever willing to sacrifice his own feelings to the wishes of his friend, Mr. Pickwick at once took a pretty long taste.

"What is it?" inquired Ben Allen, interrupting him with some impatience.

"Curious," said Mr. Pickwick, smacking his lips, "I hardly

know, now. Oh, yes!" said Mr. Pickwick, after a second taste. "It *is* punch."

Mr. Ben Allen looked at Mr. Pickwick; Mr. Pickwick looked at Mr. Ben Allen; Mr. Ben Allen smiled; Mr. Pickwick did not.

"It would serve him right," said the last-named gentleman, with some severity, "it would serve him right to drink it every drop.'

"The very thing that occurred to me," said Ben Allen.

"Is it indeed?" rejoined Mr. Pickwick. "Then here's his health!" With these words, that excellent person took a most energetic pull at the bottle, and handed it to Ben Allen, who was not slow to imitate his example. The smiles became mutual, and the milk-punch was gradually and cheerfully disposed of.

"After all," said Mr. Pickwick, as he drained the last drop, "his pranks are really very amusing; very entertaining indeed."

"You may say that," rejoined Mr. Ben Allen. In proof of Bob Sawyer's being one of the funniest fellows alive, he proceeded to entertain Mr. Pickwick with a long and circumstantial account how that gentleman once drank himself into a fever and got his head shaved; the relation of which pleasant and agreeable history was only stopped by the stoppage of the chaise at the Bell at Berkeley Heath, to change horses.

"I say! We're going to dine here, aren't we?" said Bob, looking in at the window.

"Dine!" said Mr. Pickwick. "Why, we have only come nineteen miles, and have eighty-seven and a half to go."

"Just the reason why we should take something to enable us to bear up against the fatigue," remonstrated Mr. Bob Sawyer.

"Oh, it's quite impossible to dine at half-past eleven o'clock in the day," replied Mr. Pickwick, looking at his watch.

"So it is," rejoined Bob, "lunch is the very thing. Hallo, you sir! Lunch for three, directly, and keep the horses back for a quarter of an hour. Tell them to put everything they have cold, on the table, and some bottled ale, and let us taste your very best Madeira." Issuing these orders with monstrous importance and bustle, Mr. Bob Sawyer at once hurried into the house to superintend the arrangements; in less than five minutes he returned and declared them to be excellent.

The quality of the lunch fully justified the eulogium which Bob had pronounced, and very great justice was done to it, not only by that gentleman, but Mr. Ben Allen and Mr. Pickwick also. Under the auspices of the three, the bottled ale and the Madeira were promptly disposed of; and when (the horses being once more put to) they resumed their seats, with the case-bottle full of the best substitute for milk-punch that could be procured on so short a notice, the key-bugle sounded, and the red flag waved, without the slightest opposition on Mr. Pickwick's part.

At the Hop Pole at Tewkesbury, they stopped to dine; upon which occasion there was more bottled ale, with some more Madeira, and some Port besides; and here the case-bottle was replenished for the fourth time. Under the influence of these combined stimulants, Mr. Pickwick and Mr. Ben Allen fell fast asleep for thirty miles, while Bob and Mr. Weller sang duets in the dickey.

It was quite dark when Mr. Pickwick roused himself sufficiently to look out of window. The straggling cottages by the road-side, the dingy hue of every object visible, the murky atmosphere, the paths of cinders and brick-dust, the deep-red glow of furnace fires in the distance, the volumes of dense smoke issuing heavily forth from high toppling chimneys, blackening and obscuring everything around; the glare of distant lights, the ponderous waggons which toiled along the road, laden with clashing rods of iron, or piled with heavy goods—all betokened their rapid approach to the great working town of Birmingham.

As they rattled through the narrow thoroughfares leading to the heart of the turmoil, the sights and sounds of earnest occupation struck more forcibly on the senses. The streets were thronged with working-people. The hum of labour resounded from every house, lights gleamed from the long casement windows in the attic stories, and the whirl of wheels and noise of machinery shook the trembling walls. The fires, whose lurid sullen light had been visible for miles, blazed fiercely up, in the great works and factories of the town. The din of hammers, the rushing of steam, and the dead heavy clanking of engines, was the harsh music which arose from every quarter.

The postboy was driving briskly through the open streets, and past the handsome and well-lighted shops which intervene between the outskirts of the town and the Old Royal Hotel, before Mr. Pickwick had begun to consider the very difficult and delicate nature of the commission which had carried him thither.

The delicate nature of this commission, and the difficulty of executing it in a satisfactory manner, were by no means lessened by the voluntary companionship of Mr. Bob Sawyer. Truth to tell, Mr. Pickwick felt that his presence on the occasion, however considerate and gratifying, was by no means an honour he would willingly have sought; in fact, he would cheerfully have given a reasonable sum of money to have had Mr. Bob Sawyer removed to any place at not less than fifty miles' distance, without delay.

Mr. Pickwick had never held any personal communication with Mr. Winkle, senior, although he had once or twice corresponded with him by letter, and returned satisfactory answers to his inquiries concerning the moral character and behaviour of his son; he felt nervously sensible that to wait upon him, for the first time, attended by Bob Sawyer and Ben Allen, both slightly fuddled, was not the most ingenious and likely means that could have been hit upon to prepossess him in his favour.

"However," said Mr. Pickwick, endeavouring to re-assure himself, "I must do the best I can. I must see him to-night, for I faithfully promised to do so. If they persist in accompanying me, I must make the interview as brief as possible, and be content to hope that, for their own sakes, they will not expose themselves."

As he comforted himself with these reflections, the chaise stopped at the door of the Old Royal. Ben Allen having been partially awakened from a stupendous sleep, and dragged out by the collar by Mr. Samuel Weller, Mr. Pickwick was enabled to alight. They were shown to a comfortable apartment, and Mr. Pickwick at once propounded a question to the waiter concerning the whereabout of Mr. Winkle's residence.

"Close by, sir," said the waiter, "not above five hundred yards, sir. Mr. Winkle is a wharfinger, sir, at the canal, sir. Private residence is not—oh dear no, sir, *not* five hundred yards, sir." Here the waiter blew a candle out, and made a feint of lighting it again, in order to afford Mr. Pickwick an opportunity of asking any further questions, if he felt so disposed.

"Take anything now, sir?" said the waiter, lighting the candle in desperation at Mr. Pickwick's silence. "Tea or coffee, sir? Dinner, sir?"

"Nothing now."

"Very good, sir. Like to order supper, sir?"

"Not just now."

"*Very* good, sir." Here, he walked softly to the door, and then stopping short, turned round, and said, with great suavity:

"Shall I send the chambermaid, gentlemen?"

"You may if you please;" replied Mr. Pickwick.

"If *you* please, sir."

"And bring some soda water," said Bob Sawyer.

"Soda water, sir? Yes, sir." With his mind apparently relieved from an overwhelming weight, by having at last got an order for something, the waiter imperceptibly melted away. Waiters never walk or run. They have a peculiar and mysterious power of skimming out of rooms, which other mortals possess not.

Some slight symptoms of vitality having been awakened in Mr. Ben Allen by the soda water, he suffered himself to be prevailed upon to wash his face and hands, and to submit to be brushed by Sam. Mr. Pickwick and Bob Sawyer having also repaired the disorder which the journey had made in their apparel, the three started forth, arm in arm, to Mr. Winkle's; Bob Sawyer impregnating the atmosphere with tobacco smoke as he walked along.

About a quarter of a mile off, in a quiet, substantial-looking street, stood an old red-brick house with three steps before the door, and a brass plate upon it, bearing, in fat Roman capitals, the words, "Mr. Winkle." The steps were very white, and the bricks were very red, and the house was very clean; and here stood Mr. Pickwick, Mr. Benjamin Allen, and Mr. Bob Sawyer, as the clock struck ten.

A smart servant girl answered the knock, and started on beholding the three strangers.

"Is Mr. Winkle at home, my dear?" inquired Mr. Pickwick.

"He is just going to supper, sir," replied the girl.

"Give him that card if you please," rejoined Mr. Pickwick. "Say I am sorry to trouble him at so late an hour; but I am anxious to see him to-night, and have only just arrived."

The girl looked timidly at Mr. Bob Sawyer, who was expressing his admiration of her personal charms by a variety of wonderful grimaces; and casting an eye at the hats and great coats which hung in the passage, called another girl to mind the door while she went up stairs. The sentinel was speedily relieved; for the girl returned immediately, and begging pardon of the gentlemen for leaving them in the street, ushered them into a floor-clothed back parlour, half office and half dressing-room, in which the principal useful and ornamental articles of furniture, were a desk, a wash-hand stand and shaving glass, a boot-rack and boot-jack, a high stool, four chairs, a table, and an old eight-day clock. Over the mantel-piece were the sunken doors of an iron safe, while a couple of hanging shelves for books, an almanack, and several files of dusty papers, decorated the walls.

"Very sorry to leave you standing at the door, sir," said the girl, lighting a lamp, and addressing Mr. Pickwick with a winning smile, "but you was quite strangers to me; and we have such a many trampers that only come to see what they can lay their hands on, that really—

"There is not the least occasion for any apology, my dear," said Mr. Pickwick good humouredly.

"Not the slightest, my love," said Bob Sawyer, playfully stretching forth his arms, and skipping from side to side, as if to prevent the young lady's leaving the room.

The young lady was not at all softened by these allurements, for she at once expressed her opinion that Mr. Bob Sawyer was an "odous creetur;" and, on his becoming rather more pressing in his attentions, imprinted her fair fingers upon his face, and bounced out of the room with many expressions of aversion and contempt.

Deprived of the young lady's society, Mr. Bob Sawyer proceeded to divert himself by peeping into the desk, looking into all the table-drawers, feigning to pick the lock of the iron safe, turning the almanack with its face to the wall, trying on the boots of Mr. Winkle, senior, over his own, and making several other humorous experiments upon the furniture, all of which afforded Mr. Pickwick unspeakable horror and agony, and yielded Mr. Bob Sawyer proportionate delight.

At length the door opened, and a little old gentleman in a snuff-coloured suit, with a head and face the precise counter-part of those belonging to Mr. Winkle, junior, excepting that he was rather bald, trotted into the room with Mr. Pickwick's card in one hand, and a silver candlestick in the other.

"Mr. Pickwick, sir, how do you do?" said Winkle the elder, putting down the candlestick and proffering his hand. "Hope I see you well, sir. Glad to see you. Be seated, Mr. Pickwick, I beg, sir. This gentleman is—"

"My friend, Mr. Sawyer," interposed Mr. Pickwick, "your son's friend."

"Oh," said Mr. Winkle the elder, looking rather grimly at Bob. "I hope *you* are well, sir."

"Right as a trivet, sir," replied Bob Sawyer.

"This other gentleman," cried Mr. Pickwick, "is, as you will see, when you have read the letter with which I am entrusted, a very near relative, or I should rather say a very particular friend of your son's. His name is Allen."

"*That* gentleman?" inquired Mr. Winkle, pointing with the card towards Ben Allen, who had fallen asleep in an attitude which left nothing of him visible but his spine and his coat collar.

Mr. Pickwick was on the point of replying to the question, and reciting Mr. Benjamin Allen's name and honourable distinctions at full length, when the sprightly Mr. Bob Sawyer, with a view of rousing his friend to a sense of his situation, inflicted a startling pinch upon the fleshy part of his arm, which caused him to jump up with a shriek. Suddenly aware that he was in the presence of a stranger, Mr. Ben Allen advanced, and, shaking Mr. Winkle most affectionately by both hands for about five minutes, murmured, in some half-intelligible fragments of sentences, the great delight he felt in seeing him, and a hospitable inquiry whether he felt disposed to take anything after his walk, or would prefer waiting "till dinner-time;" which done, he sat down and gazed about him with a petrified stare, as if he had not the remotest idea where he was, which indeed he had not.

All this was most embarrassing to Mr. Pickwick, the more especially as Mr. Winkle, senior, evinced palpable astonishment at the eccentric—not to say extraordinary—behaviour of his two companions. To bring the matter to an issue at once, he drew a letter from his pocket, and presenting it to Mr. Winkle, senior, said:

"This letter, sir, is from your son. You will see, by its contents, that on your favourable and fatherly consideration of it, depend his future happiness and welfare. Will you oblige me by giving it the calmest and coolest perusal, and by discussing the subject afterwards, with me, in the tone and spirit in which alone it ought to be discussed? You may judge of the importance of your decision to your son, and his intense anxiety upon the subject, by my waiting upon you, without any previous warning, at so late an hour; and," added Mr. Pickwick, glancing slightly at his two companions, "and under such unfavourable circumstances."

With this prelude, Mr. Pickwick placed four closely written sides of extra superfine wire-wove penitence in the hands of the astounded Mr. Winkle, senior. Then reseating himself in his chair, he watched his looks and manner: anxiously, it is true, but with the open front of a gentleman who feels he has taken no part which he need excuse or palliate.

The old wharfinger turned the letter over; looked at the front, back, and sides; made a microscopic examination of the fat little boy on the seal; raised his eyes to Mr. Pickwick's face; and then, seating himself on the high stool, and drawing the lamp closer to him, broke the wax, unfolded the epistle, and lifting it to the light, prepared to read.

Just at this moment, Mr. Bob Sawyer, whose wit had lain dormant for some minutes, placed his hands upon his knees, and made a face after the portraits of the late Mr. Grimaldi, as clown. It so happened that Mr. Winkle, senior, instead of being deeply engaged in reading the letter, as Mr. Bob Sawyer thought, chanced to be looking over the top of it at no less a person than Mr. Bob Sawyer himself; rightly conjecturing that the face aforesaid was made in ridicule and derision of his own person, he fixed his eyes on Bob with such expressive sternness, that the late Mr. Grimaldi's lineaments gradually resolved themselves into a very fine expression of humility and confusion.

"Did you speak, sir?" inquired Mr. Winkle, senior, after an awful silence.

"No, sir," replied Bob, with no remains of the clown

about him, save and except the extreme redness of his
cheeks.

"You are sure you did not, sir?" said Mr. Winkle, senior.

"Oh dear, yes, sir, quite," replied Bob.

"I thought you did, sir," rejoined the old gentleman, with
indignant emphasis. "Perhaps you *looked* at me, sir?"

"Oh, no! sir, not at all," replied Bob, with extreme civility.

"I am very glad to hear it, sir," said Mr. Winkle, senior.
Having frowned upon the abashed Bob with great magnifi-
cence, the old gentleman again brought the letter to the
light, and began to read it seriously.

Mr. Pickwick eyed him intently as he turned from the
bottom line of the first page to the top line of the second,
and from the bottom of the second to the top of the third,
and from the bottom of the third to the top of the fourth;
but not the slightest alteration of countenance afforded a
clue to the feelings with which he received the announcement
of his son's marriage, which Mr. Pickwick knew was in the
very first half-dozen lines.

He read the letter to the last word; folded it again with
all the carefulness and precision of a man of business; and,
just when Mr. Pickwick expected some great outbreak of
feeling, dipped a pen in the inkstand, and said as quietly as
if he were speaking on the most ordinary counting-house
topic:

"What is Nathaniel's address, Mr. Pickwick?"

"The George and Vulture, at present," replied that gentleman.

"George and Vulture. Where is that?"

"George Yard, Lombard Street."

"In the City?"

"Yes."

The old gentleman methodically indorsed the address on
the back of the letter; and then, placing it in the desk, which
he locked, said as he got off the stool and put the bunch of
keys in his pocket:

A MAN OF BUSINESS.

"I suppose there is nothing else which need detain us, Mr. Pickwick?"

"Nothing else, my dear sir!" observed that warm-hearted person in indignant amazement. "Nothing else! Have you no opinion to express on this momentous event in our young friend's life? No assurance to convey to him, through me, of the continuance of your affection and protection? Nothing to say which will cheer and sustain him, and the anxious girl who looks to him for comfort and support? My dear sir, consider."

"I will consider," replied the old gentleman. "I have nothing to say just now. I am a man of business, Mr. Pickwick. I never commit myself hastily in any affair, and from what I see of this, I by no means like the appearance of it. A thousand pounds is not much, Mr. Pickwick."

"You're very right, sir," interposed Ben Allen, just awake enough to know that he had spent *his* thousand pounds without the smallest difficulty. "You're an intelligent man. Bob, he's a very knowing fellow this."

"I am very happy to find that *you* do me the justice to make the admission, sir," said Mr. Winkle, senior, looking contemptuously at Ben Allen, who was shaking his head profoundly. "The fact is, Mr. Pickwick, that when I gave my son a roving license for a year or so, to see something of men and manners (which he has done under your auspices), so that he might not enter into life a mere boarding-school milk-sop to be gulled by everybody, I never bargained for this. He knows that, very well, so if I withdraw my countenance from him on this account, he has no call to be surprised. He shall hear from me, Mr. Pickwick. Good night, sir. Margaret, open the door."

All this time, Bob Sawyer had been nudging Mr. Ben Allen to say something on the right side; Ben accordingly now burst, without the slightest preliminary notice, into a brief but impassioned piece of eloquence.

"Sir," said Mr. Ben Allen, staring at the old gentleman,

369

out of a pair of very dim and languid eyes, and working his right arm vehemently up and down, "you—you ought to be ashamed of yourself."

"As the lady's brother, of course you are an excellent judge of the question," retorted Mr. Winkle, senior. "There; that's enough. Pray say no more, Mr. Pickwick. Good night, gentlemen!"

With these words the old gentleman took up the candlestick, and opening the room door, politely motioned towards the passage.

"You will regret this, sir," said Mr. Pickwick, setting his teeth close together to keep down his choler; for he felt how important the effect might prove to his young friend.

"I am at present of a different opinion," calmly replied Mr. Winkle, senior. "Once again, gentlemen, I wish you a good night."

Mr. Pickwick walked, with angry strides, into the street. Mr. Bob Sawyer, completely quelled by the decision of the old gentleman's manner, took the same course. Mr. Ben Allen's hat rolled down the steps immediately afterwards, and Mr. Ben Allen's body followed it directly. The whole party went silent and supperless to bed; and Mr. Pickwick thought, just before he fell asleep, that if he had known Mr. Winkle, senior, had been quite so much of a man of business, it was extremely probable he might never have waited upon him on such an errand.

CHAPTER LI.

IN WHICH MR. PICKWICK ENCOUNTERS AN OLD ACQUAINTANCE.
TO WHICH FORTUNATE CIRCUMSTANCE THE READER IS
MAINLY INDEBTED FOR MATTER OF THRILLING INTEREST
HEREIN SET DOWN, CONCERNING TWO GREAT PUBLIC MEN
OF MIGHT AND POWER.

THE morning which broke upon Mr. Pickwick's sight, at
eight o'clock, was not at all calculated to elevate his spirits,
or to lessen the depression which the unlooked-for result of
his embassy inspired. The sky was dark and gloomy, the air
was damp and raw, the streets were wet and sloppy. The
smoke hung sluggishly above the chimney-tops as if it lacked
the courage to rise, and the rain came slowly and doggedly
down, as if it had not even the spirit to pour. A game-cock
in the stable-yard, deprived of every spark of his accustomed
animation, balanced himself dismally on one leg in a corner;
a donkey, moping with drooping head under the narrow roof
of an outhouse, appeared from his meditative and miserable
countenance to be contemplating suicide. In the street,
umbrellas were the only things to be seen, and the clicking
of pattens and splashing of rain-drops, were the only sounds
to be heard.

The breakfast was interrupted by very little conversation;
even Mr. Bob Sawyer felt the influence of the weather, and the
previous day's excitement. In his own expressive language he
was "floored." So was Mr. Ben Allen. So was Mr. Pickwick.

371

In protracted expectation of the weather clearing up, the last evening paper from London was read and re-read with an intensity of interest only known in cases of extreme destitution; every inch of the carpet was walked over, with similar perseverance; the windows were looked out of, often enough to justify the imposition of an additional duty upon them; all kinds of topics of conversation were started, and failed; and at length Mr. Pickwick, when noon had arrived, without a change for the better, rang the bell resolutely and ordered out the chaise.

Although the roads were miry, and the drizzling rain came down harder than it had done yet, and although the mud and wet splashed in at the open windows of the carriage to such an extent that the discomfort was almost as great to the pair of insides as to the pair of outsides, still there was something in the motion, and the sense of being up and doing, which was so infinitely superior to being pent in a dull room, looking at the dull rain dripping into a dull street, that they all agreed, on starting, that the change was a great improvement, and wondered how they could possibly have delayed making it, as long as they had done.

When they stopped to change at Coventry, the steam ascended from the horses in such clouds as wholly to obscure the hostler, whose voice was however heard to declare from the mist, that he expected the first Gold Medal from the Humane Society on their next distribution of rewards, for taking the postboy's hat off; the water descending from the brim of which, the invisible gentleman declared must inevitably have drowned him (the postboy), but for his great presence of mind in tearing it promptly from his head, and drying the gasping man's countenance with a wisp of straw.

"This is pleasant," said Bob Sawyer, turning up his coat collar, and pulling the shawl over his mouth to concentrate the fumes of a glass of brandy just swallowed.

"Wery," replied Sam, composedly.

"You don't seem to mind it," observed Bob.

CONCERNING POSTBOYS AND DONKEYS.

" Vy, I don't exactly see no good my mindin' on it 'ud do, sir," replied Sam.

" That's an unanswerable reason, anyhow," said Bob.

" Yes, sir," rejoined Mr. Weller. " Wotever is, is right, as the young nobleman sveetly remarked wen they put him down in the pension list 'cos his mother's uncle's vife's grandfather vunce lit the king's pipe vith a portable tinder-box."

" Not a bad notion that, Sam," said Mr. Bob Sawyer approvingly.

" Just wot the young nobleman said ev'ry quarter-day arterwards for the rest of his life," replied Mr. Weller.

" Wos you ever called in," inquired Sam, glancing at the driver, after a short silence, and lowering his voice to a mysterious whisper: " wos you ever called in, ven you wos 'prentice to a sawbones, to wisit a postboy ?"

" I don't remember that I ever was," replied Bob Sawyer.

" You never see a postboy in that 'ere hospital as you *walked* (as they says o' the ghosts), did you ?" demanded Sam.

' No," replied Bob Sawyer. " I don't think I ever did."

" Never know'd a churchyard were there wos a postboy's tombstone, or see a dead postboy, did you ?" inquired Sam, pursuing his catechism.

" No," rejoined Bob, " I never did."

" No !" rejoined Sam, triumphantly. " Nor never vill ; and there's another thing that no man never see, and that's a dead donkey. No man never see a dead donkey, 'cept the gen'l'm'n in the black silk smalls as know'd the young 'ooman as kep a goat ; and that wos a French donkey, so wery likely he warn't wun o' the reg'lar breed."

" Well, what has that got to do with the postboys ?" asked Bob Sawyer.

" This here," replied Sam. " Without goin' so far as to as-sert, as some wery sensible people do, that postboys and donkeys is both immortal, wot I say is this ; that wenever they feels theirselves gettin' stiff and past their work, they

373

just rides off together, wun postboy to a pair in the usual way; wot becomes on 'em nobody knows, but it's wery probable as they starts avay to take their pleasure in some other vorld, for there ain't a man alive as ever see, either a donkey or a postboy, a takin' his pleasure in this!"

Expatiating upon this learned and remarkable theory, and citing many curious statistical and other facts in its support, Sam Weller beguiled the time until they reached Dunchurch, where a dry postboy and fresh horses were procured; the next stage was Daventry, and the next Towcester; and at the end of each stage it rained harder than it had done at the beginning.

"I say," remonstrated Bob Sawyer, looking in at the coach window, as they pulled up before the door of the Saracen's Head, Towcester, "this won't do, you know."

"Bless me!" said Mr. Pickwick, just awaking from a nap, "I'm afraid you're wet."

"Oh you are, are you?" returned Bob. "Yes, I am, a little that way. Uncomfortably damp, perhaps."

Bob did look dampish, inasmuch as the rain was streaming from his neck, elbows, cuffs, skirts, and knees; and his whole apparel shone so with the wet, that it might have been mistaken for a full suit of prepared oilskin.

"I *am* rather wet," said Bob, giving himself a shake, and casting a little hydraulic shower around, like a Newfoundland dog just emerged from the water.

"I think it's quite impossible to go on to-night," interposed Ben.

"Out of the question, sir," remarked Sam Weller, coming to assist in the conference; "it's a cruelty to animals, sir, to ask 'em to do it. There's beds here, sir," said Sam, addressing his master, "everything clean and comfortable. Wery good little dinner, sir, they can get ready in half an hour— pair of fowls, sir, and a weal cutlet; French beans, 'taturs, tart, and tidiness. You'd better stop vere you are, sir, if I might recommend. Take adwice, sir, as the doctor said."

THE SARACEN'S HEAD, TOWCESTER.

The host of the Saracen's Head opportunely appeared at this moment, to confirm Mr. Weller's statement relative to the accommodations of the establishment, and to back his entreaties with a variety of dismal conjectures regarding the state of the roads, the doubt of fresh horses being to be had at the next stage, the dead certainty of its raining all night, the equally mortal certainty of its clearing up in the morning, and other topics of inducement familiar to innkeepers.

"Well," said Mr. Pickwick; "but I must send a letter to London by some conveyance, so that it may be delivered the very first thing in the morning, or I must go forward at all hazards."

The landlord smiled his delight. Nothing could be easier than for the gentleman to inclose a letter in a sheet of brown paper, and send it on, either by the mail or the night coach from Birmingham. If the gentleman were particularly anxious to have it left as soon as possible, he might write outside, "To be delivered immediately," which was sure to be attended to; or "pay the bearer half-a-crown extra for instant delivery," which was surer still.

"Very well," said Mr. Pickwick, "then we will stop here."

"Lights in the Sun, John; make up the fire; the gentlemen are wet!" cried the landlord. "This way, gentlemen; don't trouble yourselves about the postboy now, sir. I'll send him to you when you ring for him, sir. Now, John, the candles."

The candles were brought, the fire was stirred up, and a fresh log of wood thrown on. In ten minutes' time, a waiter was laying the cloth for dinner, the curtains were drawn, the fire was blazing brightly, and everything looked (as everything always does, in all decent English inns) as if the travellers had been expected, and their comforts prepared, for days beforehand.

Mr. Pickwick sat down at a side table, and hastily indited a note to Mr. Winkle, merely informing him that he was detained by stress of weather, but would certainly be in

London next day; until when he deferred any account of his proceedings. This note was hastily made into a parcel, and despatched to the bar per Mr. Samuel Weller.

Sam left it with the landlady, and was returning to pull his master's boots off, after drying himself by the kitchen fire, when, glancing casually through a half-opened door, he was arrested by the sight of a gentleman with a sandy head who had a large bundle of newspapers lying on the table before him, and was perusing the leading article of one with a settled sneer which curled up his nose and all his other features into a majestic expression of haughty contempt.

"Hallo!" said Sam, "I ought to know that 'ere head and them features; the eye-glass, too, and the broad brimmed tile! Eatansvill to vit, or I'm a Roman."

Sam was taken with a troublesome cough, at once, for the purpose of attracting the gentleman's attention; the gentleman starting at the sound, raised his head and his eye-glass, and disclosed to view the profound and thoughtful features of Mr. Pott, of the Eatanswill Gazette.

"Beggin' your pardon, sir," said Sam, advancing with a bow, "my master's here, Mr. Pott."

"Hush, hush!" cried Pott, drawing Sam into the room, and closing the door, with a countenance of mysterious dread and apprehension.

"Wot's the matter, sir?" inquired Sam, looking vacantly about him.

"Not a whisper of my name," replied Pott; "this is a buff neighbourhood. If the excited and irritable populace knew I was here, I should be torn to pieces."

"No! Vould you, sir?" inquired Sam.

"I should be the victim of their fury," replied Pott. "Now, young man, what of your master?"

"He's a stopping here to-night on his vay to town, vith a couple of friends," replied Sam.

"Is Mr. Winkle one of them?" inquired Pott, with a slight frown.

MR. POTT IN THE BUFF CAMP.

"No, sir. Mr. Vinkle stops at home now," rejoined Sam. "He's married."

"Married!" exclaimed Pott, with frightful vehemence. He stopped, smiled darkly, and added, in a low, vindictive tone: "It serves him right!"

Having given vent to this cruel ebullition of deadly malice and cold-blooded triumph over a fallen enemy, Mr. Pott inquired whether Mr. Pickwick's friends were "blue?" Receiving a most satisfactory answer in the affirmative from Sam, who knew as much about the matter as Pott himself, he consented to accompany him to Mr. Pickwick's room, where a hearty welcome awaited him. An agreement to club dinners together was at once made and ratified.

"And how are matters going on in Eatanswill?" inquired Mr. Pickwick, when Pott had taken a seat near the fire, and the whole party had got their wet boots off, and dry slippers on. "Is the Independent still in being?"

"The Independent, sir," replied Pott, "is still dragging on a wretched and lingering career. Abhorred and despised by even the few who are cognizant of its miserable and disgraceful existence; stifled by the very filth it so profusely scatters; rendered deaf and blind by the exhalations of its own slime; the obscene journal, happily unconscious of its degraded state, is rapidly sinking beneath that treacherous mud which, while it seems to give it a firm standing with the low and debased classes of society, is nevertheless, rising above its detested head, and will speedily engulf it for ever."

Having delivered this manifesto (which formed a portion of his last week's leader) with vehement articulation, the editor paused to take breath, and looked majestically at Bob Sawyer.

"You are a young man, sir," said Pott.

Mr. Bob Sawyer nodded.

"So are you, sir," said Pott, addressing Mr. Ben Allen.

Ben admitted the soft impeachment.

"And are both deeply imbued with those blue principles,

which, so long as I live, I have pledged myself to the people of these kingdoms to support and to maintain?" suggested Pott.

"Why, I don't exactly know about that," replied Bob Sawyer. "I am—"

"Not buff, Mr. Pickwick," interrupted Pott, drawing back his chair, "your friend is not buff, sir?"

"No, no," rejoined Bob, "I'm a kind of plaid at present; a compound of all sorts of colours."

"A waverer," said Pott, solemnly, "a waverer. I should like to show you a series of eight articles, sir, that have appeared in the Eatanswill Gazette. I think I may venture to say that you would not be long in establishing your opinions on a firm and solid blue basis, sir."

"I dare say I should turn very blue, long before I got to the end of them," responded Bob.

Mr. Pott looked dubiously at Bob Sawyer for some seconds, and, turning to Mr. Pickwick, said:

"You have seen the literary articles which have appeared at intervals in the Eatanswill Gazette in the course of the last three months, and which have excited such general—I may say such universal—attention and admiration?"

"Why," replied Mr. Pickwick, slightly embarrassed by the question, "the fact is, I have been so much engaged in other ways, that I really have not had an opportunity of perusing them."

"You should do so, sir," said Pott, with a severe countenance.

"I will," said Mr. Pickwick.

"They appeared in the form of a copious review of a work on Chinese metaphysics, sir," said Pott.

"Oh," observed Mr. Pickwick; "from your pen, I hope?"

"From the pen of my critic, sir," rejoined Pott with dignity.

"An abstruse subject I should conceive," said Mr. Pickwick.

"Very, sir," responded Pott, looking intensely sage. "He

crammed for it, to use a technical but expressive term; he read up for the subject, at my desire, in the *Encyclopædia Britannica.*"

"Indeed!" said Mr. Pickwick; "I was not aware that that valuable work contained any information respecting Chinese metaphysics."

"He read, sir," rejoined Pott, laying his hand on Mr. Pickwick's knee, and looking round with a smile of intellectual superiority, "he read for metaphysics under the letter M, and for China under the letter C, and combined his information, sir?"

Mr. Pott's features assumed so much additional grandeur at the recollection of the power and research displayed in the learned effusions in question, that some minutes elapsed before Mr Pickwick felt emboldened to renew the conversation; at length, as the Editor's countenance gradually relaxed into its customary expression of moral supremacy, he ventured to resume the discourse by asking:

"Is it fair to inquire what great object has brought you so far from home?"

"That object which actuates and animates me in all my gigantic labours, sir," replied Pott, with a calm smile; "my country's good."

"I supposed it was some public mission," observed Mr. Pickwick.

"Yes, sir," resumed Pott, "it is." Here, bending towards Mr. Pickwick, he whispered in a deep hollow voice, "A buff ball, sir, will take place in Birmingham to-morrow evening."

"God bless me!" exclaimed Mr. Pickwick.

"Yes, sir, and supper," added Pott.

"You don't say so!" ejaculated Mr. Pickwick.

Pott nodded portentously.

Now, although Mr. Pickwick feigned to stand aghast at this disclosure, he was so little versed in local politics that he was unable to form an adequate comprehension of the importance of the dire conspiracy it referred to; observing which, Mr. Pott, drawing forth the last number of the Eatanswill Gazette, and referring to the same, delivered himself of the following paragraph:

"HOLE-AND-CORNER BUFFERY.

"A reptile contemporary has recently sweltered forth his black venom in the vain and hopeless attempt of sullying the fair name of our distinguished and excellent representative, the Honourable Mr. Slumkey—that Slumkey whom we, long before he gained his present noble and exalted position, predicted would one day be, as he now is, at once his country's brightest honour, and her proudest boast: alike her bold defender and her honest pride—our reptile contemporary, we say, has made himself merry, at the expense of a superbly embossed plated coal-scuttle, which has been presented to that glorious man by his enraptured constituents, and towards the purchase of which, the nameless wretch insinuates, the Honourable Mr. Slumkey himself contributed, through a confidential friend of his butler's, more than three-fourths of the whole sum subscribed. Why, does not the crawling creature see, that even if this be the fact, the Honourable Mr. Slumkey only appears in a still more amiable and radiant light than before, if that be possible? Does not even *his* obtuseness perceive that this amiable and touching desire to carry out the wishes of the constituent body, must for ever endear him to the hearts and souls of such of his fellow townsmen as are not worse than swine; or, in other words, who are not as debased as our contemporary himself? But such is the wretched trickery of hole-and-corner Buffery! These are not its only artifices. Treason is abroad. We boldly state, now that we are goaded to the disclosure, and we throw ourselves on the country and its constables for protection—we boldly state that secret preparations are at this moment in progress for a Buff ball; which is to be held in a Buff town, in the very heart and centre of a Buff population; which is to be conducted by a Buff master of the ceremonies; which is to be attended by four ultra Buff members of parliament, and the admission to which, is to be by Buff tickets! Does our fiendish contemporary wince? Let him writhe, in impotent malice, as we pen the words, WE WILL BE THERE."

"There, sir," said Pott, folding up the paper quite exhausted, "that is the state of the case!"

The landlord and waiter entering at the moment with dinner, caused Mr. Pott to lay his finger on his lips, in token that he considered his life in Mr. Pickwick's hands, and depended on his secrecy. Messrs. Bob Sawyer and Benjamin Allen, who had irreverently fallen asleep during the reading of the quotation from the Eatanswill Gazette, and the discussion which followed it, were roused by the mere whispering of the talismanic word "Dinner" in their ears: and to dinner they went with good digestion waiting on appetite, and health on both, and a waiter on all three.

In the course of the dinner and the sitting which succeeded it, Mr. Pott descending, for a few moments, to domestic topics, informed Mr. Pickwick that the air of Eatanswill not agreeing with his lady, she was then engaged in making a tour of different fashionable watering-places with a view to the recovery of her wonted health and spirits; this was a delicate veiling of the fact that Mrs. Pott, acting upon her often repeated threat of separation, had, in virtue of an arrangement negociated by her brother, the Lieutenant, and concluded by Mr. Pott, permanently retired with the faithful body-guard upon one moiety or half-part of the annual income and profits arising from the editorship and sale of the Eatanswill Gazette.

While the great Mr. Pott was dwelling upon this and other matters, enlivening the conversation from time to time with various extracts from his own lucubrations, a stern stranger, calling from the window of a stage-coach, outward bound, which halted at the inn to deliver packages, requested to know, whether, if he stopped short on his journey and remained there for the night, he could be furnished with the necessary accommodation of a bed and bedstead.

"Certainly, sir," replied the landlord.

"I can, can I?" inquired the stranger, who seemed habitually suspicious in look and manner.

"No doubt of it, sir," replied the landlord.

"Good," said the stranger. "Coachman, I get down here. Guard, my carpet-bag!"

Bidding the other passengers good night, in a rather snappish manner, the stranger alighted. He was a shortish gentleman, with very stiff black hair cut in the porcupine or blacking-brush style, and standing stiff and straight all over his head; his aspect was pompous and threatening; his manner was peremptory; his eyes were sharp and restless; and his whole bearing bespoke a feeling of great confidence in himself, and a consciousness of immeasurable superiority over all other people.

This gentleman was shown into the room originally assigned to the patriotic Mr. Pott; and the waiter remarked, in dumb astonishment at the singular coincidence, that he had no sooner lighted the candles than the gentleman, diving into his hat, drew forth a newspaper, and began to read it with the very same expression of indignant scorn, which, upon the majestic features of Pott, had paralysed his energies an hour before. The man observed too, that whereas Mr. Pott's scorn had been roused by a newspaper headed The Eatanswill Independent, this gentleman's withering contempt was awakened by a newspaper entitled The Eatanswill Gazette.

"Send the landlord," said the stranger.

"Yes, sir," rejoined the waiter.

The landlord was sent, and came.

"Are you the landlord?" inquired the gentleman.

"I am, sir," replied the landlord.

"Do you know me?" demanded the gentleman.

"I have not that pleasure, sir," rejoined the landlord.

"My name is Slurk," said the gentleman.

MR. SLURK.

The landlord slightly inclined his head.

"Slurk, sir," repeated the gentleman, haughtily. "Do you know me now, man?"

The landlord scratched his head, looked at the ceiling, and at the stranger, and smiled feebly.

"Do you know me, man?" inquired the stranger, angrily.

The landlord made a strong effort, and at length replied: "Well, sir, I do *not* know you."

"Great Heaven!" said the stranger, dashing his clenched fist upon the table. "And this is popularity!"

The landlord took a step or two towards the door; the stranger fixing his eyes upon him, resumed.

"This," said the stranger, "this is gratitude for years of labour and study in behalf of the masses. I alight wet and weary; no enthusiastic crowds press forward to greet their champion; the church-bells are silent; the very name elicits no responsive feeling in their torpid bosoms. It is enough," said the agitated Mr. Slurk, pacing to and fro, "to curdle the ink in one's pen, and induce one to abandon their cause for ever."

"Did you say brandy and water, sir?" said the landlord, venturing a hint.

"Rum," said Mr. Slurk, turning fiercely upon him. "Have you got a fire anywhere?"

"We can light one directly, sir," said the landlord.

"Which will throw out no heat until it is bed-time," interrupted Mr. Slurk. "Is there anybody in the kitchen?"

Not a soul. There was a beautiful fire. Everybody had gone, and the house door was closed for the night.

"I will drink my rum and water," said Mr. Slurk, "by the kitchen fire." So, gathering up his hat and newspaper, he stalked solemnly behind the landlord to that humble apartment, and throwing himself on a settle by the fireside, resumed his countenance of scorn, and began to read and drink in silent dignity.

Now, some demon of discord, flying over the Saracen's

383

Head at that moment, on casting down his eyes in mere idle curiosity, happened to behold Slurk established comfortably by the kitchen fire, and Pott slightly elevated with wine in another room; upon which the malicious demon, darting down into the last-mentioned apartment with inconceivable rapidity, passed at once into the head of Mr. Bob Sawyer, and prompted him for his (the demon's) own evil purposes to speak as follows:

"I say, we've let the fire out. It's uncommonly cold after the rain, isn't it?"

"It really is," replied Mr. Pickwick, shivering.

"It wouldn't be a bad notion to have a cigar by the kitchen fire, would it?" said Bob Sawyer, still prompted by the demon aforesaid.

"It would be particularly comfortable, *I* think," replied Mr. Pickwick. "Mr. Pott, what do you say?"

Mr. Pott yielded a ready assent; and all four travellers, each with his glass in his hand, at once betook themselves to the kitchen, with Sam Weller heading the procession to show them the way.

The stranger was still reading; he looked up and started. Mr. Pott started.

"What's the matter?" whispered Mr. Pickwick.

"That reptile!" replied Pott.

"What reptile?" said Mr. Pickwick, looking about him for fear he should tread on some overgrown black beetle, or dropsical spider.

"That reptile," whispered Pott, catching Mr. Pickwick by the arm, and pointing towards the stranger. "That reptile Slurk, of the Independent!"

"Perhaps we had better retire," whispered Mr. Pickwick.

"Never, sir," rejoined Pott, pot-valiant in a double sense, "never." With these words, Mr. Pott took up his position on an opposite settle, and selecting one from a little bundle of newspapers, began to read against his enemy.

Mr. Pott, of course, read the Independent, and Mr. Slurk,

of course, read the Gazette; and each gentleman audibly expressed his contempt of the other's compositions by bitter laughs and sarcastic sniffs; whence they proceeded to more open expressions of opinion, such as "absurd," "wretched," "atrocity," "humbug," "knavery," "dirt," "filth," "slime," "ditch-water," and other critical remarks of the like nature.

Both Mr. Bob Sawyer and Mr. Ben Allen had beheld these symptoms of rivalry and hatred, with a degree of delight which imparted great additional relish to the cigars at which they were puffing most vigorously. The moment they began to flag, the mischievous Mr. Bob Sawyer, addressing Slurk with great politeness, said:

"Will you allow me to look at your paper, sir, when you have quite done with it!"

"You will find very little to repay you for your trouble in this contemptible *thing*, sir," replied Slurk, bestowing a Satanic frown on Pott.

"You shall have this presently," said Pott, looking up, pale with rage, and quivering in his speech, from the same cause. "Ha! ha! you will be amused with this *fellow's* audacity."

Terrific emphasis was laid upon this "thing" and "fellow;" and the faces of both editors began to glow with defiance.

"The ribaldry of this miserable man is despicably disgusting," said Pott, pretending to address Bob Sawyer, and scowling upon Slurk.

Here, Mr. Slurk laughed very heartily, and folding up the paper so as to get at a fresh column conveniently, said, that the blockhead really amused him.

"What an impudent blunderer this fellow is," said Pott, turning from pink to crimson.

"Did you ever read any of this man's foolery, sir?" inquired Slurk, of Bob Sawyer.

"Never," replied Bob; "is it very bad?"

"Oh, shocking! shocking!" rejoined Slurk.

"Really! Dear me, this is too atrocious!" exclaimed Pott, at this juncture; still feigning to be absorbed in his reading.

"If you can wade through a few sentences of malice, mean-ness, falsehood, perjury, treachery, and cant," said Slurk, handing the paper to Bob, "you will, perhaps, be some-what repaid by a laugh at the style of this ungrammatical twaddler."

"What's that you said, sir?" inquired Mr. Pott, looking up, trembling all over with passion.

"What's that to you, sir?" replied Slurk.

"Ungrammatical twaddler, was it, sir?" said Pott.

"Yes, sir, it was," replied Slurk; "and *blue bore*, sir, if you like that better; ha! ha!"

Mr. Pott retorted not a word to this jocose insult, but deliberately folded up his copy of the Independent, flattened it carefully down, crushed it beneath his boot, spat upon it with great ceremony, and flung it into the fire.

"There, sir," said Pott, retreating from the stove, "and that's the way I would serve the viper who produces it, if I were not, fortunately for him, restrained by the laws of my country."

"Serve him so, sir!" cried Slurk, starting up. "Those laws shall never be appealed to by him, sir, in such a case. Serve him so, sir!"

"Hear! hear!" said Bob Sawyer.

"Nothing can be fairer," observed Mr. Ben Allen.

"Serve him so, sir!" reiterated Slurk, in a loud voice.

Mr. Pott darted a look of contempt, which might have withered an anchor.

"Serve him so, sir!" reiterated Slurk, in a louder voice than before.

"I will not, sir," rejoined Pott.

"Oh, you won't, won't you, sir?" said Mr. Slurk, in a taunting manner; "you hear this, gentlemen! He won't; not that he's afraid; oh, no! he *won't*. Ha! ha!"

"I consider you, sir," said Mr. Pott, moved by this sarcasm, "I consider you a viper. I look upon you, sir, as a man who has placed himself beyond the pale of society, by his most

The Rival Editors

audacious, disgraceful, and abominable public conduct. I view you, sir, personally and politically, in no other light than as a most unparalleled and unmitigated viper."

The indignant Independent did not wait to hear the end of this personal denunciation; for, catching up his carpet-bag which was well stuffed with moveables, he swung it in the air as Pott turned away, and, letting it fall with a circular sweep on his head, just at that particular angle of the bag where a good thick hair-brush happened to be packed, caused a sharp crash to be heard throughout the kitchen, and brought him at once to the ground.

"Gentlemen," cried Mr. Pickwick, as Pott started up and seized the fire-shovel, "gentlemen! Consider, for Heaven's sake—help—Sam—here—pray, gentlemen—interfere, somebody."

Uttering these incoherent exclamations, Mr. Pickwick rushed between the infuriated combatants just in time to receive the carpet-bag on one side of his body, and the fire-shovel on the other. Whether the representatives of the public feeling of Eatanswill were blinded by animosity, or (being both acute reasoners) saw the advantage of having a third party between them to bear all the blows, certain it is that they paid not the slightest attention to Mr. Pickwick, but defying each other with great spirit plied the carpet-bag and the fire-shovel most fearlessly. Mr. Pickwick would unquestionably have suffered severely for his humane interference, if Mr. Weller, attracted by his master's cries, had not rushed in at the moment, and, snatching up a meal-sack, effectually stopped the conflict by drawing it over the head and shoulders of the mighty Pott, and clasping him tight round the shoulders.

"Take away that 'ere bag from the t'other madman," said Sam to Ben Allen and Bob Sawyer, who had done nothing but dodge round the group, each with a tortoise-shell lancet in his hand, ready to bleed the first man stunned. "Give it up, you wretched little creetur, or I'll smother you in it."

Awed by these threats, and quite out of breath, the Independent suffered himself to be disarmed; and Mr. Weller, removing the extinguisher from Pott, set him free with a caution.

"You take yourselves off to bed quietly," said Sam, "or I'll put you both in it, and let you fight it out vith the mouth tied, as I vould a dozen sich, if they played these games. And you have the goodness to come this here vay, sir, if you please."

Thus addressing his master, Sam took him by the arm, and led him off, while the rival editors were severally removed to their beds by the landlord, under the inspection of Mr. Bob Sawyer and Mr. Benjamin Allen; breathing, as they went away, many sanguinary threats, and making vague appointments for mortal combat next day. When they came to think it over, however, it occurred to them that they could do it much better in print, so they recommenced deadly hostilities without delay; and all Eatanswill rung with their boldness—on paper.

They had taken themselves off in separate coaches, early next morning, before the other travellers were stirring; and the weather having now cleared up, the chaise companions once more turned their faces to London.

CHAPTER LII.

CONSIDERING it a matter of delicacy to abstain from introducing either Bob Sawyer or Ben Allen to the young couple, until they were fully prepared to expect them, and wishing to spare Arabella's feelings as much as possible, Mr. Pickwick proposed that he and Sam should alight in the neighbourhood of the George and Vulture, and that the two young men should for the present take up their quarters elsewhere. To this, they very readily agreed, and the proposition was accordingly acted upon; Mr. Ben Allen and Mr. Bob Sawyer betaking themselves to a sequestered pot-shop on the remotest confines of the Borough, behind the bar-door of which their names had in other days very often appeared, at the head of long and complex calculations worked in white chalk.

"Dear me, Mr. Weller," said the pretty housemaid, meeting Sam at the door.

"Dear *me* I vish it vos, my dear," replied Sam, dropping behind, to let his master get out of hearing. "Wot a sweet lookin' creetur you are, Mary!"

"Lor, Mr. Weller, what nonsense you do talk!" said Mary. "Oh! *don't*, Mr. Weller."

"Don't what, my dear?" said Sam.

"Why, that," replied the pretty housemaid. "Lor, do get along with you." Thus admonishing him, the pretty housemaid pushed Sam against the wall, declaring that he had tumbled her cap, and put her hair quite out of curl.

"And prevented what I was going to say, besides," added Mary. "There's a letter been waiting here for you four days; you hadn't been gone away, half an hour, when it came; and more than that, it's got, immediate, on the outside."

Vere is it, my love?" inquired Sam.

"I took care of it, for you, or I dare say it would have been lost long before this," replied Mary. "There, take it; it's more than you deserve."

With these words, after many pretty little coquettish doubts and fears, and wishes that she might not have lost it, Mary produced the letter from behind the nicest little muslin tucker possible, and handed it to Sam, who thereupon kissed it with much gallantry and devotion.

"My goodness me!" said Mary, adjusting the tucker, and feigning unconsciousness, "you seem to have grown very fond of it all at once."

To this Mr. Weller only replied by a wink, the intense meaning of which no description could convey the faintest idea of; and, sitting himself down beside Mary on a window-seat, opened the letter and glanced at the contents.

"Hallo!" exclaimed Sam, "wot's all this?"

"Nothing the matter, I hope?" said Mary, peeping over his shoulder.

"Bless them eyes o' yourn!" said Sam, looking up.

"Never mind my eyes; you had much better read your letter," said the pretty housemaid; and as she said so, she made the eyes twinkle with such slyness and beauty that they were perfectly irresistible.

Sam refreshed himself with a kiss, and read as follows:

AN AFFECTING LETTER.

"*Markis Gran*
By dorken
Wensdy.

"My dear Sammle,

"I am wery sorry to have the pleasure of bein a Bear of ill news your Mother in law cort cold consekens of imprudently settin too long on the damp grass in the rain a hearin of a shepherd who warnt able to leave off till late at night owen to his havin vound his-self up vith brandy and vater and not being able to stop hisself till he got a little sober which took a many hours to do the doctor says that if she'd svallo'd varm brandy and vater artervards insted of afore she mightn't have been no vus her veels wos immedetly greased and everythink done to set her agoin as could be inwented your farther had hopes as she vould have vorked round as usual but just as she wos a turnen the corner my boy she took the wrong road and vent down hill vith a welocity you never see and notvithstandin that the drag wos put on drectly by the medikel man it wornt of no use at all for she paid the last pike at twenty minutes afore six o'clock yesterday evenin havin done the jouney wery much under the reglar time vich praps was partly owen to her haven taken in wery little luggage by the vay your father says that if you vill come and see me Sammy he vill take it as a wery great favor for I am wery lonely Samivel n b he *vill* have it spelt that vay vich I say ant right and as there is sich a many things to settle he is sure your guvner wont object of course he vill not Sammy for I knows him better so he sends his dooty in which I join and am Samivel infernally yours

"Tony Veller."

"Wot a incomprehensible letter," said Sam; "who's to know wot it means, vith all this he-ing and I-ing! It ain't my father's writin', 'cept this here signater in print letters; that's his."

"Perhaps he got somebody to write it for him, and signed it himself afterwards," said the pretty housemaid.

"Stop a minit," replied Sam, running over the letter again, and pausing here and there, to reflect, as he did so. "You've hit it. The gen'l'm'n as wrote it wos a tellin' all about the misfortun' in a proper vay, and then my father comes a lookin' over him, and complicates the whole concern by puttin' his oar in. That's just the wery sort o' thing he'd do. You're right, Mary, my dear."

Having satisfied himself on this point, Sam read the letter all over, once more, and, appearing to form a clear notion of its contents for the first time, ejaculated thoughtfully, as he folded it up:

"And so the poor creatur's dead! I'm sorry for it. She warn't a bad-disposed 'ooman, if them shepherds had let her alone. I'm wery sorry for it."

Mr. Weller uttered these words in so serious a manner, that the pretty housemaid cast down her eyes and looked very grave.

"Hows'ever," said Sam, putting the letter in his pocket with a gentle sigh, "it wos to be—and wos, as the old lady said arter she'd married the footman. Can't be helped now, can it, Mary?"

Mary shook her head, and sighed too.

"I must apply to the hemperor for leave of absence," said Sam.

Mary sighed again. The letter was so very affecting.

"Good bye!" said Sam.

"Good bye," rejoined the pretty housemaid, turning her head away.

"Well, shake hands, won't you?" said Sam.

The pretty housemaid put out a hand which, although it was a housemaid's, was a very small one, and rose to go.

"I shan't be wery long avay," said Sam.

"You're always away," said Mary, giving her head the slightest possible toss in the air. "You no sooner come, Mr. Weller, than you go again."

Mr. Weller drew the household beauty closer to him, and entered upon a whispering conversation, which had not proceeded far, when she turned her face round and condescended to look at him again. When they parted, it was somehow or other indispensably necessary for her to go to her room, and arrange the cap and curls before she could think of presenting herself to her mistress; which preparatory ceremony she went off to perform, bestowing many nods and smiles on Sam over the banisters as she tripped up stairs.

"I shan't be avay more than a day, or two, sir, at the farthest," said Sam, when he had communicated to Mr. Pickwick the intelligence of his father's loss.

"As long as may be necessary, Sam," replied Mr. Pickwick, "you have my full permission to remain."

Sam bowed.

"You will tell your father, Sam, that if I can be of any assistance to him in his present situation, I shall be most willing and ready to lend him any aid in my power," said Mr. Pickwick.

"Thankee, sir," rejoined Sam. "I'll mention it, sir."

And with some expressions of mutual good-will and interest, master and man separated.

It was just seven o'clock when Samuel Weller, alighting from the box of a stage-coach which passed through Dorking, stood within a few hundred yards of the Marquis of Granby. It was a cold dull evening; the little street looked dreary and dismal; and the mahogany countenance of the noble and gallant Marquis seemed to wear a more sad and melancholy expression than it was wont to do, as it swung to and fro, creaking mournfully in the wind. The blinds were pulled down, and the shutters partly closed; of the knot of loungers that usually collected about the door, not one was to be seen; the place was silent and desolate.

Seeing nobody of whom he could ask any preliminary questions, Sam walked softly in. Glancing round, he quickly recognised his parent in the distance.

393

The widower was seated at a small round table in the little room behind the bar, smoking a pipe, with his eyes intently fixed upon the fire. The funeral had evidently taken place that day; for attached to his hat, which he still retained on his head, was a hatband measuring about a yard and a half in length, which hung over the top rail of the chair and streamed negligently down. Mr. Weller was in a very abstracted and contemplative mood. Notwithstanding that Sam called him by name several times, he still continued to smoke with the same fixed and quiet countenance, and was only roused ultimately by his son's placing the palm of his hand on his shoulder.

"Sammy," said Mr. Weller, "you're welcome."

"I've been a callin' to you half a dozen times," said Sam, hanging his hat on a peg, "but you didn't hear me."

"No, Sammy," replied Mr. Weller, again looking thoughtfully at the fire. "I wos in a referee, Sammy."

"Wot about?" inquired Sam, drawing his chair up to the fire.

"In a referee, Sammy," replied the elder Mr. Weller, "regarding *her*, Samivel." Here Mr. Weller jerked his head in the direction of Dorking churchyard, in mute explanation that his words referred to the late Mrs. Weller.

"I wos a thinkin', Sammy," said Mr. Weller, eyeing his son, with great earnestness, over his pipe; as if to assure him that however extraordinary and incredible the declaration might appear, it was nevertheless calmly and deliberately uttered. "I wos a thinkin', Sammy, that upon the whole I wos wery sorry she wos gone."

"Vell, and so you ought to be," replied Sam.

Mr. Weller nodded his acquiescence in the sentiment, and again fastening his eyes on the fire, shrouded himself in a cloud, and mused deeply.

"Those wos wery sensible observations as she made, Sammy," said Mr. Weller, driving the smoke away with his hand, after a long silence.

" Wot observations ? " inquired Sam.

" Them as she made, arter she was took ill," replied the old gentleman.

" Wot was they ? "

" Somethin' to this here effect. 'Veller,' she says, 'I'm afeard I've not done by you quite wot I ought to have done; you're a wery kind-hearted man, and I might ha' made your home more comfortabler. I begin to see now,' she says, 'ven it's too late, that if a married 'ooman vishes to be religious, she should begin vith dischargin' her dooties at home, and makin' them as is about her cheerful and happy, and that vile she goes to church, or chapel, or wot not, at all proper times, she should be wery careful not to con-wert this sort o' thing into a excuse for idleness or self-indulgence. I *have* done this,' she says, 'and I've vasted time and substance on them as has done it more than me; but I hope ven I'm gone, Veller, that you'll think on me as I wos afore I know'd them people, and as I raly wos by natur'.' 'Susan,' says I,—I wos took up wery short by this, Samivel; I von't deny it, my boy—'Susan,' I says, 'you've been a wery good vife to me, altogether; don't say nothin' at all about it; keep a good heart my dear; and you'll live to see me punch that 'ere Stiggins's head yet.' She smiled at this, Samivel," said the old gentleman, stifling a sigh with his pipe, "but she died arter all ! "

" Vell," said Sam, venturing to offer a little homely consolation, after the lapse of three or four minutes, consumed by the old gentleman in slowly shaking his head from side to side, and solemnly smoking; "vell, gov'ner, ve must all come to it, one day or another."

" So we must, Sammy," said Mr. Weller the elder.

" There's a Providence in it all," said Sam.

" O' course there is," replied his father with a nod of grave approval. " Wot 'ud become of the undertakers vithout it, Sammy ? "

Lost in the immense field of conjecture opened by this

reflection, the elder Mr. Weller laid his pipe on the table, and stirred the fire with a meditative visage.

While the old gentleman was thus engaged, a very buxom-looking cook, dressed in mourning, who had been bustling about, in the bar, glided into the room, and bestowing many smirks of recognition upon Sam, silently stationed herself at the back of his father's chair, and announced her presence by a slight cough: the which, being disregarded, was followed by a louder one.

"Hallo!" said the elder Mr. Weller, dropping the poker as he looked round, and hastily drew his chair away. "Wot's the matter now?"

"Have a cup of tea, there's a good soul," replied the buxom female, coaxingly.

"I von't," replied Mr. Weller, in a somewhat boisterous manner, "I'll see you—" Mr. Weller hastily checked himself, and added in a low tone, "furder fust."

"Oh, dear, dear! How adversity does change people!" said the lady, looking upwards.

"It's the only think 'twixt this and the doctor as shall change *my* condition," muttered Mr. Weller.

"I really never saw a man so cross," said the buxom female.

"Never mind. It's all for my own good; vich is the reflection vith vich the penitent schoolboy comforted his feelin's ven they flogged him," rejoined the old gentleman.

The buxom female shook her head with a compassionate and sympathising air; and, appealing to Sam, inquired whether his father really ought not to make an effort to keep up, and not give way to that lowness of spirits.

"You see, Mr. Samuel," said the buxom female, "as I was telling him yesterday, he *will* feel lonely, he can't expect but what he should, sir, but he should keep up a good heart, because, dear me, I'm sure we all pity his loss, and are ready to do anything for him; and there's no situation in life so bad, Mr. Samuel, that it can't be mended. Which is what

PERILOUS POSITION OF A WIDOWER.

a very worthy person said to me when my husband died."
Here the speaker, putting her hand before her mouth, coughed
again, and looked affectionately at the elder Mr. Weller.

"As I don't rekvire any o' your conversation just now,
mum, vill you have the goodness to re-tire?" inquired Mr.
Weller in a grave and steady voice.

"Well, Mr. Weller," said the buxom female, "I'm sure I
only spoke to you out of kindness."

"Wery likely, mum," replied Mr. Weller. "Samivel,
show the lady out, and shut the door arter her."

This hint was not lost upon the buxom female; for she
at once left the room, and slammed the door behind her,
upon which Mr. Weller, senior, falling back in his chair in
a violent perspiration, said:

"Sammy, if I wos to stop here alone vun veek—only vun
veek, my boy—that 'ere 'ooman 'ud marry me by force and
wiolence afore it was over."

"Wot! Is she so wery fond on you?" inquired Sam.

"Fond!" replied his father, "I can't keep her avay from
me. If I was locked up in a fire-proof chest vith a patent
Brahmin, she'd find means to get at me, Sammy."

"Wot a thing it is, to be so sought arter!" observed Sam,
smiling.

"I don't take no pride out on it, Sammy," replied Mr.
Weller, poking the fire vehemently, "it's a horrid sitiwation.
I'm activally drove out o' house and home by it. The
breath was scarcely out o' your poor mother-in-law's body,
ven vun old 'ooman sends me a pot o' jam, and another a pot
o' jelly, and another brews a blessed large jug o' camomile-tea,
vich she brings in vith her own hands." Mr. Weller paused
with an aspect of intense disgust, and, looking round, added
in a whisper: "They wos all widders, Sammy, all on 'em,
'cept the camomile-tea vun, as wos a single young lady o'
fifty-three."

Sam gave a comical look in reply, and the old gentleman
having broken an obstinate lump of coal, with a countenance

397

expressive of as much earnestness and malice as if it had been the head of one of the widows last-mentioned, said :

" In short, Sammy, I feel that I ain't safe anyveres but on the box."

" How are you safer there than anyveres else ? " interrupted Sam.

" 'Cos a coachman's a privileged indiwidual," replied Mr. Weller, looking fixedly at his son. " 'Cos a coachman may do vithout suspicion wot other men may not; 'cos a coachman may be on the wery amicablest terms with eighty mile o' females, and yet nobody think that he ever means to marry any vun among 'em. And wot other man can say the same, Sammy ? "

" Vell, there's somethin' in that," said Sam.

" If your gov'ner had been a coachman," reasoned Mr. Weller, " do you s'pose as that 'ere jury 'ud ever ha' convicted him, s'posin' it possible as the matter could ha' gone to that extremity ? They dustn't ha' done it."

" Wy not ? " said Sam, rather disparagingly.

" Wy not ! " rejoined Mr. Weller ; " 'cos it 'ud ha' gone agin their consciences. A reg'lar coachman's a sort o' connectin' link betwixt singleness and matrimony, and every practicable man knows it."

" Wot ! You mean, they're gen'ral fav'rites, and nobody takes adwantage on 'em, p'raps ? " said Sam.

His father nodded.

" How it ever come to that 'ere pass," resumed the parent Weller, " I can't say. Wy it is that long-stage coachmen possess such insiniwations, and is alvays looked up to—adored I may say—by ev'ry young 'ooman in ev'ry town he vurks through, I don't know. I only know that so it is. It's a reg'lation of natur—a dispensary, as your poor mother-in-law used to say."

" A dispensation," said Sam, correcting the old gentleman.

" Wery good, Samivel, a dispensation if you like it better," returned Mr. Weller ; " I call it a dispensary, and it's alvays

writ up so, at the places vere they gives you physic for nothin'
in your own bottles; that's all."

With these words, Mr. Weller re-filled and re-lighted his
pipe, and once more summoning up a meditative expression
of countenance, continued as follows:

"Therefore, my boy, as I do not see the adwisability o'
stoppin' here to be marrid vether I vant to or not, and as at
the same time I do not vish to separate myself from them
interestin' members o' society altogether, I have come to the
determination o' drivin' the Safety, and puttin' up vunce
more at the Bell Savage, vich is my nat'ral-born element,
Sammy."

"And wot's to become o' the bis'ness?" inquired Sam.

"The bis'ness, Samivel," replied the old gentleman, "good-
vill, stock, and fixters, vill be sold by private contract; and
out o' the money, two hundred pound, agreeable to a rekvest
o' your mother-in-law's to me a little afore she died, vill be
inwested in your name in—wot do you call them things
agin?"

"Wot things?" inquired Sam.

"Them things as is always a goin' up and down, in the
City."

"Omnibuses?" suggested Sam.

"Nonsense," replied Mr. Weller. "Them things as is
alvays a fluctooatin', and gettin' theirselves inwolved somehow
or another vith the national debt, and the checquers bills,
and all that."

"Oh! the funds," said Sam.

"Ah!" rejoined Mr. Weller, "the funs; two hundred
pounds o' the money is to be inwested for you, Samivel, in
the funs; four and a half per cent. reduced counsels, Sammy."

"Wery kind o' the old lady to think o' me," said Sam,
"and I'm very much obliged to her."

"The rest vill be inwested in my name," continued the
elder Mr. Weller; "and ven I'm took off the road, it'll come
to you, so take care you don't spend it all at vunst, my boy,

and mind that no widder gets a inklin' o' your fortun', or you're done."

Having delivered this warning, Mr. Weller resumed his pipe with a more serene countenance; the disclosure of these matters appearing to have eased his mind considerably.

"Somebody's a tappin' at the door," said Sam.

"Let 'em tap," replied his father, with dignity.

Sam acted upon the direction. There was another tap, and another, and then a long row of taps; upon which Sam inquired why the tapper was not admitted.

"Hush," whispered Mr. Weller, with apprehensive looks, "don't take no notice on 'em, Sammy, it's vun o' the widders, p'raps."

No notice being taken of the taps, the unseen visitor, after a short lapse, ventured to open the door and peep in. It was no female head that was thrust in at the partially opened door, but the long black locks and red face of Mr. Stiggins. Mr. Weller's pipe fell from his hands.

The reverend gentleman gradually opened the door by almost imperceptible degrees, until the aperture was just wide enough to admit of the passage of his lank body, when he glided into the room and closed it after him with great care and gentleness. Turning towards Sam, and raising his hands and eyes in token of the unspeakable sorrow with which he regarded the calamity that had befallen the family, he carried the high-backed chair to his old corner by the fire, and, seating himself on the very edge, drew forth a brown pocket-handkerchief, and applied the same to his optics.

While this was going forward, the elder Mr. Weller sat back in his chair, with his eyes wide open, his hands planted on his knees, and his whole countenance expressive of absorbing and overwhelming astonishment. Sam sat opposite him in perfect silence, waiting, with eager curiosity, for the termination of the scene.

Mr. Stiggins kept the brown pocket-handkerchief before his eyes for some minutes, moaning decently meanwhile, and then, mastering his feelings by a strong effort, put it in his pocket and buttoned it up. After this, he stirred the fire; after that, he rubbed his hands and looked at Sam.

"Oh my young friend," said Mr. Stiggins, breaking the silence in a very low voice, "here's a sorrowful affliction!"

Sam nodded, very slightly.

"For the man of wrath, too!" added Mr. Stiggins; "it makes a vessel's heart bleed!"

Mr. Weller was overheard by his son to murmur something relative to making a vessel's nose bleed; but Mr. Stiggins heard him not.

"Do you know, young man," whispered Mr. Stiggins, drawing his chair closer to Sam, "whether she has left Emanuel anything?"

"Who's he?" inquired Sam.

"The chapel," replied Mr. Stiggins; "our chapel; our fold, Mr. Samuel."

"She hasn't left the fold nothin', nor the shepherd nothin', nor the animals nothin'," said Sam, decisively; "nor the dogs neither."

Mr. Stiggins looked slyly at Sam; glanced at the old gentleman, who was sitting with his eyes closed, as if asleep; and drawing his chair still nearer, said:

"Nothing for *me*, Mr. Samuel?"

Sam shook his head.

"I think there's something," said Stiggins, turning as pale as he could turn. "Consider, Mr. Samuel; no little token?"

"Not so much as the vorth o' that 'ere old umberella o' yourn," replied Sam.

"Perhaps," said Mr. Stiggins, hesitatingly, after a few moments' deep thought, "perhaps she recommended me to the care of the man of wrath, Mr. Samuel?"

"I think that's wery likely, from what he said," rejoined Sam; "he wos a speakin' about you, jist now."

"Was he, though?" exclaimed Stiggins brightening up. "Ah! He's changed, I dare say. We might live very

401

comfortably together now, Mr. Samuel, eh? I could take care of his property when you are away—good care, you see."

Heaving a long-drawn sigh, Mr. Stiggins paused for a response. Sam nodded, and Mr. Weller, the elder, gave vent to an extraordinary sound, which being neither a groan, nor a grunt, nor a gasp, nor a growl, seemed to partake in some degree of the character of all four.

Mr. Stiggins, encouraged by this sound, which he understood to betoken remorse or repentance, looked about him, rubbed his hands, wept, smiled, wept again, and then, walking softly across the room to a well-remembered shelf in one corner, took down a tumbler, and with great deliberation put four lumps of sugar in it. Having got thus far, he looked about him again, and sighed grievously; with that, he walked softly into the bar, and presently returning with the tumbler half full of pine-apple rum, advanced to the kettle which was singing gaily on the hob, mixed his grog, stirred it, sipped it, sat down, and taking a long and hearty pull at the rum and water, stopped for breath.

The elder Mr. Weller, who still continued to make various strange and uncouth attempts to appear asleep, offered not a single word during these proceedings; but when Stiggins stopped for breath, he darted upon him, and snatching the tumbler from his hand, threw the remainder of the rum and water in his face, and the glass itself into the grate. Then, seizing the reverend gentleman firmly by the collar, he suddenly fell to kicking him most furiously: accompanying every application of his top-boots to Mr. Stiggins's person, with sundry violent and incoherent anathemas upon his limbs, eyes, and body.

"Sammy," said Mr. Weller, "put my hat on tight for me."

Sam dutifully adjusted the hat with the long hatband more firmly on his father's head, and the old gentleman, resuming his kicking with greater agility than before, tumbled with Mr. Stiggins through the bar, and through the passage, out

at the front door, and so into the street; the kicking continuing the whole way, and increasing in vehemence, rather
than diminishing, every time the top-boot was lifted.

It was a beautiful and exhilarating sight to see the red-
nosed man writhing in Mr. Weller's grasp, and his whole
frame quivering with anguish as kick followed kick in rapid
succession; it was a still more exciting spectacle to behold
Mr. Weller, after a powerful struggle, immersing Mr. Stiggins's
head in a horse-trough full of water, and holding it there,
until he was half suffocated.

"There!" said Mr. Weller, throwing all his energy into
one most complicated kick, as he at length permitted Mr.
Stiggins to withdraw his head from the trough, "send any
vun o' them lazy shepherds here, and I'll pound him to a
jelly first, and drownd him artervards! Sammy, help me
in, and fill me a small glass of brandy. I'm out o' breath,
my boy."

CHAPTER LIII.

COMPRISING THE FINAL EXIT OF MR. JINGLE AND JOB TROTTER;
WITH A GREAT MORNING OF BUSINESS IN GRAY'S INN SQUARE.
CONCLUDING WITH A DOUBLE KNOCK AT MR. PERKER'S DOOR.

WHEN Arabella, after some gentle preparation, and many assurances that there was not the least occasion for being low-spirited, was at length made acquainted by Mr. Pickwick with the unsatisfactory result of his visit to Birmingham, she burst into tears, and sobbing aloud, lamented in moving terms that she should have been the unhappy cause of any estrangement between a father and his son.

"My dear girl," said Mr. Pickwick, kindly, "it is no fault of yours. It was impossible to foresee that the old gentleman would be so strongly prepossessed against his son's marriage, you know. I am sure," added Mr. Pickwick, glancing at her pretty face, "he can have very little idea of the pleasure he denies himself."

"Oh my dear Mr. Pickwick," said Arabella, "what shall we do, if he continues to be angry with us?"

"Why, wait patiently, my dear, until he thinks better of it," replied Mr. Pickwick, cheerfully.

"But, dear Mr. Pickwick, what is to become of Nathaniel if his father withdraws his assistance?" urged Arabella.

"In that case, my love," rejoined Mr. Pickwick, "I will venture to prophesy that he will find some other friend who will not be backward in helping him to start in the world,"

The significance of this reply was not so well disguised by Mr. Pickwick but that Arabella understood it. So, throwing her arms around his neck, and kissing him affectionately, she sobbed louder than before.

"Come, come," said Mr. Pickwick, taking her hand, " we will wait here a few days longer, and see whether he writes or takes any other notice of your husband's communication. If not, I have thought of half a dozen plans, any one of which would make you happy at once. There, my dear, there!"

With these words, Mr. Pickwick gently pressed Arabella's hand, and bade her dry her eyes, and not distress her husband. Upon which, Arabella, who was one of the best little creatures alive, put her handkerchief in her reticule, and by the time Mr. Winkle joined them, exhibited in full lustre the same beaming smiles and sparkling eyes that had originally captivated him.

"This is a distressing predicament for these young people," thought Mr. Pickwick, as he dressed himself next morning. "I'll walk up to Perker's, and consult him about the matter."

As Mr. Pickwick was further prompted to betake himself to Gray's Inn Square by an anxious desire to come to a pecuniary settlement with the kind-hearted little attorney without further delay, he made a hurried breakfast, and executed his intention so speedily, that ten o'clock had not struck when he reached Gray's Inn.

It still wanted ten minutes to the hour when he had ascended the staircase on which Perker's chambers were. The clerks had not arrived yet, and he beguiled the time by looking out of the staircase window.

The healthy light of a fine October morning made even the dingy old houses brighten up a little : some of the dusty windows actually looking almost cheerful as the sun's rays gleamed upon them. Clerk after clerk hastened into the square by one or other of the entrances, and looking up at the Hall clock, accelerated or decreased his rate of walking according to the time at which his office hours nominally commenced ;

the half-past nine o'clock people suddenly becoming very brisk, and the ten o'clock gentlemen falling into a pace of most aristocratic slowness. The clock struck ten, and clerks poured in faster than ever, each one in a greater perspiration than his predecessor. The noise of unlocking and opening doors echoed and re-echoed on every side; heads appeared as if by magic in every window; the porters took up their stations for the day; the slipshod laundresses hurried off; the postman ran from house to house; and the whole legal hive was in a bustle.

"You're early, Mr. Pickwick," said a voice behind him.

"Ah, Mr. Lowten," replied that gentleman, looking round, and recognising his old acquaintance.

"Precious warm walking, isn't it?" said Lowten, drawing a Bramah key from his pocket, with a small plug therein, to keep the dust out.

"You appear to feel it so," rejoined Mr. Pickwick, smiling at the clerk, who was literally red hot.

"I've come along rather, I can tell you," replied Lowten. "It went the half hour as I came through the Polygon. I'm here before *him*, though, so I don't mind."

Comforting himself with this reflection, Mr. Lowten extracted the plug from the door-key, and having opened the door, replugged and repocketed his Bramah, and picked up the letters which the postman had dropped through the box. He then ushered Mr. Pickwick into the office. Here, in the twinkling of an eye, he divested himself of his coat, put on a threadbare garment which he took out of a desk, hung up his hat, pulled forth a few sheets of cartridge and blotting-paper in alternate layers, and sticking a pen behind his ear, rubbed his hands with an air of great satisfaction.

"There you see, Mr. Pickwick," he said, "now I'm complete. I've got my office coat on, and my pad out, and let him come as soon as he likes. You haven't got a pinch of snuff about you, have you?"

"No, I have not," replied Mr. Pickwick.

"I'm sorry for it," said Lowten. "Never mind. I'll run out presently, and get a bottle of soda. Don't I look rather queer about the eyes, Mr. Pickwick?"

The individual appealed to, surveyed Mr. Lowten's eyes from a distance, and expressed his opinion that no unusual queerness was perceptible in those features.

"I'm glad of it," said Lowten. "We were keeping it up pretty tolerably at the Stump last night, and I'm rather out of sorts this morning. Perker's been about that business of yours, by the bye."

"What business?" inquired Mr. Pickwick. "Mrs. Bardell's costs?"

"No, I don't mean that," replied Mr. Lowten. "About getting that customer that we paid the ten shillings in the pound to the bill discounter for, on your account—to get him out of the Fleet, you know—about getting him to Demerara."

"Oh? Mr. Jingle?" said Mr. Pickwick, hastily. "Yes. Well?"

"Well, it's all arranged," said Lowten, mending his pen. "The agent at Liverpool said he had been obliged to you many times when you were in business, and he would be glad to take him on your recommendation."

"That's well," said Mr. Pickwick. "I am delighted to hear it."

"But I say," resumed Lowten, scraping the back of the pen preparatory to making a fresh split, "*what* a soft chap that other is!"

"Which other?"

"Why, that servant, or friend, or whatever he is; *you* know; Trotter."

"Ah?" said Mr. Pickwick, with a smile. "I always thought him the reverse."

"Well, and so did I, from what little I saw of him," replied Lowten, "it only shows how one may be deceived. What do you think of *his* going to Demerara, too?"

"What! And giving up what was offered him here!" exclaimed Mr. Pickwick.

"Treating Perker's offer of eighteen bob a-week, and a rise if he behaved himself, like dirt," replied Lowten. "He said he must go along with the other one, and so they persuaded Perker to write again, and they've got him something on the same estate; not near so good, Perker says, as a convict would get in New South Wales, if he appeared at his trial in a new suit of clothes."

"Foolish fellow," said Mr. Pickwick, with glistening eyes. "Foolish fellow."

"Oh, it's worse than foolish; it's downright sneaking, you know," replied Lowten, nibbing the pen with a contemptuous face. "He says that he's the only friend he ever had, and he's attached to him, and all that. Friendship's a very good thing in its way: we are all very friendly and comfortable at the Stump, for instance, over our grog, where every man pays for himself; but damn hurting yourself for anybody else, you know! No man should have more than two attachments —the first, to number one, and the second to the ladies; that's what I say—ha! ha!" Mr. Lowten concluded with a loud laugh, half in jocularity, and half in derision, which was prematurely cut short by the sound of Perker's footsteps on the stairs: at the first approach of which, he vaulted on his stool with an agility most remarkable, and wrote intensely.

The greeting between Mr. Pickwick and his professional adviser was warm and cordial; the client was scarcely ensconced in the attorney's arm chair, however, when a knock was heard at the door, and a voice inquired whether Mr. Perker was within.

"Hark!" said Perker, "that's one of our vagabond friends —Jingle himself, my dear sir. Will you see him?"

"What do you think?" inquired Mr. Pickwick, hesitating.

"Yes, I think you had better. Here, you sir, what's your name, walk in, will you?"

In compliance with this unceremonious invitation, Jingle

and Job walked into the room, but, seeing Mr. Pickwick, stopped short in some confusion.

"Well," said Perker, "don't you know that gentleman?"

"Good reason to," replied Mr. Jingle, stepping forward. "Mr. Pickwick—deepest obligations—life preserver—made a man of me—you shall never repent it, sir."

"I am happy to hear you say so," said Mr. Pickwick. "You look much better."

"Thanks to you, sir—great change—Majesty's Fleet—unwholesome place—very," said Jingle, shaking his head. He was decently and cleanly dressed, and so was Job, who stood bolt upright behind him, staring at Mr. Pickwick with a visage of iron.

"When do they go to Liverpool?" inquired Mr. Pickwick, half aside to Perker.

"This evening, sir, at seven o'clock," said Job, taking one step forward. "By the heavy coach from the city, sir."

"Are your places taken?"

"They are, sir," replied Job.

"You have fully made up your mind to go?"

"I have, sir," answered Job.

"With regard to such an outfit as was indispensable for Jingle," said Perker, addressing Mr. Pickwick aloud, "I have taken upon myself to make an arrangement for the deduction of a small sum from his quarterly salary, which, being made only for one year, and regularly remitted, will provide for that expense. I entirely disapprove of your doing anything for him, my dear sir, which is not dependent on his own exertions and good conduct."

"Certainly," interposed Jingle, with great firmness. "Clear head—man of the world—quite right—perfectly."

"By compounding with his creditor, releasing his clothes from the pawnbroker's, relieving him in prison, and paying for his passage," continued Perker, without noticing Jingle's observation, "you have already lost upwards of fifty pounds."

"Not lost," said Jingle, hastily. "Pay it all—stick to

409

business—cash up—every farthing. Yellow fever, perhaps —can't help that—if not— " Here Mr. Jingle paused, and striking the crown of his hat with great violence, passed his hand over his eyes, and sat down.

" He means to say," said Job, advancing a few paces, " that if he is not carried off by the fever, he will pay the money back again. If he lives, he will, Mr. Pickwick. I will see it done. I know he will, sir," said Job, with energy. " I could undertake to swear it."

" Well, well," said Mr. Pickwick, who had been bestowing a score or two of frowns upon Perker, to stop his summary of benefits conferred, which the little attorney obstinately disregarded, " you must be careful not to play any more desperate cricket matches, Mr. Jingle, or to renew your acquaintance with Sir Thomas Blazo, and I have little doubt of your preserving your health."

Mr. Jingle smiled at this sally, but looked rather foolish notwithstanding; so, Mr. Pickwick changed the subject by saying,

" You don't happen to know, do you, what has become of another friend of yours—a more humble one, whom I saw at Rochester ? "

" Dismal Jemmy ? " inquired Jingle.

" Yes."

Jingle shook his head.

" Clever rascal—queer fellow, hoaxing genius—Job's brother."

" Job's brother ! " exclaimed Mr. Pickwick. " Well, now I look at him closely, there *is* a likeness."

" We were always considered like each other, sir," said Job, with a cunning look just lurking in the corners of his eyes, " only I was really of a serious nature, and he never was. He emigrated to America, sir, in consequence of being too much sought after here, to be comfortable; and has never been heard of since."

" That accounts for my not having received the 'page from the romance of real life,' which he promised me one morning

410

when he appeared to be contemplating suicide on Rochester Bridge, I suppose," said Mr. Pickwick, smiling. "I need not inquire whether his dismal behaviour was natural or assumed."

"He could assume anything, sir," said Job. "You may consider yourself very fortunate in having escaped him so easily. On intimate terms he would have been even a more dangerous acquaintance than—" Job looked at Jingle, hesitated, and finally added, "than—than—myself even."

"A hopeful family yours, Mr. Trotter," said Perker, sealing a letter which he had just finished writing.

"Yes, sir," replied Job. "Very much so."

"Well," said the little man, laughing; "I hope you are going to disgrace it. Deliver this letter to the agent when you reach Liverpool, and let me advise you, gentlemen, not to be too knowing in the West Indies. If you throw away this chance, you will both richly deserve to be hanged, as I sincerely trust you will be. And now you had better leave Mr. Pickwick and me alone, for we have other matters to talk over, and time is precious." As Perker said this, he looked towards the door, with an evident desire to render the leave-taking as brief as possible.

It was brief enough on Mr. Jingle's part. He thanked the little attorney in a few hurried words for the kindness and promptitude with which he had rendered his assistance, and, turning to his benefactor, stood for a few seconds as if irresolute what to say or how to act. Job Trotter relieved his perplexity; for, with a humble and a grateful bow to Mr. Pickwick, he took his friend gently by the arm, and led him away.

"A worthy couple!" said Perker, as the door closed behind them.

"I hope they may become so," replied Mr. Pickwick. "What do you think? Is there any chance of their permanent reformation?"

Perker shrugged his shoulders doubtfully, but observing Mr. Pickwick's anxious and disappointed look, rejoined:

"Of course there is a chance. I hope it may prove a good one. They are unquestionably penitent now; but then, you know, they have the recollection of very recent suffering fresh upon them. What they may become, when that fades away, is a problem that neither you nor I can solve. However, my dear sir," added Perker, laying his hand on Mr. Pickwick's shoulder, "your object is equally honourable, whatever the result is. Whether that species of benevolence which is so very cautious and long-sighted that it is seldom exercised at all, lest its owner should be imposed upon, and so wounded in his self-love, be real charity or a worldly counterfeit, I leave to wiser heads than mine to determine. But if those two fellows were to commit a burglary to-morrow, my opinion of this action would be equally high."

With these remarks, which were delivered in a much more animated and earnest manner than is usual in legal gentlemen, Perker drew his chair to his desk, and listened to Mr. Pickwick's recital of old Mr. Winkle's obstinacy.

"Give him a week," said Perker, nodding his head prophetically.

"Do you think he will come round?" inquired Mr. Pickwick.

"I think he will," rejoined Perker. "If not, we must try the young lady's persuasion; and that is what anybody but you, would have done at first."

Mr. Perker was taking a pinch of snuff with various grotesque contractions of countenance, eulogistic of the persuasive powers appertaining unto young ladies, when the murmur of inquiry and answer was heard in the outer office, and Lowten tapped at the door.

"Come in!" cried the little man.

The clerk came in, and shut the door after him, with great mystery.

"What's the matter?" inquired Perker.

"You're wanted, sir."

"Who wants me?"

Lowten looked at Mr. Pickwick, and coughed.

"Who wants me? Can't you speak, Mr. Lowten?"

"Why, sir," replied Lowten, "it's Dodson; and Fogg is with him."

"Bless my life!" said the little man, looking at his watch, "I appointed them to be here, at half-past eleven, to settle that matter of yours, Pickwick. I gave them an undertaking on which they sent down your discharge; it's very awkward, my dear sir; what will you do? Would you like to step into the next room?"

The next room being the identical room in which Messrs. Dodson and Fogg were, Mr. Pickwick replied that he would remain where he was: the more especially as Messrs. Dodson and Fogg ought to be ashamed to look him in the face, instead of his being ashamed to see them. Which latter circumstance he begged Mr. Perker to note, with a glowing countenance and many marks of indignation.

"Very well, my dear sir, very well," replied Perker, "I can only say that if you expect either Dodson or Fogg to exhibit any symptom of shame or confusion at having to look you, or anybody else, in the face, you are the most sanguine man in your expectations that *I* ever met with. Show them in, Mr. Lowten."

Mr. Lowten disappeared with a grin, and immediately returned ushering in the firm, in due form of precedence: Dodson first, and Fogg afterwards.

"You have seen Mr. Pickwick, I believe?" said Perker to Dodson, inclining his pen in the direction where that gentleman was seated.

"How do you do, Mr. Pickwick?" said Dodson in a loud voice.

"Dear me," cried Fogg, "how do you do, Mr. Pickwick? I hope you are well, sir. I thought I knew the face," said Fogg, drawing up a chair, and looking round him with a smile.

Mr. Pickwick bent his head very slightly, in answer to

these salutations, and, seeing Fogg pull a bundle of papers from his coat-pocket, rose and walked to the window.

"There's no occasion for Mr. Pickwick to move, Mr. Perker," said Fogg, untying the red tape which encircled the little bundle, and smiling again more sweetly than before. "Mr. Pickwick is pretty well acquainted with these proceedings. There are no secrets between us, I think. He! he! he!"

"Not many, I think," said Dodson. "Ha! ha! ha!" Then both the partners laughed together—pleasantly and cheerfully, as men who are going to receive money, often do.

"We shall make Mr. Pickwick pay for peeping," said Fogg, with considerable native humour, as he unfolded his papers. "The amount of the taxed costs is one hundred and thirty three, six, four, Mr. Perker."

There was a great comparing of papers, and turning over of leaves, by Fogg and Perker, after this statement of profit and loss. Meanwhile, Dodson said in an affable manner to Mr. Pickwick:

"I don't think you are looking quite so stout as when I had the pleasure of seeing you last, Mr. Pickwick."

"Possibly not, sir," replied Mr. Pickwick, who had been flashing forth looks of fierce indignation, without producing the smallest effect on either of the sharp practitioners; "I believe I am not, sir. I have been persecuted and annoyed by Scoundrels of late, sir."

Perker coughed violently, and asked Mr. Pickwick whether he wouldn't like to look at the morning paper? To which inquiry Mr. Pickwick returned a most decided negative.

"True," said Dodson, "I dare say you *have* been annoyed in the Fleet; there are some odd gentry there. Whereabouts were your apartments, Mr. Pickwick?"

"My one room," replied that much-injured gentleman, "was on the Coffee Room flight."

"Oh, indeed!" said Dodson. "I believe that is a very pleasant part of the establishment."

"Very," replied Mr. Pickwick drily.

There was a coolness about all this, which, to a gentleman of an excitable temperament, had, under the circumstances, rather an exasperating tendency. Mr. Pickwick restrained his wrath by gigantic efforts; but when Perker wrote a cheque for the whole amount, and Fogg deposited it in a small pocket-book with a triumphant smile playing over his pimply features which communicated itself likewise to the stern countenance of Dodson, he felt the blood in his cheeks tingling with indignation.

"Now, Mr. Dodson," said Fogg, putting up the pocket-book and drawing on his gloves, "I am at your service."

"Very good," said Dodson, rising, "I am quite ready."

"I am very happy," said Fogg, softened by the cheque, "to have had the pleasure of making Mr. Pickwick's acquaintance. I hope you don't think quite so ill of us, Mr. Pickwick, as when we first had the pleasure of seeing you."

"I hope not," said Dodson, with the high tone of calumniated virtue. "Mr. Pickwick now knows us better. I trust : whatever your opinion of gentlemen of our profession may be, I beg to assure you, sir, that I bear no ill-will or vindictive feeling towards you for the sentiments you thought proper to express in our office in Freeman's Court, Cornhill, on the occasion to which my partner has referred."

"Oh no, no; nor I," said Fogg, in a most forgiving manner.

"Our conduct, sir," said Dodson, "will speak for itself, and justify itself I hope, upon every occasion. We have been in the profession some years, Mr. Pickwick, and have been honoured with the confidence of many excellent clients. I wish you good morning, sir."

"*Good* morning, Mr. Pickwick," said Fogg. So saying, he put his umbrella under his arm, drew off his right glove, and extended the hand of reconciliation to that most indignant gentleman : who, thereupon, thrust his hands beneath his coat tails, and eyed the attorney with looks of scornful amazement.

"Lowten!" cried Perker at this moment. "Open the door."

"Wait one instant," said Mr. Pickwick, "Perker, I *will* speak."

"My dear sir, pray let the matter rest where it is," said the little attorney, who had been in a state of nervous apprehension during the whole interview; "Mr. Pickwick, I beg!"

"I will not be put down, sir," replied Mr. Pickwick hastily. "Mr. Dodson, you have addressed some remarks to me."

Dodson turned round, bent his head meekly, and smiled.

"Some remarks to me," repeated Mr. Pickwick, almost breathless; "and your partner has tendered me his hand, and you have both assumed a tone of forgiveness and high-mindedness, which is an extent of impudence that I was not prepared for, even in you."

"What, sir!" exclaimed Dodson.

"What, sir!" reiterated Fogg.

"Do you know that I have been the victim of your plots and conspiracies?" continued Mr. Pickwick. "Do you know that I am the man whom you have been imprisoning and robbing? Do you know that you were the attorneys for the plaintiff, in Bardell and Pickwick?"

"Yes, sir, we do know it," replied Dodson.

"Of course we know it, sir," rejoined Fogg, slapping his pocket—perhaps by accident.

"I see that you recollect it with satisfaction," said Mr. Pickwick, attempting to call up a sneer for the first time in his life, and failing most signally in so doing. "Although I have long been anxious to tell you, in plain terms, what my opinion of you is, I should have let even this opportunity pass, in deference to my friend Perker's wishes, but for the unwarrantable tone you have assumed, and your insolent familiarity. I say insolent familiarity, sir," said Mr. Pickwick, turning upon Fogg with a fierceness of gesture which caused that person to retreat towards the door with great expedition.

"Take care, sir," said Dodson, who, though he was the biggest man of the party, had prudently intrenched himself behind Fogg, and was speaking over his head with a very pale face. "Let him assault you, Mr. Fogg; don't return it on any account."

"No, no, I won't return it," said Fogg, falling back a little more as he spoke; to the evident relief of his partner, who by these means was gradually getting into the outer office.

"You are," continued Mr. Pickwick, resuming the thread of his discourse, "you are a well-matched pair of mean, rascally, pettifogging robbers."

"Well," interposed Perker, "is that all?"

"It is all summed up in that," rejoined Mr. Pickwick; "they are mean, rascally, pettifogging robbers."

"There!" said Perker in a most conciliatory tone. "My dear sirs, he has said all he has to say. Now pray go. Lowten, *is* that door open?"

Mr. Lowten, with a distant giggle, replied in the affirmative.

"There, there—good morning—good morning—now pray, my dear sirs,—Mr. Lowten, the door!" cried the little man, pushing Dodson and Fogg, nothing loath, out of the office; "this way, my dear sirs,—now pray don't prolong this—dear me—Mr. Lowten—the door, sir—why don't you attend?"

"If there's law in England, sir," said Dodson, looking towards Mr. Pickwick, as he put on his hat, "you shall smart for this."

"You are a couple of mean—"

"Remember, sir, you pay dearly for this," said Fogg.

"—Rascally, pettifogging robbers!" continued Mr. Pickwick, taking not the least notice of the threats that were addressed to him.

"Robbers!" cried Mr. Pickwick, running to the stair-head, as the two attorneys descended.

"Robbers!" shouted Mr. Pickwick, breaking from Lowten and Perker, and thrusting his head out of the staircase window.

When Mr. Pickwick drew in his head again, his countenance was smiling and placid; and, walking quietly back into the office, he declared that he had now removed a great weight from his mind, and that he felt perfectly comfortable and happy.

Perker said nothing at all until he had emptied his snuff-box, and sent Lowten out to fill it, when he was seized with a fit of laughing, which lasted five minutes; at the expiration of which time he said that he supposed he ought to be very angry, but he couldn't think of the business seriously yet—when he could, he would be.

" Well, now," said Mr. Pickwick, " let me have a settlement with you."

" Of the same kind as the last?" inquired Perker, with another laugh.

"Not exactly," rejoined Mr. Pickwick, drawing out his pocket-book, and shaking the little man heartily by the hand, "I only mean a pecuniary settlement. You have done me many acts of kindness that I can never repay, and have no wish to repay, for I prefer continuing the obligation."

With this preface, the two friends dived into some very complicated accounts and vouchers, which, having been duly displayed and gone through by Perker, were at once discharged by Mr. Pickwick with many professions of esteem and friendship.

They had no sooner arrived at this point, than a most violent and startling knocking was heard at the door; it was not an ordinary double knock, but a constant and uninterrupted succession of the loudest single raps, as if the knocker were endowed with the perpetual motion, or the person outside had forgotten to leave off.

" Dear me, what's that!" exclaimed Perker, starting.

"I think it is a knock at the door," said Mr. Pickwick, as if there could be the smallest doubt of the fact!

The knocker made a more energetic reply than words could have yielded, for it continued to hammer with surprising force and noise, without a moment's cessation.

"Dear me!" said Perker, ringing his bell, "we shall alarm the Inn. Mr. Lowten, don't you hear a knock?"

418

"I'll answer the door in one moment, sir," replied the clerk.

The knocker appeared to hear the response, and to assert that it was quite impossible he could wait so long. It made a stupendous uproar.

"It's quite dreadful," said Mr. Pickwick, stopping his ears.

"Make haste, Mr. Lowten," Perker called out, "we shall have the panels beaten in."

Mr. Lowten, who was washing his hands in a dark closet, hurried to the door, and turning the handle, beheld the appearance which is described in the next chapter.

CHAPTER LIV.

CONTAINING SOME PARTICULARS RELATIVE TO THE DOUBLE KNOCK, AND OTHER MATTERS: AMONG WHICH CERTAIN INTERESTING DISCLOSURES RELATIVE TO MR. SNODGRASS AND A YOUNG LADY ARE BY NO MEANS IRRELEVANT TO THIS HISTORY.

THE object that presented itself to the eyes of the astonished clerk, was a boy—a wonderfully fat boy—habited as a serving lad, standing upright on the mat, with his eyes closed as if in sleep. He had never seen such a fat boy, in or out of a travelling caravan; and this, coupled with the calmness and repose of his appearance, so very different from what was reasonably to have been expected of the inflicter of such knocks, smote him with wonder.

"What's the matter?" inquired the clerk.

The extraordinary boy replied not a word; but he nodded once, and seemed, to the clerk's imagination, to snore feebly.

"Where do you come from?" inquired the clerk.

The boy made no sign. He breathed heavily, but in all other respects was motionless.

The clerk repeated the question thrice, and receiving no answer, prepared to shut the door, when the boy suddenly opened his eyes, winked several times, sneezed once, and raised his hand as if to repeat the knocking. Finding the door open, he stared about him with astonishment, and at length fixed his eyes on Mr. Lowten's face.

"What the devil do you knock in that way for?" inquired the clerk, angrily.

"Which way?" said the boy, in a slow and sleepy voice.

"Why, like forty hackney-coachmen," replied the clerk.

"Because master said, I wasn't to leave off knocking till they opened the door, for fear I should go to sleep," said the boy.

"Well," said the clerk, "what message have you brought?"

"He's down stairs," rejoined the boy.

"Who?"

"Master. He wants to know whether you're at home."

Mr. Lowten bethought himself, at this juncture, of looking out of the window. Seeing an open carriage with a hearty old gentleman in it, looking up very anxiously, he ventured to beckon him; on which, the old gentleman jumped out directly.

"That's your master in the carriage, I suppose?" said Lowten.

The boy nodded.

All further inquiries were superseded by the appearance of old Wardle, who, running up stairs, and just recognising Lowten, passed at once into Mr. Perker's room.

"Pickwick!" said the old gentleman. "Your hand, my boy! Why have I never heard until the day before yesterday of your suffering yourself to be cooped up in jail? And why did you let him do it, Perker?"

"I couldn't help it, my dear sir," replied Perker, with a smile and a pinch of snuff: "you know how obstinate he is."

"Of course I do, of course I do," replied the old gentleman. "I am heartily glad to see him, notwithstanding. I will not lose sight of him again, in a hurry."

With these words, Wardle shook Mr. Pickwick's hand once more, and, having done the same by Perker, threw himself into an arm-chair; his jolly red face shining again with smiles and health.

"Well!" said Wardle. "Here are pretty goings on—a

pinch of your snuff, Perker, my boy—never were such times, eh?"

"What do you mean?" inquired Mr. Pickwick.

"Mean!" replied Wardle. "Why, I think the girls are all running mad; that's no news, you'll say? Perhaps it's not; but it's true, for all that."

"You have not come up to London, of all places in the world, to tell us *that*, my dear sir, have you?" inquired Perker.

"No, not altogether," replied Wardle; "though it was the main cause of my coming. How's Arabella?"

"Very well," replied Mr. Pickwick, "and will be delighted to see you, I am sure."

"Black-eyed little jilt!" replied Wardle, "I had a great idea of marrying her myself, one of these odd days. But I am glad of it too, very glad."

"How did the intelligence reach you?" asked Mr. Pickwick.

"Oh, it came to my girls, of course," replied Wardle. "Arabella wrote, the day before yesterday, to say she had made a stolen match without her husband's father's consent, and so you had gone down to get it when his refusing it couldn't prevent the match, and all the rest of it. I thought it a very good time to say something serious to *my* girls; so I said what a dreadful thing it was that children should marry without their parents' consent, and so forth; but, bless your hearts, I couldn't make the least impression upon them. They thought it such a much more dreadful thing that there should have been a wedding without bridesmaids, that I might as well have preached to Joe himself."

Here the old gentleman stopped to laugh; and having done so to his heart's content, presently resumed.

"But this is not the best of it, it seems. This is only half the love-making and plotting that have been going forward. We have been walking on mines for the last six months, and they're sprung at last."

MORE MARRYING.

"What do you mean!" exclaimed Mr. Pickwick, turning pale; "no other secret marriage, I hope?"

"No, no," replied old Wardle; "not so bad as that; no."

"What then?" inquired Mr. Pickwick; "am I interested in it?"

"Shall I answer that question, Perker?" said Wardle.

"If you don't commit yourself by doing so, my dear sir."

"Well then, you are," said Wardle.

"How?" asked Mr. Pickwick anxiously. "In what way?"

"Really," replied Wardle, "you're such a fiery sort of young fellow that I am almost afraid to tell you; but, however, if Perker will sit between us to prevent mischief, I'll venture."

Having closed the room-door, and fortified himself with another application to Perker's snuff-box, the old gentleman proceeded with his great disclosure in these words.

"The fact is, that my daughter Bella—Bella, who married young Trundle, you know."

"Yes, yes, we know," said Mr. Pickwick impatiently.

"Don't alarm me at the very beginning. My daughter Bella, Emily having gone to bed with a headache after she had read Arabella's letter to me, sat herself down by my side the other evening, and began to talk over this marriage affair. 'Well, pa,' she says, 'what do you think of it?' 'Why, my dear,' I said, 'I suppose it's all very well; I hope it's for the best.' I answered in this way because I was sitting before the fire at the time, drinking my grog rather thoughtfully, and I knew my throwing in an undecided word now and then, would induce her to continue talking. Both my girls are pictures of their dear mother, and as I grow old I like to sit with only them by me; for their voices and looks carry me back to the happiest period of my life, and make me, for the moment, as young as I used to be then, though not quite so light-hearted. 'It's quite a marriage of affection, pa,' said Bella, after a short silence. 'Yes, my dear,' said I, 'but such marriages do not always turn out the happiest.'"

423

"I question that, mind!" interposed Mr. Pickwick, warmly.

"Very good," responded Wardle, "question anything you like when it's your turn to speak, but don't interrupt me."

"I beg your pardon," said Mr. Pickwick.

"Granted," replied Wardle. "'I am sorry to hear you express your opinion against marriages of affection, pa,' said Bella, colouring a little. 'I was wrong; I ought not to have said so, my dear, either,' said I, patting her cheek as kindly as a rough old fellow like me could pat it, 'for your mother's was one, and so was yours.' 'It's not that, I meant, pa,' said Bella. 'The fact is, pa, I wanted to speak to you about Emily.'"

Mr. Pickwick started.

"What's the matter now?" inquired Wardle, stopping in his narrative.

"Nothing," replied Mr. Pickwick. "Pray go on."

"I never could spin out a story," said Wardle abruptly. "It must come out, sooner or later, and it'll save us all a great deal of time if it comes at once. The long and the short of it is, then, that Bella at last mustered up courage to tell me that Emily was very unhappy; that she and your young friend Snodgrass had been in constant correspondence and communication ever since last Christmas; that she had very dutifully made up her mind to run away with him, in laudable imitation of her old friend and schoolfellow; but that having some compunctions of conscience on the subject, inasmuch as I had always been rather kindly disposed to both of them, they had thought it better in the first instance to pay me the compliment of asking whether I would have any objection to their being married in the usual matter-of-fact manner. There now, Mr. Pickwick, if you can make it convenient to reduce your eyes to their usual size again, and to let me hear what you think we ought to do, I shall feel rather obliged to you!"

The testy manner in which the hearty old gentleman uttered this last sentence was not wholly unwarranted; for

Mr. Pickwick's face had settled down into an expression of blank amazement and perplexity, quite curious to behold.

"Snodgrass! Since last Christmas!" were the first broken words that issued from the lips of the confounded gentleman.

"Since last Christmas," replied Wardle; "that's plain enough, and very bad spectacles we must have worn, not to have discovered it before."

"I don't understand it," said Mr. Pickwick, ruminating; "I really cannot understand it."

"It's easy enough to understand," replied the choleric old gentleman. "If you had been a younger man, you would have been in the secret long ago; and besides," added Wardle after a moment's hesitation, "the truth is, that, knowing nothing of this matter, I have rather pressed Emily for four or five months past, to receive favourably (if she could; I would never attempt to force a girl's inclinations) the addresses of a young gentleman down in our neighbourhood. I have no doubt that, girl-like, to enhance her own value and increase the ardour of Mr. Snodgrass, she has represented this matter in very glowing colours, and that they have both arrived at the conclusion that they are a terribly persecuted pair of unfortunates, and have no resource but clandestine matrimony or charcoal. Now the question is, what's to be done?"

"What have *you* done?" inquired Mr. Pickwick.

"I!"

"I mean what did you do when your married daughter told you this?"

"Oh, I made a fool of myself, of course," rejoined Wardle.

"Just so," interposed Perker, who had accompanied this dialogue with sundry twitchings of his watch-chain, vindictive rubbings of his nose, and other symptoms of impatience. "That's very natural; but how?"

"I went into a great passion and frightened my mother into a fit," said Wardle.

"That was judicious," remarked Perker; "and what else?"

"I fretted and fumed all next day, and raised a great

disturbance," rejoined the old gentleman. "At last I got tired of rendering myself unpleasant and making everybody miserable; so I hired a carriage at Muggleton, and, putting my own horses in it, came up to town, under pretence of bringing Emily to see Arabella."

"Miss Wardle is with you, then?" said Mr. Pickwick.

"To be sure she is," replied Wardle. "She is at Osborne's hotel in the Adelphi at this moment, unless your enterprising friend has run away with her since I came out this morning."

"You are reconciled, then?" said Perker.

"Not a bit of it," answered Wardle; "she has been crying and moping ever since, except last night, between tea and supper, when she made a great parade of writing a letter that I pretended to take no notice of."

"You want my advice in this matter, I suppose?" said Perker, looking from the musing face of Mr. Pickwick to the eager countenance of Wardle, and taking several consecutive pinches of his favourite stimulant.

"I suppose so," said Wardle, looking at Mr. Pickwick.

"Certainly," replied that gentleman.

"Well then," said Perker, rising and pushing his chair back, "my advice is that you both walk away together, or ride away, or get away by some means or other, for I'm tired of you, and just talk this matter over between you. If you have not settled it by the next time I see you, I'll tell you what to do."

"This is satisfactory," said Wardle, hardly knowing whether to smile or be offended.

"Pooh, pooh, my dear sir," returned Perker. "I know you both a great deal better than you know yourselves. You have settled it already, to all intents and purposes."

Thus expressing himself, the little gentleman poked his snuff-box, first into the chest of Mr. Pickwick, and then into the waistcoat of Mr. Wardle, upon which they all three laughed, but especially the two last-named gentlemen, who at once shook hands again, without any obvious or particular reason.

"You dine with me to-day," said Wardle to Perker, as he showed them out.

"Can't promise, my dear sir, can't promise," replied Perker. "I'll look in, in the evening, at all events."

"I shall expect you at five," said Wardle. "Now, Joe!" And Joe having been at length awakened, the two friends departed in Mr. Wardle's carriage, which in common humanity had a dickey behind for the fat boy, who, if there had been a foot-board instead, would have rolled off and killed himself in his very first nap.

Driving to the George and Vulture, they found that Arabella and her maid had sent for a hackney-coach immediately on the receipt of a short note from Emily announcing her arrival in town, and had proceeded straight to the Adelphi. As Wardle had business to transact in the city, they sent the carriage and the fat boy to his hotel, with the information that he and Mr. Pickwick would return together to dinner at five o'clock.

Charged with this message, the fat boy returned, slumbering as peaceably in his dickey, over the stones, as if it had been a down bed on watch-springs. By some extraordinary miracle he awoke of his own accord, when the coach stopped, and giving himself a good shake to stir up his faculties, went up stairs to execute his commission.

Now, whether the shake had jumbled the fat boy's faculties together, instead of arranging them in proper order, or had roused such a quantity of new ideas within him as to render him oblivious of ordinary forms and ceremonies, or (which is also possible) had proved unsuccessful in preventing his falling asleep as he ascended the stairs, it is an undoubted fact that he walked into the sitting-room without previously knocking at the door; and so beheld a gentleman with his arms clasping his young mistress's waist, sitting very lovingly by her side on a sofa, while Arabella and her pretty handmaid feigned to be absorbed in looking out of a window at the other end of the room. At sight of this phenomenon, the fat boy uttered an interjection, the ladies a scream, and the gentleman an oath, almost simultaneously.

"Wretched creature, what do you want here?" said the gentleman, who it is needless to say was Mr. Snodgrass.

To this the fat boy, considerably terrified, briefly responded, "Missis."

"What do you want me for?" inquired Emily, turning her head aside, "you stupid creature!"

"Master and Mr. Pickwick is a going to dine here at five," replied the fat boy.

"Leave the room!" said Mr. Snodgrass, glaring upon the bewildered youth.

"No, no, no," added Emily hastily. "Bella, dear, advise me."

Upon this, Emily and Mr. Snodgrass, and Arabella and Mary, crowded into a corner, and conversed earnestly in whispers for some minutes, during which the fat boy dozed.

"Joe," said Arabella, at length, looking round with a most bewitching smile, "how do you do, Joe?"

"Joe," said Emily, "you're a very good boy; I won't forget you, Joe."

"Joe," said Mr. Snodgrass, advancing to the astonished youth, and seizing his hand, "I didn't know you before. There's five shillings for you, Joe!"

"I'll owe you five, Joe," said Arabella, "for old acquaintance sake, you know;" and another most captivating smile was bestowed upon the corpulent intruder.

The fat boy's perception being slow, he looked rather puzzled at first to account for this sudden prepossession in his favour, and stared about him in a very alarming manner. At length his broad face began to show symptoms of a grin of proportionately broad dimensions; and then, thrusting half-a-crown into each of his pockets, and a hand and wrist after it, he burst into a horse laugh : being for the first and only time in his existence.

"He understands us, I see," said Arabella.

"He had better have something to eat, immediately," remarked Emily.

The fat boy almost laughed again when he heard this suggestion. Mary, after a little more whispering, tripped forth from the group, and said:

"I am going to dine with you to-day, sir, if you have no objection."

"This way," said the fat boy, eagerly. "There is such a jolly meat pie!"

With these words, the fat boy led the way down stairs; his pretty companion captivating all the waiters and angering all the chambermaids as she followed him to the eating-room.

There was the meat-pie of which the youth had spoken so feelingly, and there were, moreover, a steak, and a dish of potatoes, and a pot of porter.

"Sit down," said the fat boy. "Oh, my eye, how prime! I am *so* hungry."

Having apostrophised his eye, in a species of rapture, five or six times, the youth took the head of the little table, and Mary seated herself at the bottom.

"Will you have some of this?" said the fat boy, plunging into the pie up to the very ferules of the knife and fork.

"A little, if you please," replied Mary.

The fat boy assisted Mary to a little, and himself to a great deal, and was just going to begin eating when he suddenly laid down his knife and fork, leant forward in his chair, and letting his hands, with the knife and fork in them, fall on his knees, said, very slowly:

"I say! How nice you look!"

This was said in an admiring manner, and was, so far, gratifying; but still there was enough of the cannibal in the young gentleman's eyes to render the compliment a double one.

"Dear me, Joseph," said Mary, affecting to blush, "what do you mean?"

The fat boy gradually recovering his former position,

429

THE PICKWICK CLUB.

replied with a heavy sigh, and remaining thoughtful for a few moments, drank a long draught of the porter. Having achieved this feat he sighed again, and applied himself assiduously to the pie.

"What a nice young lady Miss Emily is!" said Mary, after a long silence.

The fat boy had by this time finished the pie. He fixed his eyes on Mary, and replied:

"I knows a nicerer."

"Indeed!" said Mary.

"Yes, indeed!" replied the fat boy, with unwonted vivacity.

"What's her name?" inquired Mary.

"What's yours?"

"Mary."

"So's hers," said the fat boy. "You're her." The boy grinned to add point to the compliment, and put his eyes into something between a squint and a cast, which there is reason to believe he intended for an ogle.

"You mustn't talk to me in that way," said Mary; "you don't mean it."

"Don't I, though?" replied the fat boy; "I say!"

"Well."

"Are you going to come here regular?"

"No," rejoined Mary, shaking her head, "I'm going away again to-night. Why?"

"Oh!" said the fat boy in a tone of strong feeling; "how we should have enjoyed ourselves at meals, if you had been!"

"I might come here sometimes, perhaps, to see you," said Mary, plaiting the table-cloth in assumed coyness, "if you would do me a favour."

The fat boy looked from the pie-dish to the steak, as if he thought a favour must be in a manner connected with something to eat; and then took out one of the half-crowns and glanced at it nervously.

"Don't you understand me?" said Mary, looking slyly in his fat face.

430

Mary and the Fat Boy

Again he looked at the half-crown, and said faintly, " No."

" The ladies want you not to say anything to the old gentleman about the young gentleman having been up stairs; and I want you too."

" Is that all?" said the fat boy, evidently very much relieved as he pocketed the half-crown again. " Of course I ain't a going to."

" You see," said Mary, " Mr. Snodgrass is very fond of Miss Emily, and Miss Emily's very fond of him, and if you were to tell about it, the old gentleman would carry you all away miles into the country, where you'd see nobody."

" No, no, I won't tell," said the fat boy, stoutly.

" That's a dear," said Mary. " Now it's time I went up stairs, and got my lady ready for dinner."

" Don't go yet," urged the fat boy.

" I must," replied Mary. " Good bye, for the present."

The fat boy, with elephantine playfulness, stretched out his arms to ravish a kiss; but as it required no great agility to elude him, his fair enslaver had vanished before he closed them again; upon which the apathetic youth ate a pound or so of steak with a sentimental countenance, and fell fast asleep.

There was so much to say up stairs, and there were so many plans to concert for elopement and matrimony in the event of old Wardle continuing to be cruel, that it wanted only half an hour of dinner when Mr. Snodgrass took his final adieu. The ladies ran to Emily's bedroom to dress, and the lover taking up his hat, walked out of the room. He had scarcely got outside the door, when he heard Wardle's voice talking loudly, and looking over the banisters, beheld him, followed by some other gentlemen, coming straight up stairs. Knowing nothing of the house, Mr. Snodgrass in his confusion stepped hastily back into the room he had just quitted, and passing from thence into an inner apartment (Mr. Wardle's bed-chamber), closed the door softly, just as the persons he had caught a glimpse of, entered the sitting-room.

These were Mr. Wardle, Mr. Pickwick, Mr. Nathaniel Winkle, and Mr. Benjamin Allen, whom he had no difficulty in recognising by their voices.

"Very lucky I had the presence of mind to avoid them," thought Mr. Snodgrass with a smile, and walking on tiptoe to another door near the bedside; "this opens into the same passage, and I can walk, quietly and comfortably, away."

There was only one obstacle to his walking quietly and comfortably away, which was that the door was locked and the key gone.

"Let us have some of your best wine to-day, waiter," said old Wardle, rubbing his hands.

"You shall have some of the very best, sir," replied the waiter.

"Let the ladies know we have come in."

"Yes, sir."

Devoutly and ardently did Mr. Snodgrass wish that the ladies could know *he* had come in. He ventured once to whisper "Waiter!" through the keyhole, but as the probability of the wrong waiter coming to his relief, flashed upon his mind, together with a sense of the strong resemblance between his own situation and that in which another gentleman had been recently found in a neighbouring hotel (an account of whose misfortunes had appeared under the head of "Police" in that morning's paper), he sat himself on a portmanteau, and trembled violently.

"We won't wait a minute for Perker," said Wardle, looking at his watch; "he is always exact. He will be here, in time, if he means to come; and if he does not, it's of no use waiting. Ha! Arabella!"

"My sister!" exclaimed Mr. Benjamin Allen, folding her in a most romantic embrace.

"Oh, Ben, dear, how you do smell of tobacco," said Arabella, rather overcome by this mark of affection.

"Do I?" said Mr. Benjamin Allen, "Do I, Bella? Well, perhaps I do."

Perhaps he did; having just left a pleasant little smoking party of twelve medical students, in a small back parlour with a large fire.

"But I am delighted to see you," said Mr. Ben Allen. "Bless you, Bella!"

"There," said Arabella, bending forward to kiss her brother; "don't take hold of me again, Ben dear, because you tumble me so."

At this point of the reconciliation, Mr. Ben Allen allowed his feelings and the cigars and porter to overcome him, and looked round upon the beholders with damp spectacles.

"Is nothing to be said to me?" cried Wardle with open arms.

"A great deal," whispered Arabella, as she received the old gentleman's hearty caress and congratulation. "You are a hard-hearted, unfeeling, cruel, monster!"

"You are a little rebel," replied Wardle, in the same tone, "and I am afraid I shall be obliged to forbid you the house. People like you, who get married in spite of everybody, ought not to be let loose on society. But come!" added the old gentleman aloud, "Here's the dinner; you shall sit by me. Joe; why, damn the boy, he's awake!"

To the great distress of his master, the fat boy was indeed in a state of remarkable vigilance; his eyes being wide open, and looking as if they intended to remain so. There was an alacrity in his manner, too, which was equally unaccountable; every time his eyes met those of Emily or Arabella, he smirked and grinned; once, Wardle could have sworn he saw him wink.

This alteration in the fat boy's demeanour, originated in his increased sense of his own importance, and the dignity he acquired from having been taken into the confidence of the young ladies; and the smirks, and grins, and winks, were so many condescending assurances that they might depend upon his fidelity. As these tokens were rather calculated to awaken suspicion than allay it, and were somewhat embarrassing besides, they were occasionally answered by a frown or shake of the head from Arabella, which the fat boy considering as hints to be on his guard, expressed his perfect understanding of, by smirking, grinning, and winking, with redoubled assiduity.

"Joe," said Mr. Wardle, after an unsuccessful search in all his pockets, "is my snuff-box on the sofa?"

"No, sir," replied the fat boy.

"Oh, I recollect; I left it on my dressing-table this morning," said Wardle. "Run into the next room and fetch it."

The fat boy went into the next room; and having been absent about a minute, returned with the snuff-box, and the palest face that ever a fat boy wore.

"What's the matter with the boy!" exclaimed Wardle.

"Nothen's the matter with me," replied Joe, nervously.

"Have you been seeing any spirits?" inquired the old gentleman.

"Or taking any?" added Ben Allen.

"I think you're right," whispered Wardle across the table. "He is intoxicated, I'm sure."

Ben Allen replied that he thought he was; and as that gentleman had seen a vast deal of the disease in question, Wardle was confirmed in an impression which had been hovering about his mind for half an hour, and at once arrived at the conclusion that the fat boy was drunk.

"Just keep your eye upon him for a few minutes," murmured Wardle. "We shall soon find out whether he is or not."

The unfortunate youth had only interchanged a dozen words with Mr. Snodgrass: that gentleman having implored him to make a private appeal to some friend to release him, and then pushed him out with the snuff-box, lest his prolonged absence should lead to a discovery. He ruminated a little with a most disturbed expression of face, and left the room in search of Mary.

But Mary had gone home after dressing her mistress, and the fat boy came back again more disturbed than before.

Wardle and Mr. Ben Allen exchanged glances.

"Joe!" said Wardle.

"Yes, sir."

"What did you go away for?"

The fat boy looked hopelessly in the face of everybody at table, and stammered out, that he didn't know.

"Oh," said Wardle, "you don't know, eh? Take this cheese to Mr. Pickwick."

Now, Mr. Pickwick being in the very best health and spirits, had been making himself perfectly delightful all dinner-time, and was at this moment engaged in an energetic conversation with Emily and Mr. Winkle: bowing his head, courteously, in the emphasis of his discourse, gently waving his left hand to lend force to his observations, and all glowing with placid smiles. He took a piece of cheese from the plate, and was on the point of turning round to renew the conversation, when the fat boy, stooping so as to bring his head on a level with that of Mr. Pickwick, pointed with his thumb over his shoulder, and made the most horrible and hideous face that was ever seen out of a Christmas pantomime.

"Dear me!" said Mr. Pickwick, starting, "what a very— eh?" He stopped, for the fat boy had drawn himself up, and was, or pretended to be, fast asleep.

"What's the matter?" inquired Wardle.

"This is such an extremely singular lad!" replied Mr. Pickwick, looking uneasily at the boy. "It seems an odd thing to say, but upon my word I am afraid that, at times, he is a little deranged."

"Oh! Mr. Pickwick, pray don't say so," cried Emily and Arabella, both at once.

"I am not certain, of course," said Mr. Pickwick, amidst profound silence, and looks of general dismay; "but his manner to me this moment was really very alarming. Oh!" ejaculated Mr. Pickwick, suddenly jumping up with a short scream. "I beg your pardon, ladies, but at that moment he ran some sharp instrument into my leg. Really he is not safe."

435

"He's drunk," roared old Wardle, passionately. "Ring the bell! Call the waiters! He's drunk."

"I ain't," said the fat boy, falling on his knees as his master seized him by the collar. "I ain't drunk."

"Then you're mad; that's worse. Call the waiters," said the old gentleman.

"I ain't mad; I'm sensible," rejoined the fat boy, beginning to cry.

"Then, what the devil do you run sharp instruments into Mr. Pickwick's legs for?" inquired Wardle, angrily.

"He wouldn't look at me," replied the boy. "I wanted to speak to him."

"What did you want to say?" asked half a dozen voices at once.

The fat boy gasped, looked at the bedroom door, gasped again, and wiped two tears away with the knuckle of each of his forefingers.

"What did you want to say?" demanded Wardle, shaking him.

"Stop!" said Mr. Pickwick; "allow me. What did you wish to communicate to me, my poor boy?"

"I want to whisper to you," replied the fat boy.

"You want to bite his ear off, I suppose," said Wardle. "Don't come near him; he's vicious; ring the bell, and let him be taken down stairs."

Just as Mr. Winkle caught the bell-rope in his hand, it was arrested by a general expression of astonishment; the captive lover, his face burning with confusion, suddenly walked in from the bedroom, and made a comprehensive bow to the company.

"Hallo!" cried Wardle, releasing the fat boy's collar, and staggering back, "What's this!"

"I have been concealed in the next room, sir, since you returned," explained Mr. Snodgrass.

"Emily, my girl," said Wardle, reproachfully, "I detest meanness and deceit; this is unjustifiable and indelicate in the

436

highest degree. I don't deserve this at your hands, Emily, indeed!"

"Dear papa," said Emily, "Arabella knows—everybody here knows—Joe knows—that I was no party to this conceal-ment. Augustus, for Heaven's sake, explain it!"

Mr. Snodgrass, who had only waited for a hearing, at once recounted how he had been placed in his then distressing predicament; how the fear of giving rise to domestic dissensions had alone prompted him to avoid Mr. Wardle on his entrance; how he merely meant to depart by another door, but, finding it locked, had been compelled to stay against his will. It was a painful situation to be placed in; but he now regretted it the less, inasmuch as it afforded him an opportunity of acknowledging, before their mutual friends, that he loved Mr. Wardle's daughter, deeply and sincerely; that he was proud to avow that the feeling was mutual; and that if thousands of miles were placed between them, or oceans rolled their waters, he could never for an instant forget those happy days, when first—and so on.

Having delivered himself to this effect, Mr. Snodgrass bowed again, looked into the crown of his hat, and stepped towards the door.

"Stop!" shouted Wardle. "Why, in the name of all that's—— "

"Inflammable," mildly suggested Mr. Pickwick, who thought something worse was coming.

"Well—that's inflammable," said Wardle, adopting the substitute; "couldn't you say all this to me in the first instance?"

"Or confide in me?" added Mr. Pickwick.

"Dear, dear," said Arabella, taking up the defence, "what is the use of asking all that now, especially when you know you had set your covetous old heart on a richer son-in-law, and are so wild and fierce besides, that everybody is afraid of you, except me. Shake hands with him, and order him some dinner, for goodness gracious sake, for he looks half-starved;

and pray have your wine up at once, for you'll not be tolerable until you have taken two bottles at least."

The worthy old gentleman pulled Arabella's ear, kissed her without the smallest scruple, kissed his daughter also with great affection, and shook Mr. Snodgrass warmly by the hand.

"She is right on one point at all events," said the old gentleman, cheerfully. "Ring for the wine!"

The wine came, and Perker came up stairs at the same moment. Mr. Snodgrass had dinner at a side table, and, when he had despatched it, drew his chair next Emily, without the smallest opposition on the old gentleman's part.

The evening was excellent. Little Mr. Perker came out wonderfully, told various comic stories, and sang a serious song which was almost as funny as the anecdotes. Arabella was very charming, Mr. Wardle very jovial, Mr. Pickwick very harmonious, Mr. Ben Allen very uproarious, the lovers very silent, Mr. Winkle very talkative, and all of them very happy.

CHAPTER LV.

MR. SOLOMON PELL, ASSISTED BY A SELECT COMMITTEE OF COACH-
MEN, ARRANGES THE AFFAIRS OF THE ELDER MR. WELLER.

"Samivel," said Mr. Weller, accosting his son on the morning after the funeral, "I've found it, Sammy. I thought it wos there.

"Thought wot wos were?" inquired Sam.

"Your mother-in-law's vill, Sammy," replied Mr. Weller. "In wirtue o' vich, them arrangements is to be made as I told you on, last night, respectin' the funs."

"Wot, didn't she tell you were it wos?" inquired Sam.

"Not a bit on it, Sammy," replied Mr. Weller. "We wos a adjestin' our little differences, and I wos a cheerin' her spirits and bearin' her up, so that I forgot to ask anythin' about it. I don't know as I should ha' done it indeed, if I had remembered it," added Mr. Weller, "for it's a rum sort o' thing, Sammy, to go a hankerin' arter anybody's property, ven you're assistin' 'em in illness. It's like helping an outside passenger up, ven he's been pitched off a coach, and puttin' your hand in his pocket, vile you ask him vith a sigh how he finds hisself, Sammy."

With this figurative illustration of his meaning, Mr. Weller unclasped his pocket-book, and drew forth a dirty sheet of letter paper, on which were inscribed various characters crowded together in remarkable confusion.

"This here is the dockyment, Sammy," said Mr. Weller.

"I found it in the little black teapot, on the top shelf o' the bar closet. She used to keep bank notes there, afore she vos married, Samivel. I've seen her take the lid off, to pay a bill, many and many a time. Poor creeter, she might ha' filled all the teapots in the house vith vills, and not have incon-wenienced herself neither, for she took wery little of anythin' in that vay lately, 'cept on the Temperance nights, ven they just laid a foundation o' tea to put the spirits a-top on!"

"What does it say?" inquired Sam.

"Jist vot I told you, my boy," rejoined his parent. "Two hundred pound vurth o' reduced counsels to my son-in-law, Samivel, and all the rest o' my property, of ev'ry kind and description votsoever to my husband, Mr. Tony Veller, who I appint as my sole eggzekiter."

"That's all, is it?" said Sam.

"That's all," replied Mr. Weller. "And I s'pose as it's all right and satisfactory to you and me as is the only parties interested, ve may as vell put this bit o' paper into the fire."

"Wot are you a-doin' on, you lunatic?" said Sam, snatching the paper away, as his parent, in all innocence, stirred the fire preparatory to suiting the action to the word. "You're a nice eggzekiter, you are."

"Vy not?" inquired Mr. Weller, looking sternly round, with the poker in his hand.

"Vy not!" exclaimed Sam. "'Cos it must be proved, and probated, and swore to, and all manner o' formalities."

"You don't mean that?" said Mr. Weller, laying down the poker.

Sam buttoned the will carefully in a side pocket; inti-mating by a look, meanwhile, that he did mean it, and very seriously too.

"Then I'll tell you wot it is," said Mr. Weller, after a short meditation, "this is a case for that 'ere confidential pal o' the Chancellorship's. Pell must look into this, Sammy. He's the man for a difficult question at law. Ve'll have this here, brought afore the Solvent Court directly, Samivel."

"I never did see such a addle-headed old creetur!" exclaimed Sam, irritably, "Old Baileys, and Solvent Courts, and alleybis, and ev'ry species o' gammon alvays a runnin' through his brain! You'd better get your out o' door clothes on, and come to town about this bisness, than stand a preachin' there about wot you don't understand nothin' on."

"Wery good, Sammy," replied Mr. Weller, "I'm quite agreeable to anythin' as vill hexpedite business, Sammy. But mind this here, my boy, nobody but Pell—nobody but Pell as a legal adwiser."

"I don't want anybody else," replied Sam. "Now, are you a-comin'?"

"Vait a minit, Sammy," replied Mr. Weller, who, having tied his shawl with the aid of a small glass that hung in the window, was now, by dint of the most wonderful exertions, struggling into his upper garments. "Vait a minit, Sammy; ven you grow as old as your father, you von't get into your veskit quite as easy as you do now, my boy."

"If I couldn't get into it easier than that, I'm blessed if I'd vear vun at all," rejoined his son.

"You think so now," said Mr. Weller, with the gravity of age, "but you'll find that as you get vider, you'll get viser. Vidth and visdom, Sammy, alvays grows together."

As Mr. Weller delivered this infallible maxim—the result of many years' personal experience and observation—he contrived, by a dexterous twist of his body, to get the bottom button of his coat to perform its office. Having paused a few seconds to recover breath, he brushed his hat with his elbow, and declared himself ready.

"As four heads is better than two, Sammy," said Mr. Weller, as they drove along the London Road in the chaise cart, "and as all this here property is a wery great temptation to a legal gen'l'm'n, ve'll take a couple o' friends o' mine vith us, as'll be wery soon down upon him if he comes anythin' irreg'lar; two o' them as saw you to the Fleet that day. They're the wery best judges," added Mr. Weller in a half whisper, " the wery best judges of a horse, you ever know'd."

" And of a lawyer too ? " inquired Sam.

" The man as can form a ackerate judgment of a animal, can form a ackerate judgment of anythin'," replied his father ; so dogmatically, that Sam did not attempt to controvert the position.

In pursuance of this notable resolution, the services of the mottled-faced gentleman and of two other very fat coachmen —selected by Mr. Weller, probably, with a view to their width and consequent wisdom—were put into requisition ; and this assistance having been secured, the party proceeded to the public-house in Portugal Street, whence a messenger was despatched to the Insolvent Court over the way, requiring Mr. Solomon Pell's immediate attendance.

The messenger fortunately found Mr. Solomon Pell in court, regaling himself, business being rather slack, with a cold collation of an Abernethy biscuit and a saveloy. The message was no sooner whispered in his ear than he thrust them in his pocket among various professional documents, and hurried over the way with such alacrity, that he reached the parlour before the messenger had even emancipated himself from the court.

" Gentlemen," said Mr. Pell, touching his hat, " my service to you all. I don't say it to flatter you, gentlemen, but there are not five other men in the world, that I'd have come out of that court for, to-day."

" So busy, eh ? " said Sam.

" Busy ! " replied Pell ; " I'm completely sewn up, as my friend the late Lord Chancellor many a time used to say to me, gentlemen, when he came out from hearing appeals in the House of Lords. Poor fellow ! he was very susceptible of fatigue ; he used to feel those appeals uncommonly. I actually thought more than once that he'd have sunk under 'em ; I did indeed."

Here Mr. Pell shook his head and paused ; on which, the

elder Mr. Weller, nudging his neighbour, as begging him to mark the attorney's high connections, asked whether the duties in question produced any permanent ill effects on the constitution of his noble friend.

"I don't think he ever quite recovered them," replied Pell; "in fact I'm sure he never did. 'Pell,' he used to say to me many a time, 'how the blazes you can stand the head-work you do, is a mystery to me.'—'Well,' I used to answer, '*I* hardly know how I do it, upon my life.'—'Pell,' he'd add, sighing, and looking at me with a little envy—friendly envy, you know, gentlemen, mere friendly envy; I never minded it—'Pell, you're a wonder; a wonder.' Ah! you'd have liked him very much if you had known him, gentlemen. Bring me three penn'orth of rum, my dear."

Addressing this latter remark to the waitress in a tone of subdued grief, Mr. Pell sighed, looked at his shoes, and the ceiling; and, the rum having by that time arrived, drunk it up.

"However," said Pell, drawing a chair to the table, "a professional man has no right to think of his private friendships when his legal assistance is wanted. By the bye, gentlemen, since I saw you here before, we have had to weep over a very melancholy occurrence."

Mr. Pell drew out a pocket-handkerchief, when he came to the word weep, but he made no further use of it than to wipe away a slight tinge of rum which hung upon his upper lip.

"I saw it in the Advertiser, Mr. Weller," continued Pell. "Bless my soul, not more than fifty-two! Dear me—only think."

These indications of a musing spirit were addressed to the mottled-faced man, whose eyes Mr. Pell had accidentally caught; on which, the mottled-faced man, whose apprehension of matters in general was of a foggy nature, moved uneasily in his seat, and opined that indeed, so far as that went, there was no saying how things *was* brought about;

which observation, involving one of those subtle propositions which it is difficult to encounter in argument, was controverted by nobody.

" I have heard it remarked that she was a very fine woman, Mr. Weller," said Pell in a sympathising manner.

" Yes, sir, she wos," replied the elder Mr. Weller, not much relishing this mode of discussing the subject, and yet thinking that the attorney, from his long intimacy with the late Lord Chancellor, must know best on all matters of polite breeding. " She wos a wery fine 'ooman, sir, ven I first know'd her. She wos a widder, sir, at that time."

" Now, it's curious," said Pell, looking round with a sorrowful smile ; " Mrs. Pell was a widow."

" That's very extraordinary," said the mottled-faced man.

" Well, it is a curious coincidence," said Pell.

" Not at all," gruffly remarked the elder Mr. Weller. " More widders is married than single wimin."

" Very good, very good," said Pell, " you're quite right, Mr. Weller. Mrs. Pell was a very elegant and accomplished woman ; her manners were the theme of universal admiration in our neighbourhood. I was proud to see that woman dance ; there was something so firm and dignified, and yet natural, in her motion. Her cutting, gentlemen, was simplicity itself. Ah ! well, well ! Excuse my asking the question, Mr. Samuel," continued the attorney in a lower voice, " was your mother-in-law tall ?"

" Not wery," replied Sam.

" Mrs. Pell was a tall figure," said Pell, " a splendid woman, with a noble shape, and a nose, gentlemen, formed to command and be majestic. She was very much attached to me—very much—highly connected, too. Her mother's brother, gentlemen, failed for eight hundred pounds, as a Law Stationer."

" Vell," said Mr. Weller, who had grown rather restless during this discussion, " vith regard to bis'ness."

The word was music to Pell's ears. He had been revolving in his mind whether any business was to be transacted, or whether he had been merely invited to partake of a glass of brandy and water, or a bowl of punch, or any similar professional compliment, and now the doubt was set at rest without his appearing at all eager for its solution. His eyes glistened as he laid his hat on the table, and said :

"What is the business upon which—um ? Either of these gentlemen wish to go through the court ? We require an arrest ; a friendly arrest will do, you know ; we are all friends here, I suppose ? "

"Give me the dockyment, Sammy," said Mr. Weller, taking the will from his son, who appeared to enjoy the interview amazingly. "Wot we rekvire, sir, is a probe o' this here."

"Probate, my dear sir, probate," said Pell.

"Well, sir," replied Mr. Weller sharply, "probe and probe it, is wery much the same ; if you don't understand wot I mean, sir, I dessay I can find them as does."

"No offence, I hope, Mr. Weller," said Pell, meekly. "You are the executor, I see," he added, casting his eyes over the paper.

"I am, sir," replied Mr. Weller.

"These other gentlemen, I presume, are legatees, are they ?" inquired Pell with a congratulatory smile.

"Sammy is a leg-at-ease," replied Mr. Weller ; "these other gen'l'm'n is friends o' mine, just come to see fair ; a kind of umpires."

"Oh!" said Pell, "very good. I have no objections, I'm sure. I shall want a matter of five pound of you before I begin, ha! ha! ha!"

It being decided by the committee that the five pound might be advanced, Mr. Weller produced that sum ; after which, a long consultation about nothing particular, took place, in the course whereof Mr. Pell demonstrated to the perfect satisfaction of the gentlemen who saw fair, that unless the management of the business had been intrusted to him, it must all have gone wrong, for reasons not clearly made out, but no doubt sufficient. This important point being despatched,

Mr. Pell refreshed himself with three chops, and liquids both malt and spirituous, at the expense of the estate; and then they all went away to Doctors' Commons.

The next day, there was another visit to Doctors' Commons, and a great to do with an attesting hostler, who, being inebriated, declined swearing anything but profane oaths, to the great scandal of a proctor and surrogate. Next week, there were more visits to Doctors' Commons, and there was a visit to the Legacy Duty Office besides, and there were treaties entered into, for the disposal of the lease and business, and ratifications of the same, and inventories to be made out, and lunches to be taken, and dinners to be eaten, and so many profitable things to be done, and such a mass of papers accumulated, that Mr. Solomon Pell, and the boy, and the blue bag to boot, all got so stout that scarcely anybody would have known them for the same man, boy, and bag, that had loitered about Portugal Street, a few days before.

At length all these weighty matters being arranged, a day was fixed for selling out and transferring the stock, and of waiting with that view upon Wilkins Flasher, Esq., stockbroker, of somewhere near the Bank, who had been recommended by Mr. Solomon Pell for the purpose.

It was a kind of festive occasion, and the parties were attired accordingly. Mr. Weller's tops were newly cleaned, and his dress was arranged with peculiar care; the mottled-faced gentleman wore at his button-hole a full-sized dahlia with several leaves; and the coats of his two friends were adorned with nosegays of laurel and other evergreens. All three were habited in strict holiday costume; that is to say, they were wrapped up to the chins, and wore as many clothes as possible, which is, and has been, a stage-coachman's idea of full dress ever since stage coaches were invented.

Mr. Pell was waiting at the usual place of meeting at the appointed time; even Mr. Pell wore a pair of gloves and a clean shirt much frayed at the collar and wristbands by frequent washings.

446

A SUBSTANTIAL LUNCHEON.

"A quarter to two," said Pell, looking at the parlour clock. "If we are with Mr. Flasher at a quarter past, we shall just hit the best time."

"What should you say to a drop o' beer, gen'l'm'n?" suggested the mottled-faced man.

"And a little bit o' cold beef," said the second coachman.

"Or a oyster," added the third, who was a hoarse gentleman, supported by very round legs.

"Hear, hear!" said Pell; "to congratulate Mr. Weller, on his coming into possession of his property: eh? ha! ha!"

"I'm quite agreeable, gen'l'm'n," answered Mr. Weller. "Sammy, pull the bell."

Sam complied; and the porter, cold beef, and oysters being promptly produced, the lunch was done ample justice to. Where everybody took so active a part, it is almost invidious to make a distinction; but if one individual evinced greater powers than another, it was the coachman with the hoarse voice, who took an imperial pint of vinegar with his oysters, without betraying the least emotion.

"Mr. Pell, sir," said the elder Mr. Weller, stirring a glass of brandy and water, of which one was placed before every gentleman when the oyster shells were removed, "Mr. Pell, sir, it wos my intention to have proposed the funs on this occasion, but Samivel has vispered to me—"

Here Mr. Samuel Weller, who had silently eaten his oysters with tranquil smiles, cried "Hear!" in a very loud voice.

"—Has vispered to me," resumed his father, "that it vould be better to dewote the liquor to vishin' you success and prosperity, and thankin' you for the manner in which you've brought this here business through. Here's your health, sir."

"Hold hard there," interposed the mottled-faced gentleman, with sudden energy, "your eyes on me, gen'l'm'n!"

Saying this, the mottled-faced gentleman rose, as did the other gentlemen. The mottled-faced gentleman reviewed the company, and slowly lifted his hand, upon which every man (including him of the mottled countenance) drew a long breath, and lifted his tumbler to his lips. In one instant the mottled-faced gentleman depressed his hand again, and every glass was set down empty. It is impossible to describe the thrilling effect produced by this striking ceremony. At once dignified, solemn, and impressive, it combined every element of grandeur.

"Well, gentlemen," said Mr. Pell, "all I can say is, that such marks of confidence must be very gratifying to a professional man. I don't wish to say anything that might appear egotistical, gentlemen, but I'm very glad, for your own sakes, that you came to me: that's all. If you had gone to any low member of the profession, it's my firm conviction, and I assure you of it as a fact, that you would have found yourselves in Queer Street before this. I could have wished my noble friend had been alive to have seen my management of this case. I don't say it out of pride, but I think—however, gentlemen, I won't trouble you with that. I'm generally to be found here, gentlemen, but if I'm not here, or over the way, that's my address. You'll find my terms very cheap and reasonable, and no man attends more to his clients than I do, and I hope I know a little of my profession besides. If you have any opportunity of recommending me to any of your friends, gentlemen, I shall be very much obliged to you, and so will they too, when they come to know me. *Your* healths, gentlemen."

With this expression of his feelings, Mr. Solomon Pell laid three small written cards before Mr. Weller's friends, and, looking at the clock again, feared it was time to be walking. Upon this hint Mr. Weller settled the bill, and, issuing forth, the executor, legatee, attorney, and umpires, directed their steps towards the City.

The office of Wilkins Flasher, Esquire, of the Stock Exchange, was in a first floor up a court behind the Bank of England; the house of Wilkins Flasher, Esquire, was at Brixton, Surrey; the horse and stanhope of Wilkins Flasher, Esquire, were at an adjacent livery stable; the groom of

Weller and his Friends Drinking to Mr. Pell

ON THE STOCK EXCHANGE.

Wilkins Flasher, Esquire, was on his way to the West End to deliver some game; the clerk of Wilkins Flasher, Esquire, had gone to his dinner; and so Wilkins Flasher, Esquire, himself, cried, "Come in," when Mr. Pell and his companions knocked at the counting-house door.

"Good morning, sir," said Pell, bowing obsequiously. "We want to make a little transfer, if you please."

"Oh, come in, will you?" said Mr. Flasher. "Sit down a minute; I'll attend to you directly."

"Thank you, sir," said Pell, "there's no hurry. Take a chair, Mr. Weller."

Mr. Weller took a chair, and Sam took a box, and the umpires took what they could get, and looked at the almanack and one or two papers which were wafered against the wall, with as much open-eyed reverence as if they had been the finest efforts of the old masters.

"Well, I'll bet you half a dozen of claret on it; come!" said Wilkins Flasher, Esquire, resuming the conversation to which Mr. Pell's entrance had caused a momentary interruption.

This was addressed to a very smart young gentleman who wore his hat on his right whisker, and was lounging over the desk, killing flies with a ruler. Wilkins Flasher, Esquire, was balancing himself on two legs of an office stool, spearing a wafer-box with a pen-knife, which he dropped every now and then with great dexterity into the very centre of a small red wafer that was stuck outside. Both gentlemen had very open waistcoats and very rolling collars, and very small boots, and very big rings, and very little watches, and very large guard chains, and symmetrical inexpressibles, and scented pocket-handkerchiefs.

"I never bet half a dozen," said the other gentleman. "I'll take a dozen."

"Done, Simmery, done!" said Wilkins Flasher, Esquire.

"P. P., mind," observed the other.

"Of course," replied Wilkins Flasher, Esquire. Wilkins

Flasher, Esquire, entered it in a little book, with a gold pencil-case, and the other gentleman entered it also, in another little book with another gold pencil-case.

"I see there's a notice up this morning about Boffer," observed Mr. Simmery. "Poor devil, he's expelled the house!"

"I'll bet you ten guineas to five, he cuts his throat," said Wilkins Flasher, Esquire.

"Done," replied Mr. Simmery.

"Stop! I bar," said Wilkins Flasher, Esquire, thoughtfully. "Perhaps he may hang himself."

"Very good," rejoined Mr. Simmery, pulling out the gold pencil-case again. "I've no objection to take you that way. Say, makes away with himself."

"Kills himself, in fact," said Wilkins Flasher, Esquire.

"Just so," replied Mr. Simmery, putting it down. "'Flasher —ten guineas to five, Boffer kills himself.' Within what time shall we say?"

"A fortnight?" suggested Wilkins Flasher, Esquire.

"Con-found it, no;" rejoined Mr. Simmery, stopping for an instant to smash a fly with the ruler. "Say a week."

"Split the difference," said Wilkins Flasher, Esquire. "Make it ten days."

"Well; ten days," rejoined Mr. Simmery.

So, it was entered down in the little books that Boffer was to kill himself within ten days, or Wilkins Flasher, Esquire, was to hand over to Frank Simmery, Esquire, the sum of ten guineas; and that if Boffer did kill himself within that time, Frank Simmery, Esquire, would pay to Wilkins Flasher, Esquire, five guineas, instead.

"I'm very sorry he has failed," said Wilkins Flasher, Esquire. "Capital dinners he gave."

"Fine port he had too," remarked Mr. Simmery. "We are going to send our butler to the sale to-morrow, to pick up some of that sixty-four."

"The devil you are," said Wilkins Flasher, Esquire. "My man's going too. Five guineas my man outbids your man."

AT THE BANK OF ENGLAND.

" Done."

Another entry was made in the little books, with the gold pencil-cases ; and Mr. Simmery having, by this time, killed all the flies and taken all the bets, strolled away to the Stock Exchange to see what was going forward.

Wilkins Flasher, Esquire, now condescended to receive Mr. Solomon Pell's instructions, and having filled up some printed forms, requested the party to follow him to the Bank : which they did : Mr. Weller and his three friends staring at all they beheld in unbounded astonishment, and Sam encountering everything with a coolness which nothing could disturb.

Crossing a court-yard which was all noise and bustle ; and passing a couple of porters who seemed dressed to match the red fire engine which was wheeled away into a corner ; they passed into an office where their business was to be transacted, and where Pell and Mr. Flasher left them standing for a few moments, while they went up stairs into the Will Office.

" Wot place is this here ? " whispered the mottled-faced gentleman to the elder Mr. Weller.

" Counsel's Office," replied the executor in a whisper.

" Wot are them gen'l'men a settin' behind the counters ? " asked the hoarse coachman.

" Reduced counsels, I s'pose," replied Mr. Weller. " Ain't they the reduced counsels, Samivel ? "

" Wy, you don't suppose the reduced counsels is alive, do you ? " inquired Sam, with some disdain.

" How should I know ? " retorted Mr. Weller ; " I thought they looked wery like it. Wot are they, then ? "

" Clerks," replied Sam.

" Wot are they all a eatin' ham sangwidges for ? " inquired his father.

" 'Cos it's in their dooty, I suppose," replied Sam, " it's a part o' the system ; they're alvays a doin' it here, all day long ! "

Mr. Weller and his friends had scarcely had a moment to reflect upon this singular regulation as connected with the

monetary system of the country, when they were rejoined by
Pell and Wilkins Flasher, Esquire, who led them to a part
of the counter above which was a round black board with a
large "W." on it.

"Wot's that for, sir?" inquired Mr. Weller, directing
Pell's attention to the target in question.

"The first letter of the name of the deceased," replied Pell.

"I say," said Mr. Weller, turning round to the umpires.
"There's somethin' wrong here. We's our letter—this won't
do."

The referees at once gave it as their decided opinion
that the business could not be legally proceeded with, under
the letter W, and in all probability it would have stood over
for one day at least, had it not been for the prompt, though,
at first sight, undutiful behaviour of Sam, who, seizing his
father by the skirt of the coat, dragged him to the counter,
and pinned him there, until he had affixed his signature to
a couple of instruments; which from Mr. Weller's habit of
printing, was a work of so much labour and time, that the
officiating clerk peeled and ate three Ribston pippins while
it was performing.

As the elder Mr. Weller insisted on selling out his portion
forthwith, they proceeded from the Bank to the gate of the
Stock Exchange, to which Wilkins Flasher, Esquire, after a
short absence, returned with a cheque on Smith, Payne, and
Smith, for five hundred and thirty pounds; that being the
sum of money to which Mr. Weller at the market price of
the day, was entitled, in consideration of the balance of the
second Mrs. Weller's funded savings. Sam's two hundred
pounds stood transferred to his name, and Wilkins Flasher,
Esquire, having been paid his commission, dropped the
money carelessly into his coat pocket, and lounged back
to his office.

Mr. Weller was at first obstinately determined on cashing
the cheque in nothing but sovereigns: but it being represented
by the umpires that by so doing he must incur the expense

THE ACCOUNTS ARE AUDITED.

of a small sack to carry them home in, he consented to receive the amount in five-pound notes.

"My son," said Mr. Weller as they came out of the banking-house, "my son and me has a wery particular engagement this arternoon, and I should like to have this here bis'ness settled out of hand, so let's jest go straight avay someveres, vere ve can hordit the accounts."

A quiet room was soon found, and the accounts were produced and audited. Mr. Pell's bill was taxed by Sam, and some charges were disallowed by the umpires; but, notwithstanding Mr. Pell's declaration, accompanied with many solemn asseverations that they were really too hard upon him, it was by very many degrees the best professional job he had ever had, and one on which he boarded, lodged, and washed, for six months afterwards.

The umpires having partaken of a dram, shook hands and departed, as they had to drive out of town that night. Mr. Solomon Pell, finding that nothing more was going forward, either in the eating or drinking way, took a friendly leave, and Sam and his father were left alone.

"There!" said Mr. Weller, thrusting his pocket-book in his side pocket. "Vith the bills for the lease, and that, there's eleven hundred and eighty pound here. Now, Samivel, my boy, turn the horses' heads to the George and Wulter!'

CHAPTER LVI.

AN IMPORTANT CONFERENCE TAKES PLACE BETWEEN MR. PICK-
WICK AND SAMUEL WELLER, AT WHICH HIS PARENT ASSISTS.
AN OLD GENTLEMAN IN A SNUFF-COLOURED SUIT ARRIVES
UNEXPECTEDLY.

Mr. Pickwick was sitting alone, musing over many things,
and thinking among other considerations how he could best
provide for the young couple whose present unsettled condition was matter of constant regret and anxiety to him,
when Mary stepped lightly into the room, and, advancing
to the table, said, rather hastily :

"Oh, if you please, sir, Samuel is down stairs, and he says
may his father see you ?"

"Surely," replied Mr. Pickwick.

"Thank you, sir," said Mary, tripping towards the door
again.

"Sam has not been here long, has he ?" inquired Mr.
Pickwick.

"Oh, no, sir," replied Mary eagerly. "He has only just
come home. He is not going to ask you for any more leave,
sir, he says."

Mary might have been conscious that she had communicated
this last intelligence with more warmth than seemed actually
necessary, or she might have observed the good-humoured
smile with which Mr. Pickwick regarded her, when she had
finished speaking. She certainly held down her head, and

examined the corner of a very smart little apron, with more closeness than there appeared any absolute occasion for.

"Tell them they can come up at once, by all means," said Mr. Pickwick.

Mary, apparently much relieved, hurried away with her message.

Mr. Pickwick took two or three turns up and down the room; and rubbing his chin with his left hand as he did so, appeared lost in thought.

"Well, well," said Mr. Pickwick at length, in a kind but somewhat melancholy tone, "it is the best way in which I could reward him for his attachment and fidelity; let it be so, in Heaven's name. It is the fate of a lonely old man, that those about him should form new and different attachments and leave him. I have no right to expect that it should be otherwise with me. No, no," added Mr. Pickwick more cheerfully, "it would be selfish and ungrateful. I ought to be happy to have an opportunity of providing for him so well. I am. Of course I am."

Mr. Pickwick had been so absorbed in these reflections, that a knock at the door was three or four times repeated before he heard it. Hastily seating himself, and calling up his accustomed pleasant looks, he gave the required permission, and Sam Weller entered, followed by his father.

"Glad to see you back again, Sam," said Mr. Pickwick. "How do you do, Mr. Weller?"

"Wery hearty, thankee, sir," replied the widower; "hope I see *you* well, sir."

"Quite, I thank you," replied Mr. Pickwick.

"I wanted to have a little bit o' conwersation with you, sir," said Mr. Weller, "if you could spare me five minits or so, sir."

"Certainly," replied Mr. Pickwick. "Sam, give your father a chair."

"Thankee, Samivel, I've got a cheer here," said Mr. Weller, bringing one forward as he spoke; "uncommon fine day it's

455

been, sir," added the old gentleman, laying his hat on the floor as he sat himself down.

"Remarkably so indeed," replied Mr. Pickwick. "Very seasonable."

"Seasonablest veather I ever see, sir," rejoined Mr. Weller. Here, the old gentleman was seized with a violent fit of coughing, which, being terminated, he nodded his head and winked and made several supplicatory and threatening gestures to his son, all of which Sam Weller steadily abstained from seeing.

Mr. Pickwick, perceiving that there was some embarrassment on the old gentleman's part, affected to be engaged in cutting the leaves of a book that lay beside him, and waited patiently until Mr. Weller should arrive at the object of his visit.

"I never see sich a aggerawatin' boy as you are, Samivel," said Mr. Weller, looking indignantly at his son; "never in all my born days."

"What is he doing, Mr. Weller?" inquired Mr. Pickwick.

"He von't begin, sir," rejoined Mr. Weller; "he knows I ain't ekal to ex-pressin' myself ven there's anythin' partickler to be done, and yet he'll stand and see me a settin' here takin' up your walable time, and makin' a reg'lar spectacle o' myself, rayther than help me out vith a syllable. It ain't filial conduct, Samivel," said Mr. Weller, wiping his forehead; "wery far from it."

"You said you'd speak," replied Sam; "how should I know you wos done up at the wery beginnin'?"

"You might ha' seen I warn't able to start," rejoined his father; "I'm on the wrong side of the road, and backin' into the palins, and all manner of unpleasantness, and yet you von't put out a hand to help me. I'm ashamed on you, Samivel."

"The fact is, sir," said Sam, with a slight bow, "the gov'ner's been a drawin' his money."

"Wery good, Samivel, wery good," said Mr. Weller, nodding his head with a satisfied air, "I didn't mean to speak harsh to you, Sammy. Wery good. That's the vay to begin. Come to the pint at once. Wery good indeed, Samivel."

Mr. Weller nodded his head an extraordinary number of times, in the excess of his gratification, and waited in a listening attitude for Sam to resume his statement.

"You may sit down, Sam," said Mr. Pickwick, apprehending that the interview was likely to prove rather longer than he had expected.

Sam bowed again and sat down; his father looking round, he continued,

"The gov'ner, sir, has drawn out five hundred and thirty pound."

"Reduced counsels," interposed Mr. Weller, senior, in an undertone.

"It don't much matter vether it's reduced counsels, or wot not," said Sam; "five hundred and thirty pound is the sum, ain't it?"

"All right, Samivel," replied Mr. Weller.

"To vich sum, he has added for the house and bisness—"

"Lease, good-vill, stock, and fixters," interposed Mr. Weller.

—"As much as makes it," continued Sam, "altogether, eleven hundred and eighty pound."

"Indeed!" said Mr. Pickwick. "I am delighted to hear it. I congratulate you, Mr. Weller, on having done so well."

"Vait a minit, sir," said Mr. Weller, raising his hand in a deprecatory manner. "Get on, Samivel."

"This here money," said Sam, with a little hesitation, "he's anxious to put someveres, vere he knows it'll be safe, and I'm wery anxious too, for if he keeps it, he'll go a lendin' it to somebody, or inwestin' property in horses, or droppin' his pocket-book down a airy, or makin' a Egyptian mummy of his-self in some vay or another."

"Wery good, Samivel," observed Mr. Weller, in as complacent a manner as if Sam had been passing the highest eulogiums on his prudence and foresight. "Wery good."

"For vich reasons," continued Sam, plucking nervously at

457

THE PICKWICK CLUB.

the brim of his hat; "for vich reasons, he's drawd it out to-day, and come here vith me to say, leastvays to offer, or in other vords to—"

"—To say this here," said the elder Mr. Weller, impatiently, "that it ain't o' no use to me. I'm a goin' to vork a coach reg'lar, and ha'nt got noveres to keep it in, unless I vos to pay the guard for takin' care on it, or to put it in vun o' the coach pockets, vich 'ud be a temptation to the insides. If you'll take care on it for me, sir, I shall be wery much obliged to you. P'raps," said Mr. Weller, walking up to Mr. Pickwick and whispering in his ear, "p'raps it'll go a little vay towards the expenses o' that 'ere conwiction. All I say is, just you keep it till I ask you for it again." With these words, Mr. Weller placed the pocket-book in Mr. Pickwick's hands, caught up his hat, and ran out of the room with a celerity scarcely to be expected from so corpulent a subject.

"Stop him, Sam!" exclaimed Mr. Pickwick, earnestly. "Overtake him; bring him back instantly! Mr. Weller— here—come back!"

Sam saw that his master's injunctions were not to be disobeyed; and catching his father by the arm as he was descending the stairs, dragged him back by main force.

"My good friend," said Mr. Pickwick, taking the old man by the hand; "your honest confidence overpowers me."

"I don't see no occasion for nothin' o' the kind, sir," replied Mr. Weller, obstinately.

"I assure you, my good friend, I have more money than I can ever need; far more than a man at my age can ever live to spend," said Mr. Pickwick.

"No man knows how much he can spend, till he tries," observed Mr. Weller.

"Perhaps not," replied Mr. Pickwick; "but as I have no intention of trying any such experiments, I am not likely to come to want. I must beg you to take this back, Mr. Weller."

458

"Wery well," said Mr. Weller with a discontented look. "Mark my vords, Sammy. I'll do somethin' desperate vith this here property; somethin' desperate!"

"You'd better not," replied Sam.

Mr. Weller reflected for a short time, and then, buttoning up his coat with great determination, said:

"I'll keep a pike."

"Wot!" exclaimed Sam.

"A pike," rejoined Mr. Weller, through his set teeth; "I'll keep a pike. Say good bye to your father, Samivel. I dewote the remainder o' my days to a pike."

This threat was such an awful one, and Mr. Weller besides appearing fully resolved to carry it into execution, seemed so deeply mortified by Mr. Pickwick's refusal, that that gentleman, after a short reflection, said:

"Well, well, Mr. Weller, I will keep the money. I can do more good with it, perhaps, than you can."

"Just the wery thing, to be sure," said Mr. Weller, brightening up; "o' course you can, sir."

"Say no more about it," said Mr. Pickwick, locking the pocket-book in his desk; "I am heartily obliged to you, my good friend. Now sit down again. I want to ask your advice."

The internal laughter occasioned by the triumphant success of his visit, which had convulsed not only Mr. Weller's face, but his arms, legs, and body also, during the locking up of the pocket-book, suddenly gave place to the most dignified gravity as he heard these words.

"Wait outside a few minutes, Sam, will you?" said Mr. Pickwick.

Sam immediately withdrew.

Mr. Weller looked uncommonly wise and very much amazed, when Mr. Pickwick opened the discourse by saying:

"You are not an advocate for matrimony, I think, Mr. Weller?"

Mr. Weller shook his head. He was wholly unable to speak;

459

vague thoughts of some wicked widow having been successful in her designs on Mr. Pickwick, choked his utterance.

"Did you happen to see a young girl down stairs when you came in just now with your son?" inquired Mr. Pickwick.

"Yes. I see a young gal," replied Mr. Weller, shortly.

"What did you think of her, now? Candidly, Mr. Weller, what did you think of her?"

"I thought she wos wery plump, and vell made," said Mr. Weller, with a critical air.

"So she is," said Mr. Pickwick, "so she is. What did you think of her manners, from what you saw of her?"

"Wery pleasant," rejoined Mr. Weller. "Wery pleasant and conformable."

The precise meaning which Mr. Weller attached to this last-mentioned adjective, did not appear; but, as it was evident from the tone in which he used it that it was a favourable expression, Mr. Pickwick was as well satisfied as if he had been thoroughly enlightened on the subject.

"I take a great interest in her, Mr. Weller," said Mr. Pickwick.

Mr. Weller coughed.

"I mean an interest in her doing well," resumed Mr. Pickwick; "a desire that she may be comfortable and prosperous. You understand?"

"Wery clearly," replied Mr. Weller, who understood nothing yet.

"That young person," said Mr. Pickwick, "is attached to your son."

"To Samivel Veller!" exclaimed the parent.

"Yes," said Pickwick.

"It's nat'ral," said Mr. Weller, after some consideration, "nat'ral, but rayther alarmin'. Sammy must be careful."

"How do you mean?" inquired Mr. Pickwick.

"Wery careful that he don't say nothin' to her," responded Mr. Weller. "Wery careful that he ain't led avay, in a

innocent moment, to say anythink as may lead to a conwiction for breach. You're never safe vith 'em, Mr. Pickwick, ven they vunce has designs on you; there's no knowin'
vere to have 'em; and vile you're a-considering of it, they
have you. I wos married fust, that vay myself, sir, and
Sammy wos the consekens o' the manoover."

"You give me no great encouragement to conclude what
I have to say," observed Mr. Pickwick, "but I had better
do so at once. This young person is not only attached to
your son, Mr. Weller, but your son is attached to her."

"Vell," said Mr. Weller, "this here's a pretty sort o' thing
to come to a father's ears, this is!"

"I have observed them on several occasions," said Mr.
Pickwick, making no comment on Mr. Weller's last remark;
"and entertain no doubt at all about it. Supposing I were
desirous of establishing them comfortably as man and wife in
some little business or situation, where they might hope to
obtain a decent living, what should you think of it, Mr.
Weller?"

At first, Mr. Weller received, with wry faces, a proposition
involving the marriage of anybody in whom he took an
interest; but, as Mr. Pickwick argued the point with him,
and laid great stress on the fact that Mary was not a widow,
he gradually became more tractable. Mr. Pickwick had great
influence over him, and he had been much struck with Mary's
appearance; having, in fact, bestowed several very unfatherly
winks upon her, already. At length he said that it was not
for him to oppose Mr. Pickwick's inclination, and that he
would be very happy to yield to his advice; upon which, Mr.
Pickwick joyfully took him at his word, and called Sam back
into the room.

"Sam," said Mr. Pickwick, clearing his throat, "your
father and I have been having some conversation about you."

"About you, Samivel," said Mr. Weller, in a patronising
and impressive voice.

"I am not so blind, Sam, as not to have seen, a long time

461

since, that you entertain something more than a friendly feeling towards Mrs. Winkle's maid," said Mr. Pickwick.

"You hear this, Samivel?" said Mr. Weller in the same judicial form of speech as before.

"I hope, sir," said Sam, addressing his master: "I hope there's no harm in a young man takin' notice of a young 'ooman as is undeniably good-looking and well-conducted."

"Certainly not," said Mr. Pickwick.

"Not by no means," acquiesced Mr. Weller, affably but magisterially.

"So far from thinking there is anything wrong, in conduct so natural," resumed Mr. Pickwick, "it is my wish to assist and promote your wishes in this respect. With this view, I have had a little conversation with your father; and finding that he is of my opinion——"

"The lady not bein' a widder," interposed Mr. Weller in explanation.

"The lady not being a widow," said Mr. Pickwick, smiling. "I wish to free you from the restraint which your present position imposes upon you, and to mark my sense of your fidelity and many excellent qualities, by enabling you to marry this girl at once, and to earn an independent livelihood for yourself and family. I shall be proud, Sam," said Mr. Pickwick, whose voice had faltered a little hitherto, but now resumed its customary tone, "proud and happy to make your future prospects in life, my grateful and peculiar care."

There was a profound silence for a short time, and then Sam said, in a low husky sort of voice, but firmly withal:

"I'm very much obliged to you for your goodness, sir, as is only like yourself; but it can't be done."

"Can't be done!" ejaculated Mr. Pickwick in astonishment.

"Samivel!" said Mr. Weller, with dignity.

"I say it can't be done," repeated Sam in a louder key. "Wot's to become of you, sir?"

"My good fellow," replied Mr. Pickwick, "the recent changes among my friends will alter my mode of life in

462

future, entirely; besides, I am growing older, and want repose and quiet. My rambles, Sam, are over."

"How do I know that 'ere, sir?" argued Sam. "You think so now! S'pose you wos to change your mind, vich is not unlikely, for you've the spirit o' five-and-tventy in you still, what 'ud become on you vithout me? It can't be done, sir, it can't be done."

"Wery good, Samivel, there's a good deal in that," said Mr. Weller, encouragingly.

"I speak after long deliberation, Sam, and with the certainty that I shall keep my word," said Mr. Pickwick, shaking his head. "New scenes have closed upon me; my rambles are at an end."

"Wery good," rejoined Sam. "Then, that's the wery best reason wy you should alvays have somebody by you as understands you, to keep you up and make you comfortable. If you vant a more polished sort o' feller, vell and good, have him; but vages or no vages, notice or no notice, board or no board, lodgin' or no lodgin', Sam Veller, as you took from the old inn in the Borough, sticks by you, come what come may; and let ev'rvthin' and ev'rybody do their wery fiercest, nothin' shall ever perwent it!"

At the close of this declaration. which Sam made with great emotion, the elder Mr. Weller rose from his chair, and, forgetting all considerations of time, place, or propriety, waved his hat above his head, and gave three vehement cheers.

"My good fellow," said Mr. Pickwick, when Mr. Weller had sat down again, rather abashed at his own enthusiasm, "you are bound to consider the young woman also."

"I do consider the young 'ooman, sir," said Sam. "I have considered the young 'ooman. I've spoke to her. I've told her how I'm sitivated; she's ready to vait till I'm ready, and I believe she vill. If she don't, she's not the young 'ooman I take her for, and I give her up vith readiness. You've know'd me afore, sir. My mind's made up, and nothin' can ever alter it."

Who could combat this resolution? Not Mr. Pickwick. He derived, at that moment, more pride and luxury of feeling from the disinterested attachment of his humble friends, than ten thousand protestations from the greatest men living could have awakened in his heart.

While this conversation was passing in Mr. Pickwick's room, a little old gentleman in a suit of snuff-coloured clothes, followed by a porter carrying a small portmanteau, presented himself below; and after securing a bed for the night, inquired of the waiter whether one Mrs. Winkle was staying there, to which question the waiter, of course, responded in the affirmative.

"Is she alone?" inquired the little old gentleman.

"I believe she is, sir," replied the waiter; "I can call her own maid. sir, if you——"

"No, I don't want her," said the old gentleman quickly. "Show me to her room without announcing me."

"Eh, sir?" said the waiter.

"Are you deaf?" inquired the little old gentleman.

"No, sir."

"Then listen, if you please. Can you hear me now?"

"Yes, sir."

"That's well. Show me to Mrs. Winkle's room, without announcing me."

As the little old gentleman uttered this command, he slipped five shillings into the waiter's hand, and looked steadily at him.

"Really, sir," said the waiter, "I don't know, sir. whether——"

"Ah! you'll do it, I see," said the little old gentleman. "You had better do it at once. It will save time."

There was something so very cool and collected in the gentleman's manner, that the waiter put the five shillings in his pocket, and led him up stairs without another word.

"This is the room, is it?" said the gentleman. "You may go."

MRS. WINKLE, I BELIEVE?

The waiter complied, wondering much who the gentleman could be, and what he wanted; the little old gentleman waiting till he was out of sight, tapped at the door.

"Come in," said Arabella.

"Um, a pretty voice at any rate," murmured the little old gentleman; "but that's nothing." As he said this, he opened the door and walked in. Arabella, who was sitting at work, rose on beholding a stranger—a little confused—but by no means ungracefully so.

"Pray don't rise, ma'am," said the unknown, walking in, and closing the door after him. "Mrs. Winkle, I believe?"

Arabella inclined her head.

"Mrs. Nathaniel Winkle, who married the son of the old man at Birmingham?" said the stranger, eyeing Arabella with visible curiosity.

Again, Arabella inclined her head, and looked uneasily round, as if uncertain whether to call for assistance.

"I surprise you, I see, ma'am," said the old gentleman.

"Rather, I confess," replied Arabella, wondering more and more.

"I'll take a chair, if you'll allow me, ma'am," said the stranger.

He took one; and drawing a spectacle-case from his pocket, leisurely pulled out a pair of spectacles, which he adjusted on his nose.

"You don't know me, ma'am?" he said, looking so intently at Arabella that she began to feel alarmed.

"No, sir," she replied timidly.

"No," said the gentleman, nursing his left leg; "I don't know how you should. You know my name, though, ma'am."

"Do I?" said Arabella, trembling, though she scarcely knew why. "May I ask what it is?"

"Presently, ma'am, presently," said the stranger, not having yet removed his eyes from her countenance. "You have been recently married, ma'am?"

465

"I have," replied Arabella, in a scarcely audible tone, laying aside her work, and becoming greatly agitated as a thought, that had occurred to her before, struck more forcibly upon her mind.

"Without having represented to your husband the propriety of first consulting his father, on whom he is dependent, I think?" said the stranger.

Arabella applied her handkerchief to her eyes.

"Without an endeavour, even, to ascertain, by some indirect appeal, what were the old man's sentiments on a point in which he would naturally feel much interested?" said the stranger.

"I cannot deny it, sir," said Arabella.

"And without having sufficient property of your own to afford your husband any permanent assistance in exchange for the worldly advantages which you knew he would have gained if he had married agreeably to his father's wishes?" said the old gentleman. "This is what boys and girls call disinterested affection, till they have boys and girls of their own, and then they see it in a rougher and very different light!"

Arabella's tears flowed fast, as she pleaded in extenuation that she was young and inexperienced; that her attachment had alone induced her to take the step to which she had resorted; and that she had been deprived of the counsel and guidance of her parents almost from infancy.

"It was wrong," said the old gentleman in a milder tone, "very wrong. It was foolish, romantic, unbusiness-like."

"It was my fault; all my fault, sir," replied poor Arabella, weeping.

"Nonsense," said the old gentleman; "it was not your fault that he fell in love with you, I suppose? Yes it was though," said the old gentleman, looking rather slyly at Arabella. "It was your fault. He couldn't help it."

This little compliment, or the little gentleman's odd way of paying it, or his altered manner—so much kinder than it was, at first—or all three together, forced a smile from Arabella in the midst of her tears.

"Where's your husband?" inquired the old gentleman, abruptly; stopping a smile which was just coming over his own face.

"I expect him every instant, sir," said Arabella. "I persuaded him to take a walk this morning. He is very low and wretched at not having heard from his father."

"Low, is he?" said the old gentleman. "Serve him right!"

"He feels it on my account, I am afraid," said Arabella; "and indeed, sir, I feel it deeply on his. I have been the sole means of bringing him to his present condition."

"Don't mind it on his account, my dear," said the old gentleman. "It serves him right. I am glad of it—actually glad of it, as far as he is concerned."

The words were scarcely out of the old gentleman's lips, when footsteps were heard ascending the stairs, which he and Arabella seemed both to recognise at the same moment. The little gentleman turned pale, and making a strong effort to appear composed, stood up, as Mr. Winkle entered the room.

"Father!" cried Mr. Winkle, recoiling in amazement.

"Yes, sir," replied the little old gentleman. "Well, sir, what have you got to say to me?"

Mr. Winkle remained silent.

"You are ashamed of yourself, I hope, sir?" said the old gentleman.

Still Mr. Winkle said nothing.

"Are you ashamed of yourself, sir, or are you not?" inquired the old gentleman.

"No, sir," replied Mr. Winkle, drawing Arabella's arm through his. "I am not ashamed of myself, or of my wife either."

"Upon my word!" cried the old gentleman, ironically.

"I am very sorry to have done anything which has lessened your affection for me, sir," said Mr. Winkle; "but I will say, at the same time, that I have no reason to be ashamed of having this lady for my wife, nor you of having her for a daughter."

"Give me your hand, Nat," said the old gentleman in an altered voice. "Kiss me, my love. You *are* a very charming little daughter-in-law after all!"

In a few minutes' time Mr. Winkle went in search of Mr. Pickwick, and returning with that gentleman, presented him to his father, whereupon they shook hands for five minutes incessantly.

"Mr. Pickwick, I thank you most heartily for all your kindness to my son," said old Mr. Winkle, in a bluff straightforward way. "I am a hasty fellow, and when I saw you last, I was vexed and taken by surprise. I have judged for myself now, and am more than satisfied. Shall I make any more apologies, Mr. Pickwick?"

"Not one," replied that gentleman. "You have done the only thing wanting to complete my happiness."

Hereupon, there was another shaking of hands for five minutes longer, accompanied by a great number of complimentary speeches, which, besides being complimentary, had the additional and very novel recommendation of being sincere.

Sam had dutifully seen his father to the Bell Sauvage, when, on returning, he encountered the fat boy in the court, who had been charged with the delivery of a note from Emily Wardle.

"I say," said Joe, who was unusually loquacious, "what a pretty girl Mary is, isn't she? I am *so* fond of her, I am!"

Mr. Weller made no verbal remark in reply; but eyeing the fat boy for a moment, quite transfixed at his presumption, led him by the collar to the corner, and dismissed him with a harmless but ceremonious kick. After which, he walked home, whistling.

CHAPTER LVII.

IN WHICH THE PICKWICK CLUB IS FINALLY DISSOLVED, AND EVERYTHING CONCLUDED TO THE SATISFACTION OF EVERYBODY.

For a whole week after the happy arrival of Mr. Winkle from Birmingham, Mr. Pickwick and Sam Weller were from home all day long, only returning just in time for dinner, and then wearing an air of mystery and importance quite foreign to their natures. It was evident that very grave and eventful proceedings were on foot; but various surmises were afloat, respecting their precise character. Some (among whom was Mr. Tupman) were disposed to think that Mr. Pickwick contemplated a matrimonial alliance; but this idea the ladies most strenuously repudiated. Others, rather inclined to the belief that he had projected some distant tour, and was at present occupied in effecting the preliminary arrangements; but this again was stoutly denied by Sam himself, who had unequivocally stated when cross-examined by Mary that no new journeys were to be undertaken. At length, when the brains of the whole party had been racked for six long days, by unavailing speculation, it was unanimously resolved that Mr. Pickwick should be called upon to explain his conduct, and to state distinctly why he had thus absented himself from the society of his admiring friends.

With this view, Mr. Wardle invited the full circle to

dinner at the Adelphi; and, the decanters having been twice sent round, opened the business.

"We are all anxious to know," said the old gentleman, "what we have done to offend you, and to induce you to desert us and devote yourself to these solitary walks."

"Are you?" said Mr. Pickwick. "It is singular enough that I had intended to volunteer a full explanation this very day; so, if you will give me another glass of wine, I will satisfy your curiosity."

The decanters passed from hand to hand with unwonted briskness, and Mr. Pickwick looking round on the faces of his friends, with a cheerful smile, proceeded:

"All the changes that have taken place among us," said Mr. Pickwick, "I mean the marriage that *has* taken place, and the marriage that *will* take place, with the changes they involve, rendered it necessary for me to think, soberly and at once, upon my future plans. I determined on retiring to some quiet pretty neighbourhood in the vicinity of London; I saw a house which exactly suited my fancy; I have taken it and furnished it. It is fully prepared for my reception, and I intend entering upon it at once, trusting that I may yet live to spend many quiet years in peaceful retirement, cheered through life by the society of my friends, and followed in death by their affectionate remembrance."

Here Mr. Pickwick paused, and a low murmur ran round the table.

"The house I have taken," said Mr. Pickwick, "is at Dulwich. It has a large garden, and is situated in one of the most pleasant spots near London. It has been fitted up with every attention to substantial comfort; perhaps to a little elegance besides; but of that you shall judge for yourselves. Sam accompanies me there. I have engaged, on Perker's representation, a housekeeper—a very old one— and such other servants as she thinks I shall require. I propose to consecrate this little retreat, by having a ceremony in which I take a great interest, performed there. I wish, if my friend Wardle entertains no objection, that his daughter should be married from my new house, on the day I take possession of it. The happiness of young people," said Mr. Pickwick, a little moved, "has ever been the chief pleasure of my life. It will warm my heart to witness the happiness of those friends who are dearest to me, beneath my own roof."

Mr. Pickwick paused again: Emily and Arabella sobbed audibly.

"I have communicated, both personally and by letter, with the club," resumed Mr. Pickwick, "acquainting them with my intention. During our long absence, it had suffered much from internal dissensions; and the withdrawal of my name, coupled with this and other circumstances, has occasioned its dissolution. The Pickwick Club exists no longer.

"I shall never regret," said Mr. Pickwick in a low voice, "I shall never regret having devoted the greater part of two years to mixing with different varieties and shades of human character: frivolous as my pursuit of novelty may have appeared to many. Nearly the whole of my previous life having been devoted to business and the pursuit of wealth, numerous scenes of which I had no previous conception have dawned upon me—I hope to the enlargement of my mind, and the improvement of my understanding. If I have done but little good, I trust I have done less harm, and that none of my adventures will be other than a source of amusing and pleasant recollection to me in the decline of life. God bless you all!"

With these words, Mr. Pickwick filled and drained a bumper with a trembling hand, and his eyes moistened as his friends rose with one accord, and pledged him from their hearts.

There were very few preparatory arrangements to be made for the marriage of Mr. Snodgrass. As he had neither father nor mother, and had been in his minority a ward of Mr. Pickwick's, that gentleman was perfectly well acquainted with his possessions and prospects. His account of both was quite satisfactory to Wardle—as almost any other account would have been, for the good old gentleman was overflowing with hilarity and kindness—and a handsome portion having been bestowed upon Emily, the marriage was fixed to take place on the fourth day from that time: the suddenness of which preparations reduced three dress-makers and a tailor to the extreme verge of insanity.

Getting post-horses to the carriage, old Wardle started off, next day, to bring his mother up to town. Communicating his intelligence to the old lady with characteristic impetuosity, she instantly fainted away; but being promptly revived, ordered the brocaded silk gown to be packed up forthwith, and proceeded to relate some circumstances of a similar nature attending the marriage of the eldest daughter of Lady Tollimglower, deceased, which occupied three hours in the recital, and were not half finished at last.

Mrs. Trundle had to be informed of all the mighty preparations that were making in London, and being in a delicate state of health was informed thereof through Mr. Trundle, lest the news should be too much for her; but it was not too much for her, inasmuch as she at once wrote off to Muggleton, to order a new cap and a black satin gown, and moreover avowed her determination of being present at the ceremony. Hereupon, Mr. Trundle called in the doctor, and the doctor said Mrs. Trundle ought to know best how she felt herself, to which Mrs. Trundle replied that she felt herself quite equal to it, and that she had made up her mind to go; upon which the doctor, who was a wise and discreet doctor, and knew what was good for himself as well as for other people, said that perhaps if Mrs. Trundle stopped at home she might hurt herself more by fretting, than by going, so perhaps she had better go. And she did go; the doctor with great attention sending in half a dozen of medicine, to be drunk upon the road.

In addition to these points of distraction, Wardle was intrusted with two small letters to two small young ladies who were to act as bridesmaids; upon the receipt of which, the two young ladies were driven to despair by having no "things" ready for so important an occasion, and no time to make them in—a circumstance which appeared to afford the two worthy papas of the two small young ladies rather a feeling of satisfaction than otherwise. However, old frocks were trimmed, and new bonnets made, and the young ladies looked as well as could possibly have been expected of them. And as they cried at the subsequent ceremony in the proper places, and trembled at the right times, they acquitted themselves to the admiration of all beholders.

How the two poor relations ever reached London—whether they walked, or got behind coaches, or procured lifts in wagons, or carried each other by turns—is uncertain; but there they were, before Wardle; and the very first people that knocked at the door of Mr. Pickwick's house, on the bridal morning were the two poor relations, all smiles and shirt collar.

They were welcomed heartily though, for riches or poverty had no influence on Mr. Pickwick; the new servants were all alacrity and readiness; Sam was in a most unrivalled state of high spirits and excitement; Mary was glowing with beauty and smart ribands.

The bridegroom, who had been staying at the house for two or three days previous, sallied forth gallantly to Dulwich Church to meet the bride, attended by Mr. Pickwick, Ben Allen, Bob Sawyer, and Mr. Tupman; with Sam Weller outside, having at his button-hole a white favour, the gift of his lady love, and clad in a new and gorgeous suit of livery invented for the occasion. They were met by the Wardles, and the Winkles, and the bride and bridesmaids, and the Trundles; and the ceremony having been performed, the coaches rattled back to Mr. Pickwick's to breakfast, where little Mr. Perker already awaited them.

Here, all the light clouds of the more solemn part of the proceedings passed away; every face shone forth joyously;

nothing was to be heard but congratulations and commendations. Everything was so beautiful! The lawn in front, the garden behind, the miniature conservatory, the dining-room, the drawing-room, the bed-rooms, the smoking-room, and above all the study with its pictures and easy chairs, and odd cabinets, and queer tables, and books out of number, with a large cheerful window opening upon a pleasant lawn and commanding a pretty landscape, dotted here and there with little houses almost hidden by the trees; and then the curtains, and the carpets, and the chairs, and the sofas! Everything was so beautiful, so compact, so neat, and in such exquisite taste, said everybody, that there really was no deciding what to admire most.

And in the midst of all this, stood Mr. Pickwick, his countenance lighted up with smiles, which the heart of no man, woman, or child, could resist: himself the happiest of the group: shaking hands, over and over again with the same people, and when his own hands were not so employed, rubbing them with pleasure : turning round in a different direction at every fresh expression of gratification or curiosity, and inspiring everybody with his looks of gladness and delight.

Breakfast is announced. Mr. Pickwick leads the old lady (who has been very eloquent on the subject of Lady Tollimglower), to the top of a long table; Wardle takes the bottom; the friends arrange themselves on either side; Sam takes his station behind his master's chair; the laughter and talking cease; Mr. Pickwick, having said grace, pauses for an instant, and looks round him. As he does so, the tears roll down his cheeks, in the fulness of his joy.

Let us leave our old friend in one of those moments of unmixed happiness, of which, if we seek them, there are ever some, to cheer our transitory existence here. There are dark shadows on the earth, but its lights are stronger in the contrast. Some men, like bats or owls, have better eyes for the darkness than for the light. We, who have no such optical powers, are better pleased to take our last parting look at the visionary companions of many solitary hours, when the brief sunshine of the world is blazing full upon them.

It is the fate of most men who mingle with the world, and attain even the prime of life, to make many real friends, and lose them in the course of nature. It is the fate of all authors or chroniclers to create imaginary friends, and lose them in the course of art. Nor is this the full extent of their misfortunes; for they are required to furnish an account of them besides.

In compliance with this custom—unquestionably a bad one—we subjoin a few biographical words, in relation to the party at Mr. Pickwick's assembled.

Mr. and Mrs. Winkle, being fully received into favour by the old gentleman, were shortly afterwards installed in a newly-built house, not half a mile from Mr. Pickwick's. Mr. Winkle, being engaged in the City as agent or town correspondent of his father, exchanged his old costume for the ordinary dress of Englishmen, and presented all the external appearance of a civilised Christian ever afterwards.

Mr. and Mrs. Snodgrass settled at Dingley Dell, where they purchased and cultivated a small farm, more for occupation than profit. Mr. Snodgrass, being occasionally abstracted and melancholy, is to this day reputed a great poet among his friends and acquaintance, although we do not find that he has ever written anything to encourage the belief. There are many celebrated characters, literary, philosophical, and otherwise, who hold a high reputation on a similar tenure.

Mr. Tupman, when his friends married, and Mr. Pickwick settled, took lodgings at Richmond, where he has ever since resided. He walks constantly on the Terrace during the summer months, with a youthful and jaunty air which has rendered him the admiration of the numerous elderly ladies of single condition, who reside in the vicinity. He has never proposed again.

THE PICKWICK CLUB.

Mr. Bob Sawyer, having previously passed through the Gazette, passed over to Bengal, accompanied by Mr. Benjamin Allen; both gentlemen having received surgical appointments from the East India Company. They each had the yellow fever fourteen times, and then resolved to try a little abstinence; since which period, they have been doing well.

Mrs. Bardell let lodgings to many conversable single gentlemen, with great profit, but never brought any more actions for breach of promise of marriage. Her attorneys, Messrs. Dodson and Fogg, continue in business, from which they realise a large income, and in which they are universally considered among the sharpest of the sharp.

Sam Weller kept his word, and remained unmarried, for two years. The old housekeeper dying at the end of that time, Mr. Pickwick promoted Mary to the situation, on condition of her marrying Mr. Weller at once, which she did without a murmur. From the circumstance of two sturdy little boys having been repeatedly seen at the gate of the back garden, there is reason to suppose that Sam has some family.

The elder Mr. Weller drove a coach for twelve months, but being afflicted with the gout, was compelled to retire. The contents of the pocket-book had been so well invested for him, however, by Mr. Pickwick, that he had a handsome independence to retire on, upon which he still lives at an excellent public-house near Shooter's Hill, where he is quite reverenced as an oracle: boasting very much of his intimacy with Mr. Pickwick, and retaining a most unconquerable aversion to widows.

Mr. Pickwick himself continued to reside in his new house, employing his leisure hours in arranging the memoranda which he afterwards presented to the secretary of the once famous club, or in hearing Sam Weller read aloud, with such remarks as suggested themselves to his mind, which never failed to afford Mr. Pickwick great amusement. He was much troubled at first, by the numerous applications made to him by Mr. Snodgrass, Mr. Winkle, and Mr. Trundle, to act as godfather to their offspring; but he has become used to it now, and officiates as a matter of course. He never had occasion to regret his bounty to Mr. Jingle; for both that person and Job Trotter became, in time, worthy members of society, although they have always steadily objected to return to the scenes of their old haunts and temptations. Mr. Pickwick is somewhat infirm now; but he retains all his former juvenility of spirit, and may still be frequently seen, contemplating the pictures in the Dulwich Gallery, or enjoying a walk about the pleasant neighbourhood on a fine day. He is known by all the poor people about, who never fail to take their hats off, as he passes, with great respect. The children idolise him, and so indeed does the whole neighbourhood. Every year, he repairs to a large family merry-making at Mr. Wardle's; on this, as on all other occasions, he is invariably attended by the faithful Sam, between whom and his master there exists a steady and reciprocal attachment which nothing but death will terminate.

*This book, designed
by William B. Taylor,
is a production
of Heron Books, London*

Printed in Switzerland